BLUE
HOLLOW

A thrilling mystery with a wicked twist

CHERYL REES-PRICE

THE
BOOK
FOLKS

Published by The Book Folks

London, 2021

© Cheryl Rees-Price

ISBN 978-1-913516-58-1

www.thebookfolks.com

For Morgan, Haddy, and Meg

Prologue

The heavy blanket moulded to his thin body. It was comforting like a warm hug. He didn't want to move and let in the cold air, but the pressure in his groin was unbearable. He screwed up his eyes and tried to force himself back to sleep, maybe he could make it until the morning.

It was still dark in the room and he had no way of telling the time, no idea of how many hours he would have to lie there desperate for a pee. He had two choices, stay and hope he didn't wet the bed or get up and make his way out of the house, in the dark, to the stone building that housed the toilets. Either choice came with consequences. Those who wet the bed were beaten and their humiliation broadcast to the whole house. He knew a boy who was made to wear a nappy to bed. The towel had been pinned to him and was too bulky to fit under his pyjamas. He went to bed each night and cried himself to sleep. There was equal punishment for being caught out of bed at night.

The boy poked his head out of the blanket deciding that the beating for being caught out of bed was preferable to the shame of being known as a bed-wetter. He sat up and felt his muscles contract as the cold air seeped through the thin cotton of his pyjama top. The bare ceiling-to-floor windows let in the weak moonlight along with a draft that chilled your bones, so you never felt warm.

He glanced around the room, hoping to find one of the other boys sat up and in the same predicament. All of them were asleep, heaped under their blankets, except for the last bed. It was empty with the blanket thrown back. The thought of not being alone outside made him spring to action. He leapt out of the bed and winced as his feet landed on the freezing floorboards. He pulled a jumper over his head as he wiggled his feet into his shoes and hurried to try and catch up with the other boy.

Out in the corridor darkness closed around him. He crept along, fearful of making the slightest sound, the pressure on his bladder threatening to release. He expected to meet the other boy making his way back to bed, but all was quiet when he reached the staircase. He hurried down and pushed through the two sets of swing doors careful to let them shut silently against his hand. He was breathless when he reached the front door, more from fear than exertion. The bolt had already been pulled back. He opened the door and stepped out into the night air.

Frost glittered on the lawn and icy fingers coiled around his chest making it difficult to breathe. He made his way to the side of the house and stood in front of the stone building.

'Are you in there?' he whispered.

There was no reply, so he tried again a little louder. He stood still, listening for movement. All was silent. He hated the countryside, no sound of traffic and no streetlights. He was about to push open the door to the toilets when he heard a strange chanting. He spun around trying to determine the direction from which the noise came. It stopped abruptly and all he could hear now was his heart thudding against his ribs. Too scared to enter the building he scurried around the side and relieved himself.

A cloud of steam rose, and he felt the pressure in his bladder ease. He jiggled about trying to hurry the job, he just wanted to get back inside. Now with the pain in his groin gone he felt the cruel bite of the cold. His teeth chattered and his body shook. He hurried back to the front of the house and was about to push open the door when the chanting started, louder this time. He turned around and looked across the lawn to the old stone church. Light flickered in the windows, illuminating the stained glass. The thought occurred to him that maybe some of the older boys were inside the church and had lit a fire. The way the light danced made him think of flames. The idea of a fire was enticing. His bed would be cold, and it would take a long time to warm up. At that moment it felt like he would never be warm again.

He stepped onto the lawn. The frozen grass crunched beneath his feet as he walked. Halfway across he stopped and turned to glance back at the house. Soulless windows stared back, the house full of cold and creeping darkness. It has to be the older boys, he thought. They're always up to mischief. He was sure they wouldn't mind if he joined them. Just to get warm by the fire. He ran across the lawn and into the porch. His hands were numb, and his toes hurt. He felt like crying as he put his hand on the heavy oak door and pushed. The chanting became louder, faster, the voices an excited frenzy. The boy's eyes widened as he took in the scene before him.

All the church windows were lined with cream candles, the flames dancing, the wax spilling over the edge and pooling at the base. The wooden pews that usually lined both sides of the church had been pushed back and piled up against the back wall. The flagstone aisle led to a group of men standing inside a circle of candles. All faced inwards and wore robes which covered their heads and draped onto the floor. The boy stood transfixed as one man raised a hand in the air, fingers wrapped around the hilt of a silver dagger. The man gave a cry and his hand plummeted downwards ending in a sickening thud. Then all was silent. Two men stepped forward and knelt. Over the top of their hoods the boy saw the lifeless body of one of the younger boys. He lay strapped to a table, blood ran down the side of his chest and dripped onto the floor.

A scream rent the air, piercing the silence. The boy staggered backwards through the door and into the shadows. All eyes turned in his direction, for a moment no one moved. The men startled by the interruption and the boy frozen in terror.

'Bring our guest to join us.' The voice of the man with the blade was calm but authoritative.

Three men started down the aisle, their robes dragging in the dust. The boy bolted into the night, darting in all directions like a wild animal running from a predator. He reached the graveyard and dived behind a headstone. He crouched into a ball wishing himself invisible. He heard the men's voices getting nearer as they hunted him. His rasping breath filled the air, he was sure it would give him away, but he couldn't hold his breath or stop his body from trembling violently.

'Leave him.' That calm voice again. 'We'll soon find out which of the little bastards is out of bed. He'll probably freeze to death out here, so he won't give us any problems. We need to finish and clear up.' The voices died away as they went back into the church.

The boy stayed crouched on the grave, too terrified to move. He knew he couldn't make the run back to the house without being caught, but also that he couldn't stay out all night. He heard the men come back out of the church and risked a peek around the headstone when he heard the roar of an engine. One of the men carried the lifeless boy over his shoulder, his head lolling from side to side and his arm poking out of a blanket. He dumped him in the back of the Land Rover and slammed the door. He watched it drive away as the other men returned to the church.

He lay still now, his body had stopped shivering, he could no longer feel the cold. His mind wandered and filled with images of the person who lay in the coffin beneath him, arms coming out of the grave, wrapping around his body and keeping him safe. A warm hand grabbed his shoulder, he opened his mouth to scream but no sound came out.

Chapter One

Dora Lewis sat at her kitchen table with a purple fluffy dressing gown wrapped around her body. Her eyes scanned the words on the screen of the laptop. It was quiet in the house. The only sound came from her fingers tapping the keyboard and the purrs emitted from a large ginger cat that lay curled up on the table.

'This is rubbish.' Dora huffed. She picked up the mug next to the laptop and took a swig of cold tea before deleting the last paragraph she wrote. The words weren't flowing, no matter how hard she tried to concentrate. She looked at the wall clock. There was no chance she would finish the article today. She saved the document and shut down the laptop.

'Right, Horace, I suppose I better get dressed and go see Eddie.' She stroked the cat who unfurled, yawned and curled back into a ball.

'Just what I'd like to do,' Dora said.

Upstairs she took a quick shower and dressed in a pair of jeans and a light pink jumper. It was the first time she had bothered getting dressed in three days. She ran a brush through her long auburn hair and tied it back. She checked her reflection in the mirror, sighed, and went downstairs.

The cat fussed at her feet, so she let him out the back door before picking up a brightly wrapped parcel and leaving the house.

Outside, the crisp October air made her wish she had grabbed her coat. She quickened her pace and drew in deep breaths, allowing the cool breeze to awaken her senses. The small Welsh village of Trap was peaceful, most people having eaten a large Sunday lunch were relaxing indoors. Dora was pleased not to have to stop and talk to anyone. It was the type of village where everyone knew your business and Dora sensed she had been the subject of gossip since her husband, Gary, left her for another woman.

She walked down the hill and took a glance at Carreg Cennen Castle on her left. The ruin sat above a limestone precipice and she always marvelled at its magnificence, no matter how many times she saw it. At the bottom of the hill she crossed the bridge and turned onto the road that led to a row of bungalows. A woman with a miniature poodle walked towards her.

'Hello, Dora, how are you?'

You really mean how I have been since my husband left, Dora thought. 'I'm good thanks, Kate.' She forced a smile.

'So nice to see you. I haven't seen you out and about for ages.'

'I've been busy, working.'

'Oh, that's good. I do enjoy reading your articles. I was sorry to hear about Gary.'

Dora felt herself stiffen. 'Oh, that was months ago.'

'Yes, but you were together a long time.' Kate put a hand on Dora's arm. 'It must've been very difficult for you.'

'Honestly, I'm fine. I have to go. It's Uncle Eddie's birthday.' Dora waved the package she was carrying.

'Oh, okay,' Kate looked disappointed. 'Take care of yourself.'

Dora hurried to the end of the road, knocked the door of the last bungalow and entered.

'Hi, Uncle Eddie,' she called as she walked into the sitting room.

Eddie was sat in his usual armchair watching the television. A smile lit his face as he stood to greet Dora.

'Hello, love.'

'Happy birthday, Uncle Eddie.' Dora stepped forward and put her arms around Eddie and hugged him lightly. She could feel his rib cage through the cotton of his T-shirt. Dora pulled back and handed him the present. 'Just a little something.'

'Thanks.' Eddie opened the card, smiled and put it on the coffee table. Next, he tore open the package.

'I thought it would keep your head warm until your hair grows back.'

Eddie looked at the brightly coloured bobble hat and rubbed his head. 'I don't think it's ever going to grow back.'

Dora looked at the patchy stubble. 'It's coming,' she said.

'This will certainly attract the ladies.' Eddie stuck the hat on his head.

'It suits you. So, did you have a good holiday with Charlie?'

'Yeah, we had a great time. Went on a trip down memory lane. Visited some old mates. Let's put the kettle on and I'll tell you all about it.'

'You sit down and rest. I'll make the tea.'

'Nah, I'll keep you company when you make it. I'll rest when I'm an old man,' Eddie said.

They walked through to the kitchen. Dora could hear Eddie's laboured breathing as she filled the kettle.

'Are you okay?' She flicked the switch and turned to face Eddie who was leaning against the counter.

'I'm fine. The trip took it out of me, but a good night's rest and I'll be back to normal.'

'Okay.' Dora grabbed two mugs and put in the teabags. 'You are getting better? You'd tell me if the treatment isn't working?'

'When your number's up, that's it. Fuck all you can do about it, so it's not worth fretting. I don't want you to worry.'

'I can't help it.'

'You worry too much, you need to toughen up. You're too nice and people take advantage.'

'No they don't.'

'Yeah, what about that dick of a husband of yours? You heard from him?' Eddie raised his eyebrows.

'He wants to come around Thursday afternoon to talk about selling the house.' Dora's stomach tensed at the thought. She turned and poured the boiling water into the mugs. 'By the time we split what's left after paying off the mortgage, there's not going to be enough for me to buy a garden shed.'

'Tell him to piss off. He's the one who took up with that tart.' Eddie shook his head. 'Dickless cun—'

'Whoa!' Dora put her hands over her ears. 'You know I don't like that word.'

'Yeah, but that's the least offensive thing I can think of calling him.' Eddie chuckled.

'I can't really expect him to keep paying the mortgage while I live there. He's still helping the girls with university costs. He doesn't owe me anything.'

'You're still his wife.'

'For now.'

'You know I could arrange to get rid of the pair of them for you.' Eddie's eyes twinkled with mischief.

'You know a hit man in Trap?' Dora laughed. She scooped out the teabags and dumped them in the bin. 'It's a tempting thought.'

'Seriously, I could sort it.'

'He's still the father of my girls. I have to make an effort to keep things civilised for their sake. I don't think having their dad bumped off would go down well.' Dora laughed as she stirred in the milk.

'Just her then, but would you want him back? He's probably crawling with fuck knows what. You'd have to dip his dick in bleach.'

'Ew.' Dora tried to shake the image from her mind. 'You have such a way with words.'

'I'm just saying.' Eddie picked up a mug of tea. 'You should learn to use a couple of them yourself.'

'I don't like swearing.'

'They're just words, Dora, but they make you feel so much better. Let's go and sit down. You can bring what's left of the birthday cake Charlie gave me.'

Dora cut a couple of slices from the cake, put them on a plate, and carried it through to the sitting room. She placed the cake on the table between the armchair and sofa before sitting with her legs tucked up.

'You really don't have to worry. I'll take care of you. You can move in with me and the girls can stay during the holidays.' Eddie took a slice of cake and bit into it.

'Thanks.' Dora felt her throat constrict and tears prick her eyes. She took a sip of tea and picked up the cake. 'I think it's a better option than moving in with Mum.' She bit into the cake.

'She only worries about you. You need to get out more, have some fun, get laid.' Eddie grinned. 'You've been moping around the house for too long. Your mum said you don't bother getting dressed most days.'

Dora took another swig of tea to wash away the icing that stuck to her teeth. 'What's the point in getting dressed? I work from home and there's no one to see me in my dressing gown.'

'That's the point. You're a good-looking woman, you shouldn't be hiding in the house. You need to be out. Put some make-up on and live your life. You're too young to be on your own.'

'I'm not interested in finding someone else. I'm thirty-eight, not twenty. What do you want me to do? Join a dating site and go out on dates with a string of weirdos?' Dora took another bite of cake.

'It would be a start.' Eddie's expression became serious. 'Actually, there is something I want you to do for me.'

'Please don't tell me you've set me up on a blind date.'

'No, nothing like that, although it will get you out of the house and away for a few days. I want you to write a book about my life.'

'Oh, the thing is I only write articles for a magazine and not very good ones. I wouldn't know where to start. I could write your memoirs, put them in a file with some nice pictures if that's the sort of thing that you want.'

'No, I want a book. One that can be published and shared.'

'I see. I'm not sure how easy it would be for you to get a publisher. It's mostly celebrities that write that sort of thing.'

'Self-publish, I've heard people do that now. I'm sure you can manage that. You have loads of followers on social media. I'm not interested in the money. You can keep it all. I just want to tell my story.'

'Okay, if it means that much to you. I can do some work on it, but I have a deadline for the next article. I won't be able to give it my full attention until I've finished.'

'Fuck the magazine.' Eddie sat forward in the chair. 'What are you writing about now? Ten tips to clean your bathroom? You said you weren't making enough money to pay the bills. This story will sell. There are far worse things in life than you could ever conjure up in your imagination. Things that would give you nightmares. I need to tell you things, I wish I didn't have to, but you need to know. You might even find out where a body is buried.'

'Have you been maxing out on painkillers?' Dora asked. 'Those things can make you a bit confused.'

'I'm serious,' Eddie snapped. 'There are things about me you don't know. I want you to hear it from me. It will be too late when I'm gone, you'll never know the truth.'

Anxiety twisted Dora's stomach. 'I thought you said you were okay.'

'I am, but I'm not going to be around forever,' Eddie said.

'I've known you all my life,' Dora said. 'Do you really think I would listen to anything bad being said about you?'

'No.' Eddie's face softened. 'You know you are the closest I have to a daughter. You, Charlie, your mum and dad, rest his soul, are my family. I've done some bad shit in the past. Really bad shit. You know I did a stretch.'

'Mum did mention that you had been in prison, but she didn't say what for.' Oh God, he mentioned a body, maybe he killed someone, she thought. 'Look, it honestly doesn't matter what you've done. It's in the past. Perhaps it's best that I don't know.' Dora picked up her mug and drank down the tea.

'It does matter. I need to put things right.' Eddie stood up and walked to the cupboard that was set against the wall. 'Finish your cake.' He knelt down to open the door with a groan.

Dora picked up the cake and took a small bite. The thick icing now made her feel sick. She put it back on the plate. She didn't want to hear what Eddie had done in the past. It would ruin the memories of the man who took her on trips as a child, bought her first car, and comforted her when her father died.

Eddie took a Dictaphone from the cupboard and returned to his seat.

'You want to tape the conversation?' Dora asked. 'There are easier ways. I can bring over my voice recorder, it transfers straight to the laptop.'

'I prefer to do things the old way. It's safer.' Eddie's expression darkened. 'Computers aren't safe. Anyone can hack in and get the information. Anyway, we're not going to tape anything today. It's already done.' Eddie pulled out the miniature tape and showed it to Dora. 'This is Tape One. Keep it safe and don't tell anyone about it.' He slotted the tape back into the recorder and handed it to Dora.

'I think there's one of these in Gary's desk drawer at home. It just needs batteries. You better keep this one so you can finish your story.'

'I don't need it anymore.'

'Okay, do you want me to listen to it now?'

'No, take it home and listen, then if you have any questions you can ask me next time you come over.'

'So your whole life story is on this tape?' Dora asked.

'No, there are five tapes altogether. The thing is, it's not just my story to tell. That's why I've been away, to talk to the others that were involved. I want you to meet them first. They each have a tape. Meet them and talk to them before you make any judgements. They've agreed to talk to you and answer any questions you have. Everything we did was for a reason. You're going to have to find some of the pieces to the puzzle yourself.'

'And they have all agreed to the story being written? Are you sure you want to make it public?'

'That will be up to you. You can choose to do nothing and keep it to yourself or you can share it with the world.'

'Why is it down to me? It's your story.'

'You'll understand when you've listened to all the tapes. I've arranged for us to go to London on Saturday. We can stay with Charlie for a few days.'

'I can't just go away.'

'Why not? You've got five days to sort yourself out. We'll only be gone a few days. A week at the most.'

'What about work?' Dora sat back on the sofa.

'Bring your laptop and you can work on the train. Trust me, when you listen to the tapes you won't want to bother with your articles. This will be a story you'll want to finish. I'm sorry, Dora. I didn't want to put this on you, but I have no other choice.' Eddie looked away but not before Dora saw the tears gather in his eyes.

Dora wanted to go to him and give him a hug but knew he didn't like showing emotion. The only time she had seen him cry was at her father's funeral and then he had walked away embarrassed.

'It's alright, I don't mind. You've always been there for me. It's the least I can do. We'll go to London and have some fun when we're there. I'll meet your friends and listen to the tapes. I'll start tonight. I'll listen to the tape and type it up.'

'No.' Eddie cleared his throat. 'Don't put anything on the computer. It can be hacked, or someone could nick it.'

'I don't think anyone would be interested in hacking my computer. It is full of rubbish.'

'Just listen to the tape, nothing else.'

'Okay, if it makes you feel better.'

'Good, and not a word to anyone about this.'

'Okay.' Dora stood and tucked the Dictaphone into her handbag. 'I'll pop in and see you tomorrow.'

'No, I think it's best you stay away until Saturday. Just in case.'

'In case of what?'

'Never mind.' Eddie smiled. 'Don't worry about it. I'll see you Saturday morning. Pack for the week. We'll catch the train. You can leave your car at the station.'

'Okay, I'm sure Mum will look after the cat. At least it will get her off my case about going out.'

Dora stepped out into the dark. She hunched her shoulders against the cold as she walked up the hill with her mind whirring. Either Eddie had done something really bad in the past that he was ashamed of or the chemo was making him a bit crazy. Dora stopped as a horrible thought came into her head. Maybe the cancer had gone to his brain. She carried on walking. Eddie's words about a buried body came back to her along with images of him beating someone to death. No, not Eddie, he couldn't have killed someone, she thought.

By the time she reached home she was cold and breathless. She changed into her pyjamas and dressing gown then called the cat in. With a cup of tea and a packet of biscuits she curled up on the sofa. She picked up the Dictaphone and pressed play.

Chapter Two

Eddie 1964

I guess I should start with the last memory I have of my mother. I was eight years old. My father had left when I was a baby. Mum wasn't the type of woman to be on her own for too long. There were always lots of people in the house, they would come for parties. Then there were the uncles who would come and go. One left us with my sister, Julie, who was four years younger than me. Most of the men were okay, some would even give me a few coppers to buy sweets. All that changed when Patrick moved in. He was a nasty bastard who'd find any excuse to give me a smack. I soon learned to stay out of his way.

With him came a group of people who would hang out in our house most evenings, playing loud music, dancing, smoking, and taking drugs. The air was so thick with smoke it made me and Julie cough all the time. Mum seemed to get thinner by the day. She gave up cooking dinner and was either crashed out or partying with the others.

If I could go back and change things, I would start with the Saturday afternoon that I did something stupid.

The consequences would stay with me for the rest of my life and eventually take Julie's life.

Weekends usually meant that I could stay out all day. Sometimes I would take Julie with me, there were always younger kids out that she could play with. Weekends also meant no school. The only good thing about school was that you got to eat at lunchtime. For me that was the only meal I would have. I didn't do well at school. I just couldn't understand the mathematics and when it came to reading and writing I always got my letters jumbled up. That's why I always had welts across my knuckles from where the teacher would hit me with a ruler. Sometimes I got the cane. There were times when Mum would let me bunk off school so I could take Julie off her hands. Those days were long because there was no one else to play with and no food in the cupboards.

We lived in a mid-terraced house in Adamstown, Cardiff. It was a close community with friendly neighbours, and you could play out until all hours without coming to any harm. Mum didn't seem to want to be part of the community. She kept to her own friends and rarely bothered with the neighbours.

On that fateful Saturday, I was outside playing ball with the other boys from our street. I was a skinny boy with scabby knees and bruised legs, unwashed with shabby clothes. The other boys didn't seem to care. We were all enjoying a warm summer's day, the energetic game making our faces puce and our hands sweaty.

'Eddie, get in here!' My mum was stood at the door.

'Can I finish the game?' I didn't want to go inside.

'Now!' My mother always seemed to be shouting.

'See you later.' I left the boys and walked into the house. It was dark inside after being out in the sun. It didn't help that the curtains were still drawn.

'I want you to go to the shop and pick up some fags,' Mum said. She was dressed in a flower print cotton dress, her blond hair piled on top of her head, bright lipstick and spider eyelashes.

'Okay, can I have a glass of water first?'

'Hurry up.' She picked up her handbag.

In the kitchen I gulped down a glass of water, enjoying the feel of the cool liquid running down my throat. I splashed some water on my face and went back to the sitting room. Mum had emptied her purse onto the table and was counting the coppers. Patrick was lounging on the sofa wearing a pair of jeans and a grubby white vest, his beady eyes watching me, waiting to pounce. Julie was sat behind the sofa clutching a ragged teddy bear and sucking her thumb. Silent tears ran down her face tracking through the grime. She had learned to keep quiet.

'What's up, Jules?' I knelt down beside her.

'I'm hungry.' She stared at me with large blue eyes.

'Mum, Julie's hungry.'

Mum ignored me and started to root around in the bottom of her handbag. I went into the kitchen and searched the cupboards. They were empty apart from some old teabags, and sugar that had hardened into a block. In the fridge, half a block of lard sat next to something blue and furry in a dish.

'Give us a couple of bob,' I heard Mum ask Patrick as I walked back into the sitting room.

'I'm skint,' Patrick grunted.

Mum upturned the cushions on the chairs and pushed her hands down the side. Her frown turned to a smile and she pulled her hand out, clutching a few coppers. She handed me the carefully counted pennies with a note.

'Don't dawdle,' she warned.

I looked at Julie who was still sat behind the sofa. 'Could I have a bit more to get some food? Julie's really hungry and there's nothing in the kitchen.'

Mum stared at me for a moment. 'I haven't got any more, you can have some chips later.'

'But–'

Patrick flew off the sofa. I heard the crack before I felt the sting of his hand. 'Don't talk back to your mother,' he snarled. 'Get out before I take my belt to you.'

I walked to the shop, the side of my head smarting from the slap. I hated Patrick; sometimes I hated my mother. She would drink for the rest of the day and there would be no chips. It would be another night going to bed hungry.

The door to the shop opened with the tinkling of a bell. There was a customer at the counter talking to the shopkeeper, so I walked around looking at the food. The smell of bread made my mouth water and my stomach cramp with hunger. I desperately wanted to snatch a bar of chocolate, rip off the wrapper and stuff it in my mouth. It felt like torture, I was surrounded by food but couldn't eat anything. I walked down the tins aisle, looking at the pictures and trying to imagine the taste. My eyes fell on the tins of condensed milk stacked neatly. I thought of Julie back home, hungry and crying. I glanced at the shopkeeper, he was still busy talking so I grabbed a can and stuck it down the back of my shorts. I didn't have anywhere else to put it.

At the counter I handed the coppers and the note to the shopkeeper. He took his time counting the money. The tin was sliding further down my shorts, so I shoved my hand behind my back and wiggled it back into place. The bell sounded on the door and another customer came in, I was afraid they would stand behind me and see the bulge in my shorts, so I turned to the side. Finally, the shopkeeper turned and took a packet of cigarettes off the shelf and handed them to me.

As I turned to leave, I noticed the crate of bread near the door. The shopkeeper was busy with the next customer, so I grabbed a loaf and bolted.

'Hey, you, get back here!' The shopkeeper was at the door yelling.

I legged it all the way home and crashed through the front door. Panting for breath I put the cigarettes down on the coffee table and went into the kitchen. Mum didn't notice the loaf of bread in my hands.

In the kitchen I cut two slices of bread, opened the tin of condensed milk and spread it thickly on the bread. I crept into the sitting room and crouched down next to Julie who hadn't moved since I left the house.

'I've made you some food,' I whispered.

A smile lit her face and she followed me into the kitchen. I closed the door and sat her at the table with the sandwich and a glass of water. While she ate, I made another sandwich, cutting thick slices of bread. I took a large bite, it tasted wonderful. I had just taken another bite when I heard the banging at the door. I gulped down the mouthful and stuffed as much of the remaining sandwich in my mouth as I could. I knew I was in trouble so I was going to eat as much as I could before it got taken away.

The kitchen door flew open and Mum stood gaping at me and Julie. A policeman peered over her shoulder.

'How could you?' she shrieked. 'Nicking from the shop.' She grabbed at my hand trying to prise the rest of the bread from my fingers.

I couldn't speak. My mouth was stuffed full of bread and it was difficult to chew with Mum pulling at me and the policeman watching. I saw him look at Julie. His eyes taking in her dirty bare feet, stick-thin legs, and the bruise on the side of her face.

'I'll sort this.' Patrick stormed into the kitchen. He hit me so hard I flew across the kitchen and landed in a heap on the floor, blood mixed with the bread in my mouth. Julie started to scream. Patrick raised his hand to her, and she stopped.

'There's no need for that,' the policeman said.

'Good beating is what the boy needs.' Patrick grabbed my arm and hauled me to my feet. 'He won't do it again.'

'Let him go,' the policeman said.

Patrick let go and turned on the policeman. 'You can piss off now, I'll deal with the boy. You can tell the shopkeeper he's been punished and won't steal again.'

'The goods still have to be paid for,' the policeman said.

'Well, I'm not paying for them,' my mum said. 'It's not my fault he nicked the stuff.'

'You heard her,' Patrick growled. 'She's not paying, now out.' Patrick shoved the policeman in the chest.

I sat there watching, hoping that the policeman would give Patrick a good thumping.

'I think I've got a good idea of what's going on here.' The policeman looked at Julie who was sucking her thumb. 'The boy was obviously hungry. I think it's best I take him to the station. We can sort it out there.'

I looked from Patrick to the policeman. I didn't really want to go to the police station, but it seemed a better option than staying there with Patrick.

'I'll go.' I stepped forward.

'You stay there, you little shit.' Patrick turned on me but before he had a chance to give me another whack the policeman grabbed hold of his arm. Patrick turned and drove his fist into the policeman's face. The policeman staggered backwards; he regained his balance and withdrew his truncheon.

'No, Patrick!' My mum screeched as she tried to pull him back.

Patrick lashed out at Mum. The back of his hand caught her across the face. The policeman raised his arm and brought the truncheon down on Patrick with a crack. Enraged, Patrick flew at the policeman. I watched with fascination as the truncheon rained down on Patrick, blow after blow until Patrick slumped to the floor dazed. I wanted the policeman to keep hitting him, but he stopped. He cuffed Patrick and dragged him out of the house.

'Now look what you've done,' Mum sobbed. She stomped out of the kitchen. I followed her into the sitting room and watched her fill a glass with clear liquid and knock it back. She refilled the glass and looked at me. 'Just get out of my sight.'

I stayed in the kitchen with Julie. I mixed the last of the condensed milk with water and filled two glasses. I didn't dare go back into the sitting room. I'm not sure how long we sat there but it seemed like hours. A knock at the door filled the silence. I thought perhaps the policeman had come back to take me to the station. I peered around the kitchen door. Mum was crashed out on the sofa, an empty bottle and glass sat on the coffee table. Another knock at the door, louder this time. Mum didn't stir so I went to the door and opened it.

A woman and a man stood on the pavement, they were dressed smartly. She wore a floral dress with a pink cardigan draped over her shoulders, the man wore a suit. They didn't look like friends of Mum's, and friends usually came in without knocking. Behind them I could see a black car, the paint reflecting the sun.

'Is your mother home?' the woman asked.

'She's sleeping.'

'We're from social services,' the man said.

I had no idea what that meant. 'I'll tell her you called.'

'We really need to come in and talk to you and your sister. My name is Jenny, and this is Austin,' the woman said with a smile. 'I'm sure your mother won't mind. We'll explain things to her when she wakes up.'

'Okay.' I let them in and showed them into the kitchen.

'Hello,' Jenny said, 'what's your name?'

Julie stared at the visitors.

'That's Julie.'

'And how is old is Julie?'

'She's four,' I told them.

'And you're Edward?'

'Eddie.' I didn't like being called Edward. 'I'm eight,' I offered.

22

'How did you cut your lip?' Austin asked.

I knew I would be in trouble if I told on Patrick, so I didn't say anything.

'And that's a nasty bruise your sister has got on her cheek.' Austin gave Jenny a strange look.

Jenny sat down and started asking all sorts of questions. Questions about my father, questions about Patrick, and how often my mother drank. As she asked questions, Austin peered into the kitchen cupboards and then left the room. I wished Mum would wake up and make these people leave.

Austin came back into the kitchen and nodded to Jenny. 'Right, Eddie, you and Julie are going to come with us.'

'Why?' I asked. My stomach felt funny like it was full of worms.

'You and your sister are going to go to Bracken House for a few days. Just a little holiday,' Jenny said.

'But I don't want to go. Is it because I stole the bread?'

'Why did you steal the bread?' Austin asked.

'Julie was hungry, and she was crying.'

'You did a good thing getting your sister something to eat. You don't have to worry, you're not in any trouble. Your mother needs a little break to sort out some things. Be a good boy now and go with Jenny to the car. You don't want to upset your sister, do you? I'll wake your mother and have a little chat.'

I took Julie's hand and led her outside, Jenny followed. My stomach was churning, and I tried hard not to cry. As we sat in the car, with the hot leather seats burning my back I couldn't stop the tears. I put my arm around Julie who sucked her thumb and clutched her teddy in the other hand.

* * *

Bracken House was an enormous grey building with three floors. There were two smaller buildings on either side. A fence ran around the perimeter with a large lawn in the centre, trees on one side and a yard on the other, separated by the driveway. Austin stopped the car and I could see groups of children running around. Some stopped and approached the car to get a look at the newcomers.

'Come along.' Austin opened the door and beckoned me to come out.

Jenny took Julie from the other side and started to walk to the left of the building. I followed Jenny, aware of the children gathered behind us. Austin shooed them away.

Inside the building we were taken to a large room where a man sat. He had thick-rimmed glasses and wore a short-sleeved shirt.

'Hello, I'm Dr Williams, but you can call me Dr Ray.'

Julie moved closer to me and buried her head in my stomach.

'This is Eddie and Julie,' Jenny said.

'No need to be afraid,' Dr Ray said. 'I just need to have a look at you.'

He examined me first, looking at my face, then he checked the rest of my body. He made some notes then examined Julie. He took his time looking at Julie, talked to her, and even tickled her to make her smile.

'Okay, you can take them to see the nurse.' The doctor returned to his notes.

We were taken to another room where a nurse weighed and measured us before checking our hair for nits. After we'd been scrubbed with cold water and carbolic soap we had to sit still to have our hair cut short. Julie screamed as her blond curls fell to the floor.

'Right let's get you two settled in,' Austin said. 'You come with me, Eddie.'

Panic crushed my chest. 'What about Julie?' I didn't want to leave her alone.

'She'll be placed in the nursery,' Jenny said.

Julie began to wail. She threw her arms around my waist, clinging so tightly that Jenny had to prise her fingers apart.

'I'll come and see you later.' I turned away and followed Austin before I started to cry myself.

We walked through the doors of the main building which had a large hall lined with coat hangers and a staircase to the left. It smelled musty and the walls were grubby with peeling paint. We passed through another set of doors to where two boys were stood against the wall next to a door. One boy had brown curly hair with long dark lashes that framed mischievous blue eyes. He had a scar running from his bottom lip over his chin. The other boy was taller, thickset with brown eyes and short dark hair.

'You boys in trouble again?' Austin asked.

'Yeah, but it weren't our fault,' the smaller one said in a cockney accent.

'It never is, Charlie.' Austin smiled.

'Alright?' Charlie smiled at me.

I nodded. Maybe this place wouldn't be so bad. Before Charlie had a chance to say any more Austin knocked the door and opened it. I followed him inside and looked around. The room had a desk with a leather chair. Next to the fireplace was a comfy-looking armchair with a table holding a glass and an open book.

'This is Mr Wainwright,' Austin said. 'He is in charge of all the boys. This is Eddie.' He put his hand on my shoulder. 'I'll leave you now, I'll come back in a few days to see how you're getting on.'

I watched him leave then turned to look at Mr Wainwright. He was tall and slim with a bushy moustache that sat on his face like a furry caterpillar. His eyes were stern, he looked at me now with no hint of a smile.

'So, Eddie, I'm not sure what you're used to at home but here we have rules. If you behave and stick to the rules we'll get along fine.'

I didn't say anything.

'Well, boy?'

'Erm, yeah, okay.'

'Yes *sir*, or yes Mr Wainwright.'

'Yes, sir.'

'Good. You will get up at seven each morning and make your bed. Wash and dress before you go to breakfast. There is no talking during mealtimes. After breakfast you will wash and dry your plate then put it away. During the week you walk to school, after school you come straight back here. You stay out in the grounds until teatime. You are not to come indoors and wander around the house until you are called in. Bedtime is at eight, no one is permitted out of bed after this time. On weekends you will be given chores, after these are complete you may go outside. We do not tolerate bad language, fighting, or answering back. Is that understood?'

My mind had wandered while Mr Wainwright spoke, so I hadn't heard half of what he said. He looked at me expectantly.

'Yes, sir,' I answered.

'Good. You can go outside now.'

I stood there looking at Mr Wainwright. I didn't know what I was supposed to do, and I desperately needed a pee.

'What are you waiting for?' Mr Wainwright frowned.

'I need to go to the toilet.'

'The toilet block is at the back of the house.' He strode to the door and yanked it open. 'You two, get in here,' he ordered.

I scuttled out the door past Charlie and his friend. I could hear Mr Wainwright shouting as I stepped out the front door. I walked around the side of the house and spotted the toilet block. You could smell it before you stepped inside. Filthy urinals festering in the heat. I peed as quickly as I could whilst holding my breath. Outside I took a deep breath and walked back to the front of the house. I wasn't sure where I should go. The boys playing in groups ignored me as I walked past. I felt tired now, the day seemed endless and I had no idea of the time. I decided to walk to the edge of the lawn where large sycamore trees gave shade; I thought perhaps I could sit down and rest. As I got nearer, I spotted a group of five boys; they were shouting and jeering. Another boy stood in front of them seemingly trying to block their way. I walked closer and saw two small boys crouched at the base of the tree. One had white blond hair; the other dark hair set against a pale face. The boys didn't look much older than Julie. The pale boy was crying and the other was huddled close to him.

'What're you doing?' I asked.

Five pairs of eyes turned on me. The other boy shook his head and waved his hand at me to go.

'You a new boy?' one of them asked.

'Yeah, I'm Eddie.' I tried to force a smile.

'This is our tree and we don't allow freaks to sit here, so piss off.'

The other boys laughed.

'Go and pick on someone your own age, Malcom,' the boy defending the young ones said.

'What you going to do about it, Denny? Boris is with Wainwright.'

I looked at the two boys on the floor. 'They're only small. Why don't you leave them alone? There are plenty of trees.'

Without warning Malcom's fist slammed into my face. I fell backwards as Denny went for Malcom. I was used to getting thumped by Patrick, so I wasn't afraid, but there were five against two, so we didn't stand a chance. I got up anyway and joined in, throwing punches and kicks where I could. From behind me came a shout, I turned and saw Charlie and his friend running towards us just before I was hit to the ground. I wasn't sure which side they were on until the big boy with Charlie charged at Malcom and knocked him down. He jumped on his chest and started to pummel his face. The other boys backed off.

'You okay?' Charlie held out his hand.

'Yeah.' I wiped the blood from my nose with the back of my hand and let Charlie help me up.

'Enough, Boris.' Charlie put his hand on the big boy's shoulder.

Boris climbed off Malcom. 'You stay away from my brother.' He gave Malcom a kick before crouching down next to the two boys. 'Come on, Iosif.' He pulled up the dark-haired pale boy. 'It's okay now.' He put his arms around the boy and kissed the top of his head. 'Are you hurt, MJ?'

The smaller blond boy shook his head.

'Wainwright,' Denny said.

We all turned and saw Mr Wainwright striding towards us.

'Now we're in the shit,' Charlie said.

'Thanks for helping Denny with Iosif and MJ,' Boris said to me.

'You talk funny.' It was out of my mouth before I had a chance to stop it.

'I'm Russian,' Boris said.

'Oh.' I didn't know what he meant.

'He's from Russia,' Charlie said. 'Bleeding foreigner like me. I'm from London.'

'You should go back where you came from,' Malcom hissed.

'Get outside my office, all of you!' Wainwright boomed, his eyes blazed, and he was red in the face.

I felt sick. I was hurting all over and my legs felt too weak to walk back to the house. Whatever punishment awaited me there, I knew it wouldn't be good. We trailed behind Wainwright and stood in a line against the wall outside his office.

'What happens now?' I asked.

'You get one hundred whacks with the cane,' Malcom said.

'Shut up, Malcom,' Charlie said. 'You just get a couple. Boris and I will go before you, by the time Wainwright has finished with us he'll be too tired to hit you hard.'

'Yeah, he broke a stick on me once,' Boris added.

When it was my turn to go in, sweat was trickling down the side of Mr Wainwright's face. 'You've only been here five minutes and you're already in trouble. Is there something wrong with you, boy?'

'I'm sorry, sir.' I could feel my legs shaking.

'Shorts down and bend over the desk.'

I did what I was told. The cane swished through the air and cracked as it collided with my backside. I gritted my teeth and clenched my fists, but it didn't help. Tears stung my eyes as he delivered a second and third blow.

'Get out, straight to bed, there will be no dinner.'

Charlie, Boris, and Denny were waiting outside the door for me. They took me to the dormitory. It was a gloomy room with five beds on each side. A small set of drawers sat next to each bed.

'You can have the bed in between me and Boris,' Charlie said.

From that day the four of us stuck together. We mostly spent our time watching out for Iosif and MJ. We protected newcomers from Malcom and his gang; boys like Adam who, with bright red hair and freckles, didn't stand a chance alone.

I learned that MJ had been there the longest and had been brought to the nursery as a baby. He befriended Iosif when he arrived four years later. They had been moved to the main house when they were six years old and left to fend for themselves against the older children. They were inseparable.

Iosif was a sickly boy and often had fits. MJ would sit and stroke his head until the fit passed. Boris fiercely protected his brother, and MJ became a second brother to him. I guess all of us were like brothers. We had no one else. I worried about Julie, alone in the nursery. The boys would help me sneak in so I could spend a little time with her. She had made some friends and seemed happy, although she would throw her arms around me and cover me in kisses when she saw me.

I soon settled into the routine of the house. It wasn't difficult. School five days a week and chores on the weekend. The rest of the time we were outside in all weather, often we were soaked and shivering with cold.

Some of the kids got to go home at weekends for family visits. They were the lucky ones. They stayed for a few months then returned home. Others got visitors to the house. My mother came twice. The second time she visited she said she was sorry, and things would soon be sorted out so Julie and me could go home. That was the last time I saw her. I became like Boris, Charlie, Denny, Iosif, and MJ. No visitors, no family, no one wanted us.

The only friendly adult in Bracken House was Dr Ray. We would get to see him if we were sick or injured. Because Iosif was ill so often we got to see him more than most. Dr Ray would let us all stay with Iosif when he was sick. He would give us sweets and tell us stories. He did what he could for us boys, except speak out. He could have saved a few lives.

Two years passed quickly in that place. Boris never seemed to stop growing. I had put on a little weight and wasn't the puny boy I'd been when I arrived. Julie had been moved to the main house, so I got to see her a lot more.

Sometimes we would get important visitors to the house. Police, politicians, or local celebrities. There would be a whole week of scrubbing the house. We were made to dress in our good clothes and be on our best behaviour.

The visitors brought money from fundraising, for toys and a holiday by the sea. We never got to go.

Then things changed, boys started to disappear. They would be there at bedtime and gone the next morning. We were told their families had taken them home. We started to notice that the boys that left were always the older ones, the ones who didn't have family visits. Then Adam went missing. We knew he was an orphan, so we started to ask questions. We should have stayed quiet.

Chapter Three

Dora sat in the sitting room listening to her mother rattling around in the kitchen making tea. It always made her melancholic visiting her childhood home now that her father was no longer around. Her eyes rested on the mantle where a framed photo of her father sat next to a candle that her mother lit every evening.

For two days Dora had thought of nothing but the tape Eddie had given her. No matter how hard she tried to work on her current article, her mind kept drifting to the children's home and the sad start Eddie had in life.

'I'm glad to see you're moving on with your life.' Dora's mother, Jenny, walked into the sitting room carrying two mugs. She handed one to Dora before taking a seat in the armchair. 'You've been moping around the house for far too long.'

'That's why I thought I'd go away for a few days. You okay to feed Horace?'

'Of course, so where are you going?'

'To see Charlie with Uncle Eddie.'

'Oh,' Jenny said with a frown. 'I thought you might be going somewhere nice.'

'What, like a single's holiday?' Dora laughed. 'I think I'm past all that.'

'I'm just not sure going away with Eddie is the best thing for you at the moment.'

Dora took a sip of her tea. 'Why?'

'Eddie has his own problems.'

'Have you spoken to him?'

'He called around yesterday. You know he isn't well, and I think he's a bit down.'

Dora shuffled back on the sofa. 'I'm worried about him. I think he's worse than he's letting on. What if he's dying?'

'Oh, Dora, I know how hard it hit you when your dad died, and then Gary leaving, but you can't put all your energy and emotions into worrying about Eddie. He wouldn't want you to, and sometimes it's better to let things go. What will be will be, worry won't change anything.'

'I know, but I can't help it. We're the only family he has. Dad and Charlie are like brothers to him. His heart was breaking at Dad's funeral. Did you know that he was in a children's home?'

'I don't think he mentioned it.' Jenny took a sip of her tea. 'I know he doesn't have any family, but he's never talked about it. What's he been saying to you?'

'Nothing.' Dora wondered if she should tell her mother about the tape but she had promised Eddie she would tell no one, so decided against it. 'He's just been reminiscing about the past, his friends, and how he ended up in the children's home. Did you know he had a sister?'

'No, I already said that he didn't talk about his family,' Jenny snapped.

Dora was a little taken aback by her mother's response. 'It sounds like she died. She was in the home with Eddie, he didn't say what happened to her. Do you know how Dad and Eddie met?'

'On a construction site, as far as I know.'

'It's just that Eddie mentioned someone called MJ in the home and I wondered if it was Dad. He was Michael John.'

'No one ever called him anything but Mike. It must be someone else.'

'I suppose so, it's just that I don't know anything about Dad's side of the family.'

'That's because your father was estranged from them. He never told me why and I never asked. This is why I don't think it's a good idea for you to go away with Eddie. He wants to dwell in the past and you might end up hearing things you don't want to hear.'

'Like that Eddie was in prison?'

'Yes, exactly.' Jenny stood and grabbed the mug from Dora's hand.

'I haven't finished yet.'

'I have things to do, I'm meeting Sue for craft night.' Jenny walked into the kitchen.

Dora followed her mother. 'Do you know why Eddie was in prison?'

'No, you'll have to ask him yourself, but you may not like the answer. Please, Dora, don't get involved in Eddie's trip down memory lane. If you must go away, try and get Charlie to persuade him to concentrate on the present, he needs to enjoy life while he still can.'

'I'll do my best.' Dora kissed her mother on the cheek. 'I'll see you before I go.'

* * *

When she arrived home, she was surprised to see Eddie waiting on her doorstep. He hurried to the car and opened the door.

'Is something wrong?' Dora asked.

'Quick, get in the house.' Eddie glanced up and down the road. He took Dora's arm and marched her to the front door, his eyes continuing to dart around.

'What's going on?' Dora took her keys from her bag, dropped them, stooped to pick them up, and unlocked the front door. He was making her jittery.

'We'll talk inside.'

'Okay.' Dora shut the door. 'Come and sit down. Is it bad news from the hospital?' She could feel her stomach churning.

'No, nothing like that.' Eddie stood in the room with his hand tapping against the side of his leg. 'We have to leave first thing in the morning.'

'But everything is arranged for Saturday.' Dora perched on the edge of the chair. 'Is Charlie okay?'

'Charlie is fine.' Eddie paced the room. 'Did you tell anyone about the tape?' He stopped pacing and stared at her intensely.

'No, of course not. I've only had it two days. I didn't even tell Mum. Please, sit down. You're making me nervous.'

'They must have found out. Someone on the inside, watching.'

'Who are you talking about?' Dora thought maybe she should call her Mum, or a doctor. Eddie sounded like he needed help. 'Sit down, you're worrying me.' Dora stood up. 'I'll make us a cup of tea or get you something stronger. I think Gary left some whisky in the cupboard.'

'I don't want a drink.'

'I think I need one.' Dora forced a smile.

'Listen to me.' Eddie put his hand on her shoulder. 'It's not safe, they know where I am, and they're watching me. One came to see me today. They're everywhere. Probably some of them living here. You can't trust anyone, especially the police. There are things I should've told you a long time ago, things you need to know. I thought this would be the best way. Give you time to get used to the idea. It's too much to hear at once.'

'Why don't you come and sit down and tell me what happened today? Who came to see you?' Dora sat on the sofa, hoping Eddie would calm down.

Eddie perched on the armchair with his legs jiggling. He pulled out a tin and took out a roll up.

'I thought you'd given up?' Dora said.

'I have, I just have the odd one now and then, and I really need one now.'

'Okay, if it helps.'

Eddie lit up the cigarette, took a long drag, and his shoulders relaxed. 'A vicar came to see me today.'

'Vicar Lee?'

'No, not that one, I know him. Seen him around. This one said his name was Phillip Bevan. He said he works with the hospital and helps patients through difficult times. He asked how I was feeling and if there was anything he could do for me. I found it odd that he should be calling around. For a start I don't think the hospital would've given my name and address. I told him I didn't have any faith in the church, I trust God but not men. He quoted some Bible mumbo at me then talked about putting my life in order, addressing things in the past that I might want to talk through, a bit like a confession. He said there was a service available that helps type memoirs, something to leave for loved ones. I asked him who sent him. He insisted the hospital sent him, that it was a part of the care programme. I threw him out.' Eddie took another drag of the cigarette, coughed and stubbed it out on the tin.

Dora imagined the vicar being marched out the front door with a few choice words. She tried not to smile. 'I don't understand why this has upset you so much.'

'Don't you see? He wanted information. They must know what I'm planning, that I'm going to tell you my story.'

'I think you're reading too much into it. It's just a coincidence that he called around today. Like he said, it's a service offered by the hospital. Probably lots of patients have had a visit. Writing memoirs is one way of coping if you are facing death. So it's not an unusual suggestion.'

'No, you don't understand.' Eddie leaped from the chair. 'They know, it's not safe. We have to leave in the morning. I've already called Charlie.'

Maybe it will be a good thing to go tomorrow. Charlie will be able to calm him down and know what to do, Dora thought. 'Okay, I'll book our train tickets for the morning.'

'No, we'll buy them at the station. I don't want anyone to know our plans.'

'Right, I'll pack tonight and pick you up in the morning. Let me drive you home.' Dora stood up.

'I'll walk, I don't want you to be seen with me.'

'Then stay here the night, we'll go to your house early in the morning to pick up your things.'

Eddie frowned as he considered the offer. 'No, I'll go and pack. I need to sort a few things out, make some calls. Where's the tape I gave you?'

'On the desk in Gary's study. I've listened to it twice. It's a sad story and I have so many questions. Like what happened to Adam?'

'We'll talk about it when we get to Charlie's. That's only the beginning of the story, you're going to hear a lot of bad stuff. You'll hear things about me that will shock you, just keep an open mind until you've heard the whole story.'

'Okay, but you mustn't worry, whatever you've done in the past doesn't matter to me.'

'It will. Go get the tape.'

Dora went into the study and grabbed the tape then offered it to Eddie.

'I don't want it back, I want you to hide it, put it somewhere safe.'

Dora looked around the room and her eyes fell on the cat basket. She knelt down and pushed the tape under the cushion.

'There, no one will think of looking in Horace's basket.'

'Good, I want you to lock the door when I leave, don't open it for anyone. If anything happens to me, call Charlie. He will help you, he'll look after you, trust no one else. You have his number?'

'Yes.'

'I'll see you in the morning.' Eddie pulled her into a hug and placed a kiss on the top of her head before walking out the front door.

Dora twisted the key in the lock, more so that Eddie would hear the lock click than for concern for her safety. Upstairs in the bedroom she laid the suitcase on the bed and started to select clothes for the trip. As she collected toiletries and added them to the case an uneasy feeling crept over her, a deep foreboding that made her stop and sit down on the bed. She tried to shake away the feeling. *Eddie is just being paranoid, he's unwell. It'll be okay when we get to Charlie's tomorrow. But what if there is something in his past that someone wants forgotten? What if there is someone watching him?* she thought.

She zipped the case, took it downstairs and placed it by the door, then sat in the kitchen with her laptop. She opened her notebook and looked at the list of names she had written when listening to the tape. Next to *MJ* she had written *Dad* with a question mark. MJ could still be her father; maybe he never told her mum about the children's home.

On the laptop she opened a search engine and entered *Bracken House, Cardiff*, and *missing boy, Adam*. The top search listed Bracken House with the words *missing boy* crossed out. She opened the link and read.

> In 1936 Bracken House was an approved school for delinquent boys aged between 10 and 13. In 1956 it became a children's home for boys and girls up to the age of 16. The home was split into three buildings. A nursery for children up to age 6, the main house for children between 6

and 16, and a clinic, used for the treatment of illness and to isolate those suffering from contagious infections.

Those who worked at Bracken House came under investigation in 1998 when a large police operation, investigating abuse in children's homes across Wales, found evidence of abuse from the late seventies spanning over 10 years. In 2001 David Wainwright, manager of the home at the time, was found guilty of 21 counts of sexual and physical abuse. Wainwright, then in his mid-sixties, was sentenced to fifteen years in prison. Four other care workers at the home were also given lengthy sentences. Bracken House closed as a children's home in 1991 and the building was converted to flats.

Those poor kids, she thought, I hope Wainwright died in jail. She tried another search, this time using the words, *missing boys Cardiff 1970s*. A link came up with missing children in the UK. She clicked on the site. It was shocking to see the number of children listed as missing. A lot of them teenagers, each one had a smiling picture. Dora scanned the lists of names. There was no listing for Adam but as she reached the bottom of the page the name Iosif Orlov stood out. There was no picture, just a brief description with the words *missing since 1971, aged 12, last seen in Cardiff.* She quickly checked the rest of the names, nothing for Boris or Adam.

Dora guessed that Iosif had to be Boris's brother, even though Eddie hadn't mentioned the surname. Iosif was an unusual name. It didn't make sense to her. Boris and the other boys looked after Iosif so he couldn't have run away. Eddie hadn't said anything on the tape about Iosif going missing. Unless something happened later.

Dora shut down the laptop and packed it for the trip. She climbed into bed and pulled the covers over her shoulder. For the first time in months she felt uneasy about being alone in the house.

Chapter Four

It was just after nine when Dora parked outside Eddie's bungalow. She tooted the horn and waited for ten minutes. When he didn't come out, she got out of the car and walked to the front door thinking that he'd overslept. She tried the door. It was open, so she stepped inside. The first thing she noticed was the mess in the kitchen. All the drawers and cupboards were open, with the storage jars upturned. *What the hell has he been doing?*

'Uncle Eddie!' she called out as she walked into the passage.

There was no sound. Her heart started to thud in her chest. What if he was ill in the night and couldn't call for help? She rushed to the bedroom and flung open the door. It was in the same state as the kitchen, clothes pulled out of drawers, dressing table swept clean, the contents lying on the floor. Dora felt panic constrict her chest.

'Uncle Eddie!' She made for the sitting room and pushed open the door. 'Oh God.' She looked around wildly. Papers and photos were strewn across the floor, she stepped further in, and it was then that she saw Eddie sat in the chair. She stumbled forward, her breath caught in her throat, her brain not registering what she was seeing.

Eddie's eyes stared back, wide and still. His mouth gaped open to reveal a bloody hole, congealed blood covered his chin and soaked through his T-shirt. A scream escaped Dora's mouth. She stood, unable to move or draw her eyes away from the horror before her. Her eyes travelled down his blood-soaked body to where his hands were bound together on his lap, stubs instead of fingers had dripped blood onto his jeans.

Dora felt her skin prickle as a cold sweat covered her body. Her breath came out in short shallow gasps, her eyes started to blur. Blackness crept around the edge of her vision. She felt herself fading as her body fell. She was unconscious before she hit the ground.

She slowly became aware of her surroundings. She was lying with her cheek pressed against the carpet. It felt uncomfortable, sticky. Confusion fogged her mind. She rolled onto her back and stared up at the ceiling, put her hand to her cheek and rubbed before putting her hand in front of her face. Blood. Panic gripped her body and she struggled for breath. Don't look, she told herself. She squeezed her eyes shut but she couldn't block out the image of Eddie sat bound in the chair. She knew if she tilted her head back, she would see him behind her. She felt around for her handbag and located it by her side. She could feel the blood seeping from the carpet into her jeans, bile rose in her throat.

Dora's hands shook violently as she tried to release the zipper on her bag. She forced herself to sit up and peek through her lashes. She opened her bag and took out her mobile phone, dialling 999 as she tried to fight the dizziness. It took her a moment to realise that there was a voice on the line.

'Help, I need help.' Dora didn't recognise her own voice.

'What service do you require?'

'P… Police.' Dora peeked over her shoulder to check she hadn't imagined Eddie tied to a chair. It didn't seem real.

'Can you give me your location?'

'Number 2.' Dora's eyes trailed along the carpet to where two of Eddie's fingers lay discarded with his tongue. 'Oh, God, no.' She felt a fresh wave of dizziness and without warning she emptied the contents of her stomach on the floor.

'Hello? Hello? Are you okay, love?'

'No.' Dora just managed to finish the address before she started retching again. 'I have to get out of here.' She tried to stand but her head spun so she crawled towards the sitting room door.

'Help is on the way. Can you tell me your name?'

'Do… Dora.'

'Okay, Dora, are you hurt?'

'No.' Dora continued to crawl towards the kitchen.

'Can you tell me what's happened?'

'He's dead, someone's killed him.'

'Who's dead?'

'Uncle Eddie.'

'Is there someone there with you?'

'No, I'm on my own.'

'Have you checked for a pulse, is he breathing?'

'No, he's dead, there's blood everywhere.' Dora tried to draw in breath, but it felt like there was no oxygen. 'I can't go back in the room.'

'Okay, the police and an ambulance will be with you shortly. I'm going to stay on the phone until they get there. I want you to try and take a deep breath for me, hold it and blow out slowly.'

Dora reached the kitchen and sat slumped against the cupboard. She listened to the woman's calm voice on the line and tried to follow her instructions. She felt detached from her body, dizzy with an overwhelming fatigue.

'I don't feel well.'

'Is there somewhere you can lie down safely?'

'Yes.' Dora lay down on the floor. The cool tiles felt comforting. 'I can hear sirens.'

'They're nearly with you. Is the door open?'

'Yes, it's not locked.'

The sirens grew louder, and Dora heard a car pull up outside. 'They're here.'

'Okay, I'm going to leave you now.'

'Thank you.' The line went dead, and Dora felt alone and scared. A few moments later the door opened, and Dora saw a pair of shoes approach.

'Dora?' A policeman crouched down beside her, his radio crackling. 'Are you hurt?'

'No.' Dora shook her head. 'He's in the sitting room.'

'Okay, I'm going to take a look. Matt is going to look after you.'

'The ambulance has just arrived, we'll get the paramedics to check you over.' Matt crouched at her side. 'Do you think you can sit up?'

'No, I feel dizzy.'

'Okay, you just lie there for now.'

Dora heard a shout from the sitting room, she turned her head and saw the policeman run into the kitchen. He made straight for the door and flung it open. She heard him throw up, her own stomach contracted with the memory of what she had seen. The policeman was now talking urgently on his radio, but she couldn't make out what he was saying.

A paramedic entered the kitchen and put an oxygen mask over Dora's face, then checked her pulse and blood pressure, all the while talking in soothing tones. Dora didn't want to speak anymore, didn't want to listen to the commotion around her or think about Eddie in the sitting room. She let the paramedic wrap a blanket around her and lead her to the waiting ambulance.

* * *

'Dora.' Her mother's voice broke through the haze of her mind. She didn't want to open her eyes; if she opened them reality would seep in, Eddie would be dead, tied to a chair and tortured.

When she arrived at the hospital she had been examined by a doctor and given tranquilizers; they took effect quickly, numbing the shock and making her body feel heavy. Now she just wanted to sleep. Maybe then she could wake up from the nightmare.

'Dora.' Her mother's voice was tearful.

Dora opened her eyes. 'Oh, Mum.' She struggled to lift her head. It felt unnaturally heavy.

'Let me help you.'

Dora allowed her mother to help her sit up and prop a pillow behind her back. 'Is he really dead?'

'Yes, try not to think about it,' Jenny said.

'How are you feeling now?' A nurse walked into the room.

'A bit dazed,' Dora said.

'It will take a while for the sedative to wear off and even then you may feel a little detached. It's only natural after a shock. There are two detectives outside, are you up to talking to them?'

Dora rubbed her hands over her face. 'I don't know.'

'They said it's important they speak with you. Perhaps they can have a few minutes. I'll ask them to keep it brief.'

'Okay.'

The nurse left the room and two men entered. One was stocky with a round open face, and grey hair. He looked to be in his fifties. The other was younger with cropped brown hair and a hard expression.

'Hello, Isadora, I'm DI Wayne Price,' the older one said. 'And this is DS Rhys Sims. We won't keep you long.'

'Is it alright if I stay? I'm Dora's mother, Jenny Jones.'

'That's fine.' DI Price dragged a chair over to the bed and sat down. DS Sims did the same, taking out his notebook.

a strange thing to do. He could've just told me the whole story himself or given me all the tapes. He was adamant that I didn't use my laptop to type up notes in case it was hacked. I'm beginning to think he was right. Whoever killed him was probably after the tapes but how would anyone know about them?'

'You need to forget about this. Get rid of the tape you have, and don't mention it to anyone. You don't know what Eddie was mixed up in. Think of the type of people he met in prison.'

'But he wanted me to know. Whatever it is, he was willing to die for it.'

'There is a madman out there somewhere.' Jenny's voice rose. 'Just leave it alone. I don't want you getting involved. The police don't need to know about the tape. There's nothing on it that will help them.' She stood and let out a sigh. 'I'm going to leave you now to get some rest. I'll come back in the morning and take you to the police station then you can stay a few days with me.'

'Thanks, but I just want to go home.'

'Let's see how you feel tomorrow.'

Dora let her head rest back on the pillow, she felt drained. She couldn't forget about it. It was important to Eddie. A tear leaked from the corner of her eye. She pulled the blanket up to her neck and closed her eyes hoping that sleep would take away the pain.

* * *

Dora was glad when morning arrived. Her sleep had been disturbed by nightmares and the sounds of the hospital had filled her with fear. Each time she heard footsteps she thought someone was coming for her. Her mother had picked her up and driven her to the police station where she was fingerprinted, and a swab taken from her mouth. Now she sat in the interview room going over the events of yesterday. A pain gnawed at her stomach as she recalled the upturned drawers, scattered papers, and Eddie bound to a chair.

'Okay, Dora, that's great. I understand how difficult this must be for you,' DI Price said. 'Did you notice anyone outside Eddie's house or on the street when you visited him on Sunday?'

'No, just the neighbour walking the dog.'

'Did Eddie mention seeing anyone loitering? Any visitors?'

'He said he had a visit from a vicar.'

'The local vicar?'

'No, this one came from the hospital, said it was part of the care services.'

'Did Eddie say what they talked about?'

'Not really, just that he was there to offer support. His name was Phillip Bevan. Maybe he will be able to tell you more about the visit.' If Eddie was right, the police won't be able to trace the vicar. Maybe they'll concentrate on finding him, he could be the killer, Dora thought.

'We've talked to Eddie's neighbours and there was mention of him writing an autobiography. Did he talk to you about that?' DS Sims asked.

This didn't sound right. Eddie was adamant that the tape was to be kept secret.

'No, he never mentioned it. Who said he was writing a biography?' Dora took a sip of water.

'Like I said, we've talked to his neighbours. The thing is Eddie had a bit of a past.'

'You mean he was in prison?'

'Yes, he told you about that?' DS Sims leaned forward.

'I know he was in prison some time ago, but I don't know why. We never talked about it.'

'Eddie was in prison for armed robbery. He was convicted in 1976 along with Charlie Briar, they both served eight and a half years.'

An image of Charlie and Eddie in balaclavas skimmed across Dora's mind. She bit her lip to stop herself smiling. She just couldn't imagine the two of them as robbers. She wondered if this was what Eddie wanted to tell her. The thing he didn't want her hearing from anyone else.

'That was a long time ago and he served his time, so I don't see what that has to do with what happened to Eddie. Are you saying because he was an ex-con he got what was coming?'

'No, that's not what we're implying,' DS Sims said. 'We will treat this case the same as any other, regardless of Eddie's past. However, we cannot rule out the possibility that his previous conviction has some bearing on the case. Not all the money from the robbery was recovered and two members of the gang were never caught.'

'You think Eddie knew where the money was? Look at how he lived, he didn't have much money.'

'But he knew the names of the other gang members. If they thought he was about to reveal their names... This was a vicious attack so if Eddie told you anything, you better tell us for your own safety.' DS Sims looked hard at Dora.

'I don't know anything. I told you Eddie didn't tell me about the robbery.'

'Okay, we'll leave it there for now.' DI Price smiled. 'If you do remember anything, perhaps a name that has come up in conversation with Eddie, let us know.'

'I will.'

'We haven't been able to trace Eddie's next of kin.'

'He didn't have any family. He grew up in care.'

'We'll be going through Eddie's personal effects so maybe that will shed some light. Do you know if he made a will?'

'No, he didn't mention one. I'll talk to Charlie, maybe he'll know if Eddie had a will and what to do about the funeral.'

'It may be some time before the body is released. We'll keep you informed.'

An image of Eddie's broken body filled Dora's mind and she felt her throat constrict with emotion.

'We'll be in touch.' DI Price stood.

'I can go now?'

'Yes,' DI Price said. 'Thank you for your help. I know it must be very difficult for you.'

* * *

Dora was relieved to leave the police station and be back in her own house. Her mother insisted on staying and fussed around washing every work surface, polishing, and hoovering. Dora sat in front of her laptop giving the pretence of working. The afternoon passed to evening and she struggled to concentrate on the words on the screen.

'Mum, do you think Eddie knew his killer?'

'I don't know, perhaps it's best you try not to think about it. Let the police do their job.' Jenny continued wiping down the fridge.

'The police said Eddie was in prison for armed robbery. Eddie and Charlie. I can't imagine it. They think it could be someone connected to that, apparently two of the gang were never caught.'

Jenny put down the cloth and took a seat at the table. 'It wouldn't surprise me. Eddie and Charlie were bad boys back then. I guess they made a lot of enemies.'

'I think it's more than that. I didn't tell the police about the tape. Eddie didn't trust them, and he wouldn't want them listening to his story.'

'I expect you're right.'

'I'd like to hear the other tapes. I could ask Charlie to get them and send them to me. He'll know who Eddie gave them to. It doesn't matter now what I hear or if I don't meet the people involved. Nothing Eddie did in the past can justify what happened to him.' Dora put her hand to her stomach, the pain was raw, gnawing at her insides, and no amount of tablets could take it away.

Jenny slipped an arm around Dora's shoulder. 'You shouldn't be thinking about this now. You've had an awful shock. It's going to take time to heal. Perhaps it's best to wait for things to settle before talking to Charlie about the tapes. He was Eddie's best friend and he's taking it hard.'

'I'll leave it for now, give Charlie some time. But I will listen to the tapes. I owe it to Eddie.'

'Eddie would want you to be safe. Try and keep busy, you have your work to do. Eddie was very proud of you, as am I, and your dad of course.'

'Thank you, you should get home now. I'll be fine.'

'If you're sure.' Jenny planted a kiss on Dora's head. 'Lock up after I've gone.'

The house was quiet and still. Dora drew the curtains, switched on the TV and curled up in a blanket on the sofa. She tried to concentrate on the screen but her mind kept wandering. She put her head back and closed her eyes, she could feel herself drifting to sleep when the front door opening startled her back to consciousness. Her heart thudded in her chest as the door closed.

'Dora!'

'Gary, you gave me a fright, what are you doing here?' Dora stood up crossing her arms over her chest as he entered the room.

'It's Thursday, we arranged for me to come over to sort out the house.'

'I forgot, it's been an awful couple of days.'

'I heard about Eddie, I'm really sorry.' He stepped forward and pulled her into an embrace.

Dora stiffened in his arms. After twenty years of marriage his touch now felt alien. She pulled away and took a step back. 'I haven't had time to look at the paperwork or work anything out.'

'That's okay, we'll go through it now,' Gary said.

'Do we have to? I don't feel up to it at the moment.'

'It's best to get on with it. It will probably do you good. Take your mind off things. Put the kettle on and I'll get the paperwork from the study. We can sort out the contents while we're at it.'

Dora watched Gary move into the study. She felt like slapping his face, throwing him out, and demanding the house keys back, but she didn't want to start a fight. She went to the kitchen and filled the kettle.

She thought he'd put on weight since she last saw him and lost more hair. How long would it be until his new woman got bored of him? Dora wasn't sure she wanted him back anymore. She made the tea and placed it on the table where Gary had set out papers. He sat with a pen poised over a large writing pad.

'Let's get on with it.' Dora sighed.

Each item in the house was listed with running columns showing the value, who would take ownership, and how much the other party was owed. It was all very clinical, their lives divided up into monetary value. The hours ticked by and Dora's head hurt.

'It's getting late.' Dora stood and stretched. 'I don't think there's anything left to discuss.'

'Right, I'll organise a valuation on the house and get it on the market.'

'And what do I do with the girls' things? They won't have a home to come back to in the holidays or when they finish uni. Or are they going to stay with you?'

'I don't think that's a good idea.' Gary closed the writing pad and stood.

'I guess your girlfriend wouldn't like the idea. I'll leave you to explain the situation to the girls.'

'That's not fair,' Gary snapped.

'You think any of this is fair? I didn't ask you to leave and now you want to sell our home and for me to find some bedsit or move in with my mother.'

'I'm sorry. I never meant to hurt you. We were only teenagers when the girls were born. We didn't get to have fun, enjoy ourselves. We missed out on the best years of our lives. I can't live with Tina and not contribute to the mortgage, and I can't keep paying the mortgage on this place. Surely you understand.'

'I understand.' Dora gritted her teeth. 'You stayed until the girls went to university. You've done your job.'

'Don't be like this.'

'I'm tired, it's been a difficult day and the last thing I want to do is discuss who gets the bloody telly.'

'I'll go now and come back when you're feeling more like yourself.' Gary leaned in to kiss her on the cheek, but she moved away.

She saw him out the front door and turned the keys in the lock. She left them dangling to be sure he couldn't get back in. I should have asked him for the keys back, she thought. Eddie was right, he is a dick.

Dora washed up the cups then went upstairs and changed into her nightclothes. She was about to get into bed when she remembered the cat was still outside. She padded downstairs and into the kitchen where she opened the back door.

'Horace, puss puss.'

The cat flew into the house and began winding itself around Dora's legs.

'I expect you want food.' She stroked the cat before pushing the door shut. She was about to turn the key when the handle was forced down. The door flew open with such a force it knocked her backwards throwing her onto the kitchen tiles. She let out a scream as a figure stepped through the door. Cold eyes stared at her through the holes of a balaclava.

Chapter Five

Eight men sat around the wooden table in silence, each could feel the tension mounting in the room. Inner circle meetings were scheduled twice a year with an annual meeting of both inner and outer circles held on 18 December. The mansion house was hired under the guise of a Christmas gathering. An emergency meeting was difficult to organise, no electronic communication was allowed. A letter would be received, read and destroyed, no trace. The rules had to be strictly adhered to, the consequences dire for those who broke them. The men knew the seriousness of the situation. To be called together at such short notice meant that they would be called upon to act or make orders that would weigh on their conscience. There were many members missing, which added to the burden of those present.

The door opened and a cloaked man entered. His gaze swept around the faces at the table before he scraped back a chair and took a seat at the head. He adjusted his cloak so that the emblem, a snake wrapped around a tree trunk, was visible.

'I take it the perimeters have been checked?' The man's voice was deep and confident.

'Yes,' one of the men spoke up. 'All clear.'

'Good, then shut the door and we'll begin.'

One man shut the door and turned off the lights while another lit the three candelabras in the centre of the table. All took their seats and the leader opened with an incantation, calling on the power of knowledge to guide them. The candlelight cast an eerie glow on the ancient portraits that hung on the walls. The men joined in with the chanting, low at first, then building to the final crescendo before abruptly stopping. The room once again became silent.

'I've called this meeting this evening because, as some of you will be aware, our existence is being threatened. There are those who do not understand what we represent. They would have us treated like criminals, put on trial, destroy our reputations, and take away our freedom. There are others that would take the power for themselves. For generations we have kept our existence secret, we are the chosen ones. We cannot allow fear and rumour to penetrate the outer circle and weaken their loyalty. It happened once before and cannot happen again.'

There was a murmur of agreement around the table.

'Eddie Flint and the Russian have always posed a threat; they took something of ours which, in the wrong hands, has the power to destroy us. Only they know the location.'

Some of the men nodded while others looked on with curiosity.

'I understand that Eddie Flint has been dealt with,' one of the men spoke.

The leader narrowed his eyes. 'Your man failed to get the information, Kyle.'

'He is very persuasive. If there was anything to tell then he would have extracted the information. Eddie Flint is dead so I can't see how there's still a threat.'

'He made tapes,' the leader snapped. 'If that information gets into the wrong hands... Things are different now. One whisper of Blue Hollow will bring us all down.'

'There was only a rumour about tapes, nothing was found in the house,' Kyle said.

'And who is going to listen to an ex-con?' the man next to Kyle piped up.

'Use your head, Phillip. If enough noise is made about it someone will listen. You have social media now with their conspiracy theories. They would love a story like this, spreading theories. Then there's the woman.'

'Isadora Lewis,' Kyle said.

'What do we know about her?'

'Writes for some online magazine, married with two kids. Daughter of Michael and Jenny Jones. Her husband walked out on her six months ago, the children are grown and left home, so she's all alone.'

'You think Eddie Flint has been talking to her?' the man on the end seat asked.

'According to one of yours, Nate, yes. She was seen visiting on a number of occasions.'

'Sounds like he was going to use her to tell his story,' Phil said. 'I don't understand why he would do this now. He's been quiet for so long.'

'He was dying,' Kyle said.

'Perhaps he wanted to avenge his sister,' Phil suggested.

'It doesn't matter what he intended to do,' the leader snarled. 'You better make sure that the woman doesn't talk, and the Russian is silenced.'

'The Russian is being watched but anything else at the moment is too dangerous. As for the woman, my man is paying her a visit as we speak. If she knows anything, he'll get it out of her.' Kyle grinned.

Chapter Six

Dora sat paralysed on the floor as the man turned the key in the lock. Her brain was screaming to run but her legs wouldn't move. She tried to shuffle backwards. The man turned, stepped towards her and without a word grabbed a fistful of her hair. Dora yelped as he hauled her to her feet and forced her onto the kitchen chair.

He's going to kill me, she thought. An image of Eddie tied up filled her with terror. She could feel the pressure in her bladder, threatening to spill.

'You and I are going to have a little chat. I'm going to ask you a question and each time you give me a wrong answer you'll lose a finger.' The man took a tool belt from around his waist and laid it on the table. 'Do you understand?'

Dora nodded.

'Good, then after perhaps we can have a little fun.' He leaned over her and ran his hand up the inside of her thigh. 'The smell of fear is a powerful aphrodisiac.' He grinned showing a row of crooked teeth through the hole in the balaclava.

Dora pressed herself into the back of the chair. His touch brought a fresh wave of terror; her body was charged with adrenalin urging her to fight or run but there was no escape. He pulled his hand away and selected a bolt cutter from the tool belt. She gasped and flew out of the chair. He grabbed her arm digging his fingers into her flesh, she lashed out with her fists, but her blows had no impact on him. He dropped the bolt cutters, drew back his hand and drove his fist into her face. She reeled backwards but he still had hold of her arm.

'Going to try and fight me, are you? Then I guess I better tie you to the chair.' He forced her into the seat.

'No, please,' Dora begged.

'Eddie tried to fight me, put up quite a struggle for an old sick man.'

'Just tell me what you want.'

'Eddie gave you something before he died.'

'What?'

'So, you want to play games.'

'No, I don't know what you are talking about.'

'Eddie has been telling tales. He told you where it is.'

'He didn't tell me anything about the money. The police told me about the robbery, but I swear he never told me where the money was hidden.'

'This is much more valuable than money. I know he made a tape and gave it to you. Thought you'd make some money out of the story, did you?'

'Please, I don't know what you are talking about.' If she gave him the tape she knew he would kill her. Her mind worked furiously trying to figure out an escape.

'Maybe a little pain will jog your memory.' He picked up the bolt cutters.

Horace leaped on Dora's lap and rubbed himself against her chest. She stroked him with a trembling hand.

The man grabbed the cat by the scruff of the neck and dangled him in the air. Horace let out a squeal, his paws peddling and eyes bulging.

'No, let him go.' Dora leaped from the chair.

The man stepped back still gripping the cat. 'Maybe I'll take his paws off one by one, you can watch.'

'No, let him go. I'll give you the tape,' Dora pleaded.

'Now that was easy.' He dropped the cat who hissed and ran away.

'It's in the desk, in the other room.'

'After you.' The man grabbed a knife from the belt.

Dora could feel her heart thudding in her chest, her skin tingling and every muscle tense. Her eyes darted around searching for something to use as a weapon. She could feel him close behind, hear his breathing. Time was running out. She entered the room that Gary used as an office and switched on the light. As she approached the desk her eyes fell on the silver letter opener she had given Gary as a birthday present. She opened the middle drawer, pulled out a random tape and handed it to the man.

'Do you want the recorder?'

'I'll need to be sure you haven't given me the wrong tape.'

Dora picked out the recorder, tossed it to the man while grabbing the letter opener with her other hand. She pulled back her hand and plunged it into his eye socket. Blood spurted over her hand as the man screamed, dropped the knife, and instinctively put his hands to his eyes. Dora bolted from the room to the front door, she twisted the key and ran outside. She flew through the neighbour's gate and to the back door, screaming as she hammered the door with her fists.

The door opened and Dora pushed her way inside. 'Quick, lock the door!'

'What the fuck's going on?' Her neighbour stood staring at her.

'Lock the door, he's coming after me.'

'Okay, calm down.' He turned the key in the lock. 'Jackie! Get in here, it's Dora.'

Jackie appeared in the kitchen dressed in a pink dressing gown. 'What's happened?'

'There's a man in my house with a knife, he was going to kill me.' Panic caught the breath in Dora's throat, she tried to draw in the air, but it felt like there was no oxygen.

'I'll go and have a look.'

'No, don't be stupid, Josh. You heard what she said. He has a knife. Call the police. Come and sit down, Dora. Oh, God, you're bleeding.' Jackie looked in horror at Dora's hand. 'Better ask for an ambulance as well.' She guided Dora to the sofa in the sitting room.

'You're shaking.' Jackie fussed about, putting a blanket around Dora before taking a seat herself. Josh could be heard in the kitchen giving out the address to the police.

'I'm sorry to barge in on you,' Dora said. 'I didn't know what else to do.' She pulled the blanket tighter around her body.

'It's okay, don't worry about it. Do you think it's a serial killer?'

'What?' Dora rocked back and forth.

'First poor Eddie and now you. It could be anyone next.' Jackie shook her head. 'None of us are safe.'

'Police are on their way.' Josh stood awkwardly in the doorway. 'Do you want a cup of tea?'

Dora shook her head. 'No, thanks. I feel a bit sick.'

'A cuppa will make you feel better,' Jackie said. 'Put plenty of sugar in it.'

As Dora sat cradling a cup of tea the police arrived. The house soon became a hive of activity with paramedics first checking her then a series of questions from the police. Swabs were taken from her hands and her clothes bagged for evidence. Jackie gave her a pair of pyjamas and a dressing gown to wear. She refused to go to hospital, not wanting to spend another night lying awake in a noisy ward. She just wanted to go home and curl up in her own bed.

Dora heard the arrival of DI Price and DS Sims and sunk further into the sofa, she didn't want to answer more questions.

'We would like to talk to Dora alone,' DS Sims said.

'Oh, okay.' Jackie stood up. 'I'll give your mother a call, shall I?'

'Please,' Dora said. She watched Jackie leave the room feeling guilty that her neighbour had been shepherded out of her own sitting room.

DI Price took a seat. 'There has been a thorough search of your house. The intruder is long gone but forensics are still there, so you won't be able to go home for a while.'

'That's fine, I'll go to my mother's house.'

'Is there anything you can tell us about the man that attacked you?'

'No, I already told the policeman when he arrived. He wore a balaclava, so I didn't see his face. He was tall and muscular.'

'How tall?' DS Sims asked.

'I don't know. Taller than me. Maybe six foot.'

'What about his voice?' DI Price leaned forward in the chair. 'Was he Welsh?'

'No, he had an English accent.'

'Can you be more specific?' Sims said.

'I don't know.' Dora rubbed her hands over her face. 'Probably London. Not West Country, or Liverpool. I'm not that good with accents.'

'That's okay,' DI Price said. 'You told PC Lane that the man wanted information.'

'Yes, he wanted to know what Eddie had told me. I told him I didn't know anything, he threatened to cut off my fingers, and then, he got hold of my cat. Oh, Horace.' Anxiety snaked around Dora's chest.

'Is he a big ginger moggy?' DI Price asked.

'Yes, did he hurt him?'

'He was sitting outside on the wall when we came in. He looks fine.'

Dora let go of the breath she had been holding.

'You were in the kitchen when this happened?' DS Sims asked.

'Yes, he came through the back door.'

'There's a considerable amount of blood in your office. I understand that you stabbed the assailant in the eye with a letter opener.'

'Yes.'

'How did you get him to the office?'

'I told him Eddie had given me something.'

'What?' DS Sims straightened up.

'Erm, a letter.'

'Did you give it to him?'

'No, there wasn't a letter, I just wanted him in the office so I could have a chance to escape. I didn't know what else to do.'

'It was quick thinking on your part,' DS Sims commented.

'I was scared. I think he would've killed me anyway. I thought if I let him think I had something I could distract him.'

'Are you sure that Eddie didn't give you anything? Could he have hidden some notes, or a memory stick for you to find?' DI Price asked.

'No, Eddie didn't use a computer and he didn't leave me anything. I don't know what this man wanted from me.'

'We've been looking into Eddie's movements over the past few weeks. He's been spending a lot of time with his old friend Charlie,' Sims said.

'Yes, I know.'

'So why were you going up to London to see Charlie the day Eddie died?'

'He thought I needed a break.'

'Eddie also visited another old friend in prison. Did he tell you about that?'

'No, he didn't mention it.'

'He went to see Boris Orlov. Have you heard of him?'

'No, I don't think Eddie mentioned him.'

'He has a nickname. They call him "the Russian". One of Britain's most dangerous prisoners. A child killer. Known for taking prison officers hostage. Now why would Eddie visit him?'

'I don't know, maybe you should ask him why Eddie visited.'

'Look, Dora, Eddie obviously had some very nasty enemies. We know he was about to tell his story, and someone didn't want his secret known. Now they think you know. We can help you. Get you into a safe house, but you have to be honest with us. Help us find Eddie's killer.'

An image of the man and his bolt cutters came to Dora's mind. She could give them the tape and go to a safe house. Let them deal with it. But they knew about Eddie's plans to tell his story. She knew Eddie wouldn't have told his neighbours. The police were lying to her. 'I really don't know anything.' Dora sighed.

'We talked to Charlie, he wasn't very forthcoming,' DI Price said. 'Perhaps he might speak to you.'

'I'll try but I'm sure if Charlie knew who killed Eddie he'd tell you.'

'Okay, we'll leave it there for now. Try and get some rest.' DI Price stood. 'We'll check our database for a match to the DNA samples taken from your house. If we get a result, we'll let you know.'

The detectives left the room and Dora's mum hurried in. She thanked Josh and Jackie before leading Dora to the car.

* * *

Now Dora lay on her mother's sofa, tucked under a blanket.

'You should try and get some sleep,' Jenny said.

'I don't think I can. Why would Eddie start all this? He must've known that he would put himself and me in danger.'

'I told him I didn't think it was a good idea,' Jenny said.

Dora sat up. 'I thought you didn't know.'

'I don't know what he was going to tell you, just that he had an idea of telling his life story. With him being in prison I didn't think it would come to any good.' Jenny sat down on the edge of the sofa. 'Maybe you should give the tape to the police. You said there was nothing important on it. Perhaps then this can all go away, and we can get back to normal.'

'I think it's a bit late for that now. I've lied to the police and whoever came to the house tonight thinks I know something. They're not going to stop coming after me just because I give the tape to the police. They'll think I have more. Besides, Eddie didn't trust the police. They know about Eddie's plan to tell his story. How would they know if they weren't involved somehow?'

'Do you really think the police are involved in what happened to Eddie? I can't see it. Eddie must have told someone about his plans.'

'No, he was adamant that no one should know. Until I hear the rest of the tapes I'm not going to know what Eddie was trying to tell me, whom he was afraid of, and who is after me. I'm gonna ring Charlie, he'll know what to do. Can I use your phone? Mine's in the house.'

'It's the middle of the night. Don't you think you should wait until morning? Give yourself some time to think things over before dragging Charlie into it.'

'No, I can't wait until morning. It's important and if Charlie thinks I should give the tape to the police then I will.'

'Okay.' Jenny stood and took her phone from her handbag and handed it to Dora.

The call was answered on the second ring. 'Jenny, what's happened?' Charlie sounded tense.

'It's Dora.' She quickly explained the events of the evening.

'Bastards,' Charlie hissed. 'Pack a bag and come up to London. I'll organise a safe place for you to stay. Don't tell anyone where you're going. Don't worry, I'll take care of you.'

'What's going on, Charlie?'

'I can't go into it right now. It will take too long to explain. Eddie…' Charlie's voice broke. There was silence on the line for a few moments. 'Eddie left a tape with me, we can get the other ones. Then you can listen, let Eddie tell you the way he planned.'

'But the police know that Eddie was planning on telling his story. I don't understand what was so important that it got him killed. Why did he start all this?'

'You're gonna have to trust me. You'll understand when you've heard the whole story. Just don't judge us too harshly.'

'If you're talking about the robbery and prison, the police already told me.'

'Ah, I'm afraid it's gonna get a lot worse than that.' Charlie chuckled. 'You're in for a bumpy ride down memory lane.'

'I'm scared.'

'I know, but it's gonna be okay. Eddie loved you like a daughter and I won't let anything happen to you. Go pack your bag. I'll send instructions in a couple of hours. Don't trust anyone, especially the police. I'll see you soon.'

'So you're going to London,' Jenny said.

'Yes, at least I'll be safe with Charlie.'

'I hope you're right. I couldn't bare it if anything happened to you.' Tears pooled in Jenny's eyes.

'It will be okay.' Dora hugged her mother wishing that she believed her own words.

Chapter Seven

Dora paced the floor of the hotel room and checked her watch again. Her suitcase was packed and lay on the bed. She had been stuck there for two days while she waited for Charlie to find a safe house for the two of them. The staff had made a fuss of her and the Polish maintenance man, Janusz, had accompanied her whenever she left her room. It was clear that the hotel owners and Janusz were friends of Charlie's and went out of their way to make her feel safe and welcome. Charlie had sent a phone, an Oyster card, and an envelope of cash. He had told her to switch off her own phone and not use her bank card. Last night he had sent a text instructing her to catch the underground to Whitechapel where he would send someone to meet her. She was to travel in the rush hour where she would be protected by the crowds. Her luggage would be collected.

Dora read through the instructions one final time, memorised the route and left the room. Janusz was waiting at reception, he stepped beside her and they walked towards the station keeping the conversation light. At the entrance to the tube station Janusz gave Dora a hug and pecked her on both cheeks.

'Right, Charlie's angel, I leave you now. You take care.'

'Thank you for everything.'

'It's no problem.'

Dora joined the crowd of people jostling into the station. She tried to keep pace while watching for the signs and trying to look like she knew where she was going. She felt air thicken as the escalator descended and panic twisted her stomach. She wanted to turn and run, get away from the crowds and into the open air. When she visited London in the past with Eddie they always took a cab, he knew her fear of crowds. She wished now she had insisted on getting a cab to Whitechapel, Charlie had sent enough money. Too late now, she thought as she moved with the flow of people onto the platform.

The train arrived with a swish of air. Dora peered at the people crammed onto the train. Their bodies pressed up against the door. There was no way she was getting on in that crowd. She took a step backwards. Some people got off and others jammed themselves in through the door. The train pulled away and more people came onto the platform. What if the person Charlie sent doesn't wait? I won't know where to go. I'll have to get on the next one, she thought.

A few minutes later the next train arrived, this one as full as the last. Dora forced herself to move, pushing in amongst the crowd and stepping onto the train. She tried to move away from the door but there was no room. The doors closed with a hiss trapping her between a man in a suit and a woman with a cream coat. She tried to slow her breathing and listen to the announcements over the tannoy, and count the stops.

At the next station some people got off and Dora shuffled into the carriage. There were no seats; people stood with one hand on the grab rail and the other with either a book or their phone. She was amazed that anyone could read a book while standing on a crowded train. The train was moving again, and Dora felt perspiration gather under her arms and on the back of her neck. She longed to pull off her coat but there was no room and she was afraid of falling if she let go of the grab rail. She unbuttoned her coat, but it didn't make a difference, panic was raising her body temperature and the air on the train was thick with perfume and body odour.

She looked around; no one made eye contact or talked to the person sitting next to them.

The journey seemed endless and Dora felt her spirit lift when the tannoy announced the next stop was Whitechapel. The only problem now was getting to the door and off the train. She squeezed past people, apologising as she went, and managed to get near the door. She found herself pressed up against the woman in the cream coat who hadn't moved for the whole journey. There was nothing for Dora to hold onto so she braced herself for the stop hoping she wouldn't fall.

The train slowed as it pulled into the station. More people tried to cram into the space by the door. Just as the train entered the station, it jerked violently. Dora felt a sting in her side as she toppled sideways into the man standing next to her.

'Sorry,' she said as she righted herself. The man grunted a response.

The woman in the cream coat pitched forward into the crowd. People tried to edge away as she continued to fall to the ground. Someone let out a piecing scream as the doors opened. Dora looked down and saw blood staining the woman's coat as she lay crumpled on the floor. People started to shove in panic to get off the train. Dora was swept away with the crowd. She lost her footing in the door and landed on her hands and knees on the platform. There were shouts and screams around her as terrified people tried to flee the station.

'Keep moving.' A hand gripped her firmly on the arm and hauled her to her feet.

Dora tried to pull away.

'Charlie sent me.'

Dora looked up at the man who held her arm. He had cropped dark hair and a firm square jaw covered in what she thought was either designer stubble, or he hadn't bothered to shave. She allowed the man to guide her to the escalator. He didn't slow but kept pace with the moving crowd. She struggled to keep up with him and pain tore at her side.

'Slow down.' She put her hand to her side. It was wet. She pulled her hand away and stopped walking as she looked at the blood covering her palm. She looked down and saw blood seeping through the top of her jeans.

'Keep moving,' the man barked. People pushed past and the man tugged on her arm.

'I'm bleeding, oh God.' Dora felt a coldness creep over her body.

'Shit.' The man looked at Dora's side. They were nearing the top of the escalator. The man's eyes darted around. 'We have to get out of here, now.' He pulled her forward.

Dora stepped off the escalator and felt her skin prickle. Perspiration broke out over her body. 'I don't feel well.'

'Oh great!' The man scooped her up and continued to march forward.

Dora felt too lightheaded to protest so she lent her head against his shoulder. He was breathing heavily by the time they exited the station. The cool air felt wonderful on Dora's face. He set her down on the pavement.

'Do you think you can walk now?'

Dora felt her body tremble. People rushed past and the noise of the traffic and distant sirens echoed in her head. 'I think you should call an ambulance.'

'Come on, not too far now. I have a car waiting.' He put his arm around her shoulder and led her towards the traffic.

They stopped at the edge of the pavement and the man put his hand in the air. A few moments later a car pulled up. The man opened the door, shoved Dora on the back seat before climbing in on the opposite side. He lent forward and spoke to the driver in what Dora guessed to be Italian. Sitting back, he tugged at Dora's coat.

'What are you doing?' She pulled her coat from his hand.

'I need to see if you're badly injured.'

Dora opened her coat and lifted her jumper, turning her head so she didn't have to look.

'It's not too bad.'

'Are you a doctor?' Dora snapped.

'No.'

'Then I suggest you take me to the nearest hospital. I'll call Charlie, he can meet us there.' Dora unzipped her bag and took out the phone Charlie had given her.

The man hit the window button and cold air blew in as the window whirred down. He snatched the phone from Dora's hand and threw it out the window.

'What are you doing? Charlie didn't send you, did he?' She made a grab for the door handle.

'Don't be stupid.' The man gripped her upper arm. 'The phone was compromised, that's how they knew you were on the train.'

'No, Charlie gave me the phone, he said it was safe.'

'Yeah, well it isn't safe anymore.'

Dora was about to take out her own phone but thought the man was likely to hurl that out the window. Instead she sat back and watched the car weave in and out of traffic. She had no idea where they were going. She tried to quell the niggling doubt that this man was not here to help her.

The car pulled into an underground carpark and the driver got out of the car.

'Come on,' the man in the back said. 'We need to get you out of sight.'

Dora winced as she climbed out of the car and put her hand to her side. She was still feeling lightheaded but didn't dare mention it to the man, fearful that she would have the indignity of being scooped up and carried again. The driver keyed in a code to open the lift and they rode up to the third floor in silence. They got out into a narrow corridor. The man looked around as they walked halfway down then stopped at a door. The driver took keys from his pocket, opened the door and ushered Dora inside.

Dora stepped into the flat and looked around. They were stood in a sitting room with a wooden floor. Two black leather sofas faced each other with a heavy oak coffee table in between. On one wall was mounted a large-screen television, the other walls were decorated with modern art.

'Take a seat,' the driver said.

'Where's Charlie?' Dora turned on the man that stood behind her.

'Enzo, you better make Dora a drink. Something strong. Come on, sit down and I'll see to your cut.'

'I don't want a drink, and you are not touching me. I already told you I need to go to hospital. I need proper treatment, antibiotics, or it could get infected. You were supposed to take me to Charlie. How do I know I can trust you? You drag me out of the station and–'

'Will you shut the fuck up,' the man shouted.

'Don't swear at me.'

'I can't think straight with you going on. Just sit down and let me put a dressing on the wound then we'll figure out what to do.' The man sighed. 'You're just going to have to trust me. I'm trying to help you. I'm a friend of Charlie's, my name is Dmitri, and this is Enzo. We can't risk taking you to a hospital, they'll inform the police as soon as they see your wound. Do you have any idea how much shit you're in?'

'No, I don't. I haven't a clue what's going on, that's why I came here to see Charlie.'

'Okay, just please sit down. I'll get you something for the pain then clean up that cut, you'll feel better.'

Dora sighed and took a seat on the sofa. She could hear Dmitri and Enzo talking in the kitchen but again they were speaking Italian so she couldn't understand. A few moments later, Dmitri returned carrying a glass of fizzy clear liquid and a first aid box. He handed the glass to Dora.

'What is it?'

'A painkiller. Drink it down in one go.'

Dora took a mouthful and gagged. 'That's disgusting.'

'It's not supposed to taste nice.' Dmitri shook his head. 'Knock it back, don't sip.'

Dora drained the glass; she could feel the liquid fizzing in her throat.

'Good, now lie on your side and lift your jumper.' Dmitri set the glass on the table and opened the first aid box. He took out a bottle and poured liquid onto cotton wool and applied it to Dora's side.

'Aghh! What are you doing?'

'Cleaning the wound.'

'It hurts.'

'Don't be a pussy, man up.' Dmitri grinned.

'Man up! In the past few days I've been hit in the face, had a man threaten to cut off my fingers, found Uncle Eddie with his tongue cut out, and now stabbed. You've no idea what I've been through.'

'You're still alive so quit bitching and stay still. I'm going to put some butterfly stitches on this then cover it up. It will heal fine.'

Dora gritted her teeth as Dmitri pinched the skin together and applied the stitches. Her legs and arms started to feel heavy. Her body relaxed into the sofa as she let her head fall back. 'I don't feel right. What did you put in the drink?'

'Something to make you sleep.'

Dora wanted to answer but her tongue stuck to the bottom of her mouth. She felt Dmitri apply a strip of plaster before her eyelids closed and she let herself drift to sleep.

* * *

The light was fading in the room when Dora opened her eyes. It took her a few moments to remember where she was and what had happened. Dmitri was standing, looking out of the window, his back facing her. He wore jeans and a black T-shirt that clung to his muscular body. Tattoos covered his biceps and ran down to his wrists.

'You drugged me,' Dora said.

'You're awake at last, I was worried I'd given you too much.' He turned to face her.

Dora swung her legs off the sofa. The blanket fell away, and she looked in horror at her naked legs. 'Where are my clothes? You stripped me! You—'

'Don't flatter yourself,' Dmitri growled. 'I prefer my women conscious. I certainly have never had the need to drug them. Still, I couldn't help but notice that you have an impressive scar on your leg.'

Dora felt heat rise in her cheeks. She pulled the blanket around her legs. 'I fell through a patio door when I was a child. You've no right to take off my clothes.'

'I only took off your shoes, jumper, and jeans. I was trying to make you more comfortable. I didn't know how long you would be out.'

'And what's your excuse for drugging me?' Dora snapped.

'I needed some time to sort things out and it wasn't fair to leave Enzo to babysit a hysterical woman.'

'I was not hysterical.'

'I made you something to eat.' Enzo came in the room carrying a tray.

'I'm not hungry.'

'You need to try and eat a little.' Enzo placed the tray on her lap.

Dora looked down at the plate. Asparagus lay neatly beside chicken breast covered in a creamy herb sauce. She cut a piece of chicken and placed it in her mouth; it tasted delicious. 'It's lovely, thank you.' She picked up the glass from the tray and paused.

'It's just water.' Enzo smiled.

Dora took a sip then continued eating. 'Have you heard from Charlie?'

Dmitri took a seat opposite Dora. 'I'm so sorry, Charlie died last night.'

The fork fell from Dora's hand and hit the plate with a clatter. 'No, that can't be right. He sent me a text last night.'

'They took the phone, that's how they knew you would be on the train. You were probably followed to the station. They would've used the phone to get your location. Charlie knew they were coming for him, he called but I got there too late.'

'Was he killed like Eddie?'

'It's better you don't know the details.'

Pain gnawed at Dora's stomach. She stood and put the tray on the table. She didn't care that she only wore a T-shirt.

'Not Charlie as well. He promised to keep me safe, promised me it would be okay.' She felt the tears sting her eyes.

Dmitri stood up and approached her, but she stepped away.

'Where are my clothes?'

'In the bedroom. I picked up your suitcase and laptop.'

'Come, I'll show you,' Enzo said. He led her into the bedroom then left shutting the door.

Dora's hands shook as she pulled on her jeans and changed her T-shirt. What am I going to do? There's no one to help me now, she thought. She took a tissue from her bag, wiped her eyes, and blew her nose before brushing her hair into a ponytail and securing it with a band. She took a deep breath, slung her laptop bag over her shoulder and pulled up the handle on her case before leaving the bedroom.

'Thank you for looking after me but I think it's best I leave now.' She headed for the front door.

'Whoa, what are you doing?' Dmitri leapt off the sofa.

'Going home, then going to the police.'

'You won't make it if you leave here. You'll be dead before you reach the station. Look, I'm not happy about the situation either, I was just supposed to deliver you to Charlie.'

'I'm not a parcel. You've done what you were supposed to do, I'm not your problem.' Dora turned to leave.

'Wait.' Dimitri grabbed her arm. 'You are my problem now. Don't think you're the only one that cared about Charlie and Eddie. They looked after me when I had no one else to turn to. You think I would pay them back by letting you walk out that door and getting yourself killed?' He let go of her arm. 'I want to get the motherfuckers responsible for this.'

'Do you have to use such foul language?'

'Oh, I'm sorry if I offend you,' Dmitri snapped. 'My language is the least of your problems, so you'll just have to get used to it.'

'Come and sit down, please,' Enzo said. 'Dmitri's right, you're not safe on your own.'

'Am I supposed to stay locked up with you two forever? My best option is to go to the police.' Dora perched on the edge of the sofa.

'You think the police will keep you safe?' Dmitri laughed.

'Don't tell me, the police are in on it. I'm sorry but I don't believe in conspiracy theories. I can understand why

Eddie and Charlie didn't like the police. They'd both been in trouble. No doubt there was corruption in the seventies. I have no criminal record so I've nothing to be afraid of.'

'Don't be so naïve. You think hiding away in your cosy little house with your fat ginger cat is going save you,' Dmitri said.

'How do you know about my cat?'

'Charlie told me. He told me a lot about you.'

'Well, Charlie and Eddie never mentioned you.'

'I'm not the type of person you invite around for tea and cake,' Dmitri said with a grin. 'I expect they didn't want to taint you. There's a lot about them you don't know, but what they did in the past was for good reasons.' Dmitri sat on the sofa next to Enzo.

'Uncle Eddie already intimated that he had done something bad in the past. I don't really care what either of them did. They didn't deserve to die.'

'The people responsible for their murders are very powerful people. They have access to information. They knew where to find Eddie and Charlie and also knew your movements. Yeah, you could risk going to the police, but it only needs one person on the inside passing information and you're fucked.'

'Who are these people and what do they want? Is it about the money Eddie and Charlie stole?'

'I don't know who they are,' Dmitri said. 'I only know part of the story. We need to get hold of the rest of the tapes.'

'So you know about the tapes.'

'Charlie told me. He wanted insurance in case anything went wrong.'

'So you know where they are?'

'Not exactly, but I've got Charlie's.' He put his hand in his back pocket and pulled out the tape. He lent forward and handed it to Dora. 'I think you should listen before you decide to run off to the police.'

Dora took the tape and turned it over. 'It's got number three on it, I have number one, where is number two?'

'That's the one Charlie had, we'll have to figure out who has the others,' Dmitri said.

'What's on it?'

'I don't know, I haven't listened to it. It was given to me for safe keeping. The tapes are meant for you.'

Dora stood and took the Dictaphone out of her laptop bag.

'Would you like to use the bedroom?' Enzo offered.

'No, it's okay. I don't mind you both listening.'

She slotted the tape in, sat down and pressed play.

Chapter Eight

Eddie 1972

When I look back, I wonder how we survived the first
year. It was 1972, we were sixteen, and homeless. Social
services had washed their hands of us. We had no family,
no money, and no one to turn to. We had each other and
we were okay. Well, sort of. We were all haunted and
damaged by what had happened. We only talked about it
in terms of survival and revenge, never the details, none of
us could ever speak of that. It was worse for Boris, the
pain ate at him day after day turning his insides to lava
which boiled on the brink of eruption. We knew there
would come a time when he could no longer contain his
rage.

That first year, me, Charlie, and Boris lived in a squat.
We managed to get work on a construction site, cheap
labour for cash in hand. We pooled our money, saved, and
managed to get a flat, furnished with stuff people had
thrown out. Denny was next to join us, followed by MJ.
MJ was the opposite of Boris, the pain had broken his
spirit and he had withdrawn into himself. Boris was his
fierce protector. No one dared to take the piss out of MJ

on the site or they would be crushed under the weight of Boris as he pummelled them into the ground. In time MJ's confidence grew but he always stayed close to one of us, never leaving the flat alone.

Others that left the children's home in the same position as us came to stay. We'd see them alright, a bed and food. Once they were on their feet they would move on. The only person missing from our group was Julie. I longed for her to come and live with us but social services wouldn't release her into my care, so we had to wait until she was sixteen. We were regular visitors to the home and made it clear that we were watching. Wainwright stayed out of our way, but we made our plans. We couldn't act until Julie was away from that place.

Denny was the first to leave and set up on his own. He was the brightest of us all, always good with figures so it didn't surprise anyone that he got a job in the bank. He came around often which usually ended up in a party. He would bring a bunch of girls who were impressed with his snappy dressing, but the minute they saw Charlie and Boris he lost them. Charlie was charming, with long dark lashes framing twinkling eyes and a cheeky grin. If he wasn't my best friend, I would hate him for his looks. Boris was tall, strong, and brooding. Charlie would talk and dance with the girls but that's as far as they got. Boris on the other hand would end up in bed with at least two of the girls at the same time. He once managed four. He did Russia proud. It would have been wonderful if things had stayed like that. The four of us with Denny a regular visitor, but things changed, and I guess four good years were more than we could've hoped for.

I was twenty in the summer of 1976. It was the hottest summer on record which caused a drought and much complaining, with everyone hot and bothered. Julie had turned sixteen and came to live with us. It was a shame it hadn't been a few months earlier because Boris had got a girl into trouble and was going to do the honourable thing by marrying her. Julie was smitten with Boris and I could tell he felt the same way but didn't act on his feelings. Julie had grown into a beautiful young woman. Petite with long wavy blond hair and skin turned golden by the sun. She was kind and loving and always smiling. Boris's wife-to-be, Jean, could only be described as a bitch. It was obvious that she didn't love Boris but wouldn't have her reputation destroyed by being single and pregnant. She had great plans for a house with a garden. She liked to dress in the latest fashion and wanted it all. Boris worked longer hours than the rest of us to save for a deposit on a house. He still lived with us as Jean's father insisted they didn't move in together until they were married.

Boris often came home exhausted. Julie would cook for him and they would spend the evening talking. Jean rarely came around, she didn't like us, particularly Julie. When she did come around all she did was complain. She hated the flat, hated the people that called around and she ignored Julie. I felt sorry for Boris, soon he would have to move in with her and I doubted she would let him visit.

On those long summer days we'd forgotten about our plan, but fate was about to take a turn and change our lives again. We had all been for a dip in the River Taff after work. It was more like a puddle with the water so low, but it felt good on our skin as we splashed each other. We walked home with our clothes drying in the sun. Julie stayed close to Boris, talking and laughing. It was only a matter of weeks until Boris got married and I worried about Julie, I knew it would break her heart.

When we got back to the flat, we took some beer from the fridge, opened the windows and turned up the music. Charlie started dancing to Hot Chocolate, gyrating his hips to the rhythm of the music, Julie joined him, and I saw the longing in Boris's eyes as he watched. The flat door flew open and Denny rushed in, we could tell at once that something was wrong. His eyes were wild, sweat ran down the side of his face and he appeared to be finding it difficult to breathe.

'What's wrong?' Charlie turned off the music.

'I… I…' Denny tried to suck in air.

'Sit down.' MJ took hold of Denny's arm and sat him on the sofa. 'Take a slow breath.'

Charlie handed him a beer and Boris rolled him a joint. We all stood waiting as Denny glugged down the beer and took a hard drag on the joint. It took a few moments for him to settle and his hands to stop trembling.

'Take your time,' Charlie said.

Denny looked at us and I could see the pain in his eyes. 'We had a new manager start at the bank today, Alan Lloyd. We all stood in the banking hall waiting for him to arrive. When he walked in, I nearly shat myself. He was one of them.'

'Are you sure?' Boris asked.

I could feel my skin prickling, shame and disgust burning me from the inside. Boris's question was pointless. Those faces were burned into our minds.

'Yeah, I'm fucking sure. Bastard smiled and shook my hand, didn't recognise me. I felt sick. I had to work all day knowing he was in the same building. Then after work he asked us to go to The Crown so he could buy us all a drink.'

'Is that where he is now?' Charlie asked.

'Yeah, probably. I legged it as soon as we locked up.'

'Let's go,' Boris said.

'And do what?' I could hear the panic in Julie's voice. 'Please don't go,' she pleaded. 'If you do something stupid you'll all end up in prison. Don't you think you've suffered enough?'

'We'll just go and take a look,' Charlie said. 'Check him out, maybe follow him home, see where he lives. We've waited long enough, a few days more to work out what to do won't make any difference. Right, Boris?'

Boris nodded his agreement, but we could see he was coiled. He stood rigid, flexing his hands. I already felt sick and MJ was pale. I knew Charlie must have been recalling the faces and wondering which one we would see, but he kept it together, always the calm one.

We took Charlie's car as Denny was still in a bit of a state. We chucked Boris in the front and I sat in the back with MJ and Denny. We left Julie at home. When we pulled up outside the pub there was a crowd sitting on the benches, drinking in the sun. My heart was thudding as we went through the door. It was dark inside, the curtains drawn to keep the room cool. Laughter could be heard over the indistinguishable chatter. The atmosphere didn't fit with what I felt. Denny nudged my arm and indicated a table in the corner with a tilt of his head. A group of men sat around the table, jackets off and sleeves rolled up.

My insides turned to liquid, all I could think about was the stench of his sweat and heavy breathing. I bolted to the men's toilet where I threw up. Charlie followed me in and put his hand on my shoulder. He didn't have to say anything. I wiped my mouth and turned to face Charlie, silent tears ran down his face.

'He was the first,' I said.

'I know.' He pulled me into a hug, his arms shaking as they gripped me. 'Boris is kicking off, so MJ and Denny are dragging him back to the car. We better get him out of here before he blows up.' He pulled away and wiped the tears with the back of his hand. 'We'll get the bastard.'

'Yeah.' I took a deep breath and followed Charlie out. I couldn't look in the corner of the pub as we walked out. Outside Boris could be heard kicking off in the car. Some of the crowd were looking but didn't move, it was a rarity for someone to take on Boris. I opened the door and slid in next to MJ.

'Let's go and drag the fucker out.' Boris seethed. 'Get a rope and hang him from his balls. Then I'll cut his cock off, his hands off, his fucking head off!'

Charlie pulled off as Boris continued to rant. 'If we do anything now we'll all go down and the rest of them will get away with it,' MJ said.

'Then I'll do it alone,' Boris growled.

'No, we're all in this together. Besides, you have a kid on the way. There are ways of doing things without getting caught. We need to think about it. We will get him,' Charlie said.

I don't know how we managed to contain Boris, but he eventually calmed a little. We stopped for more booze then went back to the flat and started to plan. None of us were cold-blooded killers despite Boris's outburst. We wanted to cause the maximum amount of humiliation and pain without killing the man or getting caught. It was Charlie that came up with the idea. We'd all had a fair amount to drink. Julie was dozing on the sofa next to Boris. MJ and Denny were sitting on the floor, Charlie and me sat on the hard-wooden chairs we had rescued from the rubbish dump.

'We'll do the bank,' Charlie said.

'What, like rob it?' MJ grinned.

'Yeah and we'll implicate Alan Lloyd, set him up and give an anonymous tip off.'

'How the hell are we going to do that?' Boris asked.

'Denny works there, and he'll tell us the layout,' Charlie said.

'No fucking way.' Denny slammed down his drink. 'I'll lose my job.'

'No you won't.' Charlie laughed. 'You're going to get us in there, give us all the information, that's all. We'll rough you up a bit so no one will know that you're involved.'

'Oh, thank you,' Denny grumbled. 'As long as it's not Boris that hits me.'

'I'll be gentle.' Boris smirked and took a drag of his joint. It was his third since we'd got back from the pub, so he was mellow.

'Eddie will hit you,' Charlie said.

'Yeah okay,' I agreed. I was the smallest of us all. 'So, what's the best time to rob the bank?'

'Shit, you're serious,' Denny said.

'Yeah,' Charlie got up and fetched another beer. 'If we plan it properly it will be okay.'

'Okay, closing time on a Thursday. We have a delivery on Thursday ready for Friday payroll. If you hit it on the last Thursday of the month there will be more for the monthly wages.'

'How much money are we talking about?' Boris asked.

'I dunno, it differs, depends on how much business the bank does that day. The tills will be full at closing time, then there's the money in the vault. Could be two hundred and fifty thousand, or more.'

'Fucking hell,' Charlie said.

'If you hit a bigger branch you could get more,' Denny suggested.

'It's not about the money,' Boris snapped. 'It's about getting that bastard.'

'Yeah but the money will be useful. Don't see why we can't keep some for ourselves,' Charlie said.

'Keep what?' Julie stirred in the chair, got up and stretched.

'We're going to rob the bank,' Boris said.

'What! No, what if you get caught?' Julie turned to Charlie.

'We won't,' Charlie said. 'Why don't you get some paper and a pen, and you can take notes, help us plan.'

'I'm not your bloody secretary.'

'Go on, it will help us out.' Boris smiled.

Julie huffed but started rooting around the flat gathering odd scraps of paper. 'What am I supposed to write with?'

'Here, you can have my pen.' Denny took a pen from the inside of his jacket pocket and handed it to Julie.

Julie grumbled but took the pen and sat at the table.

'Right,' Charlie said. 'We hit the bank at closing time on the last Thursday of the month. Gives us plenty of time to plan. Who locks the doors?'

'Usually the manager. He locks the doors at 3.30 then lets out the last of the customers.'

'So, there's going to be people in the bank,' MJ said.

'A few, I guess.'

'Okay, Boris, Eddie, and me will come into the bank at 3.30. Get inside and lock the door,' Charlie said.

'What about me?' MJ asked.

'You can drive the car,' Boris said. 'Any sign of trouble, you get yourself out.'

'You're the one with a kid on the way,' Charlie said.

'No, I'm not putting MJ at risk.'

We knew better than to argue. MJ was Boris's only tie to Iosif and had become a brother to him.

'Take us through the layout,' Charlie said.

'Two doors in, the second is a swing door.'

'Good, so we go in the first door, cover our faces and burst through the second door.' Charlie nodded.

'Then you're into the banking hall. Lining the back wall there are tables for customers. Then there's a queue counter. The counter is L-shaped with reinforced glass. It runs from one wall almost to the other where it turns in. You have to get behind the counter to access the rest of the bank. There's an airlock. You go through one door, it closes, then someone buzzes you in from the other side. Only one door opens at a time.'

'How many can fit in the airlock?' I asked. I had visions of us all stuck in the airlock and suffocating.

'Better go two at a time,' Denny said.

'Okay, Boris, you take Alan Lloyd through first, he'll be shit-scared when he sees the size of you. You're going to have to keep your cool,' Charlie said. 'Eddie and me will go through next. How many cashiers?'

'Five women and me,' Denny said. 'There are panic buttons under the desk, so you'll have to make sure no one hits one. The alarm will be sent to the police and I guess they could be there in minutes.'

'We'll make them stand as soon as we get in, then when we're behind the counter they can empty the tills into bags.'

'Am I going to be sat outside the whole time?' MJ asked.

'That's a point,' Charlie said. 'Is there a back door?'

'Yeah, but I can't get you in that way or they'll know it's me.'

'Yeah, but we can go out the back door.'

'There's a small yard out the back, enough for four cars. I get in early so I can park mine.'

'That's good, MJ can drop us off at the front, drive around the back and keep the engine running for when we come out.'

I was amazed at Charlie's planning, he was so calm you'd think we were planning a trip to the seaside.

'Once we get the bags filled, Eddie can stay with the cashiers to make sure no one presses the button. Boris and me will go to the vault. How do we get to the vault?' Charlie looked at Denny.

'Down the stairs, or there's a lift we use to bring up the tills. The vault needs two keys.'

'Who has the keys?' Boris asked.

'The manager and one other. We usually take it in turns to have the key,' Denny said.

'You better make sure you have the key that day, and the keys to the back door,' Charlie said. 'You and Alan Lloyd can fill the bags, we'll mark one to plant at Alan's house. Then you and Boris can take the money out and put it in the boot of your car. I'll stay with Alan.'

'Hang on.' Denny looked confused. 'Why would we put the money in my car?'

We all looked at Charlie.

'If we put the money in Denny's boot it'll be safe. If the police come after us we won't have any of the money,'

Charlie said. 'No one will think of checking Denny's car. He'll be knocked out and a victim like the rest of them. Later Denny can drive home with the cash. We'll figure out where to hide it.'

'You didn't say that Eddie was going to knock me out,' Denny said.

'Gotta make it look good. You're lucky it's Eddie and not me, you wouldn't come around for a week.' Boris smirked.

'You got all that, Jules?'

'Yeah, I still think it's a mad idea,' Julie said.

'We'll have the money, plant some at Alan's house and give the police a tip off. Alan will go down. We'll be rich. What can go wrong?' Charlie smiled.

Chapter Nine

I woke early on the morning of the robbery with my nerves jangling. I'd slept badly, dreaming of Alan Lloyd and other faceless men. I kept waking up drenched in sweat, scared to go back to sleep. The morning came too quickly. We had been over the plan time after time, tweaking the details. We'd visited the bank and Charlie and me had approached Alan in the pub. We caused a scene which we hoped would be remembered. We wanted it to look like Alan had been setting up the bank job and there were arguments. Charlie had grown a beard to disguise himself and I had shaved mine off. We blended in so it would be unlikely that anyone would be able to give an accurate description. Alan, on the other hand, was a regular so wouldn't be forgotten. Now we were back to our regular appearances. Boris had got married and Julie had retreated into herself. I think she was worried about something going wrong, as well as pining for Boris. Now the day had come, I felt the same dread.

Boris turned up at the flat at noon carrying a holdall. He unzipped the bag, took out the balaclavas and hessian sacks before unrolling a large package that contained three sawn-off shotguns.

'Where the fuck did you get those?' I couldn't believe what I was looking at.

'Know a guy who knows a guy,' Boris said.

'Yeah but we didn't agree to take guns.' I could feel the panic twisting my stomach.

'How do you think we're going to get Alan and the cashiers to do what we want? We didn't tell you because we knew you would get wound up,' Charlie said.

'I thought we would be using a knife,' I said.

'Yeah, I didn't know about the guns,' MJ said.

'You don't have to worry, you won't be using one,' Boris said.

'But I've never used a gun.' I couldn't imagine picking the thing up and waving it about.

'You just pull the trigger.' Boris laughed. 'It's not that hard.'

'We're not going to use them,' Charlie said. 'They're just for show, to scare them. Make sure no one hits the panic button.'

'They're not loaded, then?' I went to pick one up.

'Of course they are. We're not going in with empty guns,' Boris said. 'Are you sure you're up to this?'

'I'll do it?' MJ offered.

'No!' Boris barked.

'We stick to the plan,' Charlie said.

'Does Denny know about the guns?' MJ asked.

'No, we thought we'd surprise him,' Charlie said.

Time moved slowly. We had a few drinks to calm our nerves as we watched the clock. When the time came, we piled into a car that Charlie had nicked the night before, a red Rover which Charlie reckoned could outrun the police if we were chased. We'd driven the route hundreds of times but this time we were silent. MJ pulled up in front of the bank a few minutes before closing time.

'Good luck, I'll see you round the back,' MJ said.

'You hear sirens, you drive,' Boris ordered. He patted MJ on the shoulder and opened the door.

MJ drove away and we entered the first door. We pulled on the balaclavas and grabbed a gun. With a nod from Charlie, Boris burst through the swing doors.

'Hands in the air and move back from the counter,' Charlie shouted.

Denny looked as terrified as the girls behind the counter. You'd never guess that he was expecting us.

'Lock the door,' I ordered Alan.

He didn't move so I pointed the gun at him; he soon shifted. He locked the door with trembling hands. I felt a thrill having power over him.

There were two customers in the banking hall. Boris ordered them to the floor, and they now sat huddled against the table. Boris turned his gun on Alan. His eyes were wild, pumped up on adrenalin. For a moment I thought Boris was going to shoot him. Sweat trickled down the back of my neck.

'Move,' Boris ordered. 'Behind the counter.'

Alan moved and keyed in the code to the door. I was relieved when they went through the airlock. Charlie and me were next. We left the customers. They couldn't go anywhere with the door locked. By the time we got through the doors, Charlie had already ordered Denny and the cashiers to empty the tills into the hessian bags. They moved swiftly, tipping each drawer. When the tills were empty Charlie turned on Alan.

'Open the vault.'

'I can't, you need two keys,' Alan stuttered.

Boris nudged Charlie away and shoved the gun in Alan's face. I saw a wet patch appear in the crotch of his trousers and spread down his legs. I enjoyed his humiliation.

'Okay, please. I'll open the vault, but I need the second set of keys.' Sweat trickled down the side of Alan's face.

'Who has the other set of keys?' Charlie pointed the gun at the cashiers who were huddled together.

'Me,' Denny squeaked.

'Move,' Charlie ordered. He indicated with the gun that Denny should move next to Alan. Keeping the gun on them, he led them through the door with Boris following.

I knew from the plan that they would first unlock the back door then head down the stairs to the vault. I didn't like being left alone. The cashiers were crying, and my balaclava was soaked in sweat. I just wanted to tear it from my head. It felt like I couldn't breathe. Time moved slowly and panic made my hands shake. The gun was heavy, but I couldn't put it down. I was worried that we had been in the bank too long. One of them could have pressed the panic button when we entered, and the police could be waiting outside.

I heard Boris shout then a gunshot, it seemed to shake the building. The cashiers screamed. Without thinking, I left the room and ran down the stairs. Denny and Charlie crashed through the back door running behind me.

'Where's Iosif?' Boris yelled.

My stomach turned over when I entered the vault. Alan lay on the floor, his face contorted with pain as he gripped what was left of his leg. The vault floor was sprayed with flesh, blood, and bone.

I grabbed the gun from Boris. 'Get him out of here,' I yelled at Charlie.

Charlie pulled at Boris, who refused to move, his whole body shook with rage. I saw a bag stuffed with wads of notes on the vault floor. It was the one that had been marked to plant in Alan's house. I grabbed the bag and thrust it at Boris.

'You've got to get outta here,' I yelled. 'They would have hit the panic buttons and the police are on the way.'

Boris seemed to snap out of it and let Charlie pull him from the vault. The colour drained from Denny's face as he stood staring at Alan.

'Please help me,' Alan begged.

I looked at the pathetic figure lying on the floor, begging and pleading. I felt nothing but disgust. I raised my gun and pointed it at him. Even if I had pulled off the balaclava and shouted my name at him he'd probably have no idea who I was. He wasn't haunted by what happened, he went to bed each night carefree. The gun shook in my hand, my finger poised to squeeze the trigger. In that moment I wanted to blow him out of existence.

'No!' Denny stepped over Alan putting himself in line of the shot. His eyes silently pleading.

I don't know why Denny put himself between me and Alan, but I guess it was more about stopping me from going down for murder than to save Alan's life. I could hear police sirens getting closer and thought of Boris, MJ, and Charlie waiting for me. Denny nodded and I turned the gun and drove it into the side of his head. He staggered for a moment then fell to the floor, blood trickled down his face. I thought I'd hit him too hard and killed him. Alan was whimpering and the sirens echoed in my head. I was about to check that Denny was breathing when I heard Charlie yelling. He appeared behind me.

'Move, go!'

We flew up the stairs and out of the back door. The sirens were close. Charlie ripped off his balaclava.

'I told MJ to get Boris outta here, I had to get another car. Dump the gun.' He threw the balaclava into the bin.

I pulled off mine and dumped it with the gun, then followed Charlie to the car. I'd barely shut the car door when Charlie put it into gear and screeched out of the carpark.

'Nice car,' I said as I slid sideways on the leather seats.

'Yeah, probably belongs to that bastard.' Charlie laughed. He shot out onto the main road almost hitting the oncoming police car. The engine screamed as he floored the accelerator, overtook a car and tore up the high street.

I turned around and saw the police car was keeping pace. 'Shit, what are we going to do?' I looked at Charlie who was gripping the steering wheel, eyes fixed ahead as he dodged oncoming traffic trying to outrun the police.

'It's okay, if they're following us, MJ and Boris are clear. We have nothing on us, no money and we dumped the guns.'

'I don't think they'll buy that. We're running from them.' I knew the situation was hopeless.

'I'll think of something,' Charlie said.

He turned into a side road, the back end of the car skidded, and he had to fight to regain control. It lost us valuable seconds. The police were so close I could see their faces.

'If they catch us, we keep our mouths shut for as long as possible. It will give the others time to plant the money and hide the rest. Then we'll say that Alan planned the robbery. There were another two members of the gang, but we didn't meet them. We only took instructions from Alan. The cashiers will say there were three of us. We'll say there was a getaway driver and they left us behind after they shot Alan. We were seen in the pub with Alan so there will be enough evidence with the money for him to go down.'

'You think that'll work? My prints are all over the gun.'

'And so are Boris's, we have to keep it simple. Alan is going to say the big one shot him.'

I turned again and saw that two more police cars had joined the chase. 'I'm scared.'

'So am I,' Charlie said. 'Put the radio on.'

'What?'

'I want music,' he said.

I turned on the radio and found a station with some decent music. It made me smile to see Charlie singing among all the madness. He pulled back on the main street and we seemed to be getting ahead of the police, even though we were driving in a big circle. The traffic up ahead slowed, and a lorry was coming the other way. Charlie swung the car into the next turning. He was flooring the accelerator when a woman with a pushchair and holding the hand of a small child stepped into the road. She looked on in horror as we sped towards her, sirens blaring behind us, she froze. Charlie pulled hard on the wheel and we mounted the pavement, missing the woman and child, but we were going too fast to right the car and smashed into a lamppost. The last thing I remember is the sound of breaking glass.

Chapter Ten

Dora turned off the tape. Dmitri and Enzo were watching her – they had sat silent throughout the tape.

'Well, that doesn't really help.' Dora sighed and rubbed her hands over her face. 'I already knew from the police that Charlie and Eddie went down for robbery and that the others got away. I need the second tape to see what happened before that.'

'Yes,' Dmitri agreed, 'but Eddie wanted you to listen to that so there must've been something he said that was important. You've listened to the first tape so you must have an idea of what's going on.'

'I don't,' Dora snapped. 'There's nothing on the first tape or this one to explain why someone wanted them dead. No big secret.'

'Come on.' Dmitri stood. 'It's time to make a move.'

'Where?'

'Some place safe for a few days until you work out what you want to do next.'

Dora stayed seated. Her side ached, her head hurt, and she was weighted with grief. 'I don't know, I should just let them find me, give them the tapes and maybe they'll leave me alone.'

'Yeah, like that's gonna work. They'll kill you anyway. They think you know something. The best thing you can do is find out what they are after, then you'll have something to bargain with. Just now, you don't have a choice but to come with me,' Dmitri said.

'I can't just go with you, I've things to do. I need to attend the inquest. Charlie was supposed to come with me.'

'There's no point in going to the inquest. You won't hear anything you don't already know. Why put yourself through that and risk your life going. Go with Dmitri,' Enzo said. 'He's a good man, he'll look after you. Keep you safe.'

'Charlie said he would keep me safe and look what happened to him.' Dora felt like curling into a ball and crying.

'Charlie sent me to look after you and I've kept you safe so far,' Dmitri said.

'Nearly a day and I was drugged for half of it. For all I know, you could be using me to get the tapes before you kill me.'

'I would've killed you by now, trust me,' Dmitri said with a grin. 'Come on, we have to leave.'

If Charlie sent him, then Dora was going to have to trust him. She stood and picked up her handbag. 'I better call my mother to let her know I'm alright.'

'I've disabled your phone, stopped it being tracked,' Dmitri said. 'I've put another phone in your bag. All your contacts are inputted. Any messages you get will be bounced around and routed to the new phone.'

'And what have you done with my phone? I suppose you threw it out the window like the one Charlie gave me.'

'No, it's in your bag. It's just not working at the moment.' Dmitri huffed. 'I suppose a thank you is too much to ask.'

'Fine, thank you for the phone, but you could've at least had the courtesy to ask me before looking through my personal information.'

Dmitri turned to Enzo and spoke in Italian. Enzo laughed and gave Dmitri a hug before turning to Dora.

'You take care.'

'Thank you for letting me stay and for the food.'

'You're welcome.'

Dora followed Dmitri who had picked up her case and laptop bag. They went back down to the carpark, but this time got into a black jeep.

'What do you think Eddie meant when he said Alan was the first one?' Dora broke the silence as they exited the carpark.

'I don't know.' Dmitri joined the traffic keeping his eyes fixed ahead. 'It sounds like they had good reason to set him up.'

'Maybe it has something to do with Iosif. On the first tape Eddie talks about Iosif, he's Boris's younger brother. They were all in the children's home together – Bracken House. The brothers were close, yet he wasn't with them in the flat. It sounds like he went missing. Eddie said something about children going missing. Boris seemed to think that Alan knew where Iosif was. Bracken House came under investigation in the nineties for child abuse, maybe Alan Lloyd worked there before the bank and did something to the boys. Do you think they managed to set up Alan? He might have served his time and be out for revenge. If he's still alive – it was 1976. Or it could be his family.' Dora's mind was whirring with possibilities.

'It's possible. I'll see what information I can get on him, and if he had anything to do with the children's home.'

They travelled in silence for a while with Dora watching the road signs trying to guess where they were heading. They had left the M25 and A21 and were now travelling towards Tunbridge Wells.

'How much further?' Dora asked.

'Not far now. Then you can rest and decide what to do.'

'Eddie was supposed to be with me when I listened to the tapes so he could answer any questions.' Dora felt her throat constrict as grief gnawed at her stomach. 'I still can't believe he's gone.'

'I'm sorry, I understand that this must be difficult for you.' Dmitri glanced at her then fixed his eyes back on the road.

'Do you? There's no one to help me now. You said you'll keep me safe, but I don't know anything about you. You seem to know a lot about me.'

'What do you want to know?'

'I don't know. Anything. What do you do? I mean work.'

'You're probably better off not knowing.' Dmitri laughed. 'I sort of work with computers. I speak four languages.'

'Oh, well that's a start. You said Eddie and Charlie helped you out. How long did you know them?'

'Since I was a teenager. I was troubled, maybe more trouble than troubled. They took me in hand.'

Dora looked at his profile. She guessed him to be late thirties, maybe forty. 'So you knew the others on the tape?'

'Some.'

'Denny?'

'Dennis Pritchard.'

'He has a lot to lose if the story got out. He had the money and got away. The police said only Charlie and Eddie were caught.'

'You think Denny is behind this?' Dmitri laughed.

'What's so funny?'

'Nothing, I just can't see Denny taking out Charlie and Eddie as well as being able to track you down.'

'You know him well, then?'

'No, I've only met him a few times.'

'I think we should talk to him. If he's not involved, then maybe Eddie left a tape with him. There are five of them and Eddie would only have given them to someone he trusted. Even if he doesn't have a tape, he may be able to answer some of my questions.'

'I would imagine Denny has gone into hiding. It's likely that he knows what Eddie and Charlie were involved in, probably part of it himself. It'll take me a few days to track him down. What about Boris and MJ? You suspect Denny because he had the money but so did they; all three of them got away.'

'I know Boris is in prison. The police told me. I couldn't find out that much about him, only that he was serving life for the murder of his girlfriend and her child. Most of the information was about what he got up to in prison. Holding a prison officer hostage, starting a riot, stuff like that. He sounds like a very dangerous man. The police did say that Eddie had visited him recently. Maybe Eddie was going to warn him about giving me the tapes.'

'And MJ?'

Dora didn't want to say that MJ might be her father. She couldn't imagine him being involved in an armed robbery. She remembered him as a quiet well-mannered man, who never raised his voice at her.

'We only have his initials. It's not a lot to go on. Unless you know who he is, and where he is?'

'No, we'll ask Denny when we find him.'

'In the first tape Eddie mentioned a Dr Ray Williams. He worked in the children's home and Eddie implied he knew something. Maybe he knows what happened to Iosif.'

'Okay, I'll see if I can track him down, I could also arrange for you to visit Boris in prison. He may have some information.'

'No, Boris killed a woman and her child. He's a dangerous criminal. I very much doubt he would help us.'

'You forget that Eddie and Charlie were in prison and that would have been a category A. You can't just make judgements on people you don't know,' Dmitri said. 'Expect everyone to come up to your standards. I bet you haven't even had a parking ticket.'

Dora looked at Dmitri. His hands were curled tightly around the steering wheel, his jaw set.

He's probably been in prison himself, that's why he's so defensive, she thought. What was Charlie thinking sending some criminal to look after me? I'll probably end up buried under concrete and never be discovered. I should've left when I had the chance.

Dora ran her hands through her hair and huffed. Dmitri was her only hope of getting the tapes. She turned her head and looked out of the window.

'Are you going to sulk and not speak to me now? I'm just saying you shouldn't make judgements on people you don't know. You don't know why Boris did what he did, or the circumstances of any prisoner, come to that. It sounds like Boris was close to Eddie and Charlie, why wouldn't he want to help?'

'People change.' Dora turned to look at Dmitri. 'Maybe Boris didn't bother with Charlie and Eddie when they were in prison. Eddie said on the tape Boris had anger issues. It's clear he left his wife and child for someone else. Without Charlie and Eddie to control him he could've lost it. And for the record, no, I haven't had a parking ticket, speeding fine, or broken any laws. I don't see why I should be ashamed of that.'

'I'm not saying you should be ashamed. You've just never had cause to break the law. You live in a quiet village with your husband, two children, and a cat. Go for a meal once a week and have sex on a Saturday night. You've never had to worry about sleeping rough or where your next meal is coming from.'

'Now who's making judgements?' Dora seethed. 'You don't know anything about my life. My husband left me, my children are grown up and are away at university. I live alone in a house I'm about to lose. I have worries like everyone else.'

'See, you don't like it when someone makes an assumption about you,' Dmitri said.

'I was not making assumptions. Something went wrong. It's a fact that Boris is serving life for murder. Eddie went to see him and days later he was murdered. What if Boris ordered a hit on Eddie and Charlie?'

'A hit?' Dmitri laughed.

'You know what I mean. Just because he's in prison doesn't mean he doesn't know people on the outside.'

'I think you've been watching too much TV.'

'Boris was the one to get the guns, the one that shot Alan Lloyd.'

'Yeah, and Charlie and Eddie kept him out of prison. Do you think he would repay them by getting them killed?'

'I don't know. We don't know what happened after. Then there's the money. We don't know what he did with his share, he could have invested it, or he could have put it in a trust for his child. Yeah, now the child wouldn't want Boris's part in the robbery known or they could lose their money. That child is going to be... well, older than me. You better see if you can find out what happened to Boris's child. They could be behind this.'

'I think you are making things complicated. We need to find the other tapes before we drag anyone else into this mess.'

'I didn't want to be dragged into this mess,' Dora snapped. 'I don't know why Eddie started this. He said he wanted to put things right, for the truth to be told, but all he has achieved is getting himself and Charlie killed. And now someone's after me for information that I don't have. So I have no choice but to drag other people into this mess.'

'Right, I'll put it on my to-do list, shall I?' Dmitri huffed. 'At the moment you're all over the place, babbling on and coming up with wild theories. You need to concentrate on one thing at a time.'

'I don't know what to concentrate on. A few days ago all I had to worry about is how to pay the bills and get my work finished before the deadline. Now two people I love are dead and I'm probably next. I don't know what to do or think. It's like someone picked me up and dumped me in a horror movie and I can't get out!' Dora sucked in a deep breath. She felt lightheaded and her skin prickled with anxiety.

'Okay, don't get hysterical,' Dmitri said.

'I'm not hysterical. I'm scared.'

'Of course you are.' Dmitri's face softened. 'I wouldn't expect you not to be, but fear isn't going to help you. You need to find a way of fighting back, use the information they're after against them.'

'For that we need the tapes and I don't know where they are. I suppose we better find Denny first and hope he has a tape, or at least knows what was so important that Eddie and Charlie gave their lives to protect it. There was something that man said.'

'What man?'

'The one who broke into my house and tried to kill me, it was something about the money.'

'What about the money?' Dmitri glanced across at Dora.

'I don't know, I was terrified at the time, he was threatening to cut off my fingers. Let me think for a moment.' Dora screwed up her eyes forcing her mind back to the house. The man loomed over her, cold eyes staring out of the balaclava. She felt her body tense as the memory became clearer. 'More valuable than money.' Dora opened her eyes.

'What is?'

'I don't know. I said I didn't know where the money was, and he said that this far more valuable than money. Maybe they took something from the vault. People keep papers in vaults, don't they?'

'I guess. The only person who would know what else was taken is Denny. We can't do anything until I track him down.'

'What am I supposed to do in the meantime?'

'I told you, I'm taking you somewhere safe. You can chill out, give your side time to heal.'

The idea of being stuck with Dmitri didn't appeal to Dora. She turned again to look out of the window and Dmitri turned on the radio to fill the silence. They had left the A26 and the last sign Dora had seen had been for Groombridge. Now they drove deeper into the countryside where the roads narrowed and there were no streetlights, the way ahead illuminated only by the headlights of the jeep.

I hope he's not taking me to some cabin in the woods, Dora thought as she glanced at Dmitri who seemed more relaxed now. Anyone following them could be easily seen on this road.

They turned off the road and up a long narrow drive until they reached a set of tall gates. Dmitri opened the window, pressed a buzzer, put his head out and gave the camera a wave. The gates parted. Dora saw a large house looming in the darkness. She counted eight windows across the top, with three bay windows either side of the door. Dmitri stopped the jeep and turned off the engine.

'Where are we?'

'A friend's house. He's gonna put you up for a few days. Come on.' Dmitri stepped out of the jeep and grabbed Dora's case from the back seat.

Dora climbed out and winced as pain pulled at her side. As they approached the house the door opened, and a man stepped out. He wore grey joggers and a baggy T-shirt. Dreadlocks hung down to his shoulders. He smiled and his face lit up.

'Mee Tree, my man.'

Dmitri stepped forward and pulled the man into a hug, thumping him on the back. 'What are you doing here?'

'Heard there was a spot of bother, I thought you could do with an extra set of peepers around the place. You must be Dora.' He held out his hand. 'I'm Dray.'

Dora shook his hand.

'Let's get you inside, girl. Ben's just gone down the cellar to get a few bottles.' Dray turned and led the way.

Dora stepped inside into a large hallway. Coats were hung on rustic hooks with a pile of wellington boots beneath. The floor was laid with worn terracotta tiles. A wide dark wood staircase led the way past gilt-framed portraits. The smell of the house reminded Dora of a museum, old and musty. She followed Dray into a sitting room where flames danced in an open log fire; her eyes swept the room. There were sofas and comfy chairs placed near the fire. The walls were painted olive with landscape pictures hanging below a dado rail. A chandelier hung from the centre of the ceiling. Rugs covered the parquet floor, and a large oak dresser housed crystal cut glasses and decanters.

'I thought I heard visitors.' A thickset man entered the room. He had dark grey hair and a round boyish face. He was dressed in jeans and a taupe waistcoat.

'I'm Ben.' He held out his hand to Dora. 'I'm so sorry about Charlie and Eddie. Great guys.' He shook his head sadly.

'Thank you.' Dora tried to keep the emotion out of her voice.

'Come and sit down, make yourself comfortable. Dray, fetch some glasses, I've got a good bottle here to toast them.'

Dora chose a high-backed chair near the fire. Dray offered her a glass. 'Erm, I don't really drink. Thanks.'

'I have a nice bit of green if that's your thing,' Dray said.

'He doesn't mean tea,' Dmitri said. 'She doesn't smoke, doesn't like the word "fuck" either.'

Dray laughed. 'Damn, girl, you gonna have to cover your lugs around here.'

Dora felt her cheeks burn and hoped no one would notice. She turned her head and gazed into the fire.

'I'll make you a cup of tea,' Dmitri said.

'Can I get you something to eat?' Ben asked.

'No, thanks, I've already eaten.' Dora forced a smile, she felt uncomfortable in this strange house and had no idea what to say to the two strangers in the room.

'I expect you've lost your appetite.' Ben poured himself a glass of wine and sat down in the chair opposite Dora. 'What you need is rest and some space to grieve. The shock of finding Eddie and the news of Charlie on top of being attacked has probably knocked you senseless.'

'It's enough to fuck anyone up,' Dray added.

Dora let the tears come. She didn't have the energy to stop them.

'If it makes you feel better, Charlie had planned to bring you here before... he knew we would keep you safe.'

'Do you know who killed Charlie and Eddie?' Dora sniffed.

'No.' Ben took a sip of wine. 'But we'll find out. There are a lot of people who owe Charlie and Eddie, they won't rest until they track them down.'

'Owe, you mean money?'

'Nah,' Dray said. 'They helped people, like me. I was on the streets. I won't make you blush by telling you the things I did to get cash for a hit. I did what I did to survive, and I took all sorts of shit to make me forget. One day I'm down on my arse and rattling. I see this guy come out of a pub, I follow him then pull a knife. That guy was Charlie, kicked the shit out of me.' Dray laughed. 'He picked me up, gave me food and somewhere to sleep. He helped me get clean. When you're down in the gutter you stay there, know what I mean? No one wants to stick their hand in the filth to pull you out but not Charlie, or Eddie. I figure they must have been through some shit in their time to understand what it means to be that low. Respect, man.'

Dmitri came back into the room and handed Dora a mug of tea before filling a glass and taking a seat.

'To Charlie and Eddie.' Ben raised his glass.

The other two men raised their glasses and knocked back the wine.

Dora turned to Ben. 'How did you meet Charlie and Eddie?'

Ben smiled. 'That's a story for another time.'

Dora took a sip of her tea and sat back in the chair as the men recounted stories of Eddie and Charlie. It seemed that Eddie had a whole different life she knew nothing about. She tried to picture him as a young man, but the image of him tied to the chair kept invading her thoughts. She watched the flames dance around the burning logs, the warmth made her drowsy, so she let her head fall back against the chair.

'You must be tired,' Ben said. 'Come on, I'll show you your room.' He drained his glass and stood up. There were now three empty bottles on the table and Dray was opening another.

Dora stood, stretched and put her hand to her side, the pain making her feel nauseous.

'I've left some dressings and painkillers in your room,' Ben said. 'You're gonna be sore for a few days.'

An image of the woman lying motionless on the train floor came to Dora's mind.

'Is there any way we can find out what happened to the woman on the train? If the knife was aimed at me then it's my fault she got hurt. I feel awful, with everything that happened I didn't think about her until now.'

'It's not your fault,' Ben said.

'Apparently, the woman is still alive but in a critical condition,' Dmitri said. 'The police are appealing for witnesses. They'll probably pick us up on CCTV so that's another reason to stay out of sight. It didn't help that I had to carry you out. That's really going to make us stand out.'

'Well, maybe you should have left me there,' Dora snapped.

'Ignore Mee Tree, he's a moody fucker,' Dray said. 'You'll get used to him.'

I don't think I want to, Dora thought. 'Well, erm, goodnight.'

Dora followed Ben upstairs, it was cold after being in the heat of the fire and she felt a chill spread down her arms.

'Here we go.' Ben opened a door, stepped into the room, and placed Dora's case on a wooden-framed bed.

The room was decorated in the same old-world style as the rest of the house. Large oak furniture and heavy velvet curtains.

'Thank you,' Dora said.

'The bathroom is the fourth door on the right. I've put out towels for you. Have a good rest.' Ben patted her on the shoulder and left the room.

Dora took her washbag from the case and went into the bathroom, had a quick wash and brushed her teeth. Back in the room she pulled on her pyjamas and climbed into the bed. She was surprised by the comfort. Her body sunk into the mattress and the fluffy duvet covered her like a hug. Despite her strange surroundings she fell into a deep sleep until a noise outside her door woke her and left her sitting upright, her heart thudding in the darkness.

Chapter Eleven

The man hurried along the pavement, his eyes darting around checking for signs of being followed. At this time of the night the road was quiet. Most of the houses were set back and in darkness, only a few had lights behind the curtains. The man hoped the lights were for security and no one was peeking out watching. Despite the cold night air he was perspiring beneath his woollen coat. It didn't help that he wore a hat with a scarf wrapped around his mouth, but he couldn't take the chance that he would come upon someone taking a dog for a midnight walk and be recognised.

He reached the house he had been instructed to attend and scuttled up the driveway. The door opened before he had a chance to knock and he was ushered inside. The hallway was in semi-darkness, the only light came from an open door at the rear of the house. He followed the occupant into the room where another man sat cradling a glass of red wine.

'Is that your idea of a disguise, Nate?' the man asked.

'It's not a laughing matter, Kyle,' the man behind Nate growled. 'Where did you park?'

'Down by the lake.' Nate unwrapped his scarf and shrugged off his coat. 'This is not a good idea. We agreed no communication, and this is the second time we've met in the last few days.'

'Are you questioning my decision?' The man's eyes narrowed.

'No, Master,' Nate said. 'It's just in my position—'

'Your position,' Kyle growled. He got up from the chair and stepped forward. 'You're the one who assured us you could clear up this mess. You've made it worse.'

'And the gorilla you sent to sort out the woman didn't do any better,' the master said.

'She caught him off guard. He wasn't to know she had a weapon.'

'A weapon?' Nate laughed. 'A letter opener is what I heard.'

'Yeah, getting her stabbed on the underground was a great plan,' Kyle retorted.

'Enough,' the master snapped. He poured a glass of wine and handed it to Nate before picking up his own. 'What did you get from Charlie Briar?'

'Nothing, he wouldn't give up the location of the tapes or the girl,' Kyle said. 'We searched the place and all his other properties, including those occupied. Nothing. It was just luck that we had the phone with the instructions he sent, or we wouldn't have been able to get to her on the train. I should've passed the information on to someone else.' He looked pointedly at Nate.

'So where is the woman now?' the master asked.

'I don't know,' Nate said. 'She had help.'

'Who?'

'Don't know.' Nate took a sip of his wine.

'You better find out.'

'There are only two left,' Kyle said. 'If we silence them, then that should be the end of it, no witnesses left.'

'One you can't find and the other we can't get to,' the master said. 'We don't know what the woman knows and how many of the tapes she has. She might know the whole story and is just collecting evidence or witnesses. My instructions were clear, she was to be kept alive until we find out what Eddie told her.'

'I'm sorry,' Nate said. 'My man got a little overzealous.'

'Overzealous!' the master roared. 'There's a woman lying in a critical condition. Now there is an investigation I can't contain. If any of it is traced back to you, you stand alone.'

Nate knew this meant that he would be taken out before he had a chance to be arrested. 'There is no trail, you have my word. I was careful.'

'You better hope for your sake you were.' Kyle smirked.

'So now we have to wait until she comes out of hiding. She'll have to return home at some time.' The master refilled his glass and sipped, leaving a burgundy stain on his lips. 'Is she a person of interest to the police?'

'No,' Kyle answered. 'She was questioned but she didn't reveal anything useful. Didn't mention the tapes.'

'I expect she was warned not to trust the police,' Nate said.

'She was the last to see Eddie Flint alive and was in London when Charlie Briar was murdered. She was also on the train when that woman got stabbed. I think you should involve yourself with the investigation. Make sure she's a person of interest,' the master said.

'I'm not sure I can pull that off,' Kyle said. 'I'm going to have to have a good reason for taking an interest in the investigation. She's not a likely suspect, look at the way Eddie and Charlie were killed, plus she was injured on the train.'

'Well you better come up with something,' the master said.

'Yes,' Kyle said.

'Good, as soon as she is pulled in for questioning we'll know where she is. This time I want no mistakes.'

'Perhaps it would be prudent to wait and see if she has the tapes. We could have her followed. See who she speaks with. She may even lead us to Dennis,' Nate suggested.

'You could have a point,' the master agreed. 'That's if she knows where the tapes are.'

'But what if she releases the information before we get to her? It only takes one click. We can't take that risk,' Kyle said.

'She's kept the information she has so far to herself. I'm guessing she doesn't know the full story or the location,' Nate added.

'Of course she doesn't know,' the master said. 'And when she does find out she's going to check it out first. It's the only proof. Find out who is helping her and get rid of them. She'll be easy to get to when she's on her own. She'll lead us to the tapes and the location and then we kill her.'

Chapter Twelve

Dora woke with a strip of light shining through the gap in the curtains. She sat up and looked around the room. The chair was still jammed under the door handle. She felt foolish now after getting so frightened when she'd heard Dray bumping along the passage and crashing into the bedroom the night before. She imagined he had drunk too much and was struggling on his feet.

After showering and dressing she gave her mother a quick call to reassure her she was okay then headed downstairs. She followed the noise of clattering plates and smell of frying bacon to the back of the house. She found Ben stood by an Aga, shaking a pan over the heat.

'Good morning,' Dora said.

'Oh good, you're up.' Ben turned and smiled. 'Just in time for breakfast.'

The thought of eating made Dora feel queasy. 'I'm not very hungry, just a cup of tea will be fine, thank you.'

'You're going to need a good breakfast, it's chilly outside and we'll be out most of the day.'

'We're going out? I thought I had to stay indoors.'

'You're not a prisoner.' Ben laughed. 'We have a surprise for you, take your mind off things. Grab a seat, it'll be ready in a minute.'

Dora sat down at the long pine table and watched Ben cook and make the tea.

'Where's Dmitri and Dray?'

'Dmitri left early this morning, he had to take care of some things. Dray is out in the field.' Ben placed a mug of tea on the table then served up the breakfast.

'Will Dmitri be back later?' Dora cut through the bacon and took a bite.

'I'm not sure. Don't worry, he hasn't abandoned you. He'll be back. How is your side?'

'Still sore. I changed the dressing, it looks okay.'

'Good, just keep an eye out for signs of infection. Don't look so worried, I'm sure Dmitri did a good job of cleaning you up.'

'It's a lovely house.' Dora buttered some toast and added it to her plate. Now she had started eating she found that she was hungry.

'Thanks, I've tried to keep the original features and stay away from modern furniture. Clients seem to like it.'

'You have people come to stay?'

'Yes, it's a sort of hunting lodge. I have fishing rights on the river, and over nine hundred acres of fields and woodland. It's also close to Tunbridge Wells so I attract visitors who want a country break and to take in the sites.'

'And you run it yourself?'

'We're closed at the moment. I have staff in to cook and take care of the rooms in peak times.'

Dora wondered how he came to own the property. She wanted to ask about his connection to Eddie and Charlie, but it didn't seem the right time. She finished her breakfast then helped Ben with the washing up.

'Right, grab your coat and we'll go and find Dray.'

'My coat got ripped on the train and it's, erm, stained.'

'No problem, we'll find something for you.' Ben looked at Dora's feet. 'Those boots should be okay.' He left the kitchen and came back with a wax jacket. 'This should fit.'

Dora put on the jacket and turned up the cuffs before leaving the house. In the daylight she could see that the house was surrounded by fields and woodland. She breathed in the fresh air and tucked her hands into the jacket pockets. They walked across two fields then picked up a track which led to a long wooden cabin with a battered Land Rover parked outside.

The cabin door opened, and Dray poked his head out. 'Thought I heard you two. It's all set up, come on in.'

Dora stepped through the door. The back of the cabin was open and looked onto a field with targets at different heights and distances. A wide ledge ran the length of the cabin with various guns laid out next to ammunition.

'Oh,' Dora squeaked and took a step back. 'You're arms dealers.' It was out of Dora's mouth before she had a chance to think about what she was saying.

There was a moment of silence then Ben laughed, a booming laugh that shook his body.

'Damn girl, you can't be blurting out shit like that.' Dray laughed. 'These are legit.'

'Come on,' Ben said. 'No need to be afraid. They are CO_2 air guns, perfectly legal.'

'But don't you need a firearms licence?' Dora asked.

'Not for these. If it makes you feel better, I do have a firearms licence. This is the shooting range. I told you the house was a sort of hunting lodge. It's just us so there's no need to worry.'

'So they're not real guns?'

'They're real enough and you could do some damage, so you've still got to be careful.'

'We didn't think it was a good idea to start you off with the serious stuff,' Dray said.

'Start me off? I'm scared just looking at them. I appreciate all the effort you've gone to trying to entertain me but I think it's best if I stay indoors, read a book, or do some work on my laptop.'

'This isn't just for fun,' Ben said. 'Look at you, you're what? Five foot three, about eight stone. You have no chance of defending yourself.'

'I'm five foot four, and besides I can't be walking around with a gun and shooting people. You can go to prison for just possessing one. Oh, no. I can't go near one of those things.'

'Yes, you can,' Ben said.

'Come on, we'll start with something simple.' Dray stepped up to the bench.

* * *

By the next day Dora was feeling confident with the handguns and was enjoying a contest with Dray while Ben checked the surrounding fields on a quad bike. For a brief time, the horror of the last few days was tucked at the back of her mind. She felt relaxed, the purpose of the exercise temporarily forgotten along with the danger.

'Damn, bitch, that was a good shot.' Dray laughed as he put down his gun. 'I think it's time to introduce you to the big boys.'

'The real guns? No, I think I'm happy to carry on with these.'

Dray ignored her comment and left the cabin. He came back carrying a wooden crate. He placed it on the bench, opened the lid, and took out a pair of safety goggles and ear protectors.

'You're gonna need these or you'll get some serious damage to your lugs. We're talking up to 150 decibels,' Dray said. He took three handguns from the box and laid them on the bench.

Dora felt her stomach churn. 'I really don't think I'm ready.'

'Ben's making sure the area is clear. No one is watching you so you're not going to get into any trouble. You're gonna have to learn to handle one of these beauties. Glock, SIG, Webley.' He pointed to the guns.

'Looks like something from an old Western movie.' Dora picked up the Webley; the cold metal weighed heavy in her hand.

'Yeah, I thought we'd start with that one for practice, then move to the semi. I reckon the SIG is gonna be your best option, 99mm 10 rounds. Fit nicely in your handbag.'

'I hope you're joking.'

'Nah, this is some serious shit you're dealing with.' He picked up the Webley and showed Dora how to load it and take off the safety. 'You got six shots, it's gonna be loud and watch out for the kickback. Best use two hands.'

Dora put on the safety goggles and ear protectors. She stood with her arms outstretched, gripping the gun tightly with her whole body tense. She could just about hear Dray shouting instructions. The gun shook in her hand. She took a breath and tried to steady her grip then gritting her teeth she pulled the trigger. The gun went off driving her hands upwards and back smacking her in the face. She squealed as she jumped backwards dropping the gun. She turned and saw Dray clutching his stomach as he howled with laughter. She yanked off her ear protectors. Ben was chuckling and Dmitri stood with a smirk on his face.

'Oh, you're back,' Dora said. She felt her cheeks burn with embarrassment. She was surprised to find herself pleased to see him and embarrassed that he had witnessed her making a fool of herself with the gun.

'Just as well. What the fuck are you trying to do?' Dmitri growled. 'You could've done yourself some serious damage.'

'Give her a break, man,' Dray said. 'She's been practicing on the air guns. She was doing really well.'

'Yeah, a toddler could fire one of those.'

'You're right.' Dora tore off the goggles and threw them on the bench. 'This was a bad idea. I could end up killing someone.'

'That's the point.' Dray laughed. 'Don't give up, give it another go. You'll be prepared this time.'

'Try the SIG,' Dmitri said. 'Here, I'll show you.' He stepped up to the bench. 'Put the glasses back on and cover your ears.' He picked up the gun and placed it in Dora's hand.

'Step apart.' He moved behind her and pressing up against her back put his arms around her body placing his hands over hers.

Dora could feel the warmth of his body and smell the woody scent of his aftershave. A quiver ran through her.

Dimitri moved her hands on the gun. 'You need to keep a firm grip on the handle. Wrap your other hand around and use it to weight down the gun when you fire. You'll be ready for the recoil this time. Squeeze the trigger, don't snap it back.'

Dora could feel her heart thudding in her chest. She gritted her teeth and screwed up her eyes, her whole body tensed.

'Relax a little,' Dmitri instructed. 'Open your eyes. You're going to have to look if you want to hit the target.'

'Okay.' Dora nodded. She tried to steady her breathing as she aimed the gun with Dmitri guiding her hand. She squeezed the trigger and the bullet exploded from the gun. The barrel sprung up, but Dmitri's grip stopped it moving too far back.

'I hit the target,' Dora squealed in delight.

'We hit the target,' Dmitri said. 'Again.'

They fired another three shots then Dmitri let go of her hands and stepped back. 'Now try on your own.'

Dora felt cold air replace the warmth of Dmitri's body. 'I'm going to end up hitting myself in the face again.'

'Just remember, weight the gun down, firm grip,' Ben said.

'Hold up a mo,' Dray said. He dashed out of the cabin and appeared in the shooting range with a target shaped as an outline of a man. He placed it in the centre then walked back into the cabin. 'Now you've got something to aim for. Imagine he's broken into your house. What you gonna say?'

'Don't move or I'll shoot you,' Dora said.

'You gotta sound like you mean it,' Dray said. 'You can't be pussying around.'

Dmitri stepped forward, picked up the Glock and aimed. 'Move and I'll blow your fucking brains outs.' The gun went off hitting the target in the head.

'I don't see why you have to swear to get your point across,' Dora said.

'This guy.' Ben pointed to the target. 'Broke into your house, tortured and killed Eddie.'

Dora aimed the gun. 'Bastard!' She fired five shots, one hitting the target in the centre of the chest.

'You didn't want to question him?' Dray laughed.

'You did good,' Dmitri said. 'I think that's enough practice for the day. We better get back to the house, you're gonna need an early night. We're hitting the road early in the morning for a funeral. I found Denny and the doc.'

Chapter Thirteen

At five in the morning Dora showered, dressed in the black suit Dmitri had bought for her and applied make-up. She checked her appearance in the mirror and decided on pinning up her hair to look more formal. She sprayed on perfume and left the room.

Dmitri was waiting at the bottom of the stairs, dressed in a black suit and crisp white shirt.

Dray appeared next to Dmitri. 'Nice pair of pins.'

Dora looked down at her legs feeling self-conscious. 'The skirt's a bit short.'

'It's a good fit, you look nice,' Dmitri said.

'Did you just dish a compliment?' Dray laughed.

'I was admiring my choice of clothes.'

Dora saw a hint of a smile on Dmitri's lips. 'I'm impressed with your ability to correctly guess my size.'

'He's taken off enough women's clothes to be an expert,' Dray said.

'Let's go.' Dmitri turned and opened the front door.

'Are you sure you don't want to slip the SIG into your handbag?' Dray asked.

'I don't think a gun in my bag is appropriate for a funeral,' Dora said. 'I'm sure we'll be safe.'

'Look after yourself.' Dray put his arms around Dora and pulled her into a warm hug. 'See you back here soon.'

The gesture brought on a wave of emotion and Dora felt her throat tighten. 'Thank you.' She kissed Dray on the cheek before leaving.

Dmitri was sat waiting in the jeep with the engine running. Dora climbed in and secured her safety belt.

'I don't see the point of going to the funeral. It's not like he can tell us anything now. He died of a heart attack, so it's not like he was murdered. He probably hasn't had contact with Eddie and Charlie since they left the home. We'd be better off just going to see Denny.'

'I didn't tell you the whole story last night. I didn't want you to get worked up.'

Dora huffed. 'After finding Eddie, I don't think there's anything worse I could see or hear.'

'Don't be too sure.' Dmitri put the jeep in gear and pulled off down the drive. 'We have another three tapes to find and listen to. The doctor's house was broken into the night he died. The intruder wrecked the place but didn't take money or valuables. I imagine the shock killed him before they had a chance to extract information.'

'What were they looking for? I don't think Eddie would've given the doctor one of the tapes.'

'Well, they were looking for something. You said Eddie talked about the doctor knowing things but not speaking out. Maybe he was involved, and they wanted to silence him.'

'Oh God, they could be there watching. We shouldn't go.'

'This is why I didn't tell you last night. We just need to be careful. Watch who turns up and talks to the family. See what sort of man he was. Anyway, we're not meeting Denny until late afternoon. We can't change our plans.' He glanced at Dora. 'Don't look so worried. I doubt they'd turn up at the funeral. The most they'd do is send someone who doesn't look out of place to keep an eye on the family and listen. Even if that's the case, they won't be expecting you and won't act on impulse. These people plan.'

'I hope you're right. We're going to stand out. What reason are we going to give for turning up to a funeral of a man we don't know?'

'Our story is your uncle Ben knew the doctor from the children's home. There must have been hundreds of children going through Bracken House over the years. No one will question it. We say your uncle is too ill to travel and asked that we come on his behalf to pay respects. Your name is Sue.'

'And who are you supposed to be?'

'I'm your husband, Dave.'

'My husband?' Dora laughed.

'What's wrong with that? You should be flattered,' Dmitri said with a grin.

They arrived in Cardiff half an hour before the funeral was due to start. They sat in the jeep watching the mourners arrive.

'There aren't many,' Dora commented.

'He was old,' Dmitri said. 'That's what happens when you get old, all your friends are dead so there's no one to come to your funeral.'

'That's a cheerful thought.'

'Just stating a fact. Look, there are a few of his friends still standing, just about.'

Dora looked at the group approaching the church. Three elderly ladies were accompanied by two old men, one with a walking stick. 'I haven't seen anyone suspicious,' Dora said.

'I don't know, that old man could do some damage with that stick.' Dmitri laughed. 'Come on, we better go in before the funeral car arrives.'

They stepped into the church and slid into the back pew. Dora looked at the stained-glass windows as the organ played softly in the background. Her thoughts turned to Eddie and she imagined him stuffed in a large freezer with a tag. She shuddered and wrapped her arms around herself.

'Are you okay?' Dmitri asked.

'Yes, I was just thinking about Uncle Eddie and when we'll be able to hold his funeral.'

'A few weeks, I expect. As they haven't caught the person responsible there'll be a second independent post-mortem, for evidence.'

'You seem to know a lot about the subject.'

'You'd be surprised by the knowledge I've collected,' Dmitri said.

'I don't think I want to know,' Dora teased.

'Those two women sat at the front are the doctor's daughters,' Dmitri whispered.

'Shouldn't they be following the coffin in?'

Dmitri shrugged his shoulders.

'I am the resurrection and the life, sayeth the Lord.' The vicar's voice echoed around the church as he led in the coffin.

Dora stood and looked at the mourners. The daughters at the front had turned to watch the coffin proceed down the aisle, both with stony faces.

'There are no flowers on the coffin,' Dora said.

'Maybe he didn't like flowers.' Dmitri picked up an order of service.

The undertakers placed the coffin on the left of the altar, bowed and retreated. The vicar made his address then said a prayer. A half-hearted attempt to sing a hymn followed. The vicar then read the eulogy from a sheet. First there was an outline of his early years then training as a doctor before taking up the role of local GP.

'He may as well be reading a menu,' Dora whispered. 'No emotion.'

The vicar then mentioned his work in Bracken House which got Dora's attention. The doctor had looked after the health of the children until 1981. I wonder what made him leave, did something happen? Dora's thoughts were interrupted by the mention of the doctor's work in prisons, looking after the health of the inmates. The rest of his work was with charities and then he retired. Dora stood as they were instructed to sing the next hymn. 'Do you think he came across Eddie and Charlie in prison?'

'He might have.'

'Or he might have known Boris.'

Dmitri started singing so Dora joined in. When the music ended, they followed the coffin outside to the graveyard. The family gathered around as the coffin was lowered. One sister had a hint of a smile on her face. The vicar said a final prayer and those gathered moved away.

'Let's go and talk to the daughters,' Dmitri said.

They approached the two women and Dmitri gave Dora a nudge.

'I'm sorry for your loss,' she said to the women.

'Oh don't be, we're just here to make sure the bastard is really dead and in the ground.'

'Oh.' Dora didn't know what to say.

'I take it from your reaction you didn't know my father,' the other sister said.

'Erm... no, my uncle knew him. He was in the children's home when your father worked there. My uncle is too ill to come today so sent me to pay respects.'

'That figures, young boys weren't his thing. Have you come far?'

'Kent,' Dmitri said.

'You've had a long journey. We're going to the Working Men's Club down the road. You're welcome to join us for a cup of tea and some food.'

'Thank you.'

'There are some of my father's old friends and some I don't know.' She looked at the group of people who stood talking at the entrance to the church. 'Maybe one of them will remember your uncle. I'm Elaine and this is my sister Judy.'

'I'm Dave and this is my wife Sue,' Dmitri said before Dora had a chance to respond.

'We'll see you there,' Judy said.

Dmitri took hold of Dora's hand as they walked back to the jeep. 'Better make our story look realistic,' he said.

'As long as you are not planning to kiss me,' Dora replied. His hand felt warm and comforting. She couldn't remember the last time someone held her hand. Dmitri let go of her hand and she climbed into the jeep. 'Do you think she was implying that her father was a pervert?'

'Or worse, she said young boys weren't his thing, so the implication is young girls, but how young?'

'Oh, that's sick,' Dora said.

'Yes, but it would explain the sisters' behaviour. Their open lack of respect and aversion to their father. Let's hang around awhile and see what we can find out.'

They drove the short distance to the club, parked in the carpark at the rear of the building and got out of the jeep. Elaine, parked next to them, was leaning into the boot of her car.

'Can I help you with anything?' Dmitri asked.

'You can take this in, thanks.' Elaine handed him a box and picked up another one before closing the boot.

It was warm inside, and the mourners were sat in groups at tables. At the back of the room a lady stood behind a table filling a stainless-steel teapot from an urn. Another table was laden with sandwiches and cakes.

'Go and grab a seat and I'll get us a cuppa,' Dmitri said as he placed the box on the nearest table.

Dora took a seat by the table where the old man with the stick sat flanked by two elderly ladies. Another man was drinking tea as he listened to their conversation. By the time Dmitri returned with the tea Dora had learned that the old man was a friend of the doctor's, one lady was the doctor's receptionist until she retired, the other the practice nurse. The younger man was the doctor's grandson but hadn't seen his grandfather for a number of years. She was trying to listen in on the conversation coming from the table behind where the sisters sat but they were talking too quietly. Dmitri set the cups down and took a seat.

'What did you say your uncle's name is?' the old man asked.

'Ben,' Dora said.

'And he was at Bracken House?'

'Yes. My uncle said that the doctor was very kind to him. The vicar mentioned that he also worked with prisoners. Can't have been easy work. Sounds like he did a lot of good deeds.'

The old man nodded. 'Yes, he was a good man.'

'Wonderful to work for,' the receptionist said.

There was a snorting noise from the grandson. They all turned to look at him.

'According to my mum he was a dirty old man. We weren't allowed to visit him when we were young. Mum didn't want anything to do with him. He liked to take photos of young children, had his own darkroom.'

'Nonsense,' the nurse said. 'I worked with him for years, in the surgery and Bracken House. He was always kind to the kids, and he took pictures of all of us. It was his hobby, nothing inappropriate about it. They're just spiteful stories made up by two ungrateful girls.' She shook her head, tutting.

'He brought those girls up on his own when their mother died, gave them everything they wanted, and they took what they could from him. He had no money of his own, gave it all to the pair of them. When he got sick they moved him to a flat, sold the big house and split the money. Pair of vultures, and now they excuse their behaviour by making up vicious stories and taking what was left before he was cold. I'm not staying around to listen to any more of this.' She scraped back her chair, grabbed her coat and left the room, the double doors swinging in her wake.

'What would she know? She only worked with him,' the grandson said. 'My mum said he made her skin crawl. Why would she say that about her own father?'

Dora watched the old man's reaction. He remained quiet, sipping his tea. She wondered why he didn't defend his friend. She thought he probably agreed with the grandson and the doctor was a pervert. But his own daughters... The thought turned Dora's stomach.

'We only came for Auntie Elaine,' the grandson continued. 'And to see if the old bugger left us anything. That's if he even remembered he had grandchildren. Auntie Elaine got all religious a few years ago. Said she wanted to forgive her father and try and build bridges. I reckon she thought he would leave everything to her. He had stocks and shares and a few quid in the bank. I don't know what that old hag was on about. Mum and Auntie Elaine didn't take all his money. Auntie Elaine moved him to a flat for his own good. He couldn't manage the house on his own. The stairs were too dangerous for him. He told her to sell the house and split what was left with my mother after he bought the flat.'

Dora thought that the grandson was trying too hard to justify his mother's and auntie's actions and that perhaps there was some truth in what the old nurse said. She looked over to the next table and saw Elaine was emptying the contents of the boxes and laying them on the table, she could make out a carriage clock, some rings and watches among the items.

'You better come and take what you want,' Judy called over to her son. 'I'm not taking it back with me. I've collected anything of value, the rest I asked the cleaners to give to charity shops or take down the rubbish dump.'

'I thought any good stuff would have been nicked when he was broken into.' The grandson stood up.

'No, they didn't take anything, some of this stuff has been in my attic since he moved to the flat,' Elaine said.

'He wanted me to keep it safe, don't know why. It's just a pile of photos and some jewellery.'

The grandson moved to the table to join the rest of the family who were picking up and examining the items. Judy was looking through the photos and showing them to her sister. They were smiling for the first time that day and Dora guessed the sisters were reminiscing over family shots.

'Disgusting,' the old man commented. 'Dumping all his stuff on a table and scrabbling for it like a jumble sale.'

'I expect they don't get together very often, and this was the easiest way of sorting out the last of his belongings,' Dora said.

'Odd lot.' The old man kept his eyes on the family.

Elaine stepped over to their table clutching a bunch of photos. 'These might be of interest to you and your uncle.' She placed the photos in front of Dora. 'They're of the children's home, you might be able to pick out your uncle.'

'Thank you.'

'You can keep them, they're of no use to me.' Elaine returned to her own table.

Dora picked up the photographs. The first lot were coloured and dated on the back from 1982 running back to the seventies. The photos then changed to black and white, they were larger than the coloured ones, the image sharper. Dora imagined the doctor developing them in a darkroom. The first of these photos showed a group of boys playing ball on a lawn, a large building visible in the background. She flipped it over and saw *Bracken House 1968* written on the back. Was Uncle Eddie there then? she thought as she turned the photo back and scrutinised the faces. When she looked up she noticed the old man had moved closer to her chair and was staring at the photo. She handed the photo to Dmitri and looked at the next one. It showed four boys sitting under a tree, on the back was written *Charlie, Eddie, Boris, and Denny. Bracken House 1967*. A lump formed in Dora's throat as she turned the photo over and looked at their smiling faces. She picked out Charlie first. Dark curly hair and a scar on his chin. He had the same twinkling eyes and mischievous smile that she remembered. Sat next to Charlie was Eddie with his knobbly knees and stick-thin legs poking out of his short trousers. He was the smallest of the four. The next boy she guessed to be Boris, serious eyes and towering over the others. That left Denny on the end. She handed the photo to Dmitri.

'Lovely photo of them,' he said.

'Lovely place, Bracken House,' the old man commented.

'You know it?'

'I worked there, voluntary.' He glanced at the remaining photos on the table. 'Helped out with the kids.' He smiled. 'I'd like to have some of the photos.'

'If you give me your contact details, I'll have some copies made and send them on to you,' Dmitri offered.

'Surely you don't want them all.'

'We don't know which ones would interest my uncle,' Dora said. 'He's very sick and it will be nice for him to see them.'

'It won't take us long to make copies,' Dmitri said. 'I'll get them sent to you in a couple of days.'

A flicker of annoyance crossed the old man's face before he put on a smile. 'That's very kind. I'll just fetch a pen and paper to write the address for you.' He excused himself from the table.

The only other person sat at their table was the receptionist, quietly sipping her tea. Dora picked up the next photo. It showed a man in police uniform with the children and staff standing behind him, apart from one boy who stood at his side. On the reverse: *Chief Constable Graham North and his ten-year-old son, Scott, visit to Bracken House to hand over funds raised for the children's annual holiday. April 1968.*

The next set of photos showed a different building. This one had a clock tower and rows of dark windows. She flicked through; the subjects in these photos seemed unaware that their picture was being taken. One showed a couple of boys chopping wood while a man stood by and watched. The boys were barechested, their ribs showing. Another showed a solemn-looking group, their eyes haunted. Next was a group of men who stood smoking as they looked at boys lined up against the wall of the house. There was something about the atmosphere captured in the photos that made Dora feel uncomfortable. On the reverse was written *Blue Hollow 1969, Harold Rolland, Robert Powell and Jack Quinn.* The photos ran through the years with names of the men and boys. Later, groups of girls appeared.

'What is this place?' She handed the photos to Dmitri.

'Looks like another children's home.' He leaned in close and whispered, 'This time the doctor was keeping a record of visitors.'

'Do you think that the intruder was after these?'

'Could be.'

'We could ask the old man about it when he comes back.'

'He's been gone awhile. Stay here and I'll go and look for him.'

Dora was left sitting at the table with the receptionist who was struggling to grip the cup with gnarled fingers.

'Did the doctor visit many children's homes?' Dora asked.

'No, only Bracken House. Why?'

'I thought he might have worked at Blue Hollow.'

'No dear, only the one. I can't say I've heard of that home. Is it local?'

'I'm not sure, my uncle mentioned it.'

'I kept all the doctor's appointments. It was only the one home. There were a lot of children to take care of on top of the practice. He was a very busy man.'

'He stopped working there before he retired?'

'Yes, after he took on the prison visits it was too much. There is only so much a man can do. The children would have missed him, not everyone that worked there was kind. I know the manager Mr Wainwright was a little free with the use of the cane. It worried the doctor. Of course such treatment wouldn't be allowed today.'

'No,' Dora agreed. 'So the doctor's wife died when the children were young. It must have been difficult. Who took care of the children?'

'His parents for a while, he did marry again but it didn't last. Nice lady, I thought they made a nice couple and they seemed happy, but something happened. She wouldn't say much but whatever it was had frightened her.'

'When was this?'

'In the eighties.'

'Do you remember her name?'

'We have to go,' Dmitri hissed behind Dora.

'In a minute.' She turned back to the receptionist.

'Now,' Dmitri growled.

Dora scraped back her chair. 'It was nice to meet you,' she said before she thanked Elaine for the photographs and hurried after Dmitri. 'What's the rush?'

'The old man has disappeared, and he was a bit too interested in the photographs. He could have made a call.'

Dora felt a cold creep over her skin. They left the building and were walking across the carpark when a door slammed. She turned and saw two men coming towards them.

'Get in the jeep,' Dmitri said. 'Now!'

Dora ran to the jeep, the photos clutched in her hand. She saw the lights flash and heard the whir of locks. She yanked open the door and jumped in slamming it behind her. The locks clicked into place trapping her in the jeep.

Chapter Fourteen

Dora sat in the jeep with her heart thudding in her chest. She forced herself to turn in the seat and look. The two men were upon Dmitri and she could just make out what they were saying through the closed windows. One man had a shaven head, the other a ponytail and beard. Both were thickset with menacing eyes.

'You've got something of ours,' the bald man said.

'I don't think so,' Dmitri said.

The bearded man stepped sideways. 'I guess I'm gonna have to get it myself.' He tapped an iron bar on the palm of his hand.

Do they want me or the photos? Dora thought, as she looked around the carpark. It was deserted. Oh God, he can't fight two of them, they'll kill him then come for me.

Panic constricted her breathing. She looked back in time to see Dmitri kick high. His foot impacted the hand holding the iron bar, and it fell to the floor. He delivered a second kick to the man's groin, before spinning and driving his fist into the other man's face. There followed a tangle of bodies as fists flew. The bald one grabbed Dmitri from behind wrapping his thick arms around him in a bear hug, the other man punched at his face and torso.

Dora was horrified, and couldn't bear to just sit there and watch. She thought if she got out and threw the photos at them, it might give Dmitri time to get away. She wished now she had brought the gun.

She yanked on the handle of the door. The jeep let out a series of loud beeps as the lights flashed. It was enough of a distraction for the men to look her way. Dmitri used the bald one as leverage bringing up both legs and kicking the bearded guy in the head. He drove his elbow into the stomach of the bald guy.

There were shouts as people came out of the building. The two men sprinted back to their car and left in a spray of gravel. Dmitri clicked the key fob and the jeep fell silent.

Dora jumped out of the jeep. 'Are you okay?'

'Yeah.' Dmitri wiped blood from his mouth.

'I've called the police.' Elaine approached them. 'What happened?'

'They were after my wallet. They'll be long gone by the time the police get here.'

'Probably, but you got a good look at them, you can give a description to the police,' Elaine said.

Dora knew they would end up at the police station, she clutched her shaking hands as she tried to think of a way to leave. 'I think it's best we go straight to the hospital. Come on, darling, we better get you checked out.'

'Shouldn't you wait for the police?' Elaine said.

'No, you can tell them where we are. He could have internal injuries. We can be at the hospital by the time the police get here.'

'I think you're right,' Dmitri said. 'I don't feel so good.'

Dora made a show of helping him into the passenger seat, then got in the driver's side and adjusted the seat.

'Good thinking,' Dmitri said.

'I didn't think it was a good idea to be here when the police arrive.' Dora backed the jeep out of the parking space.

'No, and you better move quickly. You're not insured to drive.'

'Oh shit.' She hit the brakes.

'Keep driving.' Dmitri laughed. 'At least until we're out of sight. You won't go to hell, but I do believe I heard you use bad language.'

'It was a minor expletive and I'm stressed.' She drove away from the club and took the first turning, rounded a bend and pulled over. 'You better take over. If you are okay to drive.' She looked at his swelling face.

'I've had worse,' he said before getting out of the jeep.

Dora slid to the passenger side and fixed her belt.

'How short are your legs?' Dmitri slid the driver's seat back. 'You were right on top of the steering wheel.'

'Nothing wrong with my legs,' Dora retorted. 'The pedals are too far away on this thing. Do you think those men were after the photos or me?' she asked as he pulled away from the kerb.

'Both. The old man took a lot of interest in the photos. I reckon he made a call and legged it.'

'There's nothing in the photos that's incriminating. It's just children and the home with visitors.'

'The names and dates on the back were probably of people that shouldn't have been there.'

'This one.' Dora waved the photo. 'Blue Hollow, I asked the receptionist about it. She said she had never heard of the place, and the doctor only visited Bracken House. He must have been there at some time to take the photos.'

'Yeah and they weren't posed photos. It's like he was keeping a record.'

Dora's phone trilled interrupting the conversation. She dug it out of her bag and listened to the two messages. Her stomach twisted with anxiety.

'What is it?' Dmitri glanced at her.

'The police want to see me. They've asked that I contact them urgently and arrange to go to the station. The other message was from someone named Adam Roberts, he says he's Uncle Eddie's solicitor and needs to meet with me to discuss the will. He also mentioned Blue Hollow. He said he knew about it. That's a bit odd after what just happened.'

'It could be a way of getting to you. I'll check him out.'

'Something must have happened at this Blue Hollow place for the photos to be so important. I can ask Denny about it. I think after we've seen Denny I should go home and go to the police.'

'No, that's not a good move.'

'If I arrange to go to the station they aren't going to do anything to me there. They can't all be in on it.'

'The photo showed the Chief Constable visiting the kids' home, what does that tell you?'

'It was years ago, the guy's probably dead.'

'We don't know what we are dealing with or how many are involved. It only takes one to have access to information and pass it on.'

'It will be worse if I don't go in. They'll have an excuse to have every police officer looking for me. Next thing they'll put something on the news and there will be eyes everywhere. They post on Facebook and Twitter. People will share and nowhere will be safe.'

'Yeah, you've got a point, but I'm coming with you.'

'There's no need. I'll be okay. I can shoot now.' Dora laughed. 'Shame I left the gun with Dray.'

'I'll ask Dray to meet us there and get some people to sort the security on your house. It can be done before we get back.' Dmitri gave a command to his phone and a ring tone came over the radio speakers. Dora placed a call to the police station and left a message for DI Price then listened as Dmitri gave his requirements and reeled off her address. There were no questions asked.

'How do you know my address?' Dora asked when the call ended.

'Easy to get that information. I can tell you your National Insurance number if you like,' Dmitri said.

'You've been spying on me.'

'No. When Charlie asked me to help out I found out all I could about you. If I could get the information then someone else could. I needed to be prepared to protect you.'

'It's still creepy.'

'Are you calling me a creep?' Dmitri raised his eyebrows. 'You should be a bit more careful with security.'

'Well, you forgot one important detail. I have the keys to my house in my bag so your friends will have to wait until we arrive.'

'They don't need keys.'

They drove through the Gloucestershire countryside on narrow roads until they turned down a track leading to an old farm.

'Looks a bit run-down,' Dora said.

'It's out of the way and you can see any vehicle coming down the track.' He parked the jeep. 'Come on, time to meet Denny.'

As they approached the farmhouse the door opened, and a man stepped out. He was slim and wiry with a ring of grey hair around his bald head. He wore frameless glasses that were perched halfway down his nose.

'Dora.' He smiled. 'I'm so pleased to see you're safe.' He turned to Dmitri. 'You look like you've had some trouble.'

'Nothing I couldn't take care of. Let's get inside.'

They entered the sitting room. It was spacious with an open staircase and beamed ceiling. The furniture was minimalistic with no pictures on the walls.

'One of Charlie's projects,' Denny said. 'I think he planned on doing it up, get a few animals and move out of London. I can't imagine Charlie in a pair of wellies.' His voice faltered.

'He always liked to dress smart,' Dora said. Up close she could see that Denny's eyes were bloodshot. Grey stubble covered his chin and his clothes looked slept in. Now she had met him she couldn't imagine that he had any part in Charlie's and Eddie's death.

'I expect you have a lot of questions after listening to the tapes,' Denny said.

'Yes, I've only listened to tapes one and three. Do you have number two?'

'Yeah, Eddie left it with me. He was supposed to bring you to see me before you listened to Charlie's tape. I can't believe they are gone.' He rubbed his hands over his face.

'Dora thought you might have had something to do with it,' Dmitri said.

Dora shot him a look.

'What? Why would you think that? They were my brothers. Only family I had.'

'I'm sorry,' Dora said. 'I didn't know about you and Eddie's other friends. Then, when I listened to Charlie's tape… well, the robbery… you didn't get caught and the money was never recovered.'

'You thought I wouldn't want anyone knowing the part I played in the robbery. I suppose it does look bad. I became a hero, kept my job and eventually took over as manager. It's not important now, I've had a good life. I told Eddie to do what he needed, and you could do what you liked with the information. No amount of money or even losing my freedom would make me harm those two. I loved them.'

'Then tell me, what is it that Eddie wanted me to know? I don't care what he's done.' Dora threw her hands up. 'Eddie and Charlie were hiding something that got them both killed. Clearly you know what it is and that's why you're hiding.'

'I can answer some of your questions but not all. There are parts that are not my story to tell. Please, sit down. Can I get you anything to drink?'

'No, thanks.' Dora perched on the edge of an armchair. Dmitri took the sofa and Denny took a chair from under a table and placed it opposite Dora. The room fell silent, there were so many questions Dora wanted to ask but she didn't know where to start. 'Maybe we should listen to the tape first,' she suggested.

'Perhaps it's better to discuss what you heard on Charlie's tape. I'm sure you have a lot of questions. I'll answer what I can, some answers you'll find on the tape. The rest you'll have to listen to on the next two tapes.'

'I don't know where they are. There's Boris and MJ, they were involved in the robbery so it makes sense that Eddie would leave the tapes with them.'

'Yes,' Denny agreed. 'So you have your answer.'

'But Boris is in prison. The police did say that Eddie visited him, but I can't see that he could have handed over a tape. I think Eddie told him what he planned to do and maybe he didn't want the story told. He would know people that had been inside. He could've had Charlie and Eddie killed.'

'You thought that about me.'

'Yes but you're not a murderer. He killed a woman and her child. Why did he do that?'

'That's his story to tell.'

'Who did he kill?'

Denny looked at Dmitri, then back to Dora. 'You don't know?'

'No, it's not like they had internet then and I guess he isn't important enough to be put on Wikipedia. Do you know?' She turned to Dmitri.

'Like Denny says, it's Boris's story to tell.'

'Then I'm just going to have to ask the police for the details.' Dora folded her arms and sat back.

'Good luck with that,' Denny said. 'You won't get the truth from them. You owe it to Eddie to at least go and visit Boris and hear what he has to say.'

'I think I'll take my chances with the police. So that leaves MJ, what happened to him?'

'You know what happened to MJ.'

'Michael John Jones?'

'Yes.'

'My father.' She glanced at Dmitri who didn't looked surprised. 'You knew this?'

'Yeah.'

'So, why didn't you tell me?'

'I thought it best you figure it out on your own.'

'What else are you not telling me?' Anger spiked her skin. She looked from Dmitri to Denny. 'You're all in on some private joke. Watching me scrabble around for answers you know. See how long I can survive when all along you know what Eddie was keeping secret and you could do something about it. You're just protecting yourselves.' Dora stood up. 'I've had it, I'm going home, giving the tapes to the police and they can sort it out.'

'Sit down,' Dmitri growled. 'You don't know what the fuck you're talking about. Yes, there are some things that we know but are too hard to talk about. Eddie wanted you to hear the whole story, not just a bit that would scare the hell out of you and send you running.' He looked at Denny.

'I promise you, you'll have all the answers when you listen to the tapes. Please, just be patient.'

'Fine.' Dora huffed. 'So my father grew up in a children's home and robbed a bank. I guess I can understand why Uncle Eddie thought that would freak me out. So that's everyone, apart from Iosif. He was Dad's best friend in the home. What happened to him? Does he have something to do with what's going on?'

'Partly, but I honestly don't know what happened to Iosif. None of us do. Perhaps you'll be able to get some answers.'

'Well, I'm not having any luck so far. What about Julie?'

Denny looked at Dmitri.

'That's a bit complicated and again not our story to tell.'

'Okay, what about the bank manager, Alan Lloyd, can you tell me what happened to him?'

'Yes.' Denny smiled. 'We set him up. By the time I left the hospital, and met up with Boris and MJ, we worked out that Eddie and Charlie had been caught. We went back to the bank and picked up my car. Charlie was right, no one guessed that the money would be so close to the bank. We planted a share of the money in Alan's house. He was still in hospital and his wife was there with him. Next day we made an anonymous call to the police tipping them off about Alan Lloyd's part in the robbery. He went down for it.'

'And could he be seeking revenge?'

'Last I heard he was dead.'

'Why did you set him up?'

'That's all on the tape.'

'Okay, so what happened to the rest of the money?'

'MJ, Boris, and me bought a rundown house for cash. We did it up, using cash for materials and any extra labour. Then we sold it, made a profit and bought another two. By the time Eddie and Charlie came out of the nick we had a shit-ton of money and property, all legal. One of the boys in the home trained to be a solicitor. He set up the paperwork to transfer Eddie and Charlie's share. He made up some crap about a relative leaving them an inheritance. The original amount plus the investments we shared equally.'

'But Uncle Eddie didn't have any money. He was renting his bungalow. I know Charlie was wealthy.'

'Yeah, Charlie kept going with the property investment, he was minted. I think you'll find that Eddie's money is safely tucked away.'

'I had a call from an Adam Roberts claiming to be Eddie's solicitor.'

'Yeah, Adam is sound. He's been looking after us for years. You can trust him.'

'Did my mother know about all this?'

'I don't know how much MJ told her. There were things we never talked about. Even to each other. I expect you never went without.'

'No, although she doesn't discuss her finances with me. She stayed in the house after Dad died and she never seems concerned about bills. I guess it makes sense if there is a pile of money stashed somewhere.'

'I've answered all I can. I think you should listen to the tape now.' Denny left the room briefly and came back with the tape. He handed it to Dora. 'If you don't mind I'll leave you to listen to it alone. I don't think I can bear to hear it again.'

'Do you want me to leave?' Dmitri asked.

'No, you probably know what's on it.'

'I don't,' he said.

Dora took the Dictaphone from her bag, slipped in the tape and pressed play. Eddie's voice filled the room.

Chapter Fifteen

Eddie 1967

We searched for Adam, checking the building where they isolated the kids that had infectious diseases, like measles. No one had seen him there. We asked questions but were told that Adam had been taken away by his family. Adam never had a visit the whole time he was there. He was one of the kids that you knew would be there until they were old enough to leave and get a job. We even asked Dr Ray. He explained that sometimes a relative is found that will take on a child. We were sure this wasn't the case. Adam had been in the system for too long.

After that we kept watch. We nicked a pencil and some paper from school and took note of all the children that were in the home, watching which ones had family visits. Over time a couple more boys went missing. Same as Adam, no family. They went to bed at night and were gone by morning. We knew it was no good talking to Wainwright and even the doctor didn't seem concerned. We thought perhaps we should talk to one of the teachers but back then they weren't approachable. We finally decided that our best option was to go to the police station, but we didn't know where it was. An opportunity came when we got a special visitor to the home.

Chief Constable Graham North and his son, Scott, came to give a cheque to the home from funds raised by the police force. It was to be for a holiday. I was pissed off by the time they arrived. We had spent the week cleaning the home. Charlie and me got stuck with the toilets. We had to polish our shoes, scrub our bodies, and have our hair cut. We were under strict instructions to behave, no talking unless asked to do so.

Wainwright stood beaming as he took the cheque and posed with Graham North. All us kids lined up behind pretending that we were happy. Even the doctor had his camera out. Graham North made a show of posing with a group of boys, his hands resting on their shoulders. Scott North was allowed to wander around the grounds to play with the kids. Even at that age he was an evil little shit. He talked down to us, calling us names. His delight seemed to be taunting the younger kids, pinching them till they squealed.

We figured as Graham North was from the police he would be the best person to help us find Adam and the other missing boys. We waited around for our chance to talk to him, but Wainwright was always by his side. We got Boris to tell Wainwright that MJ had hurt himself by falling from a tree. MJ agreed to lie under the tree pretending his arm was hurt. Iosif stayed by his side.

We watched Wainwright excuse himself with a thunderous look on his face as he walked away. We chose Denny as spokesperson as he was good with words. Charlie nudged him forward, the rest of us stood close by listening.

'Can I ask you something, sir?' Denny fidgeted with nerves.

Graham North looked down at Denny and smiled. 'Of course you can, what's your name boy?'

'Dennis.'

'What would you like to ask me, Dennis?'

'Do the police find missing people?'

'Yes, that's one of our jobs.'

'Would you be able to find someone?'

'It depends. Sometimes a person doesn't want to be found. Is it your parents you want to find?' He put his arm around Denny. 'I know it must be very difficult for you, but you have to understand that you have been placed here for your own good. You're a lucky boy, this is one of the best homes in the country. I hear that Mr Wainwright takes good care of you all.'

'He gives us the cane.'

Graham North's lips twitched. 'He wouldn't be doing his job if he didn't punish you when you've been naughty.'

'I suppose. It's not my family I want to find, it's my friend. Will you help find him?'

'What's your friend's name?'

'Adam Roberts.'

'Is he one of Bracken House's boys?'

'Yeah.'

'Ah well, he isn't missing. Children are sometimes allowed to go back to their family. I expect that's what's happened here. He just didn't get a chance to say goodbye.'

'He didn't have any family.'

'Everyone has a family. A mother and father somewhere, or he could have gone to live with an aunt or an uncle.'

'I don't think that happened to Adam. There are other boys that have disappeared. They always go in the night. They go to bed and in the morning they're gone. If family had turned up to get them it would be in the day, wouldn't it? We've made a list with the names and dates they went missing. We were going to take it to the police station but it's a long way to walk and we keep getting lost. We can only go on Saturdays but now you're here we won't need to go.'

'We?'

'Yeah, me and my friends.' Denny pointed to me and Charlie; Boris was walking towards us.

'Can you get the list for me?'

'Yeah.' Denny turned and gave us the thumbs up before running into the house. While we waited, Wainwright came back; he looked furious, so we stepped back. We watched as he talked to Graham North, his eyes narrowed, and his jaw set in a hard line. We guessed Graham North must have told him about Denny and the list. Denny came back and stopped abruptly when he saw Wainwright, but North beckoned him over, took the list and ruffled his hair. We scarpered after that.

That afternoon all the kids were called into the dining room where the tables were laid with sandwiches, sausage rolls, and cakes. We were never given treats like this, I couldn't wait. My mouth was watering as I took my seat but before I could fill my plate Wainwright called my name together with Charlie, Boris, Denny, MJ, and Iosif. We were sent to wait outside his office.

'I bet they're all stuffing their faces. There won't be anything left for us,' Denny complained.

'I'm hungry.' Iosif turned to Boris.

'Maybe there will be some cake in the kitchen. I'll go when no one's looking and get you some,' Boris said.

'No, you'll get in trouble. I'd rather go hungry.'

'He won't get in trouble, we'll keep watch,' Charlie said.

'Maybe we should go into his office and look through the drawers?' Denny suggested.

'What for?' I asked.

'He could have sweets.'

'I doubt it,' Charlie said, 'and if he comes, we'll be in more shit than we're in already.'

It must have been over an hour before Wainwright turned up and ordered us all in the office. He slammed the door and turned his mean eyes on us.

'So you thought it would be fun to make up stories and cause me embarrassment, did you?'

'We weren't making up stories. We thought Chief Constable North would be able to help find Adam,' Denny said.

'Who is with his family.' Wainwright picked up his cane and MJ and Iosif took a step back. 'You all knew the importance of this day. The police have raised money for all the children to be taken on holiday and you go and lie and try to ruin the reputation of this house.' He slammed the cane against the desk making us all jump. 'One thing's for certain: none of you will be going on the holiday. The next time we have a visitor you will all remain in the dormitory. You,' – he pointed the cane at Iosif – 'trousers down, bend over the desk.'

'No!' Boris stepped in front of Iosif and MJ. 'These two didn't have anything to do with it.'

'Don't take me for a fool,' Wainwright roared. 'Those two played their part. Pretending to be hurt.'

'I'll take his thrashing,' Boris said, 'and MJ's too.'

Wainwright's lips curled into a cruel smile. He stepped forward, grabbed Iosif by the ear and threw him over the desk. Boris dived at Wainwright and it took Charlie, Denny, and me to hold him back. Iosif was squealing as Wainwright yanked down his trousers. I closed my eyes, but I couldn't block out the swish and thwack of the cane and Iosif's pitiful yelps. It made me feel sick. I'm sure it hurt Boris more than the thrashing he received himself.

When Wainwright had finished he was red in the face and beads of sweat trickled down his forehead. MJ and Iosif were sobbing and Boris was shaking with rage. A movement at the window caught my eye. I turned in time to see Scott North peeking through, his face was lit up with pleasure. I glared back and he ducked out of sight.

I expect you will wonder why we didn't fight harder. There were six of us and we could have overpowered Wainwright, but we were kids and powerless. We had no one to tell and nowhere to run to. If we fought back the punishment would've been worse and we knew Wainwright would use Iosif to get at Boris.

We were ordered back to our dormitories. The younger boys had a separate room, so we stayed with MJ and Iosif.

'It will stop stinging soon,' Charlie said.

'I hate it here.' Iosif sniffed.

'So do I.' Boris paced the room. 'I wish Wainwright was dead. When I grow up I'm going to come back and kill him.'

'Yeah,' I agreed. 'First we have to make him suffer. We'll thrash him with his own cane.'

'Yeah and make him eat shit from the toilet,' Boris said.

'Make him lick the toilet clean,' Charlie said.

We all came up with ways of making Wainwright pay, some of them were so ridiculous, we had MJ and Iosif rolling with laughter on the bed. Later Charlie and Boris sneaked out of the room and down to the kitchen. They returned with food. It wasn't much so we let MJ and Iosif eat most of it. It made us feel a little better, like we had got one up on Wainwright. When the light started to fade we left the younger ones and went back to our own dorm, we didn't want to risk getting caught out of our room. The other boys would be up soon, and Wainwright would check. It was going to be a long night. I was so hungry, and my backside stung. Some of the whacks had caught me on the back so I knew it would be hard to sleep. We had settled on the bed all lying on our stomachs when the door crashed open. Wainwright stepped in and glared at us.

'Go to the isolation room, all of you.'

'But we're not sick,' Charlie said.

Wainwright's eyes narrowed. 'Do as I say unless you want another caning.'

We left the room and found MJ and Iosif stood in the corridor looking terrified. None of us spoke as we followed Wainwright down the stairs, out the door, and to the next building. The beds in the isolation room were all empty, there was no one down with an illness. A table had been put against the wall with six glasses of milk and a plate of scones.

'The Chief Constable has taken pity on you missing out on lunch, so he has sent you a treat. I will come and fetch you when it's time to go.' A smile played on Wainwright's lips before he left the room.

We rushed to the table and scoffed the scones washing them down with milk. We were afraid Wainwright would come back and take them away. He liked to play tricks. After we'd eaten we sat on the beds. I felt contented and all the anger at Wainwright seemed to slip away. MJ and Iosif fell asleep. I watched them lying peacefully on the bed, their chests rising and falling. My arms and legs felt heavy and it was too much of an effort to talk. The last thing I remember is seeing Denny keel over on the bed.

* * *

When I woke I thought I was dreaming. I was lying on the floor, it was cold and hard. My eyelids felt like they were weighted down, it was a struggle to force them open. Charlie's face was close to mine. I could hear a voice but couldn't make out the words. There was a sound of an engine, vibrations and bumps that shook my body. I wanted to reach out to Charlie, but the movement was rocking me back to sleep.

The next time I woke I was lying on top of a bed in my clothes. I knew I wasn't in my dorm or the isolation room. I sat up and looked around. There were rows of metal-framed beds on both sides of the room, Charlie and Denny lay either side of me still asleep. Boris was opposite, sitting up and looking as bewildered as I felt. Behind Boris were ceiling-to-floor windows with vertical bars. Some had cracked glass; there were no drapes. Yellowing walls with patches of mould surrounded the room. The other beds were occupied with heads sticking out of grey blankets.

'Where are we?' I asked.

Charlie and Denny sat up, confusion on their faces. I rubbed at my arms trying to stop the chill spreading through my body.

'Iosif!' Boris jumped off the bed and started pulling the blankets back on the other beds. The boys shrank away from him. I recognised a couple of them from Bracken House.

'Have you seen my brother?' Boris asked the startled faces.

'No,' one said. 'There's another room. Maybe they put him in there.'

Boris bolted from the room. I chased after him with Charlie and Denny. The next two doors were locked, the third one we tried opened. The room was similar to the one we just left. Iosif and MJ were still asleep. Boris shook his brother awake.

'Boris, is that really you?'

We turned to see Adam sat up in bed. He seemed to have shrunk since we last saw him.

'Adam.' Charlie went to the bed.

Adam looked at each of us. 'I can't believe you're here.' He started to cry.

We looked at each other not knowing what to do. Charlie was the first to speak.

'Where are we?'

'In a bad place.' Adam sniffed. 'It's called Blue Hollow. One of the men told me it used to be an asylum. Filled with crazy people. He said you can still hear them screaming in the night.'

'They've brought us to a nuthouse,' Denny said. 'Why?'

'To punish you.'

'It's okay, we told the police you were missing. They'll come to look for us,' I said.

'I think that's why we're here,' Charlie said. 'Because we told.'

'Nobody will come for us, no one cares,' Adam said. 'No one ever leaves. There are boys from different homes. Some have been here a long time.'

'How did we get here?' MJ asked.

'Milk,' Adam said.

'Milk?' Boris laughed.

'They give you milk here sometimes. It makes you sleep and have nightmares, that's if you're lucky.'

'Wainwright gave us milk,' Denny said.

'Wainwright comes here sometimes with the other men.'

'What men?'

'I don't want to talk about it.' Adam pulled his knees up to his chest.

'It can't be worse than Bracken House,' I said.

'It's much worse.' Adam trembled. 'I wish I was dead.'

The door opened and a man stepped in. He had dark cropped hair and wore thick-rimmed glasses. I later found out his name was Reg. He was in charge of Blue Hollow. The other boys all jumped out of bed and stood erect against the wall with their eyes downcast.

'So, you're the new boys. Up against the wall with the others.'

I took my place next to Charlie. Reg walked up and down the line inspecting all the boys. I hadn't a clue what he was looking for, but it made me nervous. When he stopped at me his eyes travelled up and down my body. I had a sudden urge to pee so rocked from foot to foot.

'Stay still, boy.' He grabbed hold of my arm digging his fingers into my flesh. I gritted my teeth against the pain.

'What's your name?'

'Eddie.'

'Eddie, you stand still for inspection or you'll stand all night in the graveyard until you can learn to stay still. Is that clear?'

'Yes.'

'Yes, *sir*!'

'Yes, sir.'

He let go of my arm and stood back. 'Right, move it.'

We followed Adam out of the room and down a wide staircase. 'Where are we going?' I asked.

'Toilet then showers,' Adam whispered.

We walked outside and queued up to use the toilets at the side of the house. While we stood, I looked around. The house was enormous, I counted fourteen windows on the upper floor. From the side the house was an E shape, with the building protruding out at both ends and the middle. Each end had a bay window, the front door was set into a stone archway and a clock tower loomed on the roof. I stepped back to get a better look.

'You better hurry,' Adam urged.

I used the toilet and joined the others going back in the house. We walked to the far end of the house to the open shower room. Steel heads jutted out of grimy yellowing tiles. A man stood watching as we gathered under the freezing water struggling to hold the soap with numb hands. We had to stay in the water until we were told we could leave. There were towels hanging on pegs which were already wet and rough against the skin. I dried the best I could then hurried back to the room where I found my clothes had been placed in a wooden crate under the bed. I didn't want to change but Adam said we should, or we would be in for a beating if we were seen in the same clothes.

As soon as we were dressed, we left the room again. I followed the boys who walked like robots. This time we went out the front door and followed the concrete drive around the lawn to a church that stood opposite the house. To one side of the church was a graveyard with old stone headstones sticking out like rows of teeth. The church had arch windows with leaded panes, some with glass missing. The roof was covered in moss with its slates barely clinging on. We stopped outside the front of the church and stood in a row.

'I'm hungry,' Iosif said.

'We don't have breakfast on a Sunday morning,' Adam whispered, 'but lunch is the best you get all week.'

A man in a long black robe appeared and ushered us inside. We were silent as we walked in and slid into the pews. The church smelled damp and churned my stomach. I looked around at the stone walls. Crude drawings and symbols decorated the lower half with candle wax running off the window ledges, solidifying into wax waterfalls. The floor was worn flagstone that dipped in places. At the front of the church the altar was draped with a black cloth. A golden tree had been embroidered into the centre with a red snake circling the trunk. Behind the altar, a man stood with the hood of his black robe covering part of his face. Other robed men were sat in the front pews. I looked at Boris who was staring with his mouth agape, Iosif and MJ pressed against him on each side.

The man behind the altar muttered something and everyone stood up, I quickly followed. He started to pray but it was unlike any prayer I'd ever heard. There was no mention of God or Jesus. There was talk of the master, the bond of brothers and thanks given for the fruits delivered. We then sat down, and he delivered some sort of sermon. I heard some talk of a garden, knowledge, and power, then my mind drifted until we all had to kneel on the floor. My knees hurt and I could hear my stomach growl. I peered over the top of the pew and watched the men in the front get up and kneel before the altar. The speaker then muttered some words while touching each of their heads in turn. He then took a goblet from the altar, held it up in the air, chanted some strange words then sipped. Each man took a sip before the goblet was put back and they returned to their seats. A final prayer and we left the church. I was relieved to get outside, my skin felt like a thousand insects were crawling over me. I didn't know why I felt this way. It was like a cloud of doom hovered over the building and its occupants.

I had no time to dwell or discuss this feeling as we were put to work, chopping and carrying wood to the room where the men sat drinking wine and smoking. The fire in the dining room as well as the Aga in the kitchen had to be kept burning. Then there was vegetables to be peeled and the table to be set.

Another room was set for us boys to eat, this one didn't have a fire, just a wobbly table and mismatched chairs. We followed Adam's instructions, and a boy named Ben showed us how to boil the veg and cook meat. Some of the boys were sent to clean the rooms where the men had stayed. Bed sheets had to be hand-washed and hung. Iosif and MJ were set the task of scrubbing, their hands were red by the time they finished. A few of the boys walked slowly as if they were in pain. I asked Adam about it, but he didn't answer.

When the food was cooked, we served the men first. By the time we sat down to eat, the food was cold. I didn't care, I scoffed it down as I was so hungry by then. After food we had to wash up and scrub the kitchen and dining room. It seemed pointless to me, the house was crumbling, with mouldy walls, and buckets that caught the rainwater coming through the ceiling. I went to bed exhausted that night and for the first time in my life I couldn't wait to go to school the next day. At least there you got to sit down.

In the morning, I was in for a shock. There was no school, only endless chores including trying to scrub mould off the walls with Reg's beady eyes watching. He watched and waited for an opportunity to dish out punishment if he thought the job wasn't done properly. There were so many rules I couldn't remember them all.

I'm sure Reg made up new ones each day to have the opportunity to beat or humiliate one of us.

We managed to get a couple of hours free time during the late afternoons when Reg had drunk enough to fall asleep and wouldn't wake up until his dinner was placed in front of him. We used this time to explore the house and the surrounding area. The house was enormous and split into two wings. One wing was kept locked during the week and was only opened on Friday mornings. The only rooms we saw were the bedrooms that we had to prepare for the visitors. Next to the house was a dilapidated building, it gave me the creeps. We were told it was a morgue and that experiments were carried out on the previous inhabitants of the house. Those who didn't make it were laid out in the building to be dissected. I'm not sure if the story was true but there were enough graves in the graveyard.

The toilets were on the other side of the building. Five stone cubicles with rotting wooden doors that had gaps in the top and bottom leaving you exposed to the wind and rain. They stank, no matter how many times you cleaned them, and were always inhabited by monstrous spiders.

Past the church a narrow track led up to the mountain and an enormous lake. In the summer we would sneak up there to swim. I loved that place, it was the only time I felt safe and free. The road that led away from the house was wide enough for one vehicle. We followed the road as far as we could but couldn't find any other houses, just endless fields and mountains. No cars came that way except on Fridays when the sound of the engines drove fear into our bellies.

Chapter Sixteen

The first Friday we were at Blue Hollow I saw a change come over the boys. Most of them didn't eat breakfast and those who did I saw throwing up in the toilets. The atmosphere was tense as beds were made and food prepared for the visitors. Even Adam was withdrawn, walking with his shoulders hunched. The cars arrived and I watched through the window with Charlie. We saw Chief Constable Graham North get out of one of the cars along with Austin, the social worker who had taken me from my mother.

'Do you think he's come to get us?' I nodded towards North.

'Nah, he's the one who sent us here. He wouldn't be talking and laughing with the other men if he was here looking for us.'

'I'm never trusting the police again,' I said.

'The police are supposed to help you.' Denny had crept up behind us.

'That's Wainwright,' Charlie said. 'What's that bastard doing here?'

'Probably come to laugh at us,' Denny said.

We watched them gather into a group until we heard Reg shout. We jumped away from the window.

'Get outside and line up with the others,' Reg ordered before turning his back on us.

Outside the other boys were already lined up against the house with MJ and Iosif on the end. I took my place next to Charlie. Boris squeezed himself next to his brother. The men stopped talking and took it in turns to walk up and down the line, each one placing a hand on a boy's shoulder. One of the men stood in front of me, he had a round face with piggy eyes, his belly straining his jacket.

'A new one.' He beamed. 'Yes, he'll do nicely.' He put his hand on my shoulder and gave it a squeeze. I could still feel the warmth from his hand when he removed it.

We were all ordered back inside to serve dinner. I noticed some of the boys that had been touched on the shoulder were crying. I tried to find out why, but no one would tell me. We served the men dinner then ate our own in silence. When the clearing was finished, we were told to go to the hallway. A table had been set with glasses of milk. One by one the boys knocked back the milk and walked upstairs.

'I'm not touching it,' Boris said. 'Not after what happened last time.'

'It's better if you drink it,' Adam said.

'What should we do?' Denny turned to Charlie.

'Better not,' Charlie said. 'We'll tip it down the sink and put the glasses back.' We moved swiftly to the kitchen and replaced the empty glasses then hurried up the stairs before Reg came back.

'Now what?' Denny asked.

'We pretend to be asleep when Reg comes to check, then we can find out what the men are up to and why the other boys are so frightened.'

'What about MJ and Iosif?' Boris asked.

'They're in with Adam, they'll be alright. It's best they don't get caught wandering around.'

We all crept to the top of the stairs and crouched down. We could hear the men's laughter coming from the sitting room. Cigar smoke drifted up the stairs; it reminded me of home when Mum used to have parties and some of the men would sit with fat cigars poking out of their mouths. I thought then of Julie, left in Bracken House. Maybe they told her I had run away, and she'd be thinking I didn't care about her. My throat felt tight as I tried to swallow back the tears.

'You okay?' Charlie asked.

'Yeah, don't like the smoke, it stinks.'

'Maybe they're just having a party,' Boris whispered. 'No point in us waiting out all night.'

'There must be a reason they want us all to stay asleep,' Denny said.

We were about to give up when the voices grew louder as the sitting room door was opened and the men appeared dressed in black robes. They each pulled up their hoods before walking out the front door. We scarpered back to the bedroom and pressed our faces as close to the window as we could. I could feel the bars digging into my cheekbones as I strained to make out the figures drifting across the lawn. The only sound came from the rhythmic breathing of the sleeping boys. The men disappeared into the church and a few moments later lights flickered in the windows. Then the chanting began.

'What are they doing in there?' I asked.

'Dunno,' Charlie said, 'but it's giving me the creeps.'

'Maybe they're calling up spirits,' Denny said. 'That's why they want us all asleep, so the ghosts won't get us.'

We all turned to look at Denny and I couldn't help laughing at the look on Boris's face. Charlie started to giggle.

'It's not funny,' Boris said.

'You can sleep in my bed with me if you're scared,' Charlie said.

'I'm not scared.' Boris scowled. 'But maybe we should try and go to sleep just in case.'

We all turned back to the window and watched the church, every now and then I glanced at the graveyard. I didn't want to look but I couldn't help myself. The chanting came to an end and the hooded figures started to emerge from the church.

'Quick, get into bed, they're coming back,' Charlie said.

I got under the covers and screwed up my eyes. I could hear footsteps coming up the stairs and towards the bedroom. I tried to make my breathing even as I peeked through my lashes. The door opened and Reg came in. I saw him throw back the blanket on Denny's bed. Denny yelped and Reg put his hand over his mouth as he yanked him out of bed. Part of me wanted to get out of bed and help Denny but I was terrified, so I sunk further into the bed. It was Boris that leapt out of bed first.

'What are you doing with Denny?'

Reg let go of Denny and advanced on Boris, in one swift movement he locked his hand around Boris's throat and pinned him to the wall. I sat up in bed, I could see Boris's eyes bulging as he struggled to get free.

'It will be your turn soon enough,' Reg sneered.

Charlie sprung from his bed and leapt on Reg's back. He sunk his teeth into his shoulder as he tore at his face. I joined in, grabbing hold of Reg's leg and sinking my teeth into his ankle. Reg roared in outrage as he let go of Boris who slumped to the floor, he managed to shake off Charlie and punch him in the face sending him crashing to the floor. I felt his shoe drive into my stomach, I folded in two as I tried to catch a breath. Reg then grabbed Denny and dragged him out of the room. Before we had a chance to recover, more men rushed into the room. I caught sight of Wainwright's face under the hood. The other boys started to stir and sit up.

'Get back to sleep,' one of the men ordered. They sank back into their beds.

I was grabbed by the hair and dragged from the room, my stomach still hurting. We were taken to the other wing, through the door that was usually kept locked. As we were dragged along a door would open and one of us would be slung inside. I saw Wainwright follow Boris into one room. I was the last to go. The door opened and I was flung onto the floor.

'Got a live one here for you, Alan.' The man who released me laughed before closing the door.

The man who had squeezed my shoulder earlier that day stood looking down at me, his eyes gleaming with excitement. 'You didn't drink your milk.' He tutted as he wiped his brow with a white handkerchief.

I looked around the room my heart pulsating in my throat. The windows had been blacked out and the only light came from candles that were dotted around the room on saucers, the flames swaying in the draft. Their glow illuminated strange symbols painted on the walls. The same ones I had seen in the church. A metal-framed bed with a bare mattress stood in the centre of the room, leather straps hung down the sides.

'Come on, up you get,' Alan coaxed.

I scrabbled backwards to the door, the pain in my stomach forgotten. My body shook uncontrollably as he stepped forward and hauled me to my feet. My legs wobbled as he dragged me towards the bed. I looked at the straps and started to fight. I scratched, bit, and kicked but my blows had no impact. He laughed as he undid the buckle on his belt, his eyes gleaming as he slid the leather from its loops. I braced myself for the beating, but none came, I think I would have preferred it. He spun me around and looped the belt so tight around my wrists it dug into the flesh and stopped the blood flow. My hands prickled as he threw me face down on the bed and ripped off my pyjama bottoms. I tried to wriggle but I was no match for him. I'll spare you the details of what happened next, but the pain was like nothing I had ever felt in my life. I would forever remember his smell, his sweating flesh against mine.

When it was over he untied my wrists. My hands were numb, making getting dressed difficult. He left the room without a word and another man came in and dragged me back to my bed. I curled up into a ball, I wanted to die. The others came back one at a time. No one spoke, there were no words. Boris was the last to be brought back to the room, he was badly beaten, blood smeared across his face. I turned away and pulled the blanket over my head. After that night we were no longer children, sometimes I didn't even feel human, we knew the evils of this world. There were no dreams to fulfil, our only ambition was to survive.

We never spoke about what happened in those rooms, but we drank the milk after that. It would make our brains hazy so the weekends would pass in some strange nightmare. Boris often gave half his milk to Iosif. He thought it would put him into a deeper sleep and he wouldn't remember.

Two years passed in that hell. Sometimes Dr Ray would visit to deal with the injuries the men inflicted on us. We begged him to take us away, but he said he couldn't, that he was as much a prisoner as we were. I didn't understand at the time. I guess I still don't understand. He could've tried but maybe he knew he didn't stand a chance. With Graham North being involved I doubt anyone would listen.

More boys came to the house, they arrived one by one during the night. This was matched by an increase of men that came on the weekend. They weren't always the same men, but Graham North was always present. It was clear that he was the leader of the group.

I began to wonder what would happen when we all grew up. Would we be kept there forever? It seemed that way, although Boris was getting bigger by the day and all the hard work turned his body into hard muscle. I noticed a change in Charlie too. Denny remained wiry and I didn't seem to grow as fast as the others. Reg left us alone when we were together and only dished out punishment if he caught one of us alone. Looking back, I guess we could have made a stand then, and got out, maybe the outcome would have been different, but our spirit was broken. We had nowhere to run, we thought life couldn't get any worse for us but we were wrong.

Another winter came upon us bringing frost in the mornings and a bitter chill so that you never felt warm. Chopping wood in the snow, washing bedclothes, and scrubbing floors with icy water took its toll. All of us had constant running noses and coughs. Iosif suffered the most and seemed more prone to fits. Most nights MJ would snuggle in Iosif's bed to try and keep him warm, but he grew weaker by the day. The other boys in the house pulled together to cover Iosif's chores. We would hide him away during the day wrapped in a blanket and steal extra food from the kitchen to feed him. Adam swapped beds so Iosif didn't have to sleep in the draft from the window. I wish I could go back in time and tell them how wonderful they all were. Brave, kind boys, who should have been loved and protected.

The last time we were all together was December. When the men came this time they were charged with excitement. There was something about the way they spoke and watched us. All the rooms were taken, with extra beds put into some bedrooms. We had to prepare a large feast, more food than we had seen before. The men ate, washing it down with wine, their faces glowing in the warmth of the fire. We knew something was happening but didn't know what. The usual lining up and choosing of boys seemed to have been forgotten. I hoped that we weren't part of their plans and would be spared. Maybe it would be a Christmas treat but Christmas wasn't usually a part of Blue Hollow so this change from the norm made me nervous.

The milk was left in the usual place, so I didn't hold out much hope of a peaceful night. Boris gave all his milk to Iosif so Denny, Charlie, and me left a quarter each of ours and persuaded Boris to drink it. We couldn't bear to think of him fully awake. We went up to the bedroom, said goodnight to Iosif and MJ who were in separate beds in case the men came, then we went to our own room. The chores of the day had worn me out, so the milk didn't take long to work.

'Wake up, Eddie, wake up!' I was woken by Charlie shaking me, the urgency in his voice chased away the sleep fog.

'What is it?' I sat up in bed, the cold air snaked around my back.

'Iosif is missing, MJ woke up and saw the empty bed. Adam is gone too.'

I swung my legs out of bed, my toes curling against the cold floor. I didn't know what we were going to do. If one of the men had Iosif then we would have to fight to get him back. I didn't want to go into one of those rooms in the locked wing, but we had no choice. I pulled on my jumper, slipped on shoes and followed Charlie to the next room. Boris and Denny were trying to wake the other boys, demanding to know who had taken Iosif and Adam but they had been asleep and hadn't heard anything.

'We have to go and look for them. We'll check all of the wing and find which rooms they're in.'

'Then what?' Denny asked.

'We fight the bastards and get Iosif and Adam out of there. I don't care what happens to me. I can't leave my brother to be…'

'It's okay,' Charlie said. 'We'll get him back, all of us.'

'You stay here, MJ,' Boris said.

'No, I want to come.'

'I need to know you're safe,' Boris said. 'Please stay, Iosif might come back.'

'Yeah,' Denny agreed. 'Maybe he just went for a piss.'

The sound of voices drifting through the cracked window stopped the conversation and we rushed to the other side of the room and pressed our faces to the bars. We could see shadowy figures moving around the grounds.

'What are they doing?' I asked.

'Looks like they're searching for something,' Charlie said.

'Or someone. We have to find Iosif and Adam before they do.' Boris hurried out of the room.

'Wait,' Charlie cried as we all ran after Boris. 'We don't want to be seen. At least it doesn't look like they're in the rooms with the men. They could be hiding in the house. Let's spread out and look, we'll meet at the bottom of the stairs. Be careful.' Charlie nodded at me.

I didn't want to wander around the house in the dark. I was scared but I wanted to find Adam and Iosif, so while Charlie and Denny searched the rest of the upstairs I went down with Boris. We split at the bottom and I headed for the kitchen. I called out for the boys peering in cupboards and under the table. All the while fear prickled my skin and every small noise magnified in the darkness, the creaks from upstairs and my shoes on the flagstones. I was sure Reg was going to appear at any moment and grab me. I checked the shower room then ran back to the staircase where the others were waiting.

'We have to go outside,' Boris said. 'MJ, go back to the bedroom. If we get caught, stay in bed, don't move.'

'But—'

'Go!' Boris opened the door.

MJ left us and I held my breath as we stepped out into the icy night. The men were retreating back to the church where light flickered in the windows. We crept along the building and to the toilets checking inside and behind.

162

'I'm going in the church to ask them what they've done with Iosif and Adam,' Boris said.

'Wait.' Charlie grabbed his arm. 'There are too many of them. Let's get closer and look inside, see what's going on in the church.'

We moved in a group hoping the darkness would shield us. We were nearly at the church when the door opened. We all dived for cover in the graveyard. I ran for the nearest headstone and tripped over. I looked down and saw Adam curled into a ball. I thought he was dead – he hadn't made a sound when I collided with him. I crouched down next to him and put my hand on his shoulder, he didn't move. I saw the men walk past, one of them carrying a box. I tried to make myself smaller, pressing my body in the ground. I heard them come back.

'What about the other boy?' one said.

'We'll finish cleaning up then check the rooms, see which one is missing. Then we lock the door, little bastard will freeze to death out here. We'll say he ran away.'

The other man laughed, and they went back into the church. I stood up and waved the others over.

Charlie knelt down and shook Adam. 'He's frozen, feel him, he's like ice.'

'Adam!' Boris said. He rolled Adam onto his back. Adam raised his fists to his face.

'We thought you were dead,' Boris said. 'Where is Iosif?'

Adam didn't answer so Boris pulled his hands away from his face. 'Adam, where is Iosif?'

Adam just stared at Boris, he seemed to be trying to talk. His bottom lip moved but no sound came out.

'What's wrong with him?' Denny asked.

'Dunno,' Charlie said, 'but we need to get him back inside. He's freezing and the men are going to check on us soon then they'll lock the door. We'll all freeze to death.'

'You take him, I'm going to look for Iosif.' Boris started searching behind the other headstones.

'Come on,' Charlie said.

We tried to get Adam to his feet but each time we let go he just slumped to the floor. Charlie grabbed him under the arms, and I took his feet. Together we carried him to the house and up the stairs leaving Denny with Boris. We got him into bed and climbed in each side of him, pressing our bodies up against his to try and get some warmth into his skin. He didn't utter a word.

Boris and Denny came back to the room. Boris started to shake the other boys awake when Denny kept watch on the stairs. Once all the boys were awake, Boris went to the next room, woke the boys and brought them back.

'They're coming.' Denny flew through the door.

Charlie and I jumped out of Adam's bed as Reg came thundering into the room followed by another two men.

'What's going on in here?' His head swivelled around looking at each boy.

'Where is Iosif?' Boris stepped forward.

'Back into bed.' Reg's hand shot out smacking Boris across the side of the head. Boris swayed but held his ground.

'What have you done with Iosif?' Charlie and I stepped next to Boris and were joined by Denny and MJ. The other boys moved forward. The show of defiance appeared to unnerve Reg, he stood staring at us, his jaw set.

One of the men stepped forward and pulled his hood down. 'He was taken ill, we had to take him to hospital.' Graham North smiled. 'Now, there is nothing to be done so you should all go back to bed.'

'I want to see him,' Boris said. 'I want to go to the hospital.'

'We will let you know how he is in the morning.' Graham North turned away and with a swish of his robes left the room.

'You heard him, now get back to bed before I thrash the skin off your backs,' Reg shouted. He retreated from the room with the other men and we heard the key twist in the lock.

There were too many of us in the room, so we had to share the beds. Denny, Charlie, and me, stayed up with Boris all night. He refused to sleep and paced the room. When morning came the door remained locked. No matter how hard we hammered on the door and shouted, no one came. We were locked in the room for two days with no food or water. Adam didn't speak the whole time. He lay in bed with his skin burning. When we were let out Boris flew at Reg, but he was too weak to make an impact. Reg just laughed and wouldn't give any information about Iosif, but he did at least call in Dr Ray for Adam. We stood around Adam's bed while the doc examined him.

'What's wrong with him?' Charlie asked.

'He's very sick, I think pneumonia. I'm going to take him to hospital.'

'What about Iosif?' Boris asked. 'Is he getting better? Reg won't tell us. Take me with you so I can see him.'

'I don't know anything about Iosif.' Dr Ray looked worried and it made my stomach flip.

'They said he was sick,' Boris ranted. 'That he went to hospital, where is he?'

'I don't know anything about that,' Ray said. 'I can't take you with me, but I will try and find out about Iosif and let you know.'

It was over a week before we saw Dr Ray again. He told us Adam was getting better and that Iosif had been taken back to Bracken House. He hurried away then, and we all had the feeling he was lying.

Boris's anger grew by the day and we were afraid for him. It didn't matter how many times he was beaten, he wouldn't give up demanding to see Iosif. Most days Reg locked him in a room. MJ was withdrawing from the world. Not speaking and hardly eating. He and Iosif had been inseparable since Iosif arrived at Bracken House and he was lost without his friend.

'We have to do something,' Charlie said one night as he sat in my bed sharing the blanket.

'There's nothing we can do.' Denny sat hunched at the end of the bed, his blanket pulled around his shoulders.

'We could run away,' Charlie said.

'Yeah, get away from this place. Go back to Bracken House and find Iosif.' Boris got out of bed and joined us.

'And then what?' I asked.

'Maybe they will keep us there. It's better than this place,' Denny said.

'I guess,' I said. 'But what if they send us back here?'

'Then we are no worse off than we are now,' Charlie said.

'What about MJ?' Denny asked.

'We take him with us,' Boris said. 'Don't care if I have to carry him. I'm not leaving him here.'

'Okay,' Charlie said. 'We go.'

Denny and I agreed so we made our plans. We stole food from the kitchen, hiding it under our bed. We decided the best time to leave was during the night when Reg was asleep. We didn't know how far away we were from Cardiff or how many days we would have to walk in the cold. We figured, if we followed the road coming in, it would eventually lead us to a village and we could ask for directions.

That night we packed up the food and rolled it up in our blankets. We put on an extra jumper under our coats, then crept out of the house and into the darkness. As we walked along the path we heard a sound of an engine. We ducked behind the toilets and watched the drive illuminate with headlights before a van pulled up in front of the house. We peered around the building and watched two men get out of the van and walk to the back. I recognised Wainwright. He opened the back door and slid out a child, throwing her over his shoulder like a rag doll. I saw the blond hair hanging down and gasped. 'Julie.'

Chapter Seventeen

There was an audible click where Eddie had turned off the recording. Dora dropped the Dictaphone and ran from the house sobbing. She tried to gulp in the fresh air as raw emotion shook her body. Dmitri came out behind her, turned her around, and pulled her against his chest. She let him hold her as she cried, her tears soaking into his jacket, his body warm against her.

'It's just so…'

'I know,' Dmitri said. 'I'm sorry.'

'Those poor kids, what they all went through and for Charlie and Eddie's life to end the way it did. It's not fair. I can't do this anymore. I can't listen to another tape.'

'That's why Eddie couldn't tell you. He couldn't sit face to face and relive the details.' Denny stood in the doorway. 'The tapes were the only way. We never talked about what happened in Blue Hollow. It took a lot for him to put it on tape and ask us all to share the story. Even now, after all these years, it gives me nightmares. Come back inside and have a drink. I could do with one.'

Dora pulled away from Dmitri and wiped her face with the palms of her hands. She followed Denny into the kitchen and accepted a tissue to blow her nose.

'You see now why I could never hurt Charlie and Eddie.' Denny poured whisky into three glasses.

'I'm sorry I thought that.' Dora took the drink from Denny.

'And that is why you can trust Adam.'

'The solicitor, he's the boy in the graveyard. So, you found him?'

'Yes, he came back to Blue Hollow.'

'Drink, it will make you feel better,' Dmitri said.

Dora took a small sip of the drink. The amber liquid burnt her throat, but she felt the warmth spread through her body so she took another sip.

'What about Iosif?'

Denny knocked back his drink and poured another one. 'We never found him and Boris, well, you can imagine.'

'Did Adam tell you what happened that night?'

'No, and we never asked him. It's obvious now that he was traumatised. We didn't know that at the time, we were just kids. God only knows what those sick bastards did to him.'

'And they all got away with it.' Dora shook her head.

'Not all.'

'You mean the bank manager, Alan Lloyd, that's what Eddie meant by saying he was the first.'

'Yeah.'

'It must have been horrendous to have him turn up at the bank. Eddie should have shot him in the head while he had the chance.'

'You've changed your views.' Dmitri smiled.

'Well, not really but I can understand why Boris shot him and why Eddie was tempted to kill him. The man was evil. Why did you stop Eddie pulling the trigger?'

'Because Eddie wasn't a killer, none of us were. Yeah, we've done some bad shit, but we wouldn't take another life.'

'And the others?'

169

'We dealt with the ones we could track down. Wainwright got what was coming. We made sure he would never touch another kid. Some of them we couldn't get to like Graham North.'

'Why didn't you report it to the police? It would've been investigated.'

'Things were different then. It wasn't just Graham North that was a high-ranking officer. Can you imagine how many coppers he had in his pocket? We did try, we reported Iosif missing but they wouldn't look into it, said he was a runaway.'

'But things are different now, you could've tried again. Graham North must be at least retired if not dead.'

'Yeah and guess who took his place?'

Dora shrugged her shoulders.

'His son, Scott North, Chief Inspector North, so no one would listen to us now. It's so long ago, and we're seen as a bunch of crooks. Police would think Eddie was getting revenge for being nicked and there's no evidence.'

'I don't understand why Eddie wanted me to know this now. What did he hope to achieve. Did he think the police would listen to me if I went to them with the story? He must have known that they would come after me. He knew he was being watched.'

'There is more to the story. You're going to have to listen to the other tapes.'

'I don't think I can.'

'I'm sorry, there's nothing else I can tell you.'

Dora looked at him and saw the years of pain etched on his face, she knew what it must have cost him to let her hear his story. 'It's okay. You've done more than enough. I'm so sorry for all of you. Whatever happens, I'll keep your name out of the robbery but if I do take this to the police then I expect they will want to talk to you.'

'Not yet,' Denny said.

'It's too risky,' Dmitri said.

'Could you take us to Blue Hollow?'

'No, I'm not sure I could find it and to be honest I couldn't go back there.'

'I understand. Do you think my mother knew about Blue Hollow?'

'Jenny? No, I don't think MJ would've told her the whole story. I never told my wife. She thinks there has been a fraud committed at the bank and I'm a witness, that I'm hiding out until the police make an arrest. I've sent her for a long holiday,' Denny said.

'We better get going,' Dmitri said.

'Will you be alright?' Dora asked.

'I don't think they'll find me here,' Denny said. 'You go now, hopefully we will meet again.'

'I'm sure we will. Thank you.' Dora put her arms around Denny and kissed him on the cheek. 'You take care of yourself. You are the last connection I have to Eddie and Charlie.'

'Not the last,' Denny said. 'Go and see Boris.'

* * *

'Are you okay?' Dmitri's eyes were fixed ahead as he weaved in and out of the traffic on the motorway. 'You haven't said a word since we left Denny.'

'Yeah, I'm okay. Well no, I'm not okay. I expected to hear some great revelation from Eddie. What he had done, taken, or knew. I didn't expect that, it's unthinkable what those boys went through. How long did it go on for? How many boys went through that place? It makes me feel sick. Now I know why Eddie and Charlie went to prison. Is that what he wanted me to know? To understand his actions. But all this happened nearly fifty years ago.'

'It doesn't make it any less horrific than if it happened yesterday.' Dmitri glanced at her.

'That's not what I'm saying. Did he want me to write his story and name and shame those responsible? Maybe those who are alive could be investigated and punished. Scott North wouldn't want the story coming out about his father. I guess he could be behind the murder of Charlie and Eddie.'

'I think Scott North is not the only person who would want this information kept secret. Think about it, think about what you heard on the tape.'

'I don't want to,' Dora said. 'I doubt I'll ever be able to get it out of my head.'

'Not what happened to the boys. What were the men doing in that old church?'

'You mean the robes and the symbols?'

'It sounds like they were performing some sort of ritual. Eddie mentioned chanting, the use of candles, symbols on the wall, and on the altar. Sounds like a cult. That would explain a lot. The way Eddie and Charlie were killed, silenced.'

'A cult?' Dora laughed. 'Well maybe fifty years ago, but not now.'

'Of course cults still exist, even here in the UK. You'd be surprised by how many.'

'It's a good theory but I think this was just a group of sick men. Eddie wouldn't have got me involved with some sort of cult.'

'Maybe he didn't know. Perhaps we should go to Blue Hollow, see if the building and church are still standing. There could still be symbols on the walls. It would give us a lead, see what the symbols represent.'

'How are we going to do that? You heard Denny, he won't go back and he's not even sure where the place is. We have no chance of finding it.'

'There is another person who's been there.'

'Boris? Yeah like he can take us there.'

'He could tell you where to find it.'

'Forget it, he's a lunatic.'

'After everything you've heard today you're still going to judge and condemn him?'

Dora could see she had upset Dmitri, the way his jaw was set, and his hands gripped the steering wheel.

'What happened to those boys was horrendous and I can understand why they took revenge on those involved but to kill an innocent child, no matter what he went through, it cannot excuse that.'

'You don't know the whole story.'

'No, and after today I don't think I want to. I know enough. I don't need to know the details. You're also forgetting that Adam was at Blue Hollow. I'll make arrangements to meet with him. He might have one of the tapes. It would make sense.'

'And what are you going to tell the police when you see them?'

'I don't know. We have the photos, the men's names, and the tapes. That should be enough for them to look into it.'

'You think?' Dmitri shook his head. 'They're not going to take Eddie's word. Both he and Charlie were ex-cons. Boris is serving time and Denny doesn't want to speak to them. The police will think it's some elaborate story to get their own back for being banged up.'

'The photos don't show anything incriminating, and you haven't a clue where to find Blue Hollow. On top of that, we don't know how many are involved, not only then but now. There's at least one high-ranking police officer involved who will go to any lengths to protect his father's name. How many do you think he has in his pocket? I thought you would've learnt by now that the world is not black and white with the good guys and the bad guys. You think if someone has a criminal record they should be written off, deserve to rot in jail and that every policeman is good because they wear a uniform or carry a badge. The people that have helped you so far all have a record, even me. So maybe it's time you understood that we are not the bad guys.'

'Well, what do you want me to do?' Dora said. 'You can rant all you like but I didn't ask to get involved in this. I've got people trying to kill me. I've lost Eddie and

173

Charlie and all I want to do is go home and try to get back to some sort of normality.'

'Yeah, that's not going to happen. You need to stop pissing about, find the tapes and finish it. You're going to have to man up and visit Boris. I don't care what you think of the man. There's more at stake than your feelings.'

'If you feel that way then you go to the prison.'

'It's your problem. I'm just hanging around to make sure you don't get yourself killed.'

'Then don't bother, you can just drop me home and leave.' Dora could feel the anger bubbling away under her skin. She turned her head and looked out of the window.

They drove in silence for the rest of the journey and Dora was relieved when they pulled up in front of her house.

'Looks quiet,' Dmitri said. 'Dray's car is here.' He pointed across the road.

Dora got out of the jeep and grabbed her case from the back seat.

'Let me take that,' Dmitri said. 'You shouldn't be carrying it with your injured side.'

'I'm fine, it's much better now.'

'Good.' Dmitri pulled the case from her. 'I told you that you didn't need to go to hospital,' he said with a grin. 'I'm sorry if I upset you. It's just been a difficult few days and the tape was upsetting. I also cared for Charlie and Eddie. It wasn't easy to listen to and I know it must have been worse for you.'

'Thank you, but I meant what I said. You don't have to keep looking after me.'

'I made a promise and I always keep my word.'

Relief flooded Dora. As much as he made her angry, she was happy not to be totally on her own. The door opened as they approached, and Dray popped his head around.

'All sound here, nice pad you've got.'

Dora was about to protest about people going into her house uninvited but kept quiet. 'Thanks,' she muttered as she passed him and went through to the kitchen.

'Boys are all finished. New locks and sensors on the windows and doors. Keys are on the table. Do you wanna cuppa?'

Dora looked at the cups and plates stacked next to the sink. 'I see you made yourself at home.'

'Gave the boys a bite. Not that you had much in. You need to do some shopping.' Dray laughed.

While Dora made the tea Dmitri checked the windows before picking up a package on the table and emptying the contents. 'Give me your phone.' He held out his hand.

Dora handed over the phone and sat down at the table. Tiredness stung her eyes and all she wanted to do was change into her pyjamas and curl up in bed.

'I brought the SIG for you.' Dray opened the kitchen drawer and took out the gun. He placed it on the kitchen table with a couple of magazines. 'Not sure where you wanted to keep it.'

Dora stared at the gun, it looked alien in the kitchen and far more frightening than it had done on the shooting range.

'I'm not sure I want to keep it anywhere in my house. What if the police come?'

'Shoot them,' Dray said.

'I meant if they search the house. I could go to prison for possessing a firearm.'

'Relax.' Dray placed a hand on her shoulder. 'No one's gonna know it's here.'

Dora stood, picked up the gun and ammunition and placed it back in the drawer.

'Here.' Dmitri handed back the phone. 'The sensors on the doors and windows will set off an alert on the phone if anyone tries to come in.'

'Will it alert the police?'

'It will alert me,' Dmitri said.

'And what am I supposed to do until you get here?'

'That's why you have the gun.' Dmitri shook his head. 'Maybe I better stay with you until you've seen the police and Adam, then I'll take you back to stay with Ben.'

'I can stay too,' Dray said. 'It will give your neighbours something to yak about.'

'I'll be okay. You go and do what you need to do. I don't think they'll try to get in again.'

'Don't be too sure,' Dmitri said. 'I won't be far away. I need to check out the names of the men on the tape, see if they were part of a cult and if that cult still exists. Meanwhile, leave the cat at your mother's so you don't have to open the back door.'

'How did you know? Oh, never mind.'

'Right, we'll be on our way. Call me as soon as you finished with the police and let me know the arrangements to meet with Adam. I don't want you going on your own.'

'Take care, girl.' Dray gave her a hug. 'Anyone come in here, shoot the fucker. Don't worry about the mess, we'll clean it up.'

Dora saw the two men out and locked the door. The house felt too still and quiet. She made a call to Adam and set up a meeting before changing into her pyjamas. She didn't want to stay in the kitchen with the memories of the man in the balaclava. The thought of him still out there somewhere made her nervous. She grabbed the gun and loaded the magazine before going upstairs and placing it on the bedside table next to her phone. Sitting in bed with her laptop open she googled cults in the UK. A list came up, together with an advice site. As she read, a coldness crept over her skin.

Chapter Eighteen

Dora sat in the interview room waiting for DI Price and DS Sims. She had been given a cup of tea that sat untouched on the table. She knew they were deliberately keeping her waiting. She could feel the panic prickling her skin, making her want to run from the room.

Stop it, you're getting paranoid like Eddie, she thought. But Eddie had reason to be paranoid.

She looked around the room trying to find something to concentrate on as she breathed in and counted to four and let her breath out slowly. The walls were bare and in need of redecoration, the window frosted so she couldn't see outside. Dmitri and his cult theories kept coming into her mind. The sound of the door opening made her jump. DI Price and DS Sims walked in.

'Sorry to keep you waiting.' DI Price sat down and set a file on the table. DS Sims gave her a tight smile before taking his seat.

'That's okay.' Dora forced a smile and hoped they couldn't hear the thumping of her heart.

'Thank you for coming in, we were getting a little concerned about you,' DI Price said.

'I went away for a few days. I needed a break. Get away from it all.'

'You went up to London?'

'Yes.'

'To see Charlie Briar?' DI Price fingered the file on the desk.

Dora looked at the two men and thought at least one of them could be involved. DI Price looked old enough. 'Yeah, and some of Uncle Eddie's friends.'

'Did you talk to Charlie?'

'No, as you'll be aware Charlie was murdered Sunday night.'

'Yes.' DS Sims leaned forward. 'It's a bit of a coincidence that you plan to visit Charlie Briar and he gets murdered in the same manner as Eddie.'

'What are you implying?'

'I'm not implying anything, just stating the facts.'

DI Price opened the file and took out a photograph. He placed it on the table and pushed it towards Dora.

'Do you recognise this man?'

Dora looked down. Cold eyes stared out of the photo. The man had a shaved head with a tattoo visible on his neck. His mouth was set in a hard line.

'No, I haven't seen him before. Who is he?'

'Ewan Lacey, found dead on Monday. He had his throat cut. He also had an injury to his right eye consistent with being stabbed with a letter opener. You said in your statement that you stabbed the intruder in the right eye.'

An image of the man in the study came to Dora's mind, her hand driving the letter opener into his eye. Warm blood spurting over her hand. 'Yes.' She wrapped her arms around her body. 'Is this him? The man that broke into my house?'

'It would seem so,' DI price said. 'Ewan Lacey is a known thug, served time for GBH, long list of arrests which never got a conviction because the witnesses were too terrified to testify.'

'Do you think he killed Eddie?'

'That we don't know,' DS Sims said. 'It's not like we can question him. What we do know is that he didn't kill Charlie. He'd been dead a couple of days before he was found.'

'So you don't think that Charlie and Eddie's deaths are connected?'

'Oh, we think they are connected. We're working closely with the Met. The thing that connects all three murders is you.'

'Me? You don't think I had anything to do with it?'

Dora's comment was ignored. DI Price opened the file and his eyes scanned the top sheet. Dora tried to read it upside down, but he closed the file before she had a chance to make out the words.

'You're aware that you are the sole beneficiary of Eddie Flint's will?'

'No but given that he had no family, it's not a big surprise. Like I told you Eddie didn't have any money, not that I know about, if that's what you're getting at.'

'It seems he had a little tucked away.' DS Sims sat back in the chair. 'I understand your husband left you six months ago.'

'What's that got to do with it?'

'You must be finding things difficult.'

'I manage.' Dora sat back and folded her arms.

'Can't be easy, mortgage on the house and the loss of the main income. I imagine you will have to sell. Start again.'

'I really don't see how that's any of your business.'

'You're going to need a place to live. Eddie was renting the bungalow from you. You couldn't ask him to leave, not when he was so unwell.'

'What? No, Eddie wasn't renting the bungalow from me. I don't even own my own house. Whoever told you that had their facts wrong.'

'No, we checked it out. The property is in your name, with no charge over it. It appears you own it outright. No mortgage.'

'There must be some mistake.' Dora could feel panic snake around her chest.

'No, no mistake,' DS Sims said. 'In your current situation Eddie's death came at a convenient time. Did you ask him to move out, did he refuse, and you couldn't wait any longer for him to die?'

'No.' Dora shot out of the chair. 'I told you I don't know anything about the bungalow being in my name. This is ridiculous. I came in as you asked and answered your questions, but I would like to go now.'

'Please sit down,' DI Price said. 'We have to ask these questions. You can see how it looks. First Eddie, then a man you claim broke into your house turns up dead and then Charlie.'

'You think I could have done that to Eddie, or Charlie?' Dora felt tears sting her eyes. She rubbed her hands over her face. 'I didn't kill them.' She sank down into the chair.

'Maybe not yourself.'

'You think I hired some killer.' Dora laughed. 'I think maybe I should have a solicitor.'

'You think you need a solicitor?' DS Sims smiled.

'I thought I was coming in to help you with information to find Eddie's killer, not be grilled and accused of murder.'

'Who has accused you of murder?' DI Price asked.

'You're implying it.'

'We have to look at everyone who knew Eddie or had a motive to kill him. You have a connection to all three dead men, and you've been keeping company with some unsavoury characters. So you must understand why we have to ask these questions.'

'What unsavoury characters? Are you referring to Eddie and Charlie?'

DI Price took another photo from the file and slid it towards Dora. She looked down and saw an image of herself being assisted by Dmitri as she left the train platform.

'He's a friend of Charlie's. He came to meet me off the train to tell me what had happened to Charlie.'

'A train in which a woman was stabbed,' DS Sims said. 'Just another coincidence?'

'I wasn't responsible for what happened. I think I was the intended victim.' Dora stood and lifted her jumper to reveal the wound. 'Somebody is trying to kill me. The same person that probably killed Eddie and Charlie.'

'And why do you think that is?' DI Price asked.

'I don't know.' Dora covered her side and sat down.

'It's a nasty wound. Did you get it treated in hospital?'

'No.'

DI Price raised his eyebrows.

'I was afraid. Eddie had been killed a few days earlier and a man broke into my house threatening me. Then some lunatic tries to stab me on the train.'

'I understand you would be shaken,' DI Price said, 'but why not go to hospital to get treatment and inform the police? There were calls for witnesses to the incident on the news and you didn't come forward.'

'I didn't see the news. As I said I was scared. I thought the man that tried to stab me was still after me. I just wanted to go somewhere where I felt safe.'

'With this man?' He pointed to Dmitri.

'Yes, I told you he's a friend of Charlie's. I stayed with him for a few days until I felt well enough to come home. I came in as you requested as soon as I got your message.'

'The thing is, Dora, your story doesn't make a lot of sense. At any time you could have reported it to the police, phoned for help. You could've stayed in the train station until the police arrived. You would have been safe.'

'I lost my phone.'

'Even so, you chose to leave with this man. Dmitri Orlov. He is known to us,' DI Price said.

'Orlov?'

'Yes, the son of Boris Orlov who as you know is a convicted murderer. Why would you think it safer to go with him?'

A cold fist twisted Dora's stomach and heat prickled the back of her neck. She pulled at the collar of her jumper. Dmitri had been using her to get information, to get the tapes.

'Are you okay?' DI Price asked.

'Yes, it's just a little warm in here.' She picked up the cup and took a sip of cold tea. 'I didn't know he was Boris's son.'

'He gave you a false name?'

'No, he didn't tell me his surname. So I didn't make the connection.'

'I think it's time you told us the truth,' DS Sims said.

Dora fidgeted in her chair as she wrestled with the decision of telling them everything or keeping quiet.

'I have told you the truth. I honestly don't know who killed Eddie and Charlie and I didn't have anything to do with it. I think it has to do with something that happened in the children's home where Eddie and Charlie were placed.'

'Go on,' DI Price said.

'They were in Bracken House children's home in Cardiff with Boris and his younger brother Iosif. They were then moved to a place called Blue Hollow. There the boys were abused. Then Iosif went missing. It was reported to the police a few years later when the boys left the home, but the police didn't investigate. They said that Iosif was a runaway.'

The two detectives looked at each other. 'Where did you get this information?' DS Sims asked.

'Eddie left a tape with one of his friends who also confirmed the story.'

'Name?'

'I can't tell you that. This person is afraid so doesn't want to speak to the police. There were also photographs of men that visited Blue Hollow with names and dates.'

'Have you seen these pictures?' DI Price leaned forward.

'Yes.'

'And where are they now?'

'I left them with the person for safe keeping.'

'I see,' DI Price said. 'I'm afraid unless you produce the pictures and the tape there's not a lot we can do.'

'You could at least look into Iosif Orlov's disappearance.'

'Where is this Blue Hollow?'

'I don't know.'

DI Price sat back in his chair. 'So you think Eddie and Charlie were murdered because of something that happened... how many years ago?'

Dora shrugged her shoulders. 'In the early seventies. I know what it sounds like, but they must've known who was responsible for Iosif's disappearance and that person didn't want them to talk.'

'A lot of children run away from homes,' DI Price said.

'Yeah and that's what the police said back then. Then there's the abuse, the men responsible would want that kept quiet.'

'Men who are likely dead now,' DS Sims smiled. 'And why would Eddie keep that information to himself for all these years?'

'I don't know. He was afraid before he died. He said someone was watching him. The abuse could have gone on for years after the boys left the home so there may still be some alive who were involved that don't want the information getting out.'

'Is there anything else you haven't told us?' DI Price asked.

'No, I've told you everything. Please at least look into Blue Hollow, see if there were any reports of abuse.'

'We'll look into it,' DI Price said. 'But I think you'll find that Eddie and Charlie were killed because they were involved in some criminal activity and got in over their heads.'

'Or maybe for reasons a little closer to home,' DS Sims added.

'I think we'll leave it there for now. Don't go taking any more holidays. We may need to speak to you again.'

'So, that's it?' Dora said.

'For now.' DI Price stood up.

* * *

Anger churned Dora's stomach as she pulled up in front of her house. She could see her mother standing at the front door.

'I couldn't get in,' Jenny said as Dora walked down the path.

'I've had the locks changed. After that man broke in, I didn't feel safe.' Dora took the key from her bag and opened the door.

'Probably for the best and it'll also stop Gary walking in when he wants. Treating the place like he owns it.'

'Well, he does. Anyway, I feel safer now.'

'I wish you would stay with me until this is over.' Jenny followed Dora into the kitchen.

'Over?' Dora grabbed the kettle and twisted the tap with too much force. Water sprayed over her jumper. 'Shit!'

'Go and sit down, I'll make the tea.' Jenny took the kettle from Dora's hand.

'It's never going to be over. No one will tell me what's going on. I only get pieces of information that make it more complicated. I don't know who to trust and on top of that, the police think I'm responsible for Eddie and

Charlie's deaths. I doubt they're even looking for the killer.' Dora put her head in her hands.

'Surely not.' Jenny took the chair next to Dora. 'They have to eliminate you from their enquires or they wouldn't be doing their job. So they're going to ask you questions that may seem like they suspect you.'

'No, you don't understand. The man that broke into my house is dead. When I was on the way to see Charlie, someone tried to stab me on the train and injured another woman. Then two thugs tried to get me after the funeral.' Dora wiped a tear from her cheek.

'What funeral? You're starting to scare me.'

'I'm scared.' Dora looked at her mother. 'I don't know what's going on. Everywhere I go something bad happens. That's why the police think I'm involved.'

'Then you have to tell them everything, ask them for protection.'

'I've told them as much as I can, besides I think the police are in on it, well, some of them. I can't trust anyone.'

'You're not thinking straight.' Jenny put her arms around Dora. 'You had a terrible shock finding Eddie, then losing Charlie on top of that. It's no wonder you feel like the world is against you.'

'It's not that. I've heard things. I told you that Eddie made more tapes. Charlie had one and so did Denny. I've listened to them both.'

'I see.'

Dora noticed her mother didn't ask who Denny was. 'You knew, didn't you? About the abuse that happened to Dad and all of them.'

Jenny stood up and fussed around making tea. An uncomfortable silence filled the kitchen. When the tea was made Jenny placed a cup in front of Dora and sat down with a sigh.

'Your father never spoke about it. He'd just give me a glimpse now and again then he would clam up. I know what happened back then damaged them all. Your father suffered from nightmares for years.'

'Did he mention a place called Blue Hollow?'

'Only to say it was the place they had been taken. I didn't press him for details.'

'And the money?'

Jenny shifted in her seat. 'I didn't want to know where your father got his money from but yes, we lived a comfortable life. There's enough money for you not to worry about losing this place. Let that fool of a husband get a valuation and we'll give him his share of the equity and pay off the rest of the mortgage. You'll have some security then. While you're at it you can get a good solicitor and divorce him. I'll pay the legal fees.'

'That's a lovely offer,' Dora said, 'but it seems I own Eddie's bungalow and I'm the sole beneficiary of his will.'

'That doesn't surprise me.'

'It's why the police think I had something to do with his murder. For the money.'

'Do you think the police are going to look into where the money came from?' Jenny fiddled with the handle on the cup.

'You mean the robbery? You must have guessed that's where it came from.'

'Yes, but like I said I didn't ask.'

'Don't worry, I doubt they'd find out that Dad had anything to do with it. Besides he was only the getaway driver.' Dora laughed.

'It's not funny,' Jenny said.

'Well it is a bit, Dad involved in a bank robbery.'

'I suppose,' Jenny said. 'I just hope no one finds out. Can you imagine the gossip?'

'The others would've made sure that there was no connection to him. It sounds like they always protected him.'

'Yes, they did. It hit them all hard when he died. They all came to the funeral, well most of them.'

'You mean Boris wasn't there.'

'Well no, he couldn't come but he wrote to me.'

'So you know about Boris and what he did?'

'No, I don't know exactly what happened. Like I said, the less I knew about what your father's friends got up to the better. We were happy here. Your father talked about Boris, wrote to him and visited him in prison.'

'But he murdered his girlfriend and her child. Why would Dad want anything to do with him?'

'There was a strong bond between Boris and your father. I know it had something to do with Boris's missing brother Iosif. Your father never forgot him. He would light a candle every year on his birthday. I think maybe your father became a substitute, a sort of link for Boris to his brother.'

'Did you know the woman Boris killed? I can't find any information on the case. Maybe if I had the name, I could get more details.'

'Perhaps you should just leave things alone. Your father wouldn't want you raking up the past.'

'Why?'

'Because he didn't want you to know about that part of his life. I guess in his mind he thought it would taint you or you would think less of him. What happened to those boys both mentally and physically scarred them.'

'I could never think badly of Dad. I wish you had mentioned Blue Hollow when Eddie died. At least I would've been prepared for what I heard.'

'Would it have stopped you going off to see Charlie and getting the tape? You need to leave it alone now, let the police do their job. I couldn't bear it if anything happened to you.'

'It will be okay, Mum.' Dora squeezed her mother's hand. 'I'm going to see Eddie's solicitor tomorrow. I'm sure he can help me out with the police. Maybe he will talk to them, get them to look at what happened at Blue Hollow. He was there himself.'

'I'll go with you,' Jenny said.

'There's no need. I'll be fine, honest.' Dora's phone trilled, she took it from her bag and saw Dmitri's name flash across the screen. She hit decline and switched the phone off.

'Who was that?' Jenny asked.

'Another person I can't trust. I'm better off on my own.'

Chapter Nineteen

'How could you let this happen?' Scott North growled. 'You assured me it would be dealt with.'

Nate pulled the collar up on his coat as his eyes darted around the deserted picnic spot. He felt vulnerable in the dark, and worried about Scott's motive for meeting in an isolated spot at two in the morning. 'It wasn't anyone's fault. By the time the old man called to say about the photographs it was too late to do anything. I sent a couple of men, but she was leaving, and she wasn't alone.'

'I had the CCTV pulled in the area,' Kyle interrupted. 'She's with Dmitri Orlov.'

'What's she doing with him?' Scott's eyes blazed. 'You should've dealt with him years ago, before he had a chance to establish himself.'

'Yeah, he's a slippery little fucker,' Kyle said.

'So now they've got the photographs and the tapes,' Scott said.

'We should've dealt with the doc at the time, then we wouldn't have this problem,' Nate said.

'Are you questioning my decisions?' Scott turned his cold eyes on Nate.

'No, of course not.' Nate shuffled under his gaze.

'The doc had those photos for insurance, and we had no idea where he kept them. As long as we left him alone there was no danger of it coming out. The least the old bastard could've done is destroyed them before he snuffed it. I kept my side of the bargain.'

'Maybe if Kyle's thugs hadn't gone in so heavy he would've had the chance.'

'Don't put this on me,' Kyle snapped. 'I've done my job.'

'Not yet,' Scott said. 'Where is she?'

'Back home.'

'And the tapes and photos?'

'I don't think she has all the tapes. She said she left the photos with someone.'

'Denny,' Scott spat. 'It has to be him.'

'He's gone underground. No one has seen or heard from him,' Nate said.

'Yeah, she managed to find him. Unless she's lying.'

'I don't think so,' Kyle said. 'She would have handed them over if she had them.'

'Maybe she doesn't know the significance.'

'Of course she doesn't know,' Scott said. 'She hasn't been to see Boris yet. If she had all the information she would've gone squealing to the police or the press by now and we wouldn't be able to contain it. You need to act now. Kill the bitch and this time don't fuck it up.'

'Wouldn't it be prudent to wait?' Kyle said. 'Let her get the rest of the tapes and she'll lead us to it.'

'And risk it all blowing up in our faces? Do as I say, find out what she knows and kill her and anyone else she might have talked to.'

'I think it might be a bit risky to act now,' Kyle said.

'Just do it,' Scott growled. 'Just remember who you're talking to. I can take you down like that.' He clicked his fingers. 'Eddie Flint and the rest of them have been a noose around my neck holding me back for years. They ruined my life and are still doing it from the grave. I could've been so much more. I will not have some little bitch dragging my name through the dirt. I only have six months left to retirement. I've trusted you with this. You have as much to lose as me, if not more. I am granted more protection than you. Next time we meet I want to hear the job's been completed. And bring me the photos and tapes, I'll burn them myself.' Scott got in his car and drove off leaving the other two men in darkness.

'I think he's beginning to lose the plot,' Kyle said.

'Careful what you say, Kyle, he's a dangerous man. Just sort out the woman and don't mess it up this time.'

Chapter Twenty

Dora pulled into the carpark in Laugharne and looked out over the estuary. The castle sat to her left and a small bridge led to a footpath. There were two other cars parked. Both empty. She checked her watch. There were still a few more minutes to go before the arranged meeting time. She checked her rear-view mirror watching for a car to pull up, then glanced at her handbag that held the SIG. Carrying a gun made her nervous. She felt that she was going to get caught at any moment and guilt was written all over her face.

She looked behind again and then back to the front where she saw a man walking over the bridge and approaching her car. He was tall and thin with a protruding Adam's apple. He wore a blue anorak, but despite the cold, left his hood down. His face was red from the cold and what was left of his hair blew sideways in the wind. He smiled as he reached the car. Dora opened the door and was greeted by a cold blast.

'Hello, Dora, I'm Adam.' He held out his hand. 'Thank you for agreeing to meet me here.'

'It's no problem.' She shook the offered hand. 'It's a nice spot. I haven't been here in years.'

'Shall we take a walk? It's a bit nippy but there's no one about to overhear us.'

Dora stepped out of the car and grabbed her coat. She shrugged it on and pulled the zipper to her neck before putting her hood up. 'I should have brought some gloves.' She smiled before grabbing her handbag and locking the car.

'I'm so sorry about Eddie and Charlie. I've looked after their affairs for many years. I also owe my life to them. They'll be missed by a lot of people.'

'Thank you.' Dora kept pace with Adam as they crossed the bridge. 'You said on the phone that you wanted to discuss Eddie's will. I was at the police station yesterday and they said that the bungalow Eddie was renting is in my name. Do you know about that?'

'Yes, it's what Eddie wanted. He was concerned about the situation with your husband. You do know that he didn't have long left? The doctors had given him six months at the most.'

'He told me the chemo was working. I guess he didn't want to worry me, but I had an idea he wasn't telling me the whole truth. Then after he was killed the police told me that he was dying. Now they think I had something to do with his murder because I'm the sole beneficiary of his will.'

'Really?' Adam laughed. 'That's typical. Don't worry about it. I'll help you all I can. I told Eddie I didn't think it was a good idea to put the bungalow in your name, but he wanted it to be uncomplicated. He wanted you to have instant access when he died, to move in or use it as equity. The only stipulation he had was that your husband, I won't repeat the language he used, couldn't get his hands on it.'

'I can imagine what he said.' Dora smiled.

'There's also the money from the property investments as well as shares in various companies. Most of the money is in offshore accounts.'

'But I didn't think Uncle Eddie had any money. It's not like he took exotic holidays or wore designer clothes. He didn't even own a car. He used the bus and train.'

'The money didn't mean anything to him. It couldn't put right what happened and couldn't bring back those he loved. He wanted you to have it all so that you'd never have to worry about money. He wanted to make sure you were secure. You are now a wealthy woman.'

'I'd rather have Eddie back than any amount of money.'

'I'm sure you would. You are also the sole beneficiary of Charlie's will. As you will be aware Charlie was a very wealthy man.'

Dora stopped walking. 'I don't understand, why would Charlie leave everything to me?'

'He had no one else, no family. Eddie was the beneficiary of Charlie's will and if Charlie outlived Eddie then it would pass to you. Why don't we sit down, there's a bench up ahead. It must be a lot for you to take in.'

They walked in silence to the bench, Dora's mind whirring with the information and what it meant for her. She sat down and pushed her hands deep into her pockets.

'Do you think Eddie and Charlie were murdered because of the money?'

'Why would you think that?'

'I don't know. They all did well out of the robbery, and they got Alan Lloyd put away. Revenge? Then there's Boris. What happened to his share of the money? Did they divide it up among themselves? He would've served time with some serious criminals. Maybe he was so angry that they were all out there living their lives that he arranged to have them killed.'

'Why would you think that Boris, of all people, would hurt Charlie and Eddie?'

'I don't know, it's just a thought. He has a son.'

'Yes, Dmitri.'

'He was helping me. He didn't tell me he was Boris's son. I think he was after information. You know about the tapes Eddie made?'

'Yes.'

'Maybe there's something on the tapes that Boris doesn't want known. I have three of them, there's another two.' Dora looked at Adam. 'Did Eddie leave one with you?'

'No, he didn't.' Adam gazed out at the estuary. 'I think you know that this is not about the money. Boris isn't a bad man. I can't give you the details of his finances, but I can tell you that Boris had his share.'

'But there's something that Boris wants?'

'Yes, he wants to know what happened to his brother, Iosif.'

'And he thinks that Charlie and Eddie knew?'

'No, Charlie and Eddie didn't know what happened to Iosif.'

'But you do?'

'I've never spoken about it. It's so long ago I don't know how much of it is real and how much is from the nightmares I had after. I'm scared of looking into that part of my memory and bringing it all back, making it real. I had a breakdown in my thirties. I took six months off work. I learnt to shut it away. No amount of therapy could fix me. I had to bury it to survive.'

'I'm sorry,' Dora said. 'I heard some of the things that went on in Blue Hollow on the tape. It's unthinkable. It's a wonder that any of you survived, it's enough to break anyone. You all managed to achieve so much despite what happened. You should be proud of yourself. You didn't let them win. Maybe there's still a chance that some of the men responsible could be brought to justice, for the world to know what they did. If you could bring yourself to say what happened to Iosif, maybe it would help open an investigation. You're a respected professional, surely the police would have to listen to you.'

'I know that's what Eddie and Charlie would've wanted but you should know by now you can't trust the police. Well, there are some you can't trust, and if the information gets into the wrong hands… I'm afraid, even after all this time. Eddie stirred things up by recording the tapes. He was so careful but look what happened to him. I understand why he had to do it, tell the story, but they were always braver than me. I can't go to the police.'

'Then could you tell me? I've already told the police about Blue Hollow and Iosif going missing. Maybe they'll look into it. Even if there's a high-ranking police officer involved there's a slim chance that the information won't get ignored. Maybe if I make enough noise someone will listen. I don't know what else to do, and I'm not sure what you can tell me will be enough, but I have to try. Eddie and Charlie gave their lives, I can't let it go.'

'You have enough money to disappear, if you want. Somewhere they will never find you,' Adam said. 'I can make the arrangements. There's still so much that you don't know, it will put you in even more danger. Yes, Iosif is part of the story but it doesn't end there. I'll tell you what I know but there's no point unless you listen to the rest of the tapes. Only then will you have what you need to put an end to it. That will mean a visit to Boris.'

'I can't promise I can get the other tapes, but I will try.'

'That's all I can ask of you.' Adam stared out over the estuary, his body rocked as if the memory caused him physical pain. 'That Friday night was different from the ones before.'

Chapter Twenty-One

'The whole week had been filled with endless chores. Scrubbing the church flagstones with icy water and wooden brushes that tore the skin off our hands. Cleaning the windows standing on rickety chairs, and polishing silver candlesticks until they gleamed. Then there was the house. Extra rooms were opened, scrubbed clean, and beds made up. Fires laid ready to be lit and endless chopping of wood. We thought it was for a Christmas celebration. We knew it was December but had no idea of the date. We hadn't had a Christmas since we'd been there, it was just another day to us.

'We were all subdued by Friday. I had been sick twice. I rarely escaped the weekend choosing, it seemed that I was the favourite of a man called Jack Quinn. I later learned that he was a judge. More men than usual arrived that Friday so the chances of being chosen were high, but they didn't line us up. This put us all on edge. We served dinner and kept the fires stoked as they drank and smoked. The atmosphere was charged with excitement.

'We found our milk in the usual place, none of us spoke our thoughts out loud. Either we were to have a night off or all of us would be taken. I saw Boris give his milk to Iosif, he did this every week in the hope that the men wouldn't be able to wake his brother and leave him alone. Charlie and Eddie tipped a quarter of their milk into Boris's glass. I was still feeling sick when we went to the bedroom, but the milk soon took effect and I started to feel drowsy. Boris stayed in the room until Iosif and MJ were asleep. I always wished I had a big brother like Boris, but all those boys were good to me. I had swapped beds with Iosif, so I was by the window. I didn't mind too much, I knew how sick Iosif got from the cold. It was freezing that night. I could feel the cold air seeping through the window and snaking around my body. I curled up into a ball and pulled the blanket over my head.

'I don't know how long I had been asleep before I woke with a pain in my groin. Usually the milk made me sleep through the night, if the men didn't come. I tried to ignore the pain, but I was dying for a pee. I scrunched up my eyes willing myself to go back to sleep, but it felt like my bladder would burst and I was afraid I would wet the bed. The punishment would be severe, but it would be equally bad if I was caught out of bed. I decided it was better to risk getting up. There was a chance I could get to the toilet and back without being noticed. I got out of bed and felt the goosebumps cover my skin, the cold only served to make my need more desperate. I wiggled my feet into my shoes and pulled a jumper over my head. I looked around the room, all the boys were asleep except one. Iosif's bed was empty, the blanket lay heaped at the bottom of the bed. I thought perhaps he had the same problem as me and if I hurried, I would find him in the toilets and wouldn't be alone.

'I left the room and crept down the stairs. The house was still and silent. I pulled open the front door and stepped outside. Frost glistened on the path and the grass stood stiff. I remember thinking how pretty it looked. I hurried to the toilet block, my breath rising from my mouth like billowing clouds, the cold air filling my lungs and tightening my chest. I called out for Iosif, listening outside the toilet. There was no answer, no sound. I was afraid to go into the cubical in the dark, so I went around the back of the building to relieve myself. I hopped from foot to foot, I was so cold, and my fingers hurt. With the pressure gone from my bladder all I had to do was get back to the bedroom without being caught.

'I was nearing the door when I heard the chanting. I turned in the direction of the noise and saw the church windows flickering with light. I should have just gone back inside but I was curious to see what was going on. I thought maybe the older boys were up and had lit a fire, I longed to feel warm. If it wasn't the boys then I could see what the men were up to and have a tale to tell the others. Maybe I would find Iosif in the porch watching. If all the men were busy we could go to the kitchen and steal some food. They never gave us enough to satisfy our hunger.

'It was these thoughts that spurred me onwards to the church. I opened the heavy door, it creaked but the sound was disguised by the chanting. There was no second door into the church and no candles in the porch so I could hide in the shadows and watch. There was no sign of Iosif so I assumed that he must have crept back to the house when I was behind the toilet building. The men were stood in a circle with their hoods up and robes brushing the floor. I could see some of the faces illuminated in the candlelight, their eyes gleamed as they fixed their gaze to the centre of the circle. The chanting grew louder, more frenzied. The darkness around me seemed to close in, growing thicker and snaking around my body filling my lungs with fear. The chanting came to a sudden halt and all hooded heads bowed except one who raised his face to the ceiling.

'He began to whisper, strange words that floated around the church. The words grew louder and stronger as he raised his hands in the air and brought them together. It was then that I saw the dagger held firmly in his hands. He stepped forward, breaking the circle and with a shout he brought the knife plummeting downwards. There was a sickening thud then all the men knelt down to reveal a table. Bound to the table was Iosif; blood oozed from his chest, ran down the side of the table and dripped onto the floor. A scream shattered the silence and it was a moment before I realised that I was the one screaming. No one moved, it was as if we were frozen in time.

'The man with the knife spoke. "Go fetch our visitor, I'm sure he would like to join us."

'Two men came down the aisle. I'm not sure how I managed to move. It must've been survival instinct because I fled into the graveyard and threw myself behind a headstone. The men started spilling out of the church and spreading out. I curled myself into a ball. I heard them come into the graveyard, searching in the long grass and moving behind stones. In the darkness they missed me. I heard the leader come out of the church, his voice calm but full of authority.

"'Leave him, we'll soon see who's missing from bed. Lock up the house and with a bit of luck the little bastard will freeze to death."

'The men retreated to the church. I peeked around the headstone, but I was too scared to move. I could no longer feel my hands or feet. Nausea churned my stomach and bile rose in my throat. I watched as they brought Iosif out, wrapped in a blanket, one arm dangling. They threw him in the back of the Land Rover that Reg used to pick up supplies. Two of them got in and they drove off, but not towards the road. They headed up the mountain track towards the lake. Other men got into their cars and drove off, the rest of the men returned to the church. An overwhelming tiredness came over me. I no longer cared about getting back to the house and escaping the men. I wanted to join the person who lay beneath me. I curled into a ball and closed my eyes.

'I could hear someone calling my name and calling out for Iosif. I thought I was dreaming. I couldn't move or open my mouth. The voices grew closer, then something hit into my side. There was silence then Eddie's voice whispering, calling. I was turned over. Boris asked where Iosif was, but there were no words. I didn't know why they were waking me up and trying to drag me from my bed. I remember Eddie and Charlie carrying me. The next time I woke I was in hospital. When I was well enough to leave, Wainwright picked me up. He asked lots of questions, but I told him I didn't remember anything other than drinking my milk and going to bed. He seemed satisfied. I thought he would take me back to Bracken House, but we drove to Blue Hollow. This time I saw how isolated the building was, miles from the next house where no one would hear us scream.

'There were some new residents when I arrived, young girls. Among them, Eddie's sister, Julie. Eddie, Charlie, Boris, and Denny came running out of the house when they saw me. Boris asked me if I had seen Iosif in hospital, I told him no, but no more than that. I was so afraid that if I said something the same would happen to me. The boys never asked me what happened that night. It was an unspoken pact that we never talked about what went on in Blue Hollow on the weekends the men visited.

'I was put back in the same room. Iosif's bed had been filled with another boy. As I lay in bed that night looking at the bed by the window, I wondered if the men had meant to take me instead. I had been spared because I had swapped beds with Iosif. That only fuelled the fear that they would do the same again and next time they wouldn't make a mistake. That was the first of many nights that I woke myself screaming. MJ would come to my bed to try and calm me. As the weekend grew closer, I became convinced that I was going to die. I never stayed long enough to find out if that was to be my fate.

'Eddie and Charlie came to see me three days after I returned, to tell me of their plans to run away. They had collected food and wanted me to help them find the way back to Cardiff. I told them that I didn't think I could remember the way we had travelled but I would try. It was a better option than staying. They asked the other boys to come but they were too afraid. Only Ben came with us. I don't know how we survived as long as we did out in the cold, but we were determined to escape. Keeping Julie and MJ safe spurred us on. Charlie and Eddie became experts at stealing food from shops. We found old buildings to sleep in and kept off the roads during the day so we wouldn't be seen. We were eventually caught. We told the police why we had run away but they didn't believe us. I ended up back in Bracken House with MJ, Denny, and Julie. I guess they thought we were too much trouble to take back to Blue Hollow or maybe the police kept track of where we were, so it was too risky to take us back there. Wainwright made life difficult for us but at least we no longer had to worry about the men coming on the weekends. It didn't stop the nightmares though.

'Boris never gave up looking for Iosif and I couldn't tell him what I'd seen that night. I couldn't inflict those images or pain on him or any of the others. So I tried to forget that it happened. Shoved it deep in my memory until Eddie came to see me.'

Chapter Twenty-Two

Dora wiped a tear from her cheek as she gazed out at the estuary. Someone walked by with a dog. The wind whipped around them, but it couldn't blow away the words or the images of a little boy bound to a table and murdered.

Dora broke the silence. 'So you think they put Iosif in the lake?'

'It was winter, and the ground would've been too hard to dig a grave so, yes, as they went in that direction I would imagine they put him in the lake.'

'Do you think you could find Blue Hollow? If I can persuade the police to look in the lake—'

'No! I'm sorry, I don't ever want to go back to that place. I doubt I could even tell you the way.'

'It's okay. I understand. What happened to the others?'

'What do you mean?'

'You said you went back to Bracken House. What about Charlie, Eddie, and Boris?'

'They went to a borstal, a youth institution for young delinquents. They all had a record for theft, even though it was only food they stole for us to survive. Those places were run by HM Prison Service. You can imagine what life was like for them there.

'I met up with them again when I left Bracken House, I had nowhere to go. They gave me a bed and food until I got on my feet. I got a job and studied in the evenings. I thought if I studied the law, I could use it as a weapon to get back at those who had hurt us or at least try and stop it from happening again. Without Boris, Charlie, and Eddie I don't know what would've become of me. I've looked after their financial and legal affairs all these years. They even put up the money for me to start my own practice. I could never pay back their kindness. As for Boris, you have nothing to fear from him or his son.'

'What happened to Boris? I gather he must've been pushed over the edge, but I can't find any details on who he killed and why. I guess I could search the national archives, but a date would be useful as well as the name of his victims.'

'It's complicated and only fair that you go and see him for an explanation. I can however point you in the right direction.' Adam smiled. 'There's a house here, a two-bed end-terrace. It was Eddie's so is now yours. He came here with Charlie to get away from things. He said it was his little corner of the world where he felt peaceful. I think you'll find some of the answers you're looking for there. Shall we?' Adam stood.

Dora followed Adam along the path and up a steep set of steps. It was only now she was walking that she realised how cold she had become. Her backside felt numb from sitting on the cold bench and the wind had seeped through her jeans.

'Did Eddie leave instructions for his funeral?'

'Yes, as did Charlie. I can take care of the details if you like.'

'Please, I wouldn't know where to start.'

'I think it would be nice for them to have a joint funeral. It will be all the same people attending. What do you think?'

'Yes, I think that's a lovely idea. I just hope the police release them soon so they can be laid to rest.'

'I'll get onto that.' They walked down a narrow road and Adam stopped outside a house with a blue-painted door. He put his hand into his coat pocket and took out a set of keys. 'All yours.' He handed them to Dora. 'If you need anything, call. Don't go back to the police station alone. If I can't come to represent you, I'll send someone in my place. I know some of the best solicitors and barristers, so you needn't worry.'

'You're not coming in?'

'No, I think it's best you have a look around on your own.'

'Right, thank you for meeting with me. I appreciate how difficult it was for you to talk so openly with me.'

'Maybe it's time to let it out, perhaps those of us that are left can find some peace. I'll be in touch about the funeral arrangements, although I'm not sure how long it will be before the bodies are released.'

Dora watched Adam walk away then put the key in the lock. The door swung open over letters and flyers. She bent down and picked them up before closing the door and locking it. She placed the letters on the bottom of the stairs and walked into the sitting room. There was a faint smell of tobacco in the air. Dora smiled as she imagined Eddie sitting on the blue sofa, a beer in one hand and a roll-up in the other. She took off her coat and placed it on the sofa with her handbag and looked around the room. The walls were painted cream and covered with large, framed pictures of tall ships and lighthouses. There was a flat screen television against the wall with a shelving unit lined with DVDs. The opposite wall was taken up by a pine dresser. The top shelves held plates. Framed photos of Dora at various stages of her life filled the rest of the open space, some of her alone, others with Eddie, Charlie, and her father. She moved past the dresser and through the door that led to the kitchen.

The surfaces were clean with just a toaster, kettle, and tea caddy. A tea towel was draped over the edge of the sink. Dora opened the cupboards. One was filled with tins of food and dried pasta, another plates and bowls. The fridge was empty. As she stood at the sink looking at the view of the estuary through the window, a feeling of déjà vu crept over her. Had Eddie brought her here as a child? He often took her on trips. The place felt lived-in, empty for a few weeks perhaps but not months. She wondered if someone else had been living there.

She shook the thought away as she left the kitchen and went upstairs. The first bedroom had a double bed and wardrobe which creaked as she opened the door. A pair of jeans and a few jumpers hung from the rail, at the bottom a pair of walking boots sat next to slippers. She closed the door and moved to the next room, this one had a single bed and smaller wardrobe. The third room was the bathroom. Toiletries sat on the shelf next to a rusting razor blade. She couldn't see what answers Adam expected her to find there.

Back in the living room she opened the left drawer on the Welsh dresser. Inside she found a bundle of letters held together with an elastic band. The top letter had the address of the bungalow written neatly on the envelope. She flicked through them and saw they were all in the same handwriting.

Is this what Adam meant by finding answers, reading through Eddie's personal letters? They could be from a lover.

She put them to one side and pulled out a stack of photos. They were mainly of Charlie and Eddie in different locations. Some of Dora with her mum and dad. Her father's fiftieth birthday party. The faces got younger as she looked through the pile. Her mum and dad's wedding, the pair stood smiling next to a man that towered over the two of them. She flipped the photo and saw Eddie had written on the back. *MJ, Jenny, and Boris.* The next photo showed Eddie, Charlie, Boris, and Denny dressed in suits with matching cravats. The quality of the photos changed, some were blurry, others taken with a Polaroid camera. In each one the men smiled at the camera, their hairstyles and clothes changing to match the style of the time. Eddie and Charlie disappeared from the shots. Dora stopped at a photo of a young woman, she had long wavy blond hair. She sat on a wall wearing denim shorts and halterneck top. On the back of the photograph was written *Julie 1979.* Eddie's sister. She was beautiful.

Dora replaced the photos and letters, opened the next drawer and took out a blue envelope file. Inside were yellowing newspaper clippings. She picked out the first one and read.

> *Mother slain and child missing.*
> *The residents of George Street in Grangetown are in shock this morning following the murder of young mother Julie Flint. Police were called after a neighbour heard screaming. The police entered the property and found Julie Flint in the kitchen, she had been stabbed several times. She was pronounced dead at the scene. Julie's five-year-old daughter, Stephanie, is still missing. A large-scale search was launched following the discovery and police have worked through the night with many local residents joining in the search for the missing child. Neighbour Sally Grint said Julie was a quiet and friendly girl and she often saw her taking the child to play in the park. A man has been arrested in connection to the murder.*

Boris killed Eddie's sister. Dora shook her head. She looked at the date of the clipping, 14 January 1986, and calculated Julie's age. Only twenty-six, so young, she thought. A coldness crept over her as she put the clipping to one side and looked at another.

Hopes for finding little Stephanie Flint fade.

The search for missing five-year-old Stephanie Flint have been scaled down. Stephanie the daughter of Julie Flint found murdered in her home has been missing since 13 January. Police released a statement stating that the amount of blood found at the scene indicates that the child was fatally wounded and would have needed immediate medical attention. A check of all hospitals locally and further afield have no records of a child being treated. Detective Inspector Scott North who is leading the investigation said that sadly there was little hope of finding the child alive.

Police have charged Boris Orlov with the murder of Julie Flint. Orlov is believed to have been Julie's boyfriend but it is unclear if he is Stephanie's father. Orlov appeared briefly in court to be charged, he made no comment as the charges were read. An angry crowd gathered outside and attacked the police vehicle transporting Orlov to an undisclosed prison where he will await trial.

The next clipping was dated six months later.

Boris Orlov appeared in Cardiff Crown Court today charged with the murder of Julie Flint and her five-year-old daughter Stephanie. He pleaded not guilty. It is believed that he killed Julie and her daughter in a fit of jealousy, then buried the child before returning to dispose of Julie's body. Orlov has refused to give up the location of Stephanie's body and claims he is the victim of police corruption and a cover-up. Julie Flint's brother, Eddie Flint, was present at court but refused to comment. The case continues.

Dora wondered why Eddie had kept all this? It must have been hell for him to lose his sister and his niece. On top of that, one of his best friends, someone he trusted, killed them.

She flicked through the small clippings of the daily court reports until she came to the one with the verdict.

> *Boris Orlov was today convicted of the murders of Julie and Stephanie Flint. It took the jury just two hours to return with a unanimous guilty verdict. The judge thanked the jury and, speaking to Orlov, said that this was a despicable crime against a young mother and her child. He recommended that Orlov serve a minimum term of thirty years without parole.*

There was one final clipping from April 1997.

> *Boris Orlov's application for an appeal was turned down today. Orlov's defence team claimed that vital witness statements were excluded from the trial. Orlov was convicted of the murder of Julie Flint and her five-year-old daughter, Stephanie, in July 1986. Stephanie's body has never been found. Orlov was found trying to flee the scene, his clothes were soaked in Julie and Stephanie's blood. Orlov had a previous conviction for GBH and has had his sentence extended for attacking a fellow inmate and holding a prison officer hostage. The judge ruled that there was insufficient evidence for an appeal.*

A knock on the door made Dora jump and the clippings fell from her hand and fluttered to the floor. She stayed still, listening. Another knock, louder this time.

'Dora, I know you're in there.' Dmitri's voice came from the other side of the door.

'Leave me alone.' Dora moved to the sofa and grabbed the SIG from her bag.

'What the fuck is the matter with you? You don't answer my calls and you go off on your own to meet with Adam. You were supposed to let me know about the meeting.' He thumped the door again. 'Open the door before I cause a scene.'

'I know who you are.' Dora stepped closer to the door.

There were a few minutes of silence and Dora wondered if he had gone away but the letter box opened. 'Please let me in so I can explain.'

She turned the key in the lock and stepped back. The handle turned and Dora took the safety off the gun as the door swung open. Dmitri's eyes widened as he saw the gun pointed at him.

'What the fuck are you doing? Put the gun down.' He kicked the door closed.

'Stay away from me. I've taken the safety off and it's loaded.'

'Okay, calm down.' Dmitri stepped sideways then moved slowly towards the sofa.

'Keep your hands where I can see them, or I'll pull the trigger. I don't think I'll miss from here.'

'I get it, you're pissed off. Just put the gun down and let me explain.'

'No, you lied to me.'

'I didn't lie to you.' Dmitri sat down on the sofa.

'Stand up,' Dora shrieked. The gun wavered in her hand.

'For fuck sake.' Dmitri stood up.

'Don't swear at me. You lied all this time. I know you are Boris's son.'

'I never denied it.'

'You didn't tell me.'

'You didn't ask. I thought my name would have been enough of a clue. Good Russian name given to me by my father.'

'You had plenty of opportunity to tell me. Why would I have made the connection?'

'I couldn't tell you when we met. You would've freaked out. Then you've been bleating about my father being a lunatic and a murderer since we met. Anyway, what difference does it make? I'm still the same person. All I've done is try to help you.'

'Help me! You've been using me to get information. Your father killed Eddie's sister and his niece. I know why Eddie visited him before he died. To beg him to let him know where his niece was buried so he could lay her to rest. I'm guessing Boris wanted Eddie to find out what happened to Iosif in exchange for the information. He probably knew it would get Eddie killed. Or maybe he just wanted Eddie and Charlie out of the way. I bet Eddie knew why Boris killed Julie and by telling his story he would put an end to any chance of an appeal. I know he's already tried.'

'You don't know what you are talking about. My father didn't kill Julie and her daughter. After all you've heard about him, do you think he is capable of killing a five-year-old child? He was set up. Use your head. Are you doubting what Eddie has told you so far on the tapes? What happened at Blue Hollow, the type of men that were involved?'

'No, I don't doubt what Eddie says but what happened back then doesn't change anything. Your father was there that night, the police caught him covered in blood trying to flee the scene.'

'That doesn't mean he killed them.'

'So, what are you saying? The men from Blue Hollow killed Julie and her child and set your father up?'

'Yes.'

'And why would they do that?' The gun was getting heavy in her hand. She lowered it to her side keeping her eyes fixed on Dmitri.

'You need to go to the prison and talk to him. Give him a chance to explain.'

'No, he was convicted by a jury. Are you saying there was some elaborate plan to put him away? That the entire police force, judge, and jury were all in on it? Why should I trust your father? I'm sick of everyone lying to me, keeping things from me and not giving me straight answers. I can't trust you, the police told me you have a record.'

'I told you I had a record.'

'I've told the police about Blue Hollow and the pictures, they can sort out this mess.'

'What?' Dmitri ran his hand over his chin. 'They'll come for you. You're gonna have to trust me.' He took a step towards her.

'No!' She raised the gun.

'Okay, if you're not gonna let me help you then let me call Dray or Ben to come and stay with you.'

'Like I'm going to fall for that. They're your friends. More bloody criminals.'

'Like Eddie and Charlie, oh, and don't forget your father.'

'Don't bring him into this.'

'He's part of it. My father loved him, protected him, and treated him like a brother. Do you think he would wish any harm on you?'

'He was supposed to be Eddie and Charlie's friend and look what happened to them.'

'He never broke that friendship. You know what? I've had it with you, you can go and fuck yourself.' He stormed past Dora and out the front door slamming it behind him.

Dora locked the door, put the safety catch back on the gun and placed it in her handbag. Her arm ached from holding the gun and the confrontation left her body trembling. She took a few calming breaths, picked up the newspaper clippings and replaced them in the drawer, then kneeling down she opened the cupboard beneath. The first thing she saw was an old shoe box, she pulled off the lid and peered inside. There was a tiny pink knitted cardigan with pearl buttons, matching bonnet, and booties. She took them out carefully and laid them on the floor. At the bottom of the box was a hospital ID bracelet and a birth certificate. Dora looked at the information: Stephanie Jane Flint, 4 March 1980, mother, Julie Flint. The father's name was left blank.

Could she have been Boris's child? Dora thought. He was probably still married and that's why he didn't put his name on the certificate. Oh God, that would mean he murdered his own daughter.

She replaced the certificate and clothing then took out a photo album. The first picture showed Julie cradling a baby. Her hair was cut short and she looked gaunt. Underneath the picture was written, *Stephanie: age two weeks.* She flipped the pages. They were all of the child, running through the first year of her life. She felt a lump form at the back of her throat and snapped the album shut. There was nothing else of interest in the cupboard. The only thing she hadn't looked at was the letters. She slipped the top one from the bundle and sat down on the sofa to read.

My dearest friend,

It was wonderful to see you and Charlie yesterday although it broke my heart to see how the illness has ravished your body and zapped your strength. We have fought so many enemies and survived, I cannot believe that this one will beat you, and take you from us. Keep fighting. Never give up! It's what you always tell me. You, Charlie, Denny and MJ have been my strength all these years. I was ready to give up when we lost MJ, but I keep going for you all and my son. Now it's your turn to keep going even if it's just for us all to have one more party together. Do you remember the parties we had in the flat? Denny would bring the girls and we'd turn up the music and Charlie would sing and dance to Abba. That's what I think about when I'm in my cell at night. Just the good times we had.

I understand why you want to tell our story now, it's the only way but I also know the guilt you carry. Trust me, my friend, you have no reason to feel guilty, I would take this stand, this place, a thousand times again if that's what it took. If you must leave this life then you do so with a clear conscience.

Everything is in order with Dmitri, so you have no worries there. Just be careful, you know what we are up against and you're putting a lot on the girl's shoulders. Dmitri will protect her with his life, that I promise you. I hope she has the strength to carry it through, perhaps then it will end, and we'll get that chance to be together again. Just hang on a little longer.

Until we meet again,

Your friend and brother,
Boris

Dora put the letter down.
'Oh hell, what have I done?'

Chapter Twenty-Three

Back home, Dora turned over in bed and pulled the cover up to her neck. She tried to force sleep, but it wouldn't come. Her mind continued to whir with questions. If Boris didn't kill Julie, then who did? Scott North was leading the investigation so he could have tampered with the evidence. Why did Boris send Dmitri to look after me? Why not give the tapes to Dmitri, he'd be a better choice. Oh God, I pulled a gun on him, I doubt he'll talk to me again. I'd have been better off not knowing any of Eddie's past, she thought.

Dora huffed and sat up in bed grabbing her phone from the bedside table to check the time. 1.15am. I may as well get up, she thought. As she swung her legs off the bed, the phone vibrated in her hand. She looked at the screen and saw the security system had been activated, she clicked the icon and saw the kitchen window security had been breached. She held her breath listening for a noise from an intruder. Nothing but the frantic beat of her heart. The phone vibrated again making her jump. Dmitri's name flashed across the screen, she hit accept and put the phone to her ear, not daring to speak.

'Don't say anything,' Dmitri said. 'I'm on my way. Shoot if you have to, don't hesitate. Aim for the legs first.'

Dora nodded, then realised that Dmitri couldn't see her.

'Leave the line open.'

Dora grabbed the SIG from the bedside table, moved across the room and positioned herself behind the door. She laid the phone on the floor then took off the safety. She had a sudden urge to pee, the pressure on her bladder made her tense her body. She could feel the heat rise in her body and her heart beating rapidly, quickening her breath. She heard a creak on the stairs then silence before the intruder continued up. A click told her he had entered the first bedroom; he didn't stay long before moving to the next room. The pressure in her bladder increased as she heard the soft pad of footsteps approach her bedroom. The figure entered and moved towards her bed. She waited until there was a safe distance then pushed the door with one hand while holding out the gun in the other.

'Don't fucking move or I'll blow your brains out!' She flicked on the light switch.

The figure spun round, and two eyes blinked at her through peepholes in a balaclava. She could see the intruder was a man by his build. Dressed in black, he wore leather gloves and stood glaring at her.

'Put your hands on your head. I can hit a target from three hundred metres, I don't think I'll have a problem shooting off your dick.' She lowered the gun so it was pointing at his groin. 'Do it and sit on the bed.'

He raised his hands and put them to his head as he lowered himself onto the bed. 'Now what are you going to do?'

The voice sounded familiar, but she couldn't place it. 'Take off the mask.'

He didn't move.

'I said take off the mask.' She stretched out her hands, the gun pointing at his chest.

He moved one hand to his chin pushed his thumb under the material and peeled the balaclava upwards.

'You,' Dora gasped.

'Expecting someone else, were you?' DS Sims grinned. 'You're in a lot of trouble. Possession of a firearm, well actually pulling a gun on a police officer.' He tutted. 'You'll be going down for a long time. I suggest you put the gun down and give me what I want then maybe I won't have to arrest you.'

'How about I just shoot you in the head? Or maybe if you tell me why you killed Eddie and Charlie I'll let you live and just call the police and tell them what you and DI Price have been up to.'

'Price? That old fart hasn't a fucking clue. Easy for me to suggest that I look into Blue Hollow and the missing boy. Tell him that there is nothing in it. Place doesn't exist and the boy ran away from Bracken House. Nobody cares about the runaway.'

'I think they'll be interested in you breaking into my house. There will have to be an investigation. I don't care how many of you are involved. I'll make so much noise that the information will get to the right people.'

'I was just passing by. I was worried about you so I thought I would make sure everything was okay. When I didn't get an answer I went around the back and saw the broken window. I had to come in to help, no time to call for backup. I found you in the bedroom hysterical. I must have frightened the intruder and you pulled a gun on me.'

'Yeah and how do you explain the balaclava?'

'Oh I can make that disappear, it wouldn't even make it to the evidence log.'

'Then I best go for option one, shoot you.'

'You don't have the guts.'

'You think?' Dora gently squeezed the trigger. She knew there was a slight give before it fired.

'Okay, have it your way, but if I don't kill you they will send someone else. I would've made it quick.'

'What do you want from me?'

'The tapes and the photos you took from the doctor's funeral.'

'How do you know about the tapes?'

'Eddie paid a visit to Boris. There are a few people on the inside who are only too willing to share information they overhear for a price.'

The gun was heavy in Dora's hands, her arms were aching, and she longed to lower them. She had no idea how long it would take Dmitri to get there. Her only option was to keep him talking.

'You're supposed to be a detective, solve crimes, not commit them. Help people. Why? Why would you get involved, kill Eddie and Charlie? You couldn't have been involved in Blue Hollow, you're too young.'

'Blue Hollow? You think that this has to do with some crap that happened over forty years ago? This is far bigger than you can imagine, and I know which side I would rather be on. The benefits far outweigh the risks.'

'Dora!' Dmitri's voice boomed from the bottom of the stairs.

Sims jumped off the bed.

'Don't even think about it.' She took a step back. 'Up here in the bedroom.'

Dmitri thudded up the stairs and burst through the door. 'You okay?'

Dora felt relief flood her body, she let her shoulders drop but kept the gun pointed at Sims. 'Yes, I'm good.'

'I'm impressed, excellent choice of words,' he said.

'Can't believe that all came out of my mouth.'

'So, what do we have here?' Dmitri glared at Sims.

'DS Rhys Sims. Well, just Rhys Sims. I don't think he can call himself a detective.'

Dmitri stepped closer to Sims and without warning pulled back his fist and drove it into Sims' face. 'That's for breaking into the lady's house.'

Sims staggered backwards then threw himself at Dmitri. Fists flew and they crashed into the bedside table sending the lamp crashing to the floor. Dora lowered the gun and backed against the wall afraid that they would knock into her and set the gun off. Dmitri was taller than Sims so had the advantage. He wrestled him to the floor and there was a tangle of limbs before Dmitri managed to turn Sims over and sit on his back. He put his hand in his back pocket and took out a cable tie then forced Sims' hands behind his back, securing his wrist as he bucked underneath him.

'Give me something to tie his legs,' Dmitri said.

Dora took the cord off her dressing gown that hung on the back of the door and threw it to Dmitri who tied Sims' legs together as he wriggled on the floor. Sims began to holler.

'Shut him up,' Dora said. 'He'll wake half the street.'

Dmitri flipped Sims onto his back. 'Got a pair of socks?'

'I've got some packing tape somewhere.'

'That will do,' Dmitri said. He bent over Sims, pulled him up by the collar of his jumper until their faces were inches apart. 'You're going to be begging to die by the time I've finished with you.'

'They'll hunt you down.'

'Yeah, you're boring me now.' Dmitri grabbed a pillow from the bed and covered Sims' face. 'Better get that tape.'

Dora could hear Sims' muffled protests as she left the room. She hurried downstairs and laid the gun on the kitchen counter as she searched through drawers. She didn't want to think about what Dmitri was going to do with Sims. Torture him? Kill him? She wanted no part of that. She found the tape, picked up the gun and headed back upstairs. After handing the tape to Dmitri she went to the bathroom to relieve herself then splashed cold water on her face. It helped to clear her mind.

There was silence in the bedroom when she stepped in. Sims was now on the bed with the brown tape across his mouth.

'Should we just hand him over to the police? He'd have some explaining to do coming into my house wearing a balaclava.'

'And what are you going to say about the gun?'

'We'll hide it. I'll say I heard an intruder and hit him over the head with a lamp then tied him up. You don't have to stay.'

'Right, go on then, hit him with the lamp,' Dmitri said with a grin.

'No, I can't do that. You do it.'

Sims wriggled on the bed.

'Leave him to me.' Dmitri pulled up the leg of his jeans and took a knife from a sheath.

'What are you going to do?' Dora felt sick.

'Get some answers then get rid of him. He was going to kill you. You might want to go downstairs while I work.'

'Oh no, not on my bed. Not in my house.'

'Fine, I'll take him somewhere else.' He put the knife between Sims' feet and cut the cord. 'You're going to walk out of here with no nonsense.'

Sims shook his head.

Dmitri put the barrel of the gun against Sims' forehead. 'You heard what she said, she doesn't want to get blood over her nice sheets. Now get up or I'll cut off your legs and carry you out.' He hauled Sims to his feet.

Dora followed the men downstairs and to the front door. She stepped in front of Sims and turned the key.

'Better make sure there's no one about. Shoot anything that moves.'

Dora stepped outside and walked up the path. There were no lights on in the neighbouring houses and the road was quiet. 'All clear,' she said as she reached the doorstep.

Dmitri shoved Sims in the back, and he stepped outside.

'I'm sorry,' Dora said. 'For what happened earlier. What I said.'

'Forget it,' Dmitri said.

'I read the letters your father sent—'

'We'll talk later.' He looked pointedly at Sims. 'I'll be back as soon as I can.'

Dora followed them to the gate and watched Dmitri take keys from Sims' pocket and wave them in the air as he hit the button. The lights flashed on a car four doors down. 'We'll take yours, shall we?' He marched Sims to the car, opened the boot and shoved him inside.

Dora went back inside and locked the door. Now the danger was over she felt a chill run over her body. Upstairs she grabbed a jumper and put it on over her pyjamas, then sat in the kitchen cradling a mug of hot milk and tried not to think about what Dmitri was doing to Sims. She knew she wouldn't be able to sleep despite her weariness.

She cleaned through the house trying to rid any trace of Sims. When daylight crept through the windows she showered, dressed and sat in front of the TV and waited. She was dozing when a knock at the door gave her a start. She got up and peeked through the window before opening the door.

'You could've just gone around the back to the broken window or used your keys,' Dora teased.

'Yeah and have you pull a gun on me again.' Dmitri stepped past her and walked into the kitchen. 'I'll send someone around to fix that.'

'Thanks, do you want a cup of tea or coffee?'

'Coffee would be great.' He sat down at the table.

Dora flicked the switch on the kettle and heaped a spoon of coffee into a mug. 'Did you get anything from him?'

'Yeah, some but he wouldn't give me names.'

She waited for more information, but Dmitri didn't say any more. She turned to face him. 'Did you...? Is he…? Oh, never mind, I don't want to know.' She turned back and poured boiling water into the mug.

'You want to know if I killed him?'

Dora's hand clutching the milk hovered above the mug. 'I'd rather not know the details.'

'I can't believe you think I'm a killer.'

'So he's alive.' Dora spun around.

'Mostly.' Dmitri grinned. 'I don't think he'll be coming after you again.'

'But he'll tell the police what we did.'

'I doubt it. I left him in a compromising position. He'll have a lot of explaining to do. I got rid of the car so there will be no trace back to you.'

'Thank you.' She placed the mug of coffee on the table.

Dmitri took a sip and grimaced. 'I hate this instant shit.'

'It's all I've got. I don't drink the stuff, only keep a jar for visitors.'

'That's probably why visitors to this house try to kill you.'

'Ha ha.' Dora took a seat on the opposite side of the table. 'So, what did he say? Did he tell you why he wanted the tapes and photos?'

'He said he was acting on orders.'

'Whose orders?'

Dmitri shrugged his shoulders. 'He said he just gets a message. There's no personal contact.'

'What? So he gets a message, kills someone, or gets whatever he's been asked to steal then drops it off at some location and collects his money? Doesn't sound right. He's probably too afraid to give you the name of the person he's working for; either that or you didn't do a very good job at getting the information out of him. Or you could be keeping the information you got from me.'

Dmitri raised his eyebrows. 'Trust me, he was telling the truth. Would you like me to talk you through it?'

'No, thanks, I'll take your word for it.'

'Good, there's no collection. It's not for money.'

'Then what?'

'Inclusion into the Edenites.'

'The what?' Dora rubbed her hands over her face and sighed. 'This just gets more complicated.'

'Yeah, I had to make a stop to see what I could find out. It's a secret society, a cult. Not easy to find out information. I managed to get this.' He put his hand inside his jacket and pulled out a folded piece of paper. 'Have a read of that.' He threw the paper down on the table.

Dora picked it up, unfolded it and read.

The Edenites are believed to be an ancient cult. Revived in the 1960s, its origins lie in the story of the Garden of Eden and Cain and Abel. It is believed that the serpent offered up the power of knowledge to Adam and Eve. Eve succumbed to the serpent and persuaded Adam to join her. Later, after God discovered their disobedience, Adam and Eve were expelled from the Garden and its source of power. They then turned their back on the serpent.

The Garden and the source of power lay undisturbed for many years until the serpent chose a new leader. Cain the first-born human worked the soil. He was strong and offered to God, yet God favoured his brother Abel's offerings, which enraged Cain. The serpent spoke to Cain, offering him the power of knowledge, and all the fruits of his heart's desire. In order to receive 'The Mark' that would make him unique and place him above all other men he was to make a blood of blood sacrifice. Cain murdered his brother and received 'The Mark'.

It is believed that Cain was given access to the Garden of Eden where he could enjoy all the fruits and pleasures it had to offer. He gathered others to join his circle, chose those who were worthy. The mantle then was passed down, the next chosen one would have to prove himself by performing the sacrifice and then would become Brother of Cain, and rule over the Edenites. The garden became a place where they could carry out their rituals and enjoy their degraded tastes.

'This sounds like something that happened hundreds of years ago, if it happened at all. Are you saying that Rhys Sims believes that he is acting on behalf of some ancient cult?'

'Yeah.'

'He told you he was a member?'

'Yes, with some persuasion, and I did a little research. This is not the sort of information you find on Google.'

'You mean the dark web?'

'Been on there, have you?' Dmitri laughed. 'I didn't find out much. I'm going to need more time and use some other methods. There are some unsavoury individuals who are desperate to belong to the Edenites so there are some theories on who they are, what they do, and how to get in.'

'But these are just theories?'

'Yes, but they have to originate from somewhere. Maybe someone bragging about being a part of the cult. It sounds like the Edenites were revived in the sixties. It was a watered-down version of the original, but their power grew along with their immoral taste. I think that Graham North was the leader, Brother of Cain or whatever you want to call him. It would make sense – outwardly a pillar of the community, well liked and respected. He carried out a lot of charity work and was elevated to a high position in the police force. In his private life he was a sick fuck.'

Dora shook her head. 'You were doing good so far, but you had to slip in an F-word.'

'You didn't do so bad yourself with Sims. I think some of my charm must be rubbing off on you.'

'Or you've broken me. So, what you're saying is a bunch of men revived some ancient cult for an excuse to carry out their perverted acts. They're just a group of paedophiles, sick men.'

'It's also about power, carrying out rituals and trying to summon dark forces or Satan himself. Think about the Bible story. Adam and Eve were forbidden to eat from the tree of knowledge of good and evil. The Edenites believe that partaking in these rituals will give them the power over other men. Graham North would've been seen as a powerful successful man. This would only have fuelled the idea that he was rewarded in some way. Face it, there are those who would be happy to carry out acts of perversion. It's not any different than it was hundreds of years ago, in fact it's probably worse. We're surrounded by sex, drugs, and violence. You can get free porn on your phone and watch it wherever you like. Drugs are easy to come by and kids take guns into schools and kill their classmates. It's the world we now live in and you become desensitized. These men want more, a way to carry out their fantasies, and for that they will remain loyal to the group and their leader.'

'There must be a way to find out who is in the group. We have names from Graham North's time, and it sounds like his son, Scott, is part of the group and he was the Detective Sergeant working on Julie's murder,' Dora said.

'It's not going to be easy to find those involved now. I've no idea how big the group is, it could be spread out all over the country, maybe even spread to other countries. They're very careful with communication. It used to be done with a letter which was burned as soon as it was read. I doubt now they would use regular forms of electronic communication. If they do, it will be the dark web and not easy to trace.'

'They can't be completely invisible or those who want to join wouldn't be able to find them.'

'You can't join them, you are chosen and invited. Originally there was an inner circle and outer circle. Only the most influential got chosen for the inner circle. Those in the outer circle were chosen for their usefulness. It could be anyone,' Dmitri said.

'Do you think Blue Hollow was a base for their activities?'

'It does sound like they were carrying out some sort of rituals in the church. Eddie mentioned symbols and chanting.'

'So, all this is about keeping the group a secret. Charlie and Eddie must've had information or something on them. Some evidence to go with the names.'

'Yes but I don't think they knew what they were up against. They wouldn't have been able to get the information back then. I can't see Eddie or Charlie being able to access the dark web.'

'Eddie didn't own a computer. He was paranoid that it could be hacked. I doubt he'd have the technical skills to do that sort of research.'

'No, but they knew enough. They had something that would link those men to Blue Hollow, possibly link Scott North to the Edenites.'

Iosif. Dora shifted in her chair. Adam was right, she thought, it's not easy to tell what happened, to inflict that much pain on another, but he deserved to know.

'When I met with Adam he told me things, things that he had never spoken about. He saw what happened to Iosif the night he went missing.'

'Don't.' Dmitri held up a hand. 'If you know what happened to Iosif then my father should be the one you tell. He spent all of his life searching for answers.'

'I don't think I can.'

'I thought you believed that he isn't a deranged child killer after reading Eddie's letters.'

'I do, it's just I'm not sure I could tell him what happened. It might be better coming from you. It's going to be hard enough repeating what Adam told me. Does he really need to know the details?'

'Yes, he does need to know. Please go and see him. He's waiting for you.'

'Will you come with me?'

'Yeah, you don't think I would let you go alone. Even as a visitor it's quite an eye-opener.' Dmitri stood up. 'I've gotta go. I'll make the arrangements, meanwhile I'll get Dray to come and stay a few days to keep you company.'

After the night's events Dora didn't object.

Chapter Twenty-Four

Scott pulled his coat around his body as he took a seat and looked around the caravan with distaste. Kyle had brought a bottle of whisky and was pouring it into three cheap glasses.

'What are we going to do about Sims?' Kyle handed a glass to Scott.

'Nothing, he fucked up, so he pays the price. He knows the rules.' Scott took a gulp of whisky. 'If you're going to arrange a meeting in this shithole then the least you could do is bring a decent bottle of Scotch.'

'I thought it best we meet here, no one around to see us. It belongs to my aunt,' Kyle said.

'Yeah, it smells like she died in here,' Nate said with a grin.

'I think we should do something about Sims,' Kyle said. 'He's been useful, could still be useful. It's not his fault the bitch pulled a gun on him. He swears he didn't give her any information.'

'I don't give a fuck.' Scott downed the whisky and shook his glass for another. 'Who do you think you are, questioning my decisions? Just because I've trusted you with this doesn't make you my equal.'

'No, I'm only making suggestions. There's been talk among those in the inner circle of the way things have been handled. Eddie Flint and Charlie Briar's demise was seen as a positive move; however, attempts on the woman's life have been met with disapproval.'

'Disapproval.' Scott felt his blood pressure rise, anger spiked his skin. 'Did I not make it clear what is at stake?'

'Yes, but they don't know the reason, and our code has always been the sacrifice of the worthless in order to attain our goal. This woman has no criminal record, she is not a drain on the economy, and is someone who would be missed. Questions would be asked.'

'She's a threat to us and so is anyone who disagrees with my decisions. You better make that clear. Have you got anything to add, Nate?'

'No, only to tell you that she has applied for a visiting order. Do you think she knows?'

'Well if she doesn't, she soon will after speaking to Boris. Kyle you need to get rid of all the original evidence before she stirs things up.'

'I can't, he has filed for an appeal and the evidence has been moved to an independent examiner.'

'Then you better find it fast. All it takes is one bloody hair. Look at the technology they have now. We didn't have to be so careful back then.'

'What about Blue Hollow?' Nate asked. 'Shouldn't we be concentrating our efforts there?'

'There's nothing there.'

'But your father—'

'Don't you dare.' Scott glared at Nate.

'I'm only saying, you know as well as I do what happened there.'

'What are you going to do about it? Thinking of going there yourself and clearing up?'

'No, that would be foolish.'

'We can't have any connection to Blue Hollow, it's too risky to send anyone there now. Best leave it lie.'

'So, what are we going to do?' Nate asked.

'Follow her. Boris will tell her where it's buried. She'll check it out first before she acts. Once she shows us where it is, kill her and do it properly. I want you to do it yourself, Kyle.'

'What? No.'

'If you're going to be a pussy, bring her to me and I'll do it.'

'Wouldn't it be better to deal with Boris before she gets a chance to speak to him?' Nate said.

'We can't get to him. All this prisoner welfare and rights crap. He's high-security. Too many eyes and the last inmate who tried ended up in intensive care.'

'So we just wait,' Kyle said.

'Yeah, wait and watch. In the meantime, I want to see Dmitri Orlov strung up and gutted. It's about time Boris had some payback.'

Chapter Twenty-Five

The prison walls loomed before them. Dora walked beside Dmitri as her eyes travelled the height of the walls and rested on the wire that curved inwards on the top.

'See what you mean by maximum security, there's no chance of climbing over them.'

'No chance of getting near them. The prisoners are locked up most of the day. Caged liked animals,' Dmitri said.

'Well I guess the majority of them are very dangerous. There has to be punishment.'

'And I suppose you would be in favour of bringing back hanging. In which case my father would have been dead long ago,' Dmitri snapped.

'Have you visited your father a lot?'

'Smooth change of subject.' Dmitri smiled. 'Yeah, I try to visit as often as I can. He's been moved around a bit but seemed to settle here. They mostly leave him alone.'

'It must have been difficult for you growing up with your father in prison.'

'I didn't see him when I was younger. My mother didn't want anything to do with him, she cut all connections, including me. If it wasn't for Charlie I would've ended up in a children's home. Charlie sent MJ and Denny to Russia to try to track down my family. Can you imagine those two on a road trip?'

'My father never mentioned he'd been to Russia.'

'I guess it wasn't a holiday and/or an easy trip. Charlie and Eddie couldn't go because of their prison record. It would've been too risky. It turned out that my father's family didn't know that he had been placed in a home with Iosif. There was no contact and it seems my grandfather left Russia under a cloud. I never got to the bottom of it. Anyway, I went to live in Russia with my great aunt. I didn't fit in, a new boy in school with a strange accent who couldn't speak Russian. I did pick up the language, but I never settled down. By the time I hit puberty I was a nightmare, so I was sent back to Charlie. Charlie was living in London at the time so he thought the best place was the countryside where I couldn't get up to too much mischief. I lived with Ben, helped out on the shooting range. Charlie and Eddie visited often. I was a very mixed-up moody teenager.'

'It explains a lot.'

'What do you mean?'

'Well, you're still moody.'

'No, I'm not. I just have one of those faces where you can't see that I'm smiling inside.'

'If you say so.' Dora laughed.

'So, Charlie and Eddie straightened me out, but I still wanted answers. No one spoke about the children's home or the murder. As for my uncle Iosif I was just told he was missing. Over the years I began to learn more as they revealed bits of information. I thought I understood why they stuck by my father despite what he had done but it was much later that I started to believe that he was innocent. I started to visit him and trust him. He told me more of what had happened to them in the children's home and that he had been set up. He wouldn't speak about what happened the night Julie and her daughter were killed. It was obvious that he was protecting someone, but I didn't know who or why. The others would say no more on the subject.'

'But you know now who killed Julie and her daughter?'

'Yes but that's my father's story to tell. My part is to help you uncover the truth and to keep you safe.'

'And you couldn't just have told me all this at the start.'

'No, we've been through this before. You'd never understand without hearing the whole story. Look how many times you have jumped to the wrong conclusion. You thought my father had Eddie and Charlie killed for his share of the money.'

'It made sense at the time.'

'Well, just for you to be sure, all Dad's share of the money was transferred to me. They shared every penny equally.'

'So are you telling me you know everything?'

'No, I have an idea what Eddie and Charlie were hiding but I'm not certain. At the moment I am working on getting my father an appeal, having the evidence re-examined.'

'And whatever I uncover from Eddie's tapes will help.'

'I'm hoping so, yes.' They stopped outside the gates. 'Are you sure you're ready for this?'

'No, but let's get this over with.'

They went through security and were given a locker for all their personal possessions. They were then searched again before being led to a waiting room. Dora took a seat and looked at the other visitors. An older couple sat together talking quietly, she guessed them to be visiting a son. A woman dressed provocatively sat picking at her nails. The room felt warm and claustrophobic with the doors locked. Dora tried not to think about what would happen if there was a riot. She fidgeted in her seat, her unease growing.

'You okay?' Dmitri whispered.

'Yeah, this place is depressing. I feel like I've been locked away from the civilised world.'

'It's only the waiting room,' Dmitri scoffed. 'Just think yourself lucky you get to leave.'

The door opened and they were called in to a larger room where rows of plastic chairs and tables were bolted to the floor. Prison officers were positioned around the room, their faces expressionless, their eyes alert as they swept the area. Dora took a seat next to Dmitri and watched as the prisoners came in one by one and took a seat at the table. They all looked intimidating and she could feel the perspiration gathering on her back.

Boris was the last to walk in and Dora felt her breath catch in the back of her throat as he approached their table. He was tall and broad with thick muscular arms, but it wasn't the size of him that made her shrink back in her seat. The left side of his face looked like a waxwork dummy that had been melted in a fire. The skin was pink, shiny, and puckered. The eyelid drooped covering half his eye. Dmitri stood and the two men embraced, one of the prison officers stepped forward but Boris gave him a scathing look and he retreated back to his position.

'Not this table,' Boris said. He walked to a table in the centre of the room, nodded at the men each side and shuffled into the seat.

Dora stood and looked at the prison officer who nodded and she followed Dmitri to the table taking her seat opposite Boris. He stared at her for a few moments making her feel uncomfortable. Then he smiled.

'I'm so pleased you came. I've been looking forward to meeting you.' He rested his hands on the table. 'You look so much like your mother.'

'Oh, erm…' Dora tried to think of something to say. 'You were best man at Mum and Dad's wedding, I saw the photos. Uncle Eddie had loads from when you were all younger. I came across them when I was sorting through his things.' She became aware that she was babbling and stopped speaking.

'A long time ago, before this.' Boris pointed at his face. 'It's what they do to child killers. Boiling sugar water. I guess it makes me look like the monster everyone thinks I am.'

'Not everyone,' Dmitri said. 'It gives you a don't-fuck-with-me look.'

'Yeah.' Boris laughed. 'It certainly does. You should've warned her. I thought she was going to piss herself when I walked in.'

'Nah, it's more fun this way.'

Boris looked at Dora. 'You can relax, you have nothing to fear from me. I'm sorry we have to meet here. It must be quite an experience for you.'

'Just a bit.' Dora smiled.

'And you haven't had an easy time of it. Losing your father, now Eddie and Charlie. I wish you didn't have to be dragged into this mess.'

Dora was surprised by his genuine concern. 'It must be really difficult for you. I know how close you all were.'

'Yeah, I'm going to miss them.' He looked away for a moment and when he turned his head back she could see the pain in his eyes, the struggle not to show emotion. 'We don't have a lot of time.' He leaned forward, so he was closer to Dora. 'You've listened to the tapes?'

'Only three, I was hoping you could help me find the fourth one.'

'It's hidden, Dmitri will take you there.'

He could've given me the tape, there was no need to drag me here, she thought.

'Okay.'

'Is there anything you want to ask me?'

'I read one of the letters you sent to Eddie. It was only after reading it I realized that you didn't do what you've been accused of.'

'No, I could never hurt Julie or that beautiful little girl. I loved them both.'

'Do you know why they set you up?'

'Yes, but it's too long to go into here. You never know who is listening. That's why I moved tables. I trust the men on either side of us and in the centre of the room the screws are less likely to overhear. You'll have to listen to the tape. You'll get your answers.'

'You said in your last letter to Eddie that he shouldn't feel guilty. Why would Eddie feel guilty? What did he do?'

'Nothing, he felt guilty because I'm inside and it weighed him down. There was only one thing that could've thrown doubt on the case, even proved my innocence, but to reveal it would probably cost a life. We couldn't risk it.'

'I don't understand. You mean you're all protecting someone.'

'You will understand. I'm sorry I can't say any more but I really needed you to come. I wanted to be sure that you believed in my innocence. Hopefully, you'll understand why we all did what we did at the time. It mattered to Eddie that you'll forgive him, it matters to us all. Dmitri can only do so much. The rest is up to you.'

'Why does everyone talk in riddles?' She sighed. 'I just want an end to this.'

'That's what we all want.'

'Yeah,' Dmitri agreed. 'I'll be free of this one.' He nodded his head at Dora. 'Worse job I've ever had.'

'You've not been a lot of fun to know yourself,' Dora snapped.

'He really knows how to show a woman a good time, eh?' Boris laughed and sat back in his chair. 'He didn't inherit my charm.'

'I've heard you were a hit with the women,' Dora said. 'Wild parties in the flat you all shared.'

'Yeah, they were great times.' He winked with his good eye and Dora caught a glimpse of the man he had once been.

'We're almost out of time,' Dmitri said. 'Dora has something she needs to tell you. It's not going to be easy to hear.'

'Is it about Iosif?' Boris leaned forward.

Dora felt the tension return to her body. 'Yes, I talked to Adam. He told me things that he had never been able to speak about. The night Iosif went missing.' Dora wrapped her arms around her body. She understood now why Adam could never tell him.

'It's okay,' Boris said. 'I know that he's dead. I felt that hole in my life since the night he went missing. If he was alive I would have found him, I would have felt it.'

Dora nodded. 'Adam saw the men in the church that night. They were performing some sort of ritual, they had Iosif and they—'

'Bastards!' Boris's fists slammed into the table and he bent double as though her words had slashed through his stomach.

Two prison guards rushed over to the table.

'It's okay.' Dmitri held up his hands. 'He just received some bad news. Dad?'

Boris looked up. 'It's all good here.'

The prison officers returned to their positions but kept their attention on Boris.

'I'm so sorry,' Dora said.

'How did they kill him?'

'Don't do this to yourself,' Dmitri said.

'I need to know. Please just tell me.'

'A knife.' Dora's voice trembled. 'It sounds like it was instant.'

'I knew they had done something to him.' Boris rocked in the chair. 'For a time I blamed myself. I thought

I had given him too much milk; you know they drugged us.'

'Yes,' Dora said.

'I thought perhaps he had a fit or something and they didn't get him to hospital in time or if he had been ill that night he would've been too out of it to get help.'

'Adam couldn't tell you.'

'I don't blame Adam. He was traumatised. We didn't know it at the time. He couldn't speak, even when he came back he wasn't the same. Poor kid, he must have been terrified. None of us spoke about what went on in Blue Hollow. I would never have asked Adam to tell me what he remembered from that night. It must've taken some courage for him to tell you.'

'He'd tried to put it to the back of his mind. Pretend it never happened. He eventually had a breakdown. He told me he couldn't bear to tell you what happened, couldn't cause you pain.'

'Thank you for telling me, I know it couldn't have been easy.'

'There's more, he saw the men put Iosif into the Land Rover and drive up into the mountain.'

'To the lake?'

'He thinks so, as it was winter, and the ground would've been…'

'Iosif's been in Blue Hollow all this time.' Boris rubbed his hands over his face. 'Dmitri, you have to go there, find him.'

'We will. If Iosif is there, we will find him. I promise. And we will get justice.'

'Justice?' Boris gave a bitter laugh.

'Things are different now, just hang on a little longer.'

'Just promise me if I don't get outta here you'll find him, get him out of that place and lay him to rest.'

'If I have to dive into the lake or search the whole mountain myself, I'll find him.'

An announcement was made for the visitors to leave.

'I hope we will meet again.' Boris stood.

'I'm sure we will,' Dora said.

Dmitri hugged his father and watched as Boris left the room. Outside the prison gates Dora felt the tension leave her body and gave a sigh.

'It wasn't that bad, was it?' Dmitri led the way to the car.

'I guess not, it's just... telling your father about Iosif was the worst thing I've ever had to do.'

'You said the men used a knife.'

'Yes, from what Adam described they were performing some sort of ritual.'

'A sacrifice.'

'Yes, it doesn't bear thinking about. So, what do we do now?'

'We go to Blue Hollow.'

Chapter Twenty-Six

The bleak landscape stretched for miles on either side with only the occasional weather-beaten stone farmhouse.

'Are you sure you know where you're going?' Dora asked. 'We're in the middle of nowhere. The last sign I saw was for Brecon.'

'That's why they chose the place.' Dmitri changed up gear. 'The boys would've had a rough walk staying off the road. It's amazing they didn't get lost on the mountain.'

Dora tried to imagine the boys walking in the dark, the grass frozen under their feet. Cold, hungry, and frightened. They passed a large corrugated barn and she hoped it had provided some warmth and shelter all those years ago.

'I can't believe they walked all this way.' Dora rubbed her arms as her thoughts brought a chill to her body.

'I don't like to think about it,' Dmitri said, 'but they're the bravest men I've known. I guess you will go to the limits to survive. My father was driven by his need to find his brother and all this time he was leaving him behind.'

'Do you really think they would've used Iosif for a sacrifice?'

'Yeah, from what Adam described, it sounds like it. Sick bastards, and I'm guessing Iosif wasn't the only one.'

'I don't understand how they could've got away with it. Boys just disappearing.'

'No one cared. They picked boys that didn't have a family or had a family who didn't care enough to look for them. All the boys they kept in Blue Hollow weren't missed. It wasn't a registered home and I'm guessing few knew of its existence.' Dmitri turned off the road onto a narrow track with grass growing in the centre.

'Doesn't look like anyone has been down here for a long time,' Dora commented.

'No, you need to know the location or stumble on it by accident,' Dmitri said.

'You knew where this place was all along?' Dora said.

'Yeah, it took me a while to find it. I had to piece together the location from Dad, Charlie, Eddie, and Denny. Like I said before, I couldn't overload you with information. Can you imagine if I had brought you here when we first met? You would've thought I was kidnapping you. You'd probably have died from fear.' Dmitri laughed.

'Maybe not.'

'You didn't trust me.'

'Do you blame me? You're full of secrets.'

'More than you'll ever know. If you did, you'd probably pull a gun on me again,' he said.

'That's reassuring,' Dora snapped. 'I've had it with all the secrets.' They rounded a bend and the house came into view. Her anger disappeared as she stared at the building. 'It's just as Eddie described it. I thought it would be falling down, just a shell.'

'It is inside.' Dmitri stopped the car. 'It was still used until the mid-nineties.'

'They continued to bring children here?'

'No, not children. I found a report from a woman who said she was brought here from Eastern Europe with other girls. They were held against their will, used as sex slaves. Men came to the house. She escaped but couldn't give the location of the building so those involved were never caught.'

'Trafficking?'

'Yeah, no doubt Graham North and his buddies were behind it. Do you want to take a look around?'

Dora nodded, she reached for her coat then got out of the car. The first thing that struck her was the silence – no birdsong, no rustling of leaves. There was an aura of sadness reflected in the grey sky. The clock tower still stood but the hands were missing from the clock, freezing the place in time. The top windows were barred and Dora could imagine the faces of the boys peering out.

'We can go inside, but you have to be careful.' Dmitri broke the silence.

They approached the front door which was covered in a stone archway. Dora put on her coat and pulled up the zip, but it did little to warm the chill that ran through her body. Dmitri pulled back the grill that was blocking the entrance. Behind the grill a wooden door was opened halfway, the rotting bottom resting on the floor.

'I'm surprised it isn't locked up.' Dora squeezed around the door.

'It was, I removed the lock from the grill last time I was here.'

As Dora stepped over the threshold the smell of decay tickled her nostrils. 'Who owns this place?'

'It was originally built as an asylum designed to be self-sufficient. Private water, electricity, and sewerage system. Land to produce food for the patients. Workshops for those well enough to work.'

'Sounds nice.'

'In theory,' Dmitri agreed. 'I guess reality was different. It was also used in the Second World War. I guess for men suffering from shell shock. The NHS took it over, then the council. There were plans to renovate but it was considered too costly. The council still owns it although I guess its existence is buried in a filing cabinet somewhere.'

'Someone knew about it. I'm guessing someone in the council was part of the group and suggested its use.'

'You're probably right. Men were chosen for their usefulness. This place is ideal. Out of the way, no one noticing vehicles coming and going. If the building was put up for sale, they would've had plenty of notice to clear out, especially if they had someone on the inside.'

'Sounds like the place was already in a state when the boys were kept here. Eddie described scrubbing mould off the walls.'

Dora stepped through a doorway and into a room with a bay window. Decaying curtains which looked like they would disintegrate at a touch dangled from the few remaining hooks. Parts of the wooden floor had collapsed, and the walls were blackened with mould, apart from the odd green patch of moss. There was a large open fireplace and images of Eddie and the other boys stoking the fire flooded her mind.

'Come on.' Dmitri placed his hand on the small of her back.

They looked into other rooms, some with metal beds and rotting mattresses. Dora didn't want to think about the horrors that went on in these rooms, but her imagination ran on making her shudder.

'Do you think there's anything here the police could link to the group if we persuade them to look into their activities?'

'There might be,' Dmitri said. 'It depends if there are any stains on the mattresses, the DNA could be degraded. I don't know enough about forensics but I'm looking into it for Dad's appeal. Evidence taken from Julie's house was sealed and stored. I hope that's the case. I've requested that it's re-examined. This place on the other hand has been left open to the elements and, added to that, imagine how many men have passed through here. Then there are the women that were trafficked. I don't think this place will provide the evidence needed to get justice.'

'Are all the beds still upstairs?'

'Yes, but I don't think you should go up there. The stairs are rotting, and some treads are missing. The upstairs floor is unstable.'

'I've seen enough anyway. This place gives me the creeps.'

'Wait until you see the church.'

'I don't think I want to, or is that where Eddie hid the tape?'

'Come on, you've still got a lot to see and we don't want to be hanging around here when it gets dark,' Dmitri said.

They left the main house and walked past the crumbling toilet blocks, keeping to the path that led to the church.

'You can still see some of the headstones,' Dora said as she stepped off the path and into the graveyard. She moved the long grass away from the first headstone. 'Constance Grey,' she read. 'Pretty name. Do you think she was a patient here?'

'I guess. I don't think the patients ever left.'

'That's a horrible thought. All those lost forgotten souls.' She moved to the next headstone and read, 'Henry Wright, he was only thirty-four years old.'

'Are you going to read them all?' Dmitri huffed. 'I think you're delaying going into the church.'

'Just one more, you never know.'

'Are you hoping to find a newer grave? One of the boys that were here? I don't think those bastards had the decency to give them a proper burial and mark the grave. Animals, the lot of them,' Dmitri said.

'Isadora Hale, look at this. My father named me after some poor soul buried here. Why would he do that?'

'It's probably just a coincidence.'

'How many Isadoras do you know?'

'One and that's more than enough,' Dmitri said. 'Your father may have wanted to pay tribute to some poor soul who had no one who cared for her. He had no family himself, no grandmother to name you after.'

'So he names me after someone who was likely to have been insane.'

'Very fitting, don't you think?'

Dora glared at him and moved away from the headstone.

'Look, it's usually the mother who picks the name. Your mum probably got it from some romance novel.'

'Great, I don't know which is worse.' She moved back to the path and they entered the church.

All the wooden pews had been piled up on the left side. On the right side, part of the roof had collapsed, and a pool of water shimmered on the stone floor. A branch had broken through one of the windows, its gnarled fingers reaching towards the ceiling. Below the arched windows a smooth wall ran the perimeter of the church. Every available space was decorated with words and strange symbols. Dora took out her phone and snapped pictures of the walls.

'It's Latin,' Dmitri said.

'Do you know what it means?'

'I managed to get some of it translated. The words praise Cain, the first of the Edenites.'

'It makes me feel sick.' Dora wrapped her arms around her body. 'There are still candles on the windowsills.'

'Come on, let's get out of here. I think you've seen enough.'

'But we need to find the tape. Your father said it was hidden here. I'm guessing you know where.'

'You guess correctly. First I want you to look at something.'

Dora was glad to leave the church and the evil she felt that dwelled within. She kept step with Dmitri as they followed the track that led up the mountain. The wind picked up as they climbed higher and Dora struggled to keep her hood covering her head. They crossed a wide stream jumping from stone to stone, then up around the side of the mountain and a final climb brought them to the lake.

Dark grey waters rippled in the wind against a mountain backdrop that continued to rise. A stream ran down the mounting spilling water into the lake.

'It's beautiful,' Dora said. 'I can see why the boys would want to come up here in the summer. An escape from the horrors of the house.'

'It would be beautiful if it wasn't marred by what lies beneath.'

'Do you think we can persuade the police to send in divers?'

'I don't know, it's getting the information to the right people and getting them to believe what went on here. That depends on you.' He put his hand in his pocket and pulled out a tape.

'You had it all along,' Dora accused.

'Yes, but now you're ready to listen.'

'I've got the Dictaphone in my bag, but I don't want to listen to it here. It doesn't seem right. It would be like bringing Eddie back to this place.'

'Yeah, I can see that. Come on, I'll take you home.'

Chapter Twenty-Seven

Eddie 1977

The first thing I remember after the robbery was waking up in hospital with a wrist cuffed to the bed. My other arm was in a cast. I had broken ribs and stitches in my head. A copper was posted outside my room. I asked him about Charlie, but he wouldn't give me any information. All I could do was lie there and hope that Charlie had survived the crash. The police did their best to keep the nurses away, so I was left for hours without painkillers or a bedpan. That was until a plump matron with a no-nonsense face shooed away the policeman and showed me some compassion.

It wasn't long before the detectives came, and the interrogation started. I kept my mouth shut. I had no idea how long I'd been out of it. I needed to make sure Denny and Boris had enough time to set up Alan Lloyd otherwise it wouldn't have been worth it. I didn't worry about MJ as I knew the others would take care of him. I was also banking on them to take care of Julie, she would be devastated.

The only good thing about being interrogated in the hospital was that they couldn't knock me around. That came later. I was released into police custody after two days, but not before I managed to charm the matron into telling me about Charlie. He was okay, a few broken bones and another scar to add to his collection. At the police station they knew how to inflict the most pain. I feared my ribs would never repair and I was left struggling to breathe after most sessions.

When I was sure enough time had passed, I fed them the story that Charlie and I had agreed on. I told them that Alan Lloyd had set the whole thing up and I didn't know the other gang members. We only met on the day and they were wearing masks. I told them there had been an argument over money and that's how Alan had got shot. They carried on pushing me, but I always stuck to the same story, keeping it simple. I hoped Charlie would do the same.

At the trial I pleaded guilty as did Charlie; there was no way of talking our way out of it. Alan Lloyd protested his innocence and I had to stop myself from smiling when he was found guilty. I wish the bastard had been put in the same prison as me. I never saw him again after the trial that day in court. I was also separated from Charlie.

I'd be lying if I said I wasn't shit-scared of going to prison. Armed robbery meant that I landed in a category A prison with some of the most dangerous men in Britain. When I arrived I could see them eyeing me up, a twenty-one-year-old with long hair. Some of the men's biceps were as thick as my thighs but I wasn't going to be anyone's bitch even if it meant getting myself killed.

They left me alone the first day. I guess there was some battle on who was going to get the fresh meat. On the second day I was exhausted, I hadn't slept all night not knowing what would come in the morning.

After breakfast I was walking back to my cell behind a particularly nasty-looking inmate. Two men came towards us and shanked the guy in front of me before casually walking away. Blood pooled around him and by the time the guards arrived he was dead. I was hauled to the governor's office for questioning. I told him I didn't see anything. I was put in solitary for three days. At least I felt safe there. When I still refused to give names, they roughed me up a bit and put me back on the wing. I waited for the men to come for me but when they came it was to welcome me onto the wing. It seemed my silence had bought me some friends. One of the men was Big D. He was a hulking cross-eyed giant of a man who ruled the wing. I was now under his protection although that didn't keep me safe from the screws.

Back then there was no human rights. You were doing time, and no one cared what happened to you. We were like caged animals with the screws acting as gods. They decided on a whim if you were put in solitary, got a beating, or went without food for a week. I did what I had to do to survive. I'd been used to being treated as worthless in Blue Hollow. I survived that place and I was determined to survive the next nine years.

There was some light in the dark days. Boris, MJ, and Julie would come to visit bringing news of Charlie. They smuggled in tobacco and drugs, the inside currency. Julie used to buy chocolate from the canteen, go to the toilet and swap it with an identical bar she had hidden. I'd eat the chocolate during the visiting hour as you weren't allowed to take anything back on the wing. Inside the chocolate would be a block of hash. I'd swallow it and wait for nature to take its course. It certainly increased my popularity. Boris paid off some of the screws, so I'd be given favours. Denny couldn't visit as it was too risky, but he wrote often. All these little things made my life a little more bearable. That's until they decided to move me on. They had a habit of moving prisoners. I guess it was to stop us getting too comfortable and forming bonds with the other inmates.

On the third move I was told I was going to Britain's toughest prison, filled with notorious criminals and boasting of the highest suicide rate. I'd learned a few tricks, but I was still dreading the move. I arrived expecting the worse but the first person I ran into was Charlie. I hadn't seen him for over three years. He'd gained a few more scars and his body was lean and muscular, but he greeted me with the same cheeky smile. I was glad to see that prison life hadn't dulled the mischief in his eyes. Charlie had found his place in the inmate hierarchy and I was welcomed in. It wasn't an easy stretch but with Charlie by my side I began to think we could survive the next six years. That was until MJ and Boris turned up without Julie. I could see by their faces that something was wrong as soon as I entered the visiting room. My stomach twisted as I crossed the room and took my seat next to Charlie.

'What's happened? Is Julie okay?' I could hear the fear in my own voice.

'We don't know.' Boris shook his head. 'She's missing.'

'What do you mean missing?' Charlie leaned forward.

'She went out to the shop to pick up some milk and didn't come back,' MJ said. 'We searched everywhere.'

'Was she okay when she left? Did she say anything to you? Was she worried about something?' I could feel the heat prickling my neck.

'Nothing,' MJ said. 'She was fine.'

'Her bag was found under Taff's Bridge,' Boris said. 'The police say she must've jumped into the river. They're not even searching.'

'Bastards!' I smashed my fist down on the table. A screw stepped forward.

'Keep it together,' Charlie hissed.

I held up my hands, palms facing out in a peaceful gesture and the screw returned to his position.

'She wouldn't have jumped,' MJ said. 'The police are covering something up.'

'No, they've taken her to get back at us. They…' I couldn't say it, didn't even want to think that she could be dead.

'I'll find her,' Boris said. 'I'll rip the limbs off every bastard that ever set eyes on her until I have some answers.'

I knew Boris wouldn't give up. I looked at him with his bloodshot eyes, dark circles, and stubble. I guessed he hadn't slept in days.

'We know you will,' Charlie said. 'Just be careful, I don't want you ending up in here.'

'They're finding ways of punishing us, still,' MJ said. 'We'll never be free.'

I felt useless as I sat there, knowing there was nothing I could do to help. MJ was right. We had sought revenge on those in Blue Hollow and now they were getting back at us.

'You think they've taken her to Blue Hollow?' Boris's eyes flared.

'If they still use the place,' Charlie said.

'You are going to have to go there.' I looked at MJ hating that I had to ask that of him.

'How the hell are we going to find the place?' MJ said. 'It's been years since we've been there. All I can remember is being cold, hungry and tired. Walking in the dark and staying away from the road.'

'Yeah, well someone knows how to get there,' Boris said.

Time was called for all visitors to leave. All I could do was to wait for news as worry and anger gnawed away at my stomach leaving me feeling hollow.

Next visiting time brought more bad news. MJ came alone. Boris had been on the rampage beating information out of anyone who stepped in his path. He had been caught and was doing a six-month stretch. MJ and Denny continued to search for Julie but there was no trace. I wanted to hold on to the hope that she was still alive but being locked up gives you too much time to think. I was my own worst enemy. I imagined they had killed her and thrown her body in the river. That was the best scenario my mind could come up with. The rest of the time I was plagued by images of her being held and tortured. I picked fights with the other inmates just to get rid of my frustration. The physical pain helped to numb my mind. I think I would've got myself killed if it wasn't for Charlie.

A week before Boris was due to be released I got an unexpected visitor. I was called to the medical wing. I had no idea what they wanted me there for. I wasn't sick, so I was already suspicious. I was shoved into a room by a screw. The minute I saw the man standing by the window I was transported back to Blue Hollow.

'Thank you,' Dr Ray said to the screw who nodded and left the room.

Fear was overridden by anger which boiled in my belly and threatened to burst out of my chest. I was ready to beat the life out of this man who had left us to the mercy of those monsters in Blue Hollow, the man who could've put a stop to the endless torment.

Dr Ray sensed my anger and took a step back. He held up his hands. 'Please, Eddie. I'm here to help you.'

'Help me,' I spat. I charged at him pinning him against the wall with my hand around his throat. I could've killed him easily, but I wanted him to suffer.

'It's about Julie,' he croaked.

I loosened my grip, just enough to let him get his words out.

'I know where she is.' He put his hand on my wrist. 'We don't have a lot of time. I need you to calm down and listen to me.'

I released my grip. 'Why should I listen to anything you have to say?'

'Because if you don't, Julie will die. I'm so sorry there was nothing I could do to help you boys. The men involved in Blue Hollow are powerful and dangerous. They would've killed me.' His words tumbled out.

'So you just left us there, and how many more?'

'You don't understand. I have a family, they would've got to my children. I never hurt you or the others.'

'No, you just let it happen. I don't give a fuck about your excuses. You have three seconds to tell me where Julie is.'

'Graham North and his son, Scott, have her.'

I took a step back. 'They've taken her to get back at me. It's because we took a couple of the group down.'

'No, it's more than that.' Dr Ray took a hankie from his pocket and wiped his brow. 'I told them I didn't want any part of it. I couldn't stand by and see another innocent life taken.'

Fear prickled my skin. 'They're going to kill her.'

'Not yet, but there isn't much time. They plan on making a blood of blood sacrifice.'

'What the fuck are you talking about?'

'I don't have time to explain it all. They're holding Julie in Blue Hollow. You have to get her out of there.'

'And how am I supposed to do that? Are you gonna break me outta here?'

'You know I can't do that, but you can arrange something. I know you have some good friends out there, friends that will help you.'

'You're still gonna have to help. We don't know how to get to Blue Hollow. We were just kids when we left.'

'I can't, they'd know it was me. You don't know what these people are capable of.'

'Oh, I think I do.' I could feel the anger pulsating through my body. My hands shook as I struggled to control my emotions.

The doctor could sense I was about to lose it and moved quickly to the door. He flung it open with a look of relief on his face. 'All done in here,' he said to the screw.

I went quietly, a stretch in solitary wasn't going to help Julie. As soon as Boris was released he came to visit with MJ. I filled them in on the doc's visit and they came up with a plan. I'll never forget what Boris, MJ, and Denny did for Julie. What it took them to go back to that hell. I couldn't help them so all I can do is tell you their bit of the story as they told me.

Chapter Twenty-Eight

They had no idea where to start. All three had spent days skipping work to drive around trying to find Blue Hollow or some landmark that would jolt their memory. Boris was getting increasingly frustrated and MJ worried he would end up doing another stretch in prison if he didn't calm down. It was Denny that came up with the idea of finding Dr Ray. It didn't take them long to find his workplace and follow him home, then they watched and waited for an opportunity.

The doc was leaving for work when Boris grabbed him and bundled him into the car. They drove him back to the flat and tied him to a chair.

'Please don't hurt me,' Ray begged. 'I have children and I was kind to you boys. I couldn't help you, I would have if–'

'Shut the fuck up.' Boris smacked him across the face. 'I'm not interested. You're going to take us to Blue Hollow.'

'No, please.' Droplets of sweat ran down the doctor's face. 'They'll kill me.'

'If you don't then I'll cut off your balls and post them to your wife,' Boris growled.

'He's not joking,' MJ said. 'You have to take us there.'

'Just show us the way, we'll do the rest,' Denny said.

'Yeah, we'll make a good job of making it look like you had no choice.' Boris smirked. 'MJ, Denny, go get his car.'

'What for?' Denny asked.

'They won't suspect anything if the doc's car turns up.'

'Good thinking,' MJ agreed.

By nightfall they had terrified the doctor into helping them. The doctor drove with MJ and Denny lying in the back. Boris had folded himself double in the front.

'I feel sick,' MJ said.

'We'll be there soon,' Denny said. 'If it makes you feel any better, I can't feel my legs.'

'It's not the car, it's going back.'

'I know, mate, I feel the same,' Denny said.

'Yeah and this time we're not little boys,' Boris said from the front. 'Don't worry, I'll kill anyone who comes near you.'

'There are no other cars here,' the doctor said as he brought the car to a stop.

'So, who's in there?' Boris asked.

'Probably just Reg.'

'That bastard,' Boris said. 'You get the door open and we'll be right behind.' Boris gave the doctor a shove. 'Don't think of trying anything, there are three of us and only two of you.'

'I told you I will help, you just have to make it look like I had no choice,' Ray said.

'No problem,' Boris said with a grin.

As soon as the doctor got out of the car, the front door opened.

'What are you doing here?' Reg's voice boomed in the darkness.

'Come to check on the girl.'

'You're not supposed to be here until Friday,' Reg grunted.

'Yes, but it's the wife's birthday. Couldn't get away without it looking suspicious.'

The voices faded as they walked indoors.

'Come on,' Boris said as he flung open the door.

'Oh fuck, my legs are dead,' Denny complained.

'Just move,' Boris hissed.

Boris hurtled towards the door and crashed through with MJ and Denny close behind. Reg was halfway up the stairs with the doctor. He span around looking wildly from one to the other.

'Hello, Reg, do you remember us?' Boris said.

Reg took two steps at a time and launched himself at Boris. Boris was ready, he moved at the last second and caught Reg as he stumbled, spun him and drove his fist into his face. What power Reg held over Boris as a boy was gone and Boris laid into him until Reg was on the floor.

'Go and find Julie while I take care of this piece of shit.' Boris aimed a kick at Reg's ribs.

'I don't have the keys,' the doctor squealed.

Boris grabbed Reg by the collar and pulled his face close to his. 'Keys,' he snarled.

'Hanging in the kitchen,' Reg spluttered as blood ran from his mouth.

MJ ran and retrieved a bunch of keys from the kitchen.

'Move.' Denny pushed the doctor and they followed him up the stairs and to the end of the corridor. MJ tried three keys in the lock before he got the right one. He took the padlock off and opened the door.

'Julie!' MJ called as he felt around for a light switch. A whimper came from the corner of the room.

'Julie, it's MJ and Denny. We've come to take you home.' His fingers hit the switch and he gasped as he took in the scene.

'Bastards,' Denny hissed from behind.

Julie was sat on a bed, her knees drawn up as far as her protruding belly would allow. A chain was locked around her ankle, its end bolted to the floor. Her long hair clung to her head, her eyes wild in a pale face.

MJ moved forward and nearly knocked over a bucket that had been used as a makeshift toilet, its contents almost reaching the brim. He perched on the bed next to her and pulled her into his arms.

'It's okay, you're safe now,' he soothed as he rocked her back and forth. 'What have those bastards done to you? Get the chain off her leg.' His voice cracked with emotion.

Denny gave the doc a shove.

The doctor removed the chain all the while not looking at Julie.

'Can you walk?' MJ asked.

Julie nodded.

Denny picked up the blanket and wrapped it around Julie's shoulders. 'Take her to the car. I'll deal with this one.' He glared at the doc who refused to meet his gaze.

MJ gently led Julie down the stairs. When Boris saw the state of her he lost it completely. MJ didn't hang around. He settled Julie in the car and waited.

Boris dragged Reg to the shed, there he put his balls into a vice and increased the pressure until Reg passed out from the pain. Denny roughed the doctor up and chained him to the bed.

After they told me the story we sat in silence for a few moments. I was relieved that Julie was safe, but it didn't stop the anger and pain I felt.

'How is Julie?' I knew it was a stupid question, but I had to ask.

'Not so good,' Boris said. 'She's eating a little now, but she won't leave the house and is terrified of being left alone.'

'And what about the…' I couldn't bring myself to say it.

'I don't think it will be long before she has the baby,' MJ said.

'Did she tell you what happened?' Charlie asked.

'They grabbed her on the way to the shop. They must've been watching her for a while. They took her to Blue Hollow and Graham North turned up with his son, Scott. You remember him?'

'That little prick, yeah.' Charlie frowned.

'From the little bits she told me it seems Scott raped her repeatedly until she got pregnant. They wanted the baby.' Boris's fist clenched.

'Why?'

'The doctor said it was for some sick ritual,' Denny said.

'He was talking about some sacrifice when he came to see me.' I felt sick.

'Don't worry, I'll get Scott,' Boris snarled.

'He's a copper now,' MJ said.

'Don't give a fuck,' Boris said.

'Don't do anything stupid,' I said. 'Julie needs you now.'

'I'll wait,' Boris said. 'Until you two come out.'

The next visit they told me that Julie had her baby. A little girl; she named her Stephanie.

Chapter Twenty-Nine

Rain lashed against the kitchen window as Dora sat staring at the Dictaphone. Eddie had stopped speaking and the tape whirred with the odd crackle.

'Is that it?' Dora asked. 'Is that what Eddie wanted to tell me, that Scott North was the father of Julie's child?'

'It's not something he or his father would want known. It's a connection to Blue Hollow and their sick cult.' Dmitri stood. 'Have you got anything to drink in this house?'

'There's some brandy and port in Gary's study, help yourself.'

'I guess that will have to do.'

'Why the big secret? Why keep quiet about it all this time? Julie and her daughter are dead. Too late to keep them safe.' Dora followed Dmitri into the study.

'Who would listen to them? Nearly all of them had criminal records. Dad was already fitted up for the murder.' Dmitri poured a glass of brandy and took a swig.

'Yeah, but the child's blood was found at the scene. That could've been used to back up their story.'

'DNA was fairly new then. Scott North was one of the officers on the scene and Graham North was in a position to protect his son. They probably tampered with the evidence. I'm hoping when the evidence is re-tested for the appeal there will be traces of who was there that night, but I don't hold out much hope. We need names. We need to know who killed them. Did Graham North send someone to do his work or did Scott take care of things himself?'

'So we need to know what happened that night. The doctor said they wanted the baby for some ritual.'

'Yeah, remember that info I got on the Edenites. Cain was the first, he killed his brother, a blood of blood sacrifice. They wanted the child so they could do the same thing.'

'That's sick. So, do you think Eddie knows what they did with the child? Maybe she didn't die there. Maybe they took her to Blue Hollow to perform the ritual. Poor little girl, she must have been terrified, seeing her mother killed and then…' Dora felt her throat constrict.

'Don't think about it.' Dmitri touched her arm. 'You'll drive yourself insane.'

'Why did Eddie wait so long to tell me this?'

'I don't know. He was dying so I guess he didn't want to go to the grave without the truth being told.'

'We have to get the last tape. You've been one step ahead all along so I'm guessing you know where the last one is.'

'I don't. I promise you.'

'So, what do we do now?'

'I think you should get some sleep.'

'I don't think I could.'

'I'll stay.'

'There is no need.' Dora bristled.

'I'm not offering to fuck you. I'll sleep on the sofa.'

Dora opened her mouth and closed it again.

'You'll sleep better if you know there's someone here to look out for you.' Dmitri gulped down the remainder of the brandy.

'There are two spare rooms,' Dora said.

'I don't think your daughters will appreciate some strange man sleeping in their bed,' Dmitri said.

A horrible thought struck Dora and a pain stabbed at her stomach. 'You don't think they'll go after the girls, do you?'

'No, too much of a risk. They can't use them as a threat as they have no way of communicating with you. I've had someone to take a look around. They're safe. Don't worry.'

'But they'll be home for Christmas.'

'We'll worry about that when the time comes. You can always spend Christmas with Ben.'

'And how would I explain that to them?'

'Tell them you've got a new man.'

'I'm a married woman.'

'Only on paper. The sooner you get rid of that wank maggot the better. You're an attractive woman, time you moved on with your life and had some fun.'

Dora felt her skin tingle at his compliment. 'Right, erm, I'll get you a blanket.'

She pulled a blanket from the airing cupboard and placed it on the sofa before saying goodnight. Upstairs in the darkness she wriggled around the bed trying to get comfortable all the while aware that Dmitri lay in the room below.

Her dreams were filled with images of young boys huddled in a barn trying to stay warm and of her being trapped in Blue Hollow and calling for her father. She awoke feeling as tired as she had when she got into bed. The smell of cooking drifted into her room, so she put on a dressing gown and quickly brushed her teeth before going downstairs.

Dmitri was in the kitchen, stirring a saucepan with a wooden spoon.

'Morning.' He turned to look at her. 'I've made some scrambled eggs. Not much else in the fridge.'

'Well, I haven't exactly had the time to go shopping and worry about what to give a house guest for breakfast.' She grabbed a mug from the tree and threw in a teabag.

'And what were you planning on feeding yourself?'

Dora shrugged. 'I seem to have lost my appetite.'

'That won't do you any good. I've made enough for the two of us. Sit down and have a bit to eat.' Dmitri took a swig from the coffee he'd placed next to the cooker. 'You need some decent coffee in this house.'

'I told you, I don't drink the stuff.' Dora stirred her tea. 'I just keep a jar for visitors.'

'Which has been here since the nineties by the look of it,' Dmitri said.

Dora sat down at the kitchen table and watched as Dmitri served up the breakfast. He placed the food in front of her.

'Eat up.' He grabbed his plate and took a seat opposite.

'Thanks.' She took a mouthful of food. It tasted good. She gobbled down the eggs and toast. 'So, what now?' she asked.

'I'll start tracking down as many boys that were at Blue Hollow that I can find. See how many are willing to be witnesses.'

'Adam said he would.'

'Good, then there's Ben and Denny. It's a start but not enough.'

'So, I'll type up the tapes, send them to the police, the newspapers, post on social media, anyone that will listen.'

'You think that'll stop them? For a start it's going to be difficult to get anyone to believe that there is a cult operating in the UK, let alone one that has its heart in Wales.'

'But with Eddie's account and the pictures of the church in Blue Hollow, that has to be enough to at least get some interest. Maybe pressure the police to drag the lake and look into your father's case.'

'They're careful. Most of them will go to ground, then set up again. We need names.'

'We have some of the names of those involved, at least in the late sixties and seventies. Then there's Scott North. You said there was an inner and outer circle. I'm betting Scott is at the head, so we go for those at the top and bring them down.'

'Bring them down?' Dmitri laughed. 'It's not like they have a base that you can blow up.'

'That's not what I meant,' Dora snapped. 'You could break into Scott North's house. Find information. Hack his computer.'

'I can't believe you are asking me to do that. Miss Prim and Proper who's never broken the law.'

'I think I'm past that now. I pointed a gun at a police officer.'

'That doesn't count, the guy was scum, and anyway, is that who you think I am? Someone who breaks into people's houses?'

'I don't know,' Dora said. 'I haven't a clue what you get up to. You're full of secrets.'

'Look, it isn't a problem to hack his computer. I don't need to break in to do that, but these people don't send polite e-mails to each other.'

'No, I guess not.'

'We need the last tape. We need to know who killed Julie.'

'We could just ask your father.'

'I imagine there's something on that tape that will give us the evidence we need. Dad won't speak of that night. Think – who would Eddie trust enough to leave the tape with?'

'I don't know. Adam didn't have one and he trusted him. There are five tapes. The one Eddie gave me, Charlie's tape, Denny's, and your dad's. The only other person he would have trusted is my father.'

'Where is he buried?'

'He was cremated. Unless… no.'

'Unless what?'

'Unless he left one with my mother, but I can't see it. She would've said something.'

'She could've been waiting for you to find the other tapes first.'

'No, she was against the idea of me looking. She wanted me to forget about it.'

'There's only one way to find out.' Dmitri stood. 'Come on, we'll ask her.'

'We just can't barge into my mother's house and ask if Eddie gave her a tape. Anyway, she won't be home. I'll go later on my own.'

'Fine, I'll leave it to you. I'll make a start tracking down the Blue Hollow boys.'

'I'll get the tapes transcribed. I'll let you know if I get a tape from Mum.'

'Take your gun.'

'To my mother's? Are you mad?'

'Just do it. I doubt if they'll try anything but it's better to be safe. The house is secure here, but you need to be able to protect yourself when you're out. I'll see you later.'

With Dmitri gone the house felt empty.

By late afternoon she had transcribed the tapes and added the photos she had taken at Blue Hollow. The four tapes were now on a memory stick which she attached to a necklace and hung around her neck before leaving for her mother's house.

* * *

Jenny was stood at the ironing board pressing pillowcases when Dora arrived.

'You should lock your door,' Dora said.

'I do at night.'

'Do it in the day. Please, after what happened to Eddie you need to be careful.'

Horace meandered into the kitchen and rubbed against Dora's legs. She bent down and stroked the cat. 'Has he been okay?'

'No problem. Have you come to pick him up?'

'Yes, the house is quiet without him.'

'I imagine it is. I've been enjoying his company myself.' Jenny smiled. 'You shouldn't be on your own. Maybe it's about time you moved on. Go on some dates. There are plenty of dating apps you can use. Go and have some fun.'

'I think they are for young people.'

'You're not old, Dora.'

'I think I'll give it a miss. You're the second person that's suggested I need a new man.'

'You don't want to be on your own for the rest of your life.'

'You're on your own.'

'That's different. I am too old to start again, and I had a good marriage. No one could take your father's place.'

'No,' Dora agreed. She perched on a kitchen chair. 'I've got the other tapes that Eddie made, all except one.'

'Oh.' Jenny took a sheet from the basket and placed it over the ironing board.

'I need to find the last tape.'

'Haven't you heard enough?' Jenny dragged the iron roughly across the sheet. 'You need to let it go.'

'I can't.'

'Eddie and Charlie are dead. I couldn't bear it if something happened to you. They've already tried to get to you. Please, Dora. Hand what you have to the police and walk away.'

'These people are going to come after me whether I hear the last tape or not, and it's no use handing it over to the police, they can't be trusted. I think there's something on the last tape that will give me the evidence I need. Something that can't be ignored. I met Boris, I know he

266

was best man at your wedding and one of Dad's best friends.'

'Yes.' Jenny folded the sheet and placed it on the stack of laundry. 'But that was a long time ago.'

'His son is helping me.'

'I don't think you should be involved with someone like him.'

'Like him?' Dora said. 'You mean someone like Dad? He robbed the bank with the others.'

Jenny slammed down the iron. 'Don't you dare compare your father to the others. Your father idolised Boris, he would have done anything for him.'

'You must know that Boris didn't kill Julie and her little girl. He's been rotting in prison for over thirty years.'

'He was always too hot-headed. If he kept his head down and served his time quietly he could've been up for parole. He took a prison guard hostage and caused a riot and nearly beat to death another prisoner.'

'He was given two life sentences for a crime he didn't commit. It's no wonder he went a little crazy. You should see what they've done to him.'

'There is nothing you can do for Boris.' Jenny sighed.

'There might be if I can find out what happened that night. There were only four people Eddie trusted enough to keep the tapes safe. Dad was one of those people. Did Eddie tell you where he hid the last tape?'

Jenny chewed her bottom lip and looked away.

'Mum, please, if you know where the last tape is, you have to tell me. Eddie wanted me to hear that tape.'

Jenny sighed. 'He left it with me.'

'You had it all the time!' Dora thought of the conversations she had with her mother since Eddie died. How she had tried to persuade her not to go after the tapes.

Anger fizzled in her stomach. 'You could've given it to me when Eddie died. You know what's on the tape, don't you? All this time you could've told me. Could have stopped me going to London, getting stabbed in the side, threatened and…' Dora shook her head.

'I never wanted you to hear the tape. I thought you'd give up. I begged Eddie not to involve you.' She fled from the room.

'Mum!' Dora stood and followed. She heard her mother's footsteps on the stairs. 'Are you just going to lock yourself in your bedroom?' As Dora started up the stairs her mother appeared on the landing, a tape held in her hand.

'Here.' She thrust the tape at Dora. 'Take it but listen to it at home. I don't want to hear it.' A tear trickled down Jenny's cheek. 'I'm so sorry. Please don't hate your father, he was a good man.'

Dora took the tape, put Horace in his basket and drove home. In the kitchen the tape sat on the table. Dora stared at it afraid to listen.

She made a cup of tea, sat at the table and slid the tape into the machine.

Chapter Thirty

Eddie 1986

There were a lot of changes during the last few years of my sentence and I was sad to miss out. MJ met Jenny and they got married soon after. She was afraid of the rest of us to start with, but she soon accepted that we were MJ's family. For MJ she was someone of his own to love who was not tainted by his past. We were all so happy for him. I just wish I could have been there for his wedding.

Julie took a long time to recover from her experience. Had it not been for the child she would've given up. Her confidence returned slowly but she never left the house alone. Baby Stephanie grew quickly and looked just like her mother. We never mentioned her father, for the child's sake we made a pact that she would never know. Instead we all became her surrogate dads. Boris more than any of us. His marriage had broken down, all Jean cared about was money and going out. Boris had caught her with several men, but he no longer fought for her, he only cared for his son.

By the time I was let out on parole, Boris had moved in with Julie and I had never seen her so happy. Charlie and I took a flat together. The money from the robbery had been invested in property and over the years we had been inside it had grown to a considerable sum. Adam took care of the paperwork transferring our share. Denny, MJ, and Boris insisted the split was equal at the current value even though they had done all the work. Their argument was that we had to serve time, so we deserved it, probably more than them.

Charlie took well to the property business, he had the charm to pull off deals and the nerve to take risks. I bought the cottage in Laugharne, Adam took care of the paperwork so the place couldn't be traced to me. The cottage was something of my own, a place I could escape to and walk around the castle or the local beaches. I found it difficult to adjust to life outside after the same routine for nine years. Charlie understood and would often spend time with me at the cottage looking out over the estuary as we drank beer. The place brought me a sense of peace, something I had never had. I should've known it wouldn't last.

The last time we were all together was Stephanie's fifth birthday. Me, Denny, Charlie, MJ and Jenny gathered in Boris and Julie's house. They lived in a quiet neighbourhood, in a detached house with a large garden for Steph to play. Julie looked radiant as she watched Steph blow out the candles on the cake. She had persuaded Boris not to seek revenge on Scott North. She wanted to forget the past and move on, for them to be a real family. Boris agreed, and he announced that he would be formally adopting Stephanie as well as applying for full custody of his son. He was confident that Jean could be paid off. The big news was that as soon as his divorce was final he would marry Julie.

I was so happy for them. As we toasted the news with champagne, I saw a lightness in Boris I thought I would never see. Losing Iosif had left a hole in his heart that could never be filled. I knew he would never give up looking but Julie had shrunk that hole. Now when I looked at him I no longer saw the pain and rage reflected in his eyes.

It was a few weeks later that I was spending the Friday evening with Boris and Julie. Stephanie was curled up on Julie's lap, sleeping. Boris sat next to them, one arm around Julie's shoulder the other cradling a beer. Julie said she was going to take Stephanie up to bed when the phone rang.

'I'll get it.' Boris jumped up.

The atmosphere changed as Boris's tone became serious. He fired questions down the phone before slamming it down. Stephanie woke up and started to cry.

'What's wrong?' I stood with my heart thudding in my chest.

'It's Dmitri, he's been in an accident. That was the hospital.'

'What sort of accident?' Julie asked. 'Is he okay?'

'I don't know, they wouldn't say. They just asked for me to come straight away.'

'I'll come with you,' I said.

Boris looked at Julie.

'Go, I'll be fine. We'll go and have some warm milk, shall we?' she said to Steph. 'Call me as soon as you have news.'

Boris lent down and gave Steph a hug before kissing Julie.

'I'll be back soon,' I said.

Boris insisted on driving and it reminded me of the time Charlie had tried to outrun the police. That ended with us both in hospital.

'Slow down, you are going to get us both killed.' I clung onto the grab handle as we rounded a bend. 'You'll be no good to Dmitri if you end up in hospital yourself. Jean will be there with him, he's not alone.'

'Yeah and I'll kill the bitch when I see her. She hasn't a clue how to look after him. She's probably had some man around and wasn't watching him. She knows I don't like strange men around him. She agreed he would stay with me if she wanted a screw. He should be with me.' Boris thumped the steering wheel.

'It will be okay.' I tried to reassure him although I had a horrible feeling that shrouded me like thick smoke.

We had to drive across town to get to the hospital. As we passed The Crown pub we saw Jean walking towards it. Boris slammed on the brakes and leapt out of the car.

'Get in,' he screamed.

'What are you doing?' She backed away.

'Dmitri's had an accident.' I leaned out of the car window. 'We need to get to the hospital.'

'What happened? Who did you leave him with?' Boris had grabbed hold of Jean's wrist and was yanking her towards the car.

'Let go, you're hurting me,' Jean squealed. 'Dmitri is with my mother. I only just left him. She was supposed to come over to look after him, but she forgot so I had to take him over. I'm already late. So piss off and leave me alone.'

'When?' Boris said.

'Ten minutes ago, Dad dropped me on the corner.'

'That can't be right,' Boris said.

'Let's just go to Jean's mother's house,' I suggested.

Boris flung Jean in the back of the car and sped off as she shouted obscenities. She leaped out of the car as soon as it stopped, and Boris chased her into the house. By the time I joined them at the door it was clear that there had been a mistake. Dmitri had run to his father as soon as he heard his voice. Boris was hugging the boy tight, the tension leaving his body despite Jean screaming at him that he'd ruined her evening. Then his expression changed.

'How could the hospital make a mistake?'

'It happens.' I shrugged my shoulders.

'No, how many boys are called Dmitri? And how did they get my name?'

His words drove an arrow of fear through my heart. 'Julie!'

'Call the police,' Boris shouted. 'Call them, send them to Julie's house.'

'What?' Jean said.

'Tell them someone is attacking her, just do it.'

We didn't hang around to hear Jean make the call. We jumped in the car and Boris floored the accelerator. This time I didn't ask him to slow down. It didn't matter how fast Boris drove, we weren't getting there quick enough. I just hoped that Jean had made the call and the police were on their way. All thoughts rushed through my mind, but I couldn't voice them. We'd all been so careful but as the years went by with no threat to Julie and Stephanie we'd become complacent. Part of me was begging a God that I didn't believe in that the hospital had made a mistake, but a greater part of me knew the mistake was ours. I should've stayed behind.

When we pulled onto the street where Julie lived all was quiet. Neighbours were either out or watching TV behind closed curtains. There was a car parked out front which Boris nearly hit as he brought the car to a screeching halt. He opened the glovebox, took out a gun and leapt out of the car.

'Julie!' He burst through the front door.

From behind Boris I saw two men emerge from the kitchen. Scott North had Stephanie slung over his shoulder like a rag doll. Blood dripped over his gloved hand that gripped her ankle. No one moved for a moment. Scott had been taken by surprise by our sudden appearance; the other man, who I later learned was a journalist called Pete Bradshaw, looked past Boris seemingly trying to figure his way out.

Boris was the first to move, he pointed the gun at Scott. 'Put her down,' he said.

I thought for a moment Scott would do as Boris asked but he quickly moved Stephanie using her as a shield. 'You'll have to shoot through her,' he said.

Distant sirens filled the silence as Boris kept the gun on Scott.

'Just give him the kid,' Pete said. 'We can get her later.'

'No, there's barely any life in her. I have to get her to Blue Hollow to finish the job before it's too late.'

'Then she'll die here,' Boris said.

'No,' I shouted as Boris moved the aim of the gun.

Without warning Scott tossed Stephanie at Boris. Boris dropped the gun as he caught the child. I heard a faint whimper from Stephanie as I dived for the gun. Pete Bradshaw saw his chance and ran for the door. I grabbed the gun and swung it around as Scott took flight. I fired one shot. It grazed Scott's shoulder, stopping him in his tracks.

'Eddie!'

I turned back.

'Quick, take her.' Boris held out Stephanie.

So I let Scott get away and took Stephanie from Boris's arms. He stepped into the kitchen. A keening sound rent the air and mixed with the sirens that were getting closer. It took me a moment to realise the noise was coming from Boris. I followed him in, and the sight made my knees buckle. There was blood everywhere, splattered across the kitchen cupboards and wall. The worst of it was on the floor. Boris was knelt in a pool of blood cradling Julie whose head lolled back, her blond hair stained red. It was difficult to see where she had been wounded. The coroner would later report eleven stab wounds. If I didn't have Stephanie in my arms, I think I would've joined Boris. I looked at Stephanie. She was deathly pale, her eyes unfocused, but she was still breathing. I don't know where I found the strength to move.

'Boris, we need to go, we need to get Stephanie to the hospital. The police will be here in a moment.'

'No, I'm not leaving her.'

'She's gone, we have to help Stephanie.'

'Get her out of here. If the police come they'll take her, she'll never be safe.'

'Okay, let's go.'

Boris shook his head. 'Please go, Eddie, take her to Ray.'

The sirens were close and there wasn't much time, so I had no choice but to leave Boris. I put Stephanie in the front seat and covered her with my coat. As I pulled away, I saw a police car enter the street and speed towards the house. My instinct was to take Stephanie to the hospital. I didn't know how badly she was wounded but from the amount of blood she was losing it didn't look good. But Boris was right, if I took her to the hospital she wouldn't be safe. If she survived, the best case would be that she would be taken into care. I couldn't allow that. Scott North and his sick group of friends would never stop.

'Please just hang in there.' I touched her hand. It felt cold.

I knew where the doctor lived, and it was only for the fact that he helped rescue Julie that I had left him alone. Now I needed his help. I hammered on his door. When he opened it his eyes widened, and he shook his head but before he had time to close the door I barged my way in.

'You've got to help her.'

'Ray?' The doctor's wife appeared behind him. 'What's going on?'

Dr Ray looked at the blood-soaked bundle in my arms. 'No, you have to take her to hospital.'

'No, they did this. If she dies then it's your fault. They killed Julie.' The words choked me.

'What's he talking about?' The doctor's wife's voice was shrill.

The doctor turned to his wife. 'Get some blankets and my bag, then boil some water. Bring her in here.' He led me into the sitting room.

I carefully laid Stephanie on the sofa. She didn't make a sound as the doctor removed her pyjamas and examined her wounds. 'She's lost a lot of blood and is in shock.'

The doctor's wife came into the room and knelt by Stephanie.

'I need to use the phone.'

'In the hall,' the doctor said without looking at me.

I called Charlie. I could barely get the words out. When I ended the call I sank to the floor. Julie was dead, gone forever. I was still in the same position when Charlie arrived with MJ. Charlie pulled me to my feet and held me as I shook with grief. The details of the evening came out in short bursts.

'And Stephanie? Is she going to be okay?' MJ asked.

I pulled away from Charlie and looked at MJ, tears flowed freely down his face. 'She's not good. I'm not sure she'll make it. The doctor and his wife are in there with her.' I nodded towards the door.

'Come on, mate.' Charlie rubbed his nose with the back of his hand. 'We have to pull it together. Do what we can for Stephanie.'

I nodded and the three of us went into the room.

'How is she?' Charlie asked.

'In shock,' the doc said. 'Two stab wounds, one to the arm and one to the leg. I've stitched them but she's lost a lot of blood.'

'Will she be okay?' I croaked.

The doc shrugged his shoulders. 'I've given her a sedative. We need to keep her warm and see how she goes through the night. She should be in hospital, it's her best chance.'

'No,' Charlie said. 'You know she won't be safe there. Unless you're going to sit at her side and make sure nothing happens to her.'

'I can't do that, I can't be involved.'

'You're involved now,' MJ said.

'What are they talking about?' the doctor's wife asked.

'I'll explain later, what's important now is helping the child. Come and sit with her. It may help for her to see a familiar face.'

The doctor's wife moved, and I took her place. 'You're going to be okay,' I said as I stroked her hair. 'The doctor's going to make you better.' She just stared at me.

'Eddie, we need to go back to the house, see what's happening with Boris. The police will be looking for you as Julie's next of kin.' Charlie moved towards me.

'I can't go back.' I didn't ever want to go back to the house.

'You have to,' Charlie said. 'They mustn't know you have Stephanie.'

'We'll be with you,' MJ said.

They were right. I had no choice but to go back, and that was going to make Julie's death all the more real. Dr Ray gave me a change of clothes, they didn't fit well but at least they were free of bloodstains.

There were two police cars and a van parked outside the house. One policeman stood outside the door.

'You have to act like you don't know what has happened,' Charlie said.

It wasn't difficult, the grief was real. I ran towards the house and was stopped by the policeman. I gave my name and started to kick off. Eventually they told me what happened. It was when I demanded to know about Stephanie that they started to panic. They hadn't realised there was a child in the house, and she was missing. I was questioned along with Charlie and MJ. I stuck to the story that I had been with MJ all evening.

The next few days went in a blur. Boris had been arrested at the scene and charged with murder. They weren't looking for anyone else. It didn't matter what I said to the police, I was an ex-con and not worth their time. A large-scale search was launched to find Stephanie, with her face appearing in every newspaper. Stephanie grew a little stronger each day and started asking for her mother. I couldn't leave her with the doctor and his wife much longer. The risk of being seen was too great and I feared the police were watching me. We decided to move her. It was Charlie's idea to take her to the cottage in Laugharne. We travelled at night, then took it in turns to look after her so we wouldn't be missed.

It was later that I learned that Scott North was part of the investigation team so there was no chance of throwing accusations his way. He would cover his tracks. Even if his blood was at the scene, he would find a way to get rid of the evidence. The police came to tell me that Boris had confessed to murdering Julie and Stephanie. That he had buried the child and was coming back for Julie when the police arrived at the house. He refused to give up the location of Stephanie's grave. I knew what he was doing. He was sending a clear message to Scott that he would never get his hands on the child's body. He was giving Stephanie a chance to survive. The police continued the search for another week then it was scaled down. I don't like to think about what Boris went through as they interrogated him, but he kept quiet. The rest was down to us.

I stayed in the cottage with Stephanie for three months. She had stopped asking for her mother and accepted my explanation that the angels had taken her to heaven. She woke screaming every night, terrified that the bad man would get her. I was grateful for the cold weather, it meant I could wrap her up in a coat and woollen hat and take her to the local beaches. No one took any notice of us hunting shells and searching rock pools. I was still very careful, and I knew I couldn't keep her hidden forever. It was Charlie that came up with the solution. He had been my rock all those months and I couldn't have got through it without him.

Charlie, Denny, and me met in the cottage. MJ brought Jenny, and Adam sat at the kitchen table with papers spread out.

'It's the only way to keep her safe.' I looked from MJ to Jenny. 'Scott North is not stupid. I was there that night. If we're going to have him believe that Boris buried her then she can never be seen with me.'

'No way,' Jenny said. 'It will never work.'

'It makes sense,' Charlie said. 'You don't have any children.'

'Yet,' I added. I knew they had been trying and it was a sore point with MJ.

'We'll do it,' MJ said.

'How? We can't just suddenly have a five-year-old child and claim she's ours.' Jenny walked over to where Stephanie sat playing with a doll. 'Poor little mite.' She knelt down beside her. 'That's a pretty doll you have.'

I could see Jenny was softening. As much as I didn't want to let Stephanie go, I had no idea how to raise a child. She would never be safe as long as she stayed with me. They'd come after her, maybe not straight away, but they would find a way to take her from me.

'I've sorted out everything that will be needed,' Adam said.

'I don't want to know,' Jenny said. 'The less I know the better.'

'There's some things you will need to listen to,' Adam said. 'Charlie has found a house in a small village where no one will know you. It will be a fresh start. You can register her at the school there. I have her birth certificate. Her name will be Isadora.'

We all turned to look at Adam. 'What sort of a name is that?' I asked.

'She can't keep her real name,' Adam said. 'The night you found me behind the gravestone in Blue Hollow, I... erm... I was hiding behind Isadora's grave. I know it sounds stupid but I felt like she protected me that night so

I figured the name would give this little one some protection.'

Adam had never mentioned that night but now was not the time to ask questions. 'Then I think it's a great name,' I said.

'Dora.' Jenny stroked Stephanie's hair. 'Yes, I like it.' She stood up and walked to the table. 'You're going to have to let us be a family. It will confuse her if we're all together.'

'She's right,' Charlie said. 'You can still be in her life, but you'll have to take a back seat.'

'A friend of the family.' It hurt me to say it. Stephanie was all I had left of Julie but if this was going to work then I would have to walk away and watch from a distance.

'Give her a couple of years.' Charlie put his hand on my shoulder. 'She needs time to settle and forget. It's for the best.'

Adam took care of the rest.

I'm so sorry, Dora. I hope you can forgive me, forgive all of us. Your nightmares soon faded, and you became Jenny and MJ's daughter. They couldn't have loved you more if you were their own flesh and blood. I watched you grow with pride and I know your mother would be proud. It's up to you what you do now but never forget how much I love you, how much we all love you.

Chapter Thirty-One

Dora jumped up from the table as if she'd been bitten. 'No, no, no!'

The cat that had been sleeping in the chair next to her took flight. She felt everyone had lied to her, that her whole life had been a lie.

The kitchen felt airless, her skin prickled, and she pulled on the collar of her jumper. No matter how many breaths she took, it felt as if the room had run out of oxygen. Her head became light and her vision dimmed. She staggered to the sink, turned the tap on and splashed cold water on her face.

Images of Julie being stabbed flooded her mind. She reached down and felt the scar on her leg through the fabric of her jeans. I should remember, she thought. Eleven stab wounds and two to me. How hard she must have fought to try and protect me and all this time I never knew. Didn't know the sacrifice she made. They could've told me, they should've told me, she thought.

She filled a glass of water and gulped it down. Shock turned to anger, she felt it bubbling in her veins. She wanted to scream, hit something. She grabbed her mobile, it took her three tries to get the lock screen off. Dmitri answered on the second ring.

'Bastard,' she screamed.

'Dora, what's happened?'

'You knew, you knew all along.'

'I'm on my way.'

'Stay away from me.' She ended the call and threw the phone on the table.

She was still seething when Dmitri arrived. 'Get out, you've no right to come in here, get out!' She grabbed her handbag and took out the gun.

'For fuck sake. Put the gun down. I did knock. I have a key for emergencies.' He lunged towards her and grabbed the gun out of her hand. 'Now tell me what the fuck's going on.'

'Tell you! You know, everyone knows.' She balled her fist, but Dmitri grabbed her wrist before she had a chance to land a punch. He pulled her close to his chest. She struggled as she beat her fists against him. 'Let me go,' she shrieked.

'Tell me what you think I know.'

'I'm Stephanie, I'm Julie's daughter.'

'I didn't know, I swear to you. I had my suspicions, but I couldn't ask Dad. He would never had told me when there was a chance he could be overheard. I thought maybe you suspected but I didn't want to be the one to suggest it.'

'Why the hell would I suspect I was someone else.' She pulled away from him. 'Everyone lied to me. I don't even exist. I'm a made-up person, my name taken from a gravestone. How is it even possible? You can't just create a person and use a false birth certificate.'

'Easy enough if you know how,' Dmitri said. 'No computer records back then. I'm guessing you were on your parents' passports until you were old enough to have your own. They didn't phase that out until the nineties. Easy enough to get your own passport and keep renewing.

They would've set up a child's savings account. You had your school and medical records. If ever you needed anything it would be easy to apply. Except to get a copy of your original birth certificate. You might have had problems with that, then again you had no reason to request one.'

'All of that, and for what?'

'To keep you safe. They managed to pull it off, to convince Scott North that you were dead. He would never have been able to trace you. If you had kept your real name, he would've tracked you down.'

'And your father took the blame for killing me. The whole thing is…'

'Fucked up?'

'Yeah, so all of this has been to let me know I don't exist, so Eddie could go to the grave with a clean conscience.'

'No, to give you the evidence to put a stop to it. So he could be sure you were safe. You are the evidence. What else was on the tape?'

'I don't care what else was on the bloody tape. I've had it with all of this.' Dora threw her arms up in the air. 'I don't want to reveal this big secret. How's that going to work? Hello world, I'm not dead and you can call me Stephanie.'

'This isn't just about you,' Dmitri snapped. 'It's about Iosif, my father, Eddie, Charlie, MJ, Denny, and all the others that have suffered at the hands of those bastards and are probably still suffering. Do you think that stuff doesn't still happen? Open your fucking eyes. How many times have you seen a case of child abuse reported in the papers? Paedophile rings, grooming gangs, trafficking. That's just the ones that are caught.

'Scott North thought he was safe. As long as the body of the child lay rotting in a grave there was no connection to him. He's pissed, he didn't make his sick ritual and he never made it to the same position of his father. You're proof of what he did to Julie. Somewhere locked in your memory are the events of that night.'

'I don't remember, I was five years old.'

'It doesn't matter, Scott North doesn't know that. Did Eddie say who was at the house that night?'

'Yeah, Scott North and a journalist named Pete Bradshaw.'

'Then the bastard wheedles his way into the investigation, no doubt with daddy pulling some strings. Any evidence of him found in the house he could have explained.'

'I can't believe he could go back to the house after what he did, the man is evil, he has no soul. He tried to kill his own dau… oh God, that's… that's my real father.' Dora felt sick. 'I have an evil, psychopath, rapist, killer for a father.'

'It's okay.'

'It's not okay, it's never going to be okay,' Dora sobbed.

Dmitri pulled her against his chest. 'Don't do this to yourself.' He stroked her hair. 'Don't forget I have a murderer for a father.'

'That doesn't count, he's innocent.'

'Yeah but that's not what everyone believes. I believed it when I was growing up. Look, you are still you. It's the people who brought you up that count, the people who love you that make you what you are. That piece of shit is nothing to you.' He held her at arm's length and looked into her eyes. 'Don't let them win. Don't let all that has been sacrificed be in vain, you have to fight back.'

Dora nodded. 'I just don't know if I can.'

'Yes you do, you have no problem pulling a gun on someone.' Dmitri laughed. 'You know I'll stand by your side, you're not alone.' He ran a finger down her cheek. 'You've never been on your own through this. I promised Eddie and Charlie I would look after you but more than that, I want to.' He leant in.

Dora felt his mouth hard upon hers, she didn't resist. All the anger and frustration melted away and was replaced by desire. She felt his hands in her hair then over her body. She moved in closer, snaking her hands up his chest and around his back. He moved his mouth from hers to her neck then up to her ear.

'Now I'm offering to fuck you,' he whispered.

Chapter Thirty-Two

Dora looked out of the window as the funeral car slowly made its way towards the church. Up ahead two hearses carried Eddie and Charlie's coffins. Jenny sat next to her fidgeting with the hem on her skirt.

'Are you okay, Mum?'

'Yes I'm fine, it's just like your fath... well, it brings back memories. All the same people.'

'You don't have to do that.'

'Do what?'

'Get all awkward when you mention Dad. Yes, it was a shock at first but you're still my mum and Dad's still my dad, nothing has changed.'

Jenny took Dora's hand and squeezed. 'When we took you home you became our daughter, we never spoke about it again. We couldn't have any of our own, the problem lied with your father. I guess years of abuse damaged him in some way. He'd become depressed, anxious that he couldn't give me a child. You took all that away. We couldn't have loved you more.'

'I know and I never once felt that I didn't belong. I guess that's what made it so hard to believe.'

'I'm glad now it's out in the open. I don't think I've had a good night's sleep since Eddie gave me the tape.'

The car came to a stop and the door was opened. Dora stepped out and felt the grief closing her throat and running down to her stomach where it sat like a lump of ice. She didn't want to say goodbye.

Dmitri stood by Eddie with Dray and Adam at his side. Denny and Ben with Charlie. The other pallbearers she didn't recognize. She glanced behind and saw a crowd of people snaked down the side of the building. Far more than could fit inside.

'Just shows how much they were loved and respected.' Jenny put her arm around Dora's shoulder. 'Take a deep breath, head up, you can do this.'

Dora took her place at the head of the procession. As the coffins were carried in, the room filled with Queen's *A Kind of Magic*. A smile played on her lips as she recalled Eddie's account of Charlie singing and dancing. She took her place in the front row and Dmitri set down the coffin before taking a seat next to her and holding her hand.

Denny and Adam took it in turns to read the eulogies, then Dmitri stood to read a letter from Boris. His words tore at Dora's heart and she struggled to keep her composure. She was glad to get outside in the cool air even though it meant standing and accepting a long line of people offering their condolences. Adam had arranged a wake in a local pub, but she only stayed an hour. She went home and was joined by Dmitri, Denny, Adam, Ben, and Dray. They all crammed around her kitchen table.

'Do you think any of them were there?' she asked.

'I doubt it,' Ben said. 'They would've got lynched.'

'Glad to see you got some decent shit in.' Dray poured a tumbler full of whisky.

'Dmitri stocked up.' Dora smiled.

'So what's the plan?' Ben asked.

'It better be one that doesn't involve me getting beaten up, I'm too old for that crap,' Denny said. 'Never did win a fight without Boris around.'

'Don't be a pussy, man.' Dray laughed.

'I'm just saying the last grand plan ended with Eddie and Charlie going down, and me with five stitches in my head.'

'I don't want any one of you to get hurt,' Dora said.

'Denny's a sitting duck and so is Boris. They're desperate enough to find a way to get to him inside. Someone is always willing to take a fall for the cause,' Ben said. 'Better one of us gets hurt trying to stop them than wait.'

'What about the other boys in Blue Hollow, did you manage to track them down?' Dora looked at Adam.

'That's the good news,' Adam said. 'He pulled out a sheet of paper from a file. 'These are the ones that are willing to testify. There are quite a few from later years as well as some of the girls that were kept there up to 2003.'

'Girls were kept there until then?'

'Sex slaves,' Ben said. 'They moved the operation, using different properties. I've managed to locate an old mansion they hire for their meetings. I'm working on the other places.'

Dora took the paper from Adam. 'So many.' She shook her head.

'There's plenty more out there. It's your call, Dora,' Ben said.

'We have a few names of those involved in the seventies. It looks like Graham North handed the leadership of the group over to his son. We don't know how many are involved or how widespread they are. The only way to get to them is by exposing the inner circle,' Dora said.

'I've got a few names connected to Scott North, but they are careful with their communication. I can find no trace of them on the dark web,' Dmitri said.

'Phone records?' Dora suggested.

'Damn, girl, the boy's got skills but he's not a magician.' Dray laughed.

'Then that leaves only one option. I tell Scott North who I am and demand a meeting.'

'No,' Denny said. 'Why do you think we kept your secret all these years? Eddie wanted you to know the truth, not to use it to get yourself killed.'

'It's a bit late for that. The point of Eddie giving me the tapes was to put an end to it.'

'No, love,' Denny said.

'I think she's right,' Ben said. 'Eddie didn't know when he made the tapes that it would get him and Charlie killed. He wanted Dora to make the decision. They both would've been here now ready to take the fuckers down.'

'They haven't killed me yet,' Dora said. 'They got to Eddie and Charlie, but they haven't tried to get to me again. I'm sure if they wanted to, they could've killed me by now. They're holding off for some reason.'

'She's got a point,' Ben said. 'These people are fucking lunatics and they've got the resources. They could've positioned a sniper at the church and taken Dora out as well as a few of us before we knew what was happening.'

'Thanks, that makes me feel so much better,' Dora said with a grin.

'So, what are they waiting for?' Adam asked.

'I think they are watching and waiting,' Dmitri said. 'They silenced Eddie and Charlie and would get Denny and Dad if they could. They must know they can't contain what is on those tapes. They've no idea who Dora has spoken to but as long as the resting place of the child isn't revealed, there is no connection to Scott North. No one is going to rake up the past. He must have figured out that Eddie was going to tell Dora where the child is buried. I reckon he wants her to lead him to the grave. Maybe he thinks he can still perform the ritual with the remains.'

'Except there's no body,' Dora said.

'He doesn't know that. All these years there hasn't been a trace of Stephanie Flint, so he would've concluded that she was dead. If you knew the location you would check it out first to be sure.'

'I guess.'

'That's what they're waiting for.'

'That would mean they're watching my every move.'

'Yeah.' Dmitri nodded.

'So, we let him think that Dora has found the grave and we get him that way,' Denny said.

'No, we need them all together at Blue Hollow,' Dora said.

'Oh, not there.' Denny sighed.

'Yes, we need them there. I've transcribed all the tapes and added pictures I took at the church as well as all the information Dmitri got on the Edenites. I've made a few omissions, kept Denny's name out of it. I'll upload it on a self-publishing site. Just need to click a button. Copies are ready to be sent to every police force, newspaper, and social media platform. I will give a copy to DI Price two days before the meeting. Then I go to meet them with Dmitri. Of course, Ben and Dray will already be there. Plenty of places to hide in the old house. We wait until after Christmas. We should be able to finalise the details by then. The timing is a bit problematic.'

'A bit?' Denny said. 'You'll be walking to your death.'

'How are you going to convince them all to be there at the time you want?'

'For that I do have the perfect plan.'

Chapter Thirty-Three

Scott North sat in his office and looked around the neat and polished room. He loved the smell of the leather seat, the smooth oak of his desk, and being able to bark orders down the phone. With only weeks left to his retirement he felt a black cloud cloaking his mind.

All this would be gone, a life of unfulfilled potential, an opportunity snatched from his grasp. Without it, the circle's respect for him would dwindle. He could see it in their eyes, hear it in their voices.

'What the fuck is that woman doing? She should have found it by now.' He closed his eyes and let the memories of that fateful night come to mind. The night it all went wrong.

If she hadn't clung to the child, if she hadn't spat those words at him. Calling him a rapist. She had no idea of the importance of her role. He shouldn't have lost his temper, then he wouldn't have accidently driven the knife into the child. He could've been so much more.

His phone pinged bringing him back to the present. He pulled it from his pocket and saw a new email notification. He opened the app and saw *Blood of Blood* in the subject heading. Scott felt excitement tingle his skin.

She's led them to it. His excitement quickly turned to annoyance. What the hell do they think they're doing sending an email? Imbeciles, he thought. He looked at the address, *Stephanieflintdaddygirl572*. He narrowed his eyes and felt anger spike his veins as he read the mail.

Dear Scott, or should I call you Daddy?

All these years you may have wondered why you didn't reach the same position as your father. You didn't gain unwavering support from the inner circle, didn't command their respect, and didn't succeed. It's because you failed to kill a five-year-old child, to make the sacrifice and carry out the ritual. How weak that must make you feel. I am Stephanie Flint, the little girl you tried to kill. The little girl you left for dead. The little girl who survived and has remained hidden from your sight.

I remember every detail of that night. It's the one thing you can't cover up. Your blood runs in my veins. I have now gathered enough statements and evidence to bring you and the Edenites down. It's all documented and ready to be sent out across all social media platforms, newspapers, and police forces. It just needs a click of a button. My testimony and DNA are stored in a safe place, that and what lies in Blue Hollow is enough for you to see out the rest of your days in a prison cell.

It may come as a surprise to you that to expose the Edenites is not my intention. If it was, I could have done so by now. Your time as leader has reached its end. You are no longer worthy of being called Brother of Cain. If you know your history, then you are aware that if the sacrifice survives, the power is transferred to them. It's quite fitting as the first chosen one was a woman, Eve. The one strong enough to taste the forbidden fruit. The time for change has come, for a Sister of Cain. A leader more powerful than any predecessors to lead the Edenites.

How many of your members rot in jail as paedophile and trafficking rings are brought down. More and more come forward to make accusations. How long before you let the group fall? Your inner circle already doubts your ability as leader. They will no longer sacrifice themselves for you, they will rise up against you.

I have already gathered a loyal following, look how easy it is for me to send an untraceable email to your personal address. You'll also find a copy at your work address. A history of unsavoury websites now sits on your hard drive. I can remove all traces as easily as I put them there.

I will meet you at Blue Hollow, Wednesday at 7pm. There you will gather the inner circle and perform the ordination ceremony. You failed to make the sacrifice and perform the ritual. I come now to claim what is rightfully mine.

Dora

'Fucking whore!' Scott swept his hand across his desk, a photo frame crashed to the floor.

His secretary knocked on the door. 'Are you okay, sir?'

'Yes, just knocked something over by accident. Please make sure I am not disturbed for the rest of the day.'

'Yes, sir,' she called through the door.

Scott paced his office. Those bastards had kept her hidden all this time. Rage boiled in his stomach. She could be lying, but it made sense, all those years Boris kept his mouth shut about where he buried the child. He could've used that information to get out. I'll slice her open and rip her heart from her chest while she's still breathing, he thought.

He picked up his desk phone and pressed for an external line. He gave his name and was put through immediately.

'What the fuck are you playing at calling me at work?' the voice at the other end hissed.

'Don't you dare address me in that manner.' Scott felt a vein pulsing in his forehead. 'I want her picked up.'

'Has she found it?'

'Found it? She is bloody it.' There was silence. 'Did you hear what I said?'

'Yes, this changes things. If you didn't make the sacrifice then–'

'It will be made this evening. You know the consequences of disloyalty. Do I make myself clear?'

'I can't just grab her.'

'You have a bloody surveillance team watching her.'

'For drugs. You want me to arrest her and hold her. There's no evidence.'

'No, you fucking fool. Find out where she is, as soon as she makes a move intercept her. I want her alive and brought to Blue Hollow.'

'We haven't used that place in years.'

'It has to be done there. Make sure you inform the others.'

Scott slammed down the phone then took a bottle of whisky from the cabinet in his office and poured himself a large shot. Little bitch will be begging me to kill her by the time I finish.

Chapter Thirty-Four

Dora sat in the police interview room with DI Price as he flicked through the transcript.

'So, you're telling me that the people responsible for killing Eddie Flint and Charlie Briar are named in this document?'

'Yes, as well as other crimes they've committed in the past. If you'll just drag the lake at Blue Hollow you'll have your evidence.'

'In Blue Hollow?' DI Price raised his eyebrows.

'Yes,' Dora huffed. She'd been stuck in the room for hours trying to explain what was in the document. 'If you would just read it, you'll understand.'

'Oh, I think I have a good grasp. You're telling me that there is a cult operating in Wales, and possibly UK-wide. So secret no one has heard of it. And the people involved are not only high-ranking police officers but judges, politicians, and a whole host of people in prominent positions.'

'I know what it sounds like, I didn't believe it myself at first. That's why I didn't come forward sooner, that and I didn't know who to trust. Think about it, how many celebrities have been investigated for child abuse? I could name one in particular who was in a position of trust.'

'You are saying they were part of these, erm, Edenites?' A smile played on his lips.

'No, well I don't know they very well could've been. I'm just saying that this is not the first time someone in a prominent position has used it to carry out abuse.'

'I see, so you have a list of names and evidence to back it up, in here?' He held up the document.

'There are some names and there are plenty of witnesses who are willing to testify. Please read the document then call me. I will give you information on where and when the next meeting is going to take place. It's your chance to catch them and put a stop to it.' Dora stood up.

'If you wouldn't mind waiting while I take a closer look and make some enquires.'

'I would mind. I've come in here voluntarily so unless you have reason to keep me here, I think I'm free to go.'

'Fair enough.'

Dora opened the door and stopped. 'Don't leave it too late, there's not much time. When you make your enquiries, I would take a good look at your colleague DS Sims. I imagine that he's taken a long leave of absence.'

'Wait.'

Dora heard DI Price call, but she ignored him.

* * *

When she arrived home Dmitri was sat in the kitchen with Dray and Ben.

'How did it go?' Ben asked.

'Pretty much what we expected. It sounded farfetched even to my ears and I've had first-hand experience. I just hope he reads it, or we're stuffed.'

'We've still got two nights,' Dmitri said. 'He'll read it, even if it's out of curiosity.'

'Failing that, you've got us,' Ben said.

Dray laughed. 'Yeah, shoot all the motherfuckers. I'm cool with that.'

'Oh God,' Dora groaned. 'Did Scott get his email?'

'Yeah,' Dmitri said with a grin. 'Loved to have seen the look on his face.'

'He's going to be wound up. There's no telling how he's going to react. The guy's a nutter. What if the police don't come?'

'Don't worry,' Ben said. 'Dray and me will be dropped off at Blue Hollow tomorrow night.'

'With enough kit to take down an army,' Dray added. 'We'll hang out here till then.'

'I don't know, I'm beginning to think this plan is madness. There's so many things that could go wrong. What if Scott doesn't show up? We'll look like idiots.'

'He'll show,' Dmitri said. 'He won't risk you releasing the documents, and he'll see it as his chance to kill you.'

'Thanks.'

'I'll be right at your side.'

'They'll know we have guns.'

'Yeah, they wouldn't expect us to turn up unarmed. We hand them over, they won't know about Dray and Ben hiding out. You just keep him talking until the police arrive. You'll be wearing a wire. Ben will hear everything that's going on. If that tosser of a copper listens to your instructions, then Adam will deliver a kit to him. He'll have a live feed and know when to act.'

'You better watch your language then,' Dora teased.

'Come on we better get going, it's getting dark. I've had someone watch the cottage. It's clear.'

* * *

They loaded the car and Dmitri tucked his gun into the door pocket. 'Just in case.' He winked.

'There's a car following us.' Dora peered into the wing mirror.

'We'll be taking the mountain road, if it follows us, I'll stop and shoot the driver. So, stop worrying.'

'I'll try. At least I had the best Christmas since I was a little girl, so if anything happens I'll die happy.' Dora fingered the bracelet Dmitri had given her on Christmas Day. 'The girls had a fantastic time.'

'They're great kids. Told you they wouldn't have a problem with me. Even they realise their father is a dick.'

'Yeah, taking off for Christmas in the sun with his tart didn't help. You know I thought you were a dick when I met you.'

'Changed you mind now, haven't you?' Dmitri said.

'No, you're still a dick.' Dora laughed. 'You swear too much, hang around with a bunch of criminals and brood.'

'I do not brood.'

'Don't tell me, you have a resting dick face.'

'I don't think that works. I'd prefer a resting bitch face.'

They were reaching the brow of the mountain and were heading for the crossroads. With not a car in sight. Darkness closed around them and Dora relaxed in her seat. 'So, what are we going to do for two nights stuck in the cottage?'

'I've got plenty of ideas to keep you entertained.' Dmitri grabbed her hand and placed it on his crotch.

'Ever heard of romance?'

'I don't do romance.'

The next word caught in Dora's throat as the shadow of a jeep flew out of the intersection. There was a sickening thud as metal hit metal. She felt herself being thrown against the door, then roof, as the car flipped over and landed back on four wheels with a jolt. She was momentarily dazed. She could hear Dmitri shouting but couldn't move. The air bag had inflated and was hung limply on the steering wheel. Headlights illuminated the car and a shot rent the air shattering the car door window. Dora felt blood splatter the side of her face.

'Get down.' Dmitri pushed the back of her head. 'Get your gun.' He frantically scrabbled around in the door of the car with his left hand. 'The gun's gone.'

Dora heard the panic in his voice. She thrust her hand into her bag and grabbed the gun shoving it at Dmitri.

'My arm's fucked, you're gonna have to shoot.'

Dora raised her head. Two shadows approached the car. She fired off two shots and saw them take cover before they returned fire. She ducked down again, her ears ringing.

'Aim for the chest,' Dmitri said. She could hear the pain in his voice. Blood ran down the side of his head from a gash and soaked through his jacket from where the bullet had hit his shoulder.

She popped her head up and fired another two shots. 'I'm gonna make a run for it.' She grabbed the handle of the door.

'No!' Dmitri grabbed at her arm.

'They're after me, they're going to want me alive. Here.' She held the gun out to him. 'If you can hit one the other one will come after me. You can get to their car and get out of here and get help. If I stay, they'll kill us both.'

Dmitri nodded. 'Take the gun, I can't make the shot. Wait till they get closer.'

Dora fired another three shots, pulled the handle on the door and kicked. The door flew open. She scrabbled out as another bullet pierced the car. Keeping low she waited until she could hear footsteps approaching. She wrapped two hands around the gun, jumped up and shot at the nearest figure. The shot hit one of the men in the stomach, he dropped his gun and fell to his knees. She fired another shot and ran into the darkness. The ground was rough and uneven, she stumbled as she made for the copse of trees. She knew he was coming after her, could feel his presence. She pumped her legs, pushing herself on. Another shot shattered the night and she felt the bullet tear through the flesh of her calf. She fell forward, a howl of pain escaping her lips. She could hear him now, breathing hard, his footfall heavy.

Get up, get up, she told herself. She managed to get to her feet, but she couldn't run. Warm blood soaked the bottom of her jeans and her leg dragged as she tried to move forward. She turned around and pulled the trigger. The night illuminated as the bullet left the gun but missed its target. She pulled the trigger again. Click. She tried again, but she was out of ammunition.

He lunged at her, grabbed the gun from her hand and brought it crashing down on the side of her head. She fell to the ground as pain exploded in her head. He grabbed hold of her by the upper arm and started dragging her across the grass. She tried to pull back, but he was too strong. She could feel herself losing consciousness as he dragged her past her car. In the headlights she could see Dmitri slumped at the wheel, he made no movement as she started to scream.

'Shut the fuck up.' He swung her round and she saw his fist fly towards her face. There was a moment of impact and she lost consciousness.

Chapter Thirty-Five

Dora opened her eyes to find her arms bound behind her back. Her head throbbed and her foot prickled with pins and needles. She was lying on her side in the back of the jeep. She tried to move her feet, but they were bound at the ankles. A rag had been tied tightly around her wound. Using her shoulder as leverage she wiggled upright.

'Get down,' the driver said. 'Unless you want me to stop and knock you out again.'

Dora slid back down, the pressure from the seat causing more pain to her head. Panic gripped her, snaking around her body, tightening her chest and quickening her breath. No one knew where she was. Dmitri, oh God, he wasn't moving, she thought. She felt like a caged animal, trapped and terrified. Bile rose in her throat. She tried to twist her hands, but they were bound so tightly there was no movement. Her eyes fell on the door handle. She could jump. Better than dying at their hands.

She closed her eyes and tried to listen to the traffic and judge the speed. From what she glimpsed when she sat up and the speed at which the cars whizzed by, she guessed they were on the motorway.

She concentrated on listening to the road and the sound of the engine, it helped quell the panic. When she was sure they had left the motorway she started to edge towards the door. The driver changed gear and the jeep slowed. Taking her opportunity, she pushed with her legs and managed to hook the door handle.

'I wouldn't try that if I were you, child locks are on.' He gave a mirthless laugh.

Dora kicked at the door in frustration, pain shot down her leg and a whimper escaped her lips. The journey dragged on and she could feel the sweat soaking the T-shirt beneath her jumper. They had long left the main roads with streetlights, and darkness closed around them. Dora risked sitting up again. This time the driver didn't stop her. The road illuminated by the headlights didn't give her much of an idea of their location. It was only when he turned down a rough track that she realised where he was taking her. Blue Hollow. Her body trembled as the building loomed before them.

He stopped the jeep and dragged her from the back seat.

'I can't walk.' She swayed and rested against the door.

He took a knife from his pocket and sliced through the bonds around her ankles.

She tried to take a step forward. 'My leg's dead, you've bound it too tightly.'

'Tough,' he said. 'Couldn't have you bleeding to death, not yet anyway. Move.' He gave her a shove.

She shuffled along slowly but when she saw the candlelight flickering in the church windows, panic made her bolt. She didn't get far. He closed in behind her and swept her injured leg. With her hands still tied she couldn't break her fall. She landed face down in the gravel. She felt her lip split and the metallic taste of blood filled her mouth.

'For fuck's sake.' The man gave her a kick before grabbing a handful of hair and dragging her into the church. 'A gift for you.' He threw her to the floor.

Dora managed to scrabble to her bottom and pull her knees up before Scott flew down the aisle, his eyes gleaming with pleasure. She recognised him from his photos on the internet even though he now wore a long cloak with a hood shrouding his head.

'Hello, Stephanie, how nice of you to join us,' he purred.

Dmitri had said to keep him talking until help came but she was sure no one would be coming. She could taste blood in her mouth and one eye was swollen shut.

'You're making a mistake. I left instructions for the transcripts to be released if anything happens to me. If you let me go now, I can stop it. Do you want exposure?' She raised her voice. 'Every one of you is named.'

'Shut your filthy little mouth.' Scott bore down on her. 'You think you can threaten me? That I would bow down to your pathetic demands? You've no idea of the power I'll have after the ritual is complete. I'll be untouchable. The first one to complete the blood of blood sacrifice since Cain himself.'

'You think that abusing and murdering children makes you powerful. You're sick, a freak. You're going to rot in jail for the rest of your life. All of you!'

Scott laughed. 'Look around you, no one is coming to your rescue. We don't even have to use weapons here. We are protected by a higher force.'

Dora looked around the church. There were robed men lighting more candles, others refreshing the symbols on the wall, and two putting together a makeshift altar. None of them took any notice of her.

Would Ben and Dray know by now that they hadn't made it to the cottage? Was that the plan? Was Dmitri supposed to call when they arrived? Fear frazzled her brain. She shook her head and tried to concentrate through the pain that throbbed in her leg and head.

Maybe DI Price would try and call her and, when he didn't get an answer, act on her instructions. No, Adam had to send the instructions to him first. No one was going to get there on time.

More men arrived and Dora felt tears sting her eyes as hopelessness washed over her. Scott continued to talk as if he was having a civilised conversation over a cup of tea.

'Eddie and Charlie could've joined us. I never understood why they turned against us. They were one of us. We looked after them, gave them food and shelter.'

He really is insane, I'm going to die here like Iosif, she thought. 'You abused those boys, kept them prisoner here. Took their innocence, stole their lives.'

'Stole their lives? No. They had the chance of being part of something great, something wonderful. See Paul over there?' He pointed to one of the men that was positioning a table in front of the altar. 'He came to Blue Hollow as a young boy and embraced the life. He's been a loyal and faithful servant. If not for him, we wouldn't have known about how many you were trying to contact to give evidence. He made himself useful, giving names. Now we know who is speaking against us and they are easy to get to. Once you make an example of one or two, it soon stops the others. No one is going to speak against us. The police will think you've got involved with the wrong people. You've been hanging around with known criminals. They won't waste too much time looking into your disappearance.'

'You're wrong, if anything happens to me you'll be hunted down.'

Scott made a show of looking at his watch. 'It's nearly time, you'll have to excuse me while I prepare. Get her ready,' he called to the two men that were stood by the table.

The two men approached, and Dora was dragged to her feet. The bonds on her wrists were cut and the men started pulling at her clothes.

'Get off me,' Dora shouted as they continued to tear at her jumper. She screamed and lashed out, but she didn't have the strength to fight them off.

'Scream as loud as you want,' one of the men jeered. 'No one will hear you.'

'Shut her up,' Scott shouted. 'I need silence to concentrate.'

A rag was stuffed in Dora's mouth and duct tape wound around so that all she could do was emit a muffled whine. They stripped her naked and bound her to the table in front of the altar. Her whole body trembled from fear, cold, and humiliation as the men took up position in a semi-circle at the foot of the table. Scott stood behind the altar and started to chant. The others joined in and the noise grew louder until it rumbled around the church. It stopped suddenly and all the men fixed their eyes upon Scott.

'Tonight you will witness the power of Cain descend upon me. Before you lies my daughter, my own flesh and blood. Taken and hidden from me, but now our great master has deemed it time for her to be returned. No one before me has made the blood of blood sacrifice. This will be the greatest moment in the Edenites' history. Those present tonight will reap the rewards.'

There was a murmur amongst the men and the air became charged with excitement. Dora struggled against her bonds as she saw Scott lift a dagger in the air, its blade glinting in the candlelight. The chanting started up again growing frenzied as Scott moved from behind the altar and stood at the side of the table.

Oh God, please make it quick. Dora screwed up her eyes.

'And now I call upon the power of Cain.'

'Yeah, I think not.'

Dora opened her eyes and saw that the men had parted and were looking towards the back of the church to where Ben stood with a gun pointing at Scott, and Dray who held an AK-47.

'Surprise, motherfuckers,' Dray said.

Scott thrust the knife downward but before it hit Dora a shot pierced the air and the knife dropped from his hand as the bullet hit.

'Do you really think you can stop me?' Scott clutched his bloody hand. 'Are you going to shoot every single one of us?' He started up a chant, the others joined in, drawing closer to Dora.

'I don't think that's gonna save your arse, you cock womble.' Dray sprayed bullets into the church roof. Old plaster and other debris fell on the men as they scattered. Dray fired again hitting some of the men. 'Hit the floor or I'll blow your fucking brains out,' he shouted.

'Get up, you idiots,' Scott shouted.

Ben charged down the aisle, and smacked Scott with the gun. He added a kick as he fell to the floor. 'Sicko.' He turned to Dora. 'It's okay, love, we've got you.' He took a knife and cut her bonds and ripped off the gag before draping his coat over her and lifting her in his arms.

'Get her outta here,' Dray said. 'I've got this.'

Ben carried Dora out of the church and placed her gently in the porch.

Dora couldn't stop her body from shaking. She wrapped her arms around herself and rocked back and forth.

Ben examined her leg then took a look at her head. 'You're going to be okay, just hold on. Help is on the way.'

'Dmitri?' Dora stopped rocking and looked at Ben.

'I'm sorry, I don't know. He was in a bad way. He managed to make a call, but the signal was bad. We could hear shots in the background. By the time we got there you were gone and Dmitri... he wasn't conscious. We came after you, it's what he would've wanted. We called an ambulance. Denny has gone to the hospital, that's the last we heard.'

'No, he's gotta be alright.' Dora felt a pain far more intense than from her injuries. It gnawed at her stomach spreading to her chest, then filled her whole being. She cried, sobs that wracked her body and stole the breath from her lungs.

The sound of sirens filled the air and mixed with her wails. Streaks of blue lit the sky.

'It looks like Adam's done his bit. We gotta get outta here.' Dray appeared by the door.

'Dora, I'm going to leave you with Dean,' Ben said. 'He'll look after you until the police arrive.'

'Dean?' Dora looked up and for the first time noticed the two men that stood in the doorway.

Ben stood and joined Dray and the other men. Together they secured the door.

'Think we've got time to torch the place?' Dray said.

'No, besides they should face the humiliation of an arrest and trial.'

'Go,' Dean said. 'We've got this.'

'We'll see you soon.' Dray reached down and kissed Dora on the top of the head.

'Don't worry.' Dean sat down next to her. 'They'll get away. The police won't find any guns and they can check us all they like.'

All Dora could do was nod dumbly. When the police arrived, it was chaos. She lifted her hands when the armed response unit announced themselves. Ben's coat fell from her shoulders, but she didn't care. She let a police officer cover her with a blanket. As she was led to the ambulance she heard Dean explain that they had just arrived, that they'd seen two men take off, and had been asked to look after the woman.

The paramedics checked her over, applied a bandage to her leg and head. As she lay on the stretcher, DI Price appeared in the back of the ambulance.

'I need to talk to Dora.'

'Make it quick,' the paramedic said. 'We need to get her to hospital.'

DI Price crouched next to Dora. 'What happened here tonight?'

'Is Dmitri gonna be okay?' She wasn't sure she wanted to hear the answer.

'I'll try and find out for you. All I know is that he was found with two gunshot wounds. There was another man pronounced dead at the scene. He suffered a fatal gunshot wound. What can you tell me about that?'

The one I shot in the stomach, I killed a man. I'll be arrested, sent to prison, she thought.

'Dora?'

'They ran us off the road. Then shot at us. Dmitri was hit. I thought if I ran it would give Dmitri time to call for help.'

'You got out of the car when they were shooting at you?'

'I didn't think they would shoot at me, they needed to bring me here so they could… they shot me in the leg, brought me here and…' The words stuck in Dora's throat. She didn't want to talk about it.

'We really need to go,' the paramedic said.

'One more question. There are a number of men with gunshot wounds in the church. Did you see the gunman?'

'No, there were too many people and they tied me to a table.'

'Okay, I'll talk to you again when you're feeling better. I'm sorry I didn't believe you when you came to me with this.'

'We're going to give you something for the pain,' the paramedic said.

Dora felt a scratch on her arm and then she was floating.

Chapter Thirty-Six

Dora sat on the sofa in her dressing gown, her eyes fixed to the television. When the news report started, she turned up the volume and sat forward.

> *Divers today will start searching the lake at Blue Hollow. Up until now adverse weather conditions have hampered the search for missing twelve-year-old Iosif Orlov who was last seen in Blue Hollow in 1970.*
>
> *Arrests continue to be made in connection to the cult known as the Edenites. Nathaniel Edwards QC, The Reverend Phillip Bevan, and Detective Inspector Kyle Moss were among those arrested at Blue Hollow last month. The leader of the group, Chief Inspector Scott North, was arrested and charged with the attempted murder of Dora Lewis and the murder of Julie Flint. Dora Lewis is believed to be Stephanie Flint who disappeared aged five following the murder of her mother Julie Flint in 1986. Boris Orlov who was convicted of Julie and Stephanie's murder was released earlier this week following a public outcry.*
>
> *Shocking details are still emerging of the Edenites' activities which span over sixty years. Founder of the group, 87-year-old retired Chief Superintendent Graham North*

is still in a critical condition in hospital following a heart attack.

'I hope the bastard dies a slow painful death.' Dora took a sip of her tea.

A loud urgent knocking of the door gave Dora a start. She put down her cup, tied up her robe and peeked out the window. 'Oh great,' she huffed. She opened the door and Gary shoved past her.

'My keys aren't working.' He dropped a large holdall.

'I changed the locks.'

'You could at least have told me. I must look like a right idiot to the neighbours, locked out of my own home.'

Dora looked at the man who stood before her and felt nothing for him. 'It's not your home anymore. You left, remember. You've had a letter from my solicitor, and I think I've made a very generous offer to buy you out. If you would just hurry up and sign the divorce papers you could have the money.'

'I don't want a divorce. I've left Tina. I realised that I still love you. I've been a fool and we were together much too long to throw it all away. What do you say, shall we give it another go?' He smiled.

'I say you can pick up your bag and fuck off.'

The smile slid from Gary's face. 'I know you've had a difficult time these past few months but there is no need to use that sort of language.'

'You heard her, fuck off.' Dmitri appeared at the top of the stairs in a pair of boxer shorts and displaying an angry scar on his shoulder. His hair was just growing back from where a bullet had ploughed a channel in the side of his head. Doctors had shaved his hair to pack and stitch the wound.

Gary opened his mouth and shut it, then pulled himself up to his full height and puffed out his chest. 'Who are you? And what are you doing in my house?'

Dmitri bounded down the stairs. 'I'm Dora's lover.' He held out his hand.

To Dora's surprise, Gary stood his ground.

'I'm Dora's husband and I'm home now so I think you should leave.'

'Problem?' Boris ambled down the stairs. 'Morning, love.' He kissed Dora on the cheek.

Gary stared at Boris and took a step back.

'No problem,' Dmitri said. 'This wet wank was just leaving.' He lunged forward and grabbed Gary by the throat pinning him to the wall. 'That's right, isn't it?'

Gary nodded and Dmitri released him, picked up the bag and threw it out the front door.

'I'm calling the police,' Gary spluttered as he made a quick exit.

'Sign the divorce papers. Don't forget that it would be a lot easier if I was a widow,' Dora shouted as she shut the door behind him.

'That was your husband?' Boris asked.

'Yeah.'

'Dick.'

Dora laughed. 'Seems to be the general opinion.'

'Better get yourself dressed.' Dmitri slapped her playfully on the backside. 'We need to get there before they start.'

'I don't think you should be going anywhere. You're supposed to be resting.'

'Don't fuss him. Don't want my son turning into a pussy.' Boris laughed as he headed back upstairs.

'I need to be there for him,' Dmitri said. 'Besides you're the one with a shot-up leg.'

'My leg's fine,' Dora said. It was not her leg that worried her, it was going back to that place.

After they dressed and ate a quick breakfast, they left the house. Dmitri insisted on driving and as Dora's car was in the breaker's yard she didn't object. They drove to

Cardiff and picked up Denny and Adam before heading towards Brecon and into the mountains.

'I haven't been back here since the night we rescued Julie,' Denny said.

Dora felt her stomach flip as they turned onto the track. 'Don't want to think about the last time I was here.'

Dmitri took his hand off the wheel and gave her hand a squeeze. 'I'm just sorry I wasn't there for you.'

'Yeah, I guess since Dray and Ben were the heroes, I should run off into the sunset with one of them.'

'Bitch.' Dmitri laughed.

'Just as well he wasn't there,' Boris said. 'He wouldn't have left any of the fuckers alive.'

'Are you okay, Adam?' Dora turned around to face Adam who was squashed between Boris and Denny in the back seat.

'Honestly, no. I just feel… I should have–'

'Don't,' Boris cut in. 'You were just a terrified kid, like the rest of us. There's nothing you could've done back then. You've taken care of all our shit over the years. You've nothing to be sorry for.'

They got to the end of the track and were stopped by two policemen. The five of them got out of the car.

'I'm sorry, you can't go any further,' one of the policemen said as he approached them.

'Try and stop me.' Boris stepped forward.

Dmitri stepped in front of his father. 'Give your boss a call. My father has waited long enough to find his brother. I think he's entitled to be here.'

The policeman walked away as he talked into his radio. 'Okay,' he said as he walked back. 'You can go through, but DI Price asks that you keep a reasonable distance from the lake.'

Dmitri took the car as far as he could up the mountain, they walked the rest of the way.

'Can I take that for you?' Dmitri asked.

'No, it's not heavy.' Dora adjusted the rucksack on her shoulders, so it sat snuggly against her back.

'Okay, let me know if your leg is giving you trouble. I'll carry you,' he said.

They climbed to the ridge of the mountain that overlooked the lake, sat in a row and watched as two boats circled the lake, stopping to let off divers. Dora pulled her hood up against the wind and snuggled next to Dmitri.

'I wish the others could've been here,' Boris said.

'They are.' Dora unzipped the rucksack and pulled out two urns.

'Charlie would find that funny,' Boris said. 'Him and Eddie side by side in pots.'

'To be honest I don't know what to do with them,' Dora said. 'They didn't leave any final wishes.'

'Mix them together and scatter them somewhere nice,' Boris said. 'They shouldn't be parted. Longest standing couple I've ever known.'

'Couple, you mean like together?' Dora looked at the urns.

'Don't tell me you didn't know.' Denny laughed. 'Worst-kept secret.'

'I think they fell in love the first day they met.' Boris smiled. 'But back then, you know, things were different, and they had an image to keep up. We all knew even though they thought they hid it well.'

'But they didn't live together,' Dora said. 'And Eddie never said anything.'

'Didn't he?' Dmitri said. 'Maybe you should listen to the tapes again.'

'They were happy the way things were,' Denny said. 'Both set in their ways.'

A shout went out from one of the divers and they all stood as the small remains were lifted onto the boat.

'Iosif,' Boris cried.

Dora felt a piece of her heart shatter as Boris fell to his knees. She crouched down and wrapped her arms around him. She felt Dmitri cover her and Adam and Denny did the same. They huddled together as the big man's body shook with grief. When they pulled apart there were no dry eyes.

'All these years he's been here. I don't know what to do now.' Boris wiped his eyes. 'I've spent most of my life searching, wanting answers. I thought I would feel relieved, but I feel empty.'

'It's okay, Dad,' Dmitri soothed. 'We'll take him away from this place and lay him to rest. He'll be okay now. He's got MJ, Charlie, and Eddie to look after him.'

'And you've got us to look after you,' Dora said. 'Come on, let's go home.'

Epilogue

Dora hung the picture in the hallway and looked at the smiling faces of the young boys. Iosif and MJ in the front with Charlie, Eddie, Boris, and Denny grinning as they stood behind.

'It looks great there.' Dmitri stood admiring the photo.

'It was one from Dr Ray's collection. Can't believe it's been a year since we sat on the mountain watching the divers.'

'It's a good day to do it. Ready, Dad?'

'I'm shitting myself,' Boris said.

'You'll be great,' Dora said. 'Go on, open the door.'

Boris flung open the door and a pile of journalists scrambled forward. A news reporter held out a microphone and Boris took a deep breath and spoke.

'Welcome to Iosif's Place,' he said. 'Over 100,000 children go missing every year. Ten thousand last year from children's homes alone. Some of these children are not reported missing and only a very small percentage get media coverage. Most are aged between fifteen and seventeen. There are all sorts of reasons that children go missing. A high number run away from abusive homes.

These children are vulnerable and make easy prey for those all too willing to exploit them. Most often they end up on the streets with nowhere to turn to for help. Iosif's Place is a safe haven for these young people.'

'I think he'll be alright now,' Dora said. She moved away afraid that she would be recognised. The press still hounded her for her story. Out in the garden she sat under the tree where Charlie, Eddie, and Iosif's ashes lay.

'I think they would be happy with the use you made of their money.' Dmitri sat next to her.

'This place might also help you stay straight.'

'Give up the good life and waste my talent, not a chance.' Dmitri laughed.

'Yeah, I thought not,' Dora said. 'I guess being shot and shooting someone makes me one of you now.'

'Yeah, you're a badarse now, just got to work on your language.'

Boris appeared in the garden followed by the journalists, he stopped and looked over at the tree then turned back to face the camera.

'If one good thing can come out of what happened at Blue Hollow, it is the lesson that nobody is above suspicion. That it should never be allowed to happen again to even one child. It's time to stand up and take action. Find those missing children, give them a safe haven and listen to them.'

Character List

Dora Lewis
Jenny Jones – Dora's mother
Gary Lewis – Dora's husband
Dmitri
Ben
Dray
DI Wayne Price (CID)
DS Rhys Sims (CID)

Blue Hollow

Eddie Flint
Julie Flint – Eddie's sister
Boris Orlov
Iosif Orlov
MJ (Michael John Jones)
Dennis Pritchard (Denny)
Charlie Briar
Adam Roberts
Reg – Keeper of Blue Hollow

Others

Alan Lloyd – Bank manager
Raymond Williams – Doctor
David Wainwright – Children's home manager
Graham North – Chief Constable
Scott North
Phillip Bevan – Vicar
Kyle Moss – Superintendent
Nathaniel Edwards – Judge

If you enjoyed this book, please let others know by leaving a quick review on Amazon. Also, if you spot anything untoward in the paperback, get in touch. We strive for the best quality and appreciate reader feedback.

editor@thebookfolks.com

www.thebookfolks.com

Also by Cheryl Rees-Price

Following a fall and a bang to the head, a woman's memories come flooding back about an incident that occurred twenty years ago in which her friend was murdered. As she pieces together the events and tells the police, she begins to fear repercussions. DI Winter Meadows must work out the identity of the killer before they strike again.

When the boss of a care home for mentally challenged adults is murdered, the residents are not the most reliable of witnesses. DI Winter Meadows draws on his soft nature to gain the trust of an individual he believes saw the crime. But without unravelling the mystery and finding the evidence, the case will freeze over.

When a toddler goes missing from the family home, the police and community come out in force to find her. However, with few traces found after an extensive search, DI Winter Meadows fears the child has been abducted. But someone knows something, and when a man is found dead, the race is on to solve the puzzle.

When local teenage troublemaker and ne'er-do-well Stacey Evans is found dead, locals in a small Welsh village couldn't give a monkey's. That gives nice guy cop DI Winter Meadows a headache. Can he win over their trust and catch a killer in their midst?

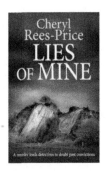

A body is found in an old mine in a secluded spot in the Welsh hills. There are no signs of struggle so DI Winter Meadows suspects that the victim, youth worker David Harris, knew his killer. But when the detective discovers it is not the first murder in the area, he must dig deep to join up the dots.

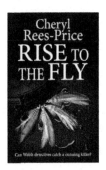

When the bodies of a retired couple are found by a reservoir, the police are concerned to discover fishing flies have been impaled on their tongues. After they find nothing in the couple's past to indicate a reason for the murder, they begin to look local. What will they turn up in this dark and secluded corner of Wales?

Printed in Great Britain
by Amazon

27022250R00189